FINE LINE

NOEL HARDING

First published in Australia 2010
This edition published November 2010
Copyright © Noel Harding 2010

Republished by Busybird Publishing 2023
Copyright © Noel Harding 2023

ISBN: Paperback: 978-1-922954-15-2
Ebook: 978-1-922954-16-9
Audiobook: 978-1-922691-10-1

Cover design, typesetting: Chameleon Print Design

Busybird Publishing
2/118 Para Road
Montmorency, Victoria
Australia 3094
www.busybird.com.au

Special thanks to

Blaise van Hecke — Sid Harta editor

Monica Dennison — The Dennison Line

Kerry Collison — Sid Harta Publishing

My Staff — Suzanne and Paula

To my wife

CHAPTER ONE

London — January 1789

eoffrey's hand reaches for the front door latch with the urgency and paralysed restraint a dreamer understands. Everything seems in place, although there is a smell of burning food.

'Claire! I'm home love,' he calls in his usual manner. There is no answer. He walks towards the kitchen.

'Claire!' he screams. His wife is lying on the floor, her new dress stretched tightly around her pregnant form.

'*What bloody monster?*' he cries out, frantically moving to her side.

With a trembling hand he feels for her pulse. Her heart has stopped. Lifting her gently, holding her tenderly, he reaches for her swollen belly.

A feeling of helplessness surges through his whole body. 'My baby *too!*' he says.

Standing, he looks down at his wife in disbelief. Placing a moist cloth on her forehead, again he listens at her chest, she is still not breathing.

'Claire, *Claire*, I'm sorry, don't leave me, *please come back.*' He shakes her again, this time almost violently.

His mind is numbed, but he will never forget the slow flickering lamp flame, the dull glow of the unstoked fire, and the smell of burnt apple pie.

The still, cold, outside air slowly permeates throughout the room as he sits in timeless shock.

The wide open door to the street attracts attention. 'Is there anybody 'ere?' calls a stern voice.

Through the eyes of an innocent man in distress, the appearance of a constable in the open doorway is agreeable. But any expectation of sympathy or support soon fades as the figure warily surveys the interior of the house. The arrival of another constable increases the official tone of their visit.

'Don't move, sir,' says the first constable as the other manoeuvres to cover the rear exit.

'There's … nothing we can do,' Geoffrey struggles with words. 'I think my child is dead too.'

'Do you live 'ere, sir?'

'Yes, this is my wife, Claire.' He looks down at her with a washed-out, mournful expression.

'Has there been a break-in, sir?'

'No, I arrived home and found her here,' he answers, oblivious to the suspicious looks that pass between the two policemen.

'What time did you find her, sir?' questions the first constable.

'At … at five after five,' he replies tenderly touching Claire's hair.

'Sir, it is five fifty-five, have you checked the premises?'

'No, I've been here … here with her … my wife is dead… don't you understand?' Geoffrey pleads.

'Has anything been stolen, sir?'

He turns his head from side to side and remains silent.

Although in shock, a part of him is becoming aware of the scepticism of the policeman, but another part of him could not care less.

Gently laying Claire down, he stands and moves towards the doorway.

'It's alright, sir … I'll have to ask you to be seated … sir, please!'

As if to invite confrontation, he continues. Suddenly he urgently needs to walk.

'I love her more than anything else in this world,' he says defiantly.

The stocky senior constable moves to block his path. With an angry energy, he heaves the policeman aside, takes two steps, and stops. Fists clenched, staring at the floor, he weeps.

'You don't know how hard I have tried … You could never know … I love her so much.'

He moves back to her side.

'I never really had you, and now, in my life, I never will,' he sobs. '*Oh God*, what have I done to you Claire?'

* * *

Geoffrey Blake is a thirty-two year old, blue-eyed Yorkshire man. His wiry but well-proportioned, muscular frame, and blue-eyed good looks could not counter his impressions of himself from his early years, a skinny, gawky, sickly child. A hint of warmth in his personality is restricted most times by the ever-present mist of over-sensitivity.

Geoff is a romantic, but this side of him, although very strong, is kept deep within. Friends he attracts usually match his conservative side, and for these reasons his relationships are predictable and boring.

Talent and ambition drives him very successfully in the world of commerce. A large shipping company, Hamsley & Co., employs him as an accounting supervisor.

Some delude themselves with illusions of grandeur … Geoffrey writes. His jottings, although improving with maturity, lack feeling.

Behaviours he picked up from his father have stuck like leaches sucking at his very soul. His inherent possessiveness continually conflicts with his firm belief that women should be treated more equally.

His father, like himself, was a hard worker as was his father before him. Geoffrey Blake has emerged from feudal England a small lord in his own right, a small lord without castle, or a large run of land.

*   *   *

'Mr Blake failed to report the death of his wife. Mr Blake, attempting to escape, assaulted an officer of the law in the course of his duty. Mr Blake was witnessed by officers, Smallbury and Coggan, to have said: 'You don't know how I have tried,' and 'God what have I done?'

'*My wife was dead when I arrived home!*' interjects Geoffrey.

'Screams were heard coming from your residence Mr Blake,' the prosecution replies.

'No! No! Cries Geoff.

'How would you know that, sir, you said you were not there? Mr Blake, we have several reports of strained relations between you and Mrs Blake.'

Underestimating the circumstantial evidence massed against him, Geoffrey now quickly realises his decision to represent himself, which he was vehemently advised against, was a grave mistake. His innocence being so obvious to him, Geoffrey's lack of preparation, coupled with the court's busy schedule, results in an irreversible catastrophe.

'Mr Blake,' the judge pauses and looks at Geoffrey. 'On the basis of the evidence presented to this court, the Court finds that the elements of the charge of murder with which you have been charged have been established beyond a reasonable doubt and therefore you are guilty of that offence. However, the jury has exercised its right to hand down a partial verdict. Mr Blake, you have been found guilty of murder with a recommendation of mercy. I hereby sentence you to seven years hard labour to be served at His Majesty's colony in New South Wales. Bailiff, take the prisoner down.'

Geoffrey is shocked as the guilty verdict is read out.

Pale and distraught he is escorted from the dock and led down a stairway to a crude holding area, given a blanket and locked up.

'The world's gon' mad,' whimpers a lad pacing back and forth in an adjoining cell.

Geoff's physical internment feels hauntingly familiar to him, although he has never been in a prison before, confronted the law, or known personally anybody that has. He stares at the roughcast wall with dry, tortured eyes. His body is now jailed, but his mind has always been imprisoned.

Geoffrey's native cunning outdoes his well-educated personality by about two to one. Flattery and placation, now less these days, flows ever so naturally from his lips in place of truth and fact sometimes, but he is not a liar. When he is wrong, only part of his mind is allowed to realise it. Deeper within, however, the score is kept ruthlessly.

In the dim light his eyes strain and scan the prison walls for soft mortar, a fault line, an imaginary trap-door, a way through. There is no way out. He is cut off and very alone. For the first time in his life, he has lost control. The future has now been taken out of his hands.

'Claire. Claire! ... *Claire*, I'm sorry, I should have done more for you ... I miss you so much,' he moans.

CHAPTER TWO

London, October 2000

Thirty-three year old Jane Turner has taken herself off to the Royal Chelsea Hospital, London. Two hours later she is relieved, the pain caused by her miscarriage and her unwanted, controversial pregnancy, has gone.

'Its all been too hard,' she says, sitting in her hospital bed. 'Why me?' She palms back her dark, oily hair. The hint of a rallying smile eases forward from behind her tired eyes and cheeks. 'You'll be just fine,' she tells herself.

The last time she experienced the sterile, scary, hollow quietness of a hospital, was twenty-nine years ago when she was four and a bit years old. Some kids glide through hospital experiences, she did not then, and does not now.

Jane's mind, nudged along by small doses of pethidine, scans back over parts of her life.

'You're jealous of the kid's looks and brains,' Dad once said in an intense argument with mum, about me. That's the only time I heard him stand up to her — well, one of the only times. Apart from that, he was a teddy bear.

Mum was always busy and did things with me when it suited her, but she always gave me quality time, and I knew in her own way she loved me — still does. She treated Dad, who is very accomplished, like a boy, and for some reason he just surrendered, putting his own fears on hold as mother's fears dragged them both along.

I love my mother and father, but declared several years ago that I would try and leave behind the negative behaviours I learnt as a child.

The last three years of Jane's life has been building to a marriage with Greg Holsworth, a fifty-one year old, successful film producer. Her need for financial security, some notoriety, and a mature love were all nudged along by a small kink in her character — fear. Through no lacking on Greg's part, her feelings for him just dried up. What he had to offer in experience, courage, financial security and his success, she no longer needed.

And then, all the stuff spread across Jane's table of life, she gathers up in an imaginary chequered tablecloth, ties all the corners neatly together, and puts it to one side.

I was loved, probably more than I want to admit, and I was given all the opportunities and education I could soak up. Who am I? she thinks.

'What's it really all about?' she says aloud. 'I have my caring nature, Ha… *Oh, that hurts.*' She reaches for her pelvic area. *I still have my looks,* she thinks. *This probably causes me more trouble than I realise. I like myself,* she affirms strongly in her mind. *I really do.* This core feeling being quite separate to the boost her confidence has experienced as a result of a new blossoming relationship, a risky relationship with handsome, sexy Michael, an acclaimed photographer, living in Australia.

I said to him, when he was staying in London, 'Michael, I don't want to have unprotected sex,' but we got carried away with the moment. I feel terrible. I'm not sure whether Michael or Greg was the father of the baby … I'm not telling a soul. I've never done anything like this before, I've always played it safe … Michael is so gorgeous though … I love him so much. Dad never took any chances.

'I want to settle down with that special person. Time for a new start in a sunny new country, *London is dull,*' she says, quietly talking to herself, but not quietly enough, a nurse pulling back the curtain, in the semi-private room, overhears her.

It's a beautiful new sunny day here in London, Jane.'

'Yes, I suppose it is.' Jane replies, a little sheepishly as they look out across the city and the river beyond.

*　　*　　*

A 747 airliner slowly turns and positions itself. With four Rolls Royce jet engines roaring, it blasts down the runway and lifts smoothly into the smoggy London skies. Jane is scared, but at the same time immensely excited, as she watches the lights of London disappear into the darkness of the night sky. She is finally on her way.

Jane is happily leaving behind a conservative society, an unful-filled love life, a loving but obsessive family background, and a cold climate. Her freedom flight is taking her away to the other end of the earth where she is convinced everything will be different. In Australia, she tells herself, the weather is warm and sunny and the population is more down to earth and liberated than that of London.

In twenty-four hours she will be in Michael's arms, a roman-tic reunion that is constantly in the forefront of her mind. She visualises Sydney Airport full of life, adorned with flowers and tropical plants, buzzing with activity, romance, colour and Michael waiting for her.

Am I running away? she thinks. *Am I being fair? Greg was so good to me. Michael's a bit cocky sometimes, and he can be possessive. Greg was always there. He gave me everything and all the freedom I needed. He was a good lover. He loved kids. And true, I know he would have always been true. God … the look on his face when I told him I was leaving London and him. What could I say? … I feel bad about that. Michael has fire in his eyes, he spoils me to bits — he's so gorgeous. Part of me is saying, look out girl, but all I can see is him. I'm sure I'm seeing things clearly. I love him so much. I'm not scared anymore.*

Michael is an Australian photographer whose work is exceptional. Jane met him when he visited London to do some photographic stills on a project for Greg's production company, seven months ago. From a previous marriage, Mike has a five-year-old daughter, Rebecca.

The massive jet engines settle as the airliner reaches its cruising speed of 680 miles per hour at an altitude of 39,000 feet. Outside it is as cold and dark as an arctic night. The aircraft banks slightly, setting a course for Singapore. Any nervous passengers are reassured by the normal routine of the flight, and the crew. An occasional bump and flutter however, reminding all that they are a long way from the ground.

Jane thinks back to the boarding lounge. *I saw a minister, some army personnel, one baby, and two children. There were no nuns, no African Americans with eyes that can open to the size of golf balls. I didn't see any movie stars. There was one Arab, but he was accompanied by his wife in national dress. That's alright. When you see all these things together in a movie there is always trouble,* she thinks, partly in jest.

She jerks her shoulders up slightly and smiles to herself. *Leaving Mum and Dad... leaving Greg, and my career ... packing ... the take-off, the magic of all this, and Michael. It's all too much,* she thinks, and sighs.

Her tired mind now focuses on Michael and the letter she wrote to him recently. She takes a copy out of her bag.

Dear Michael,
I have learnt to love you from a distance. I find that one of the hardest things I have ever had to do in my whole life.
I am warmed by thoughts of the moments I spent with you.

They were so good — so full of life and colour — especially when you were relaxed.

I have experienced part of you which is so special and beautiful, I am not sure I could find that again in another. I hope you can see that in yourself — I am sure you can.

How is Becky? I cannot wait to see her.

Be with you soon,

Love to you both,

Jane

Jane sighs again, causing the woman seated next to her to look up. She stares at the blank movie screen in front of her, and then continues to read her travel brochure.

Jane closes her eyes.

'She's a lovely little thing. Is she your daughter?' the woman next to Jane half whispers.

I must have dropped Becky's photograph, Jane thinks.

'Ah … no … no … the daughter of a friend,' she replies, reaching for her bag.

'It's in your diary dear.'

'What's in my diary?' Jane looks confused.

'The picture dear, the picture you are looking for.'

What? thinks Jane to herself, *I can't believe this.*

'I'm sorry love, I just can't help myself,' smiles the woman awkwardly.

'What do you mean?' Jane asks slowly, removing Becky's photograph from between the pages of her diary. 'Are you psychic?'

'We're all psychic love.' replies the woman, looking Jane straight in the eyes. 'Lovely kid,' she says, pointing to Rebecca's photo.

'Yes she is,' Jane replies in a loving tone. 'She is very special.'

Jane's interest is sparked in this smart-looking forty-ish

fellow passenger. She is beginning to believe this woman is very gifted.

'What's her name then?' Jane has a daring look on her face. No sooner had the words left her lips that she regretted them.

'I'm *not* a game player.' The woman is peeved.

'I'm sorry. I really am … Please accept my apology … My name is Jane, and yours … Maureen?'

The woman looks at her, hesitates and begins to laugh. 'That's very good. You got the 'M' right. My name is Margaret … Margaret Lakes. Well we only have twenty-two and three-quarter hours to go,' she says looking at her watch. 'The flight will be over before we know it.'

Jane sinks back into her seat. *She's probably reading every thought that's running through my head,* she thinks. *And I will be sitting next to her for the whole flight.* Jane outwardly doesn't like the idea, but a small tickle in her solar plexus is an indication that something else is happening.

Fifteen minutes pass while Jane struggles with the mental image of her mind's secrets being as visible as the movie screen three seats in front. Jane's concern is in vain however, for the master mind reader seems to have put her telescopic mind probe away for the time being.

That unusual, but distinguished looking gentleman in the window seat doesn't know what he is in for, sitting next to her, Jane thinks.

Quiet begins to overtake the passengers on flight 1033 to Sydney, Australia.

CHAPTER THREE

Cornwall – Port Isaacs 1787

ressed a little more conspicuously, than the many floater fishermen, Geoffrey Blake sits on the sea wall.

Behind his relaxed facade, thoughts and feelings are flashing about like the determined, restless fish that are occasionally tugging at the lines of the anglers around him.

An interest in history is one of the reasons Geoff has made this long journey from London. He is also hopeful that he may find answers to some of his life's questions.

'I'm finally here,' he says to himself.

The colourful and magical history of the Cornwall district has always fascinated him. Smugglers and great writers live on this very coastline.

But, for now, he is content to sit in the sun, breathe in the fresh air and watch life go on around him.

His reverie is suddenly interrupted with the shouts of a fisherman. 'Look out, missy! Look out!'

To avoid striking a young woman standing at the end of the breakwater, an old fisherman abruptly halts the winching of his catch. The basket tips and falls, emptying its entire contents onto the wharf like a wave swishing over a beach. She freezes, discovering it is one thing to be an interested observer, quite another to be at the centre of the smelly process. Leaping mackerel and slimy pilchards surround her.

Drawn by the commotion, Geoffrey moves up from the landing to the top of the sea wall. He will never forget the distressed, but captivating, dark-haired woman. Her shapely body hunched at the shoulders, her head back and her distorted face mouthing words that will not come. She is ankle deep in a seething, slippery, fishy mess.

'*Women!* Women!' mutters the fisherman, trying to re-basket his escaping catch.

Geoffrey's usual shyness is overtaken by an intense attraction. *I know her, she is so familiar,* he thinks.

'Geoffrey Blake at your assistance ma'm!' he announces, with the ineptness fascination can generate.

Taking a second glance, the young woman decides she likes his appearance, but with annoyance welling up inside, she retorts. 'Do you like fish?'

'Yes, I do very much,' he answers with a seemingly frivolous laugh.

She picks up a three-pound mackerel and heaves it at him, slipping as she does so. The fisherman's well-meaning, helping hand only throws her more off balance. She falls, sliding and gasping, into the partially cleaned up fishy mess.

The situation is humiliating her. Her view of Geoffrey changes from witty, handsome and novel, to annoying and provocative.

Frustrated and angry, she waves off his offer of assistance and carefully climbs onto her hands and knees, stands up, shuffles to the edge of the breakwater, and swallow dives gracefully into the cleansing cold water. She is more accustomed to diving and swimming than the amazed and concerned onlookers realise. In spite of her cumbersome skirt, she swims twenty yards to the beach.

With the mackerel still quivering in his arms, Geoffrey watches her disappear around the bluff.

For the rest of that day he cannot get her out of his mind. Images of her persist into the night and prevent him from sleeping. In the early hours of the morning, he finds himself back on the sea wall reliving those moments, and trying to understand where he may have gone wrong.

The affinity he has developed with his holiday surroundings, and now, his overwhelming attraction to this striking woman, cannot be separated out. These images and emotions, together, move uncontrollably back and forth in his mind.

It could be said that the intensity of this meeting could have resulted from an association in a previous life. Geoffrey, however, clearly remembers … *That's right, that's her*, he thinks, recalling those recurring powerful childhood thoughts. *I first met her when she was a seven-year-old, two years younger than me. She was playing in the schoolyard. She had long dark hair.*

He has never forgotten this small, innocent, vital, trusting, but vulnerable childhood friend from the past. He spent many childhood hours in fantasy thinking about his little dark haired-angel.

The young woman he met on the sea wall was a beautiful, mature woman. Geoffrey is sure the girl from his childhood days would have grown up exactly the same way.

At precisely the same hour each morning he finds himself back where he met the woman.

A week goes by and his determination to see her again has only increased. He questions many people, but locals who know of her are not going to inform a stranger.

For hours on end he sits and watches the stone breakwater, generating powerful mind pictures of her.

She does not return.

CHAPTER FOUR

hree figures move homeward along a well-worn track. The evening sun falls rapidly behind a small hill. Across the valley, and the sycamores beyond, a golden sheen brightens to a sharp climax, and then, as if in the throes of dying, the sun fades taking the day with it.

'Pa and the boys, here they come.' Claire sees the men of the family crossing the small stream at the end of the property.

One of the three figures is discernibly older, but agile. The other two are in their twenties, yet they still trail in their fathers footsteps, their youthful energies partially drained up by lack of motivation.

Their journey, in the mornings, takes them to the mine near Camelford. Claire's two brothers, William and Josh, and her father, are tin miners.

As they wearily arrive home, the evening meal is foremost in their minds. The comfort and reassurance Claire gives to her father and brothers is not always outwardly acknowledged, but it is always there at the start and end of each day, just as Claire's mother had provided for them all before she passed away.

Mother died so painfully. She was a good Christian. She attended church and took part in the ladies duties of the congregation. There was a side to mother that was very down to earth, sometimes outspoken. Claire breaths out deeply, as a look of solidarity with mother moves across her face, but she would staunchly rebuke anybody who suggested the two of them were alike.

Mother was once heard to say, after consuming several glasses of cider. 'Mary did bring Jesus up well!' I remember that moment as if it was yesterday. She shocked the whole congregation, especially the men. Reverend Michaels was very angry with her. Mother thought the church was unfair to all the women.

'And I thinks, he be the same as all those other men, clever dick, he, that Mr Geoffrey Blake standing there on the sea wall leering at me, and in those fancy clothes. He was fine though, I'm wondering where he is from. Was I too harsh … he made me so angry … *Ooh!*'

Claire has her mother's large hazel eyes, smooth light olive skin, high cheekbones, a pert nose and mischievous, well-defined lips, lips that do not always hold back the words others may expect they should.

When she smiles these attributes work together with an inner kindness to give a smile people cannot forget easily. Even the small gap between her front teeth adds to her attractiveness. In the lottery of gene allocation, she retained most of her mother's positive features and gained a few extra herself. Claire has achieved additional personality refinements, which are achievable one generation to the next, where love, perseverance, and good example are present.

There has been talk, as happens in families, that there was Celtic ancestry on Claire's mother's side. Be this true or false, Claire, with vast amounts of reading has developed an interest in Druidry.

In her early teens she taught the children at Sunday school but as the Christian doctrine began to conflict with her Celtic passion, she slowly, without any fuss, moved her mind more and more towards the world of the Druids.

To this day, she assists the schoolmaster at Camelford. This has given her access to books and an educational mentor.

Claire however is restless. She wants to move on. Books no

longer give her all the answers, especially those written by men. For many years now she has put up with pa's bossy ways, but she has had enough of that now too.

'That gentleman, if that's what you be, Mr Blake, you have quite taken my fancy,' she confesses to herself.

'Ah rabbit … rabbit again my girl.'

'Yes, rabbit Pa, you caught it, and I cooked it. A different rabbit though, and baked this time. Be happy Pa,' Claire mocks a smile with her lips.

'*Baked* rabbit? What do we think boys?'

'Don't talk to Claire so, dad,' says Josh, in a high-pitched voice that contrasts with his stocky physique.

'Pa, I'm not your wife, please do not treat me so,' Claire reminds him indifferently, as she has on many occasions.

'And how may that be girl?' His bottom jaw moves up and out to form a thinking, confronting pout … 'Tis true, tis true enough, you be my little Claire,' he reassures himself touching her hand. 'That I can see clear enough.'

'Eat up, Pa, eat up boys.' says Claire, ignoring and overriding her father's well-known carryings on.

The boys and I, William and Josh, hate Pa's tone; it makes us all uneasy sometimes. We don't like some of his looks either. I can see Josh especially, is getting more and more like Pa, he knows it too, and he hates it. Pa never treated me like Win and Joss … but we all love pa so.

Claire's ambivalent thoughts convert to subtle facial expressions, expressions her father can read, or thinks he can. But Claire's unconditional love for him has always been, and always will be, beyond his comprehension.

Rapping thunder and a delayed lightning flash indicate a storm is approaching, probably twenty minutes away. The rolling black clouds in the night sky above, dwarf the tiny hillside farmlet. The sky resembles a dark, angry seascape.

A panicked knock at the door is barely distinguishable from a banging shutter and several flapping shingles.

'*Who be there?*' calls the older brother.

The knock comes again, this time a little more intense.

'Damn it! Who is there?' repeats Josh with anger, his voice moving from baritone to soprano in the space of three words. 'Who the hell would be out on a night such as this?' he grumbles. 'It must be important.'

'Don't just sit there son, answer the bloody thing,' instructs his father.

Young William being the closest, jumps to his feet, pushes the door slightly forward and slides back the latch. A gust of howling wind bursts into the house extinguishing one candle, and threatens the glow of the table lamp.

Maybe, just maybe, it's him, Geoffrey Blake … No banish the thought, he would never know where I be living, thinks Claire, her mind fantasising to another extreme.

'Well who is it?' enquires John, relighting the candle, his question half aimed at William and half at the stranger.

The figure from out of the night enters through the small doorway, pushed forward by another strong gust. Cape swirling and hat pulled tight onto his head, he turns.

'Who the hell? … Jamie! Come in boy, come in … shut the door,' calls John.

What do *you* want Jamie? thinks Claire. For a brief moment imagining her Knight in shinning armour, that Mr Blake from the breakwater, has come to whisk her away.

'Your pony, your pony Claire, I bring him back, please come see Claire, he's hurt'n, he's gashed on his right quarter.'

It is not the first time Jamie has over-dramatised a situation to gain Claire's attention, and she well knows this is probably another one of those times.

As on most other occasions, she humours Jamie, who has

been besotted by her probably since childhood when they played mothers and fathers in the now rickety old shed at the back of the Etheridges' cottage.

Claire has matured, but poor Jamie still retains some of his pre-puberty personality. His looks also are stuck back there, so that he is good looking, but in a feminine, boyish way. He is a big man with a big heart. Warmth radiates from him with few expectations.

Claire picks up a lantern and moves outside quickly, partly out of concern for her horse, but mostly to appease Jamie. She has an inherent respect and care for him.

Unaffected by the deteriorating weather, Jamie leads the way.

'He be over here Claire … look at dis,' he says, revelling in the negative news.

Claire inspects her horse's superficial injury and relaxes.

'*See Claire … see,*' he zealously points.

'You're my dearest friend Jamie,' Claire says calmly and hugs him tight. And you watch out for me, don't you? I love you so much for that.'

Like a puppy, Jamie's soft brown eyes open and close slowly while Claire hugs him lovingly.

'Everything is alright Jamie, everything is alright,' she half whispers in his ear.

Jamie's mind switches quickly.

'Claire, I be down to Isaacs yesterday … There is talk of a drowning girl.' She fell off the breakwater, never to be seen again. They say she was very beautiful. A silent stranger is said to be watching day and night for her body. He must be her dearest friend too, Claire, as you are mine.'

'Waiting is he? He can wait till hell freezes over, see if I care.'

'What do you mean Claire, I don't understand.'

I'm only jesting Jamie, only jesting.'

Maybe I was a little brash with him on the sea wall, she thinks.

'Be off home with you, Jamie, before we both catch our death,' she says, sending Jamie packing, along with the fickle thoughts of that handsome, intriguing, but arrogant, Mr Blake, on the sea wall.

CHAPTER FIVE

he tide has turned as she moves down from her usual vantage point onto the rocks below. The mythical birthplace of King Arthur of Camelot, Tintagel Castle, towers above her.

Claire fossicks along the high water line, captivated by a collection of objects brought in by the tide. She is then drawn to explore the mysteries of the outer extremities of the reef.

Moving away from the base of the cliff, her heartbeat quickens as the lazy swell lifts and surges over the rocks beside her. She carefully selects a path between the small crevices, and moves further out.

Approaching the outer edge of the rocky reef she can see the rugged ocean floor. Long fingers of kelp move back and forth in the shifting, restless water, and for a moment the colours and mysteries of the deep mesmerise her.

Suddenly the water level drops. Looking up she sees a silent wall of water is looming. Turning, she discovers her retreat is not going to be easy. Taking a calming breath, she makes her way back over the maze of crannies and wet slippery rocks. The huge breaker thunders down behind her and white water surges all around, completely covering her retreat.

A second thundering wave sends spray twenty feet into the air. Water streams up her legs. She is surrounded, and cannot see a footing. Soaked to the skin, holding her dress up around her waist, she struggles, thigh deep, through the bubbling wash. She clambers forward and swims for her life. Reaching out with arms and legs she tries desperately to find something to hold onto.

'No! No!' she calls out, floundering helplessly, fearing she will be washed out to sea.

The water begins to recede and she finds herself secure in a large, familiar rock pool. Catching her breath, she swims carefully to an edge and drags herself up. Her first instinct is to run, but she forces herself to deal with her fear. As the water settles she can see the beauty of the pool. Small fish dart about, refreshed by the addition of oxygen and food to their temporary home. Huge boulders, worn smooth by the tide, sit like monuments amongst the patches of crushed shells, seaweed, sand and small pebbles.

For several minutes she catches her breath and waits for the adrenalin surging through her body to normalise, leaving her relaxed and fascinated. The warmth of the sun and the contained beauty of the rock pool, are enticing her back into the water. She's swum here before. Unconcerned now by the occasional wash of the receding tide over the rocks, she removes her wet clothes and lays them out to dry.

She dives to the sandy bottom of the pool, retrieving shells and coloured stones, which she places along the surface edge of a rocky shelf. She floats back and forth feeling the warm midday sun penetrating the crisp, chilly water as it laps across her belly and between her thighs. Tying her hair in a bun she places a clump of bleached seaweed over her head and parades like royalty, prancing with one hand on her hip, the other extended out, limp at the wrist. Without any warning, she flings the weed high into the air and chases after some unsuspecting gulls which are gathered hoping to be fed.

Geoffrey Blake's powerful yearnings did not bring his mystery women back to Port Isaacs, but something brought him and Claire Etheridge to King Arthur's Tintagel Promontory.

Arthur's mythical birthplace arouses intense excitement and reverence in Geoffrey. He knows the story well. As he moves about among the ruins, one hundred and fifty feet above the sea, he feels he is walking on sacred ground.

Down from the main castle area, and further out onto the promontory, he passes a tethered bay stallion, which ignores him. He continues on as the magic of Tintagel opens his senses and his psyche. The castle is one of the reasons he came to the shire.

Completely preoccupied, the sight of a young woman swimming naked in a pool on the rocks below does not register immediately.

'It's her!' he says to himself as she swims into his consciousness. 'It is her. Oh God. Can this be true?'

A warm tight sensation moves across his chest and upper arms, leaving him temporarily breathless. He sits weakened, unable to believe his eyes. The past week has seemed like an eternity. Now it only seems like minutes since he last saw her.

'Is that really her?'

Putting down a piece of the castle ruins he's been holding, he stands and moves to the edge of the cliff.

As if responding to his silent call, Claire, waist deep in the centre of the pool, turns and looks straight up at him. He puts his two arms into the air, waving them. She makes a small similar waving gesture, momentarily oblivious to everything, including her nakedness. She is excited to see him, but not surprised. This is most unusual, for he is not identifiable, being completely silhouetted against the sun. Realising she is exposed; she quickly sinks back into the water.

Geoffrey, hoping that the woman would think he had only just arrived; steps back and leaves her in privacy.

After descending a cliff stairway, he moves out over the rocks. He now feels the power and mystery of the volcanic platform, and her presence. He approaches the rock pool. Lancelot and Guinevere may have met in this very place, their romantic tryst risking the dishonour and ruin to Camelot's blossoming, but shaky existence.

'Hello, Mr Blake,' she says, moving out from behind an arch of rock.

Over the preceding week he has spoken to her repeatedly in his mind, and now she stands before him.

'I don't even know your name … Miss.' He is guarded.

'What name would you put to me *Mr* Blake?'

'You make fun of me.'

'What name *Mr* Blake?' she replies firmly, but warmly.

'Umm.' His brow wrinkles with slight frustration, but compensates with a smile.

'Oh … Emma, Anne … *Elizabeth?*'

'Claire … Claire Etheridge at your service.' She mocks at the comment he made when they first met on the sea wall.

He now perceives her even more beautiful than before. Her hazel eyes sparkle, her wet hair outlines a face relaxed, soft and proud. He senses and feels part of his deepest, finest self, in her.

She admires the strength that radiates from Geoffrey. His northern fair skin and blonde hair is not what she is accustomed to, but his face is handsome and his body trim and muscular. Beneath his facade, strong passions are evident to her, but which way they flow, she cannot tell.

'You remembered my name,' he says, flattered. 'There is so much I could say Claire, but … '

He half sits on a rock looking down directly at her. In damp clothes she seats herself several yards from him on the sand. The sounds of the wind, waves and gulls all seem to quieten. A beautiful silence falls between them.

'*Come Geoffrey*, come with me, I've something to show you.'

Her ability to move over the rocky surfaces far exceeds his.

'Am I ever going to catch up with you girl?' A moment of panic confronts his patience.

'*Maybe*,' she calls moving around a rock ledge into a small isolated cove.

Making up ground on the gravel surface he finds she is nowhere to be seen.

'Over here!' echoes her voice.

It is obvious, if he had thought to look. Her footprints, in the freshly washed gravel, lead off to the right into a large rocky chamber.

She stands in the luminous light of the huge cave.

'I came here first when I was ten … This is said to be Merlin's cave.'

'It is truly splendid, the loveliest I have ever seen,' he says looking around and then, directly at her.

He puts out his hand. She hesitates momentarily, and then takes it. 'You said Merlin's cave?' he asks, genuinely interested.

'Yes,' replies Claire. ''Tis said Merlin came here often. From this point he would move deeper into other areas of the caves to meditate. Merlin is only one of thousands who have passed through these caves over time… it's really very crowded in here,' she laughs. 'I used to pretend that if I did not judge the deeds of those who passed me by in here, they would leave me be.' She smiles warmly.

She leads him further into the cave. The cool musty air filtering out from deep within the cliffs is punctuated by the sweet smell of Claire's clothing and personal body scent. Her warm hand squeezes his every now and then.

'Just here, Geoffrey.' She stops by a blue pool. The atmosphere is breathtaking and electrifying.

'I can almost feel God's presence here,' he whispers. 'Can you feel him here?'

'Him?' Claire questions. 'I … '

Completely absorbed in his feelings for her, and his brief spiritual experience, which is more infatuation than Godly inspiration, he only hears the last part of her next comment.

'Brigid … a Druid Princess? Held your hand … *in here?*' He repeats her last words.

'Yes, Geoffrey, she spoke to me where we are now standing.'

'Who is she … who is Brigid?'

'She founded a community of women at Kildare in the year 500 AD … She was a poet … My mother gave me a small book about her life and poems.'

'How fascinating,' he answers, but his mind is in another place.

Again quietness engulfs them. They move closer together. Geoffrey's hands reach out and touch her waist then move slowly up into the small of her back. Standing on bare tiptoes, she hugs him. Claire feels a rising warm energy move through her whole body. She often dreams of romance, especially in this place. She takes a short subdued breath and closes her eyes.

They hold each other close.

CHAPTER SIX

London 1787

The sounds of stretching leather, the steamy odour, the occasional snort, and flatulence of the horse drawing their hansom cab are all that are familiar to Claire. Through the eyes of this Cornish bride, the streets of London are daunting but enticing.

In the well-to-do areas of the city, daily life moves with a new-world energy. The genie of steam and steel has stirred.

Claire is sitting close to Geoffrey. She has a radiant glow about her. Holding her hand tightly he's thrilled to be sharing the sights of London with his receptive bride.

Claire is unlike any women he has known before. She excites and inspires him. Ever since he first met her, he has been strongly attracted to her confidence and self-sufficiency, but another part of him is uneasy about those qualities. He has not experienced a love like this before.

The thoughts about his journey, meeting her again at Tintagel, introducing Claire to London, are streaming through his mind. *She is so beautiful*, he thinks.

Geoffrey's work prospects are excellent. There is talk of promotion. He has plans to write, and, *yes a family*, he pictures in his mind.

Claire misses no details. She watches the city flow with style, colour and rhythm; the buildings rise high into the sky. Beggars, merchants, the toffs all come together to form a picture of exciting, acceptable, completeness, in her mind. She admires the fine gowns, silk hats and leather shoes the women are wearing. She is feeling confident in this new city with the simple life she used to lead now far away.

Just a short distance from their residence, Geoff calls out to the driver. The carriage pulls abruptly to the left and stops against the flow of the busy traffic.

'*Tea*, madam?'

'Yes *please*.'

Geoff has often visited the Northumberland Tea Rooms.

Claire is immediately at home. Her excited eyes miss nothing. All the romantic stories she has heard about London are confirmed. Her dream to go to the big city has now come true.

Two crackling open fires, the smells of burning birch, brewing tea and coffee and fresh baking bread blend with the chatter of the patrons — the ambience of the tea-house has stood the test of time.

Exposed beams support the level above. Handcrafted crockery, brassware and porcelain figures adorn a mantle which runs completely around the walls of the teahouse. Many watercolour and oil paintings link past and present. Close to Claire and Geoffrey hangs a large oil painting of the Cornwall coastline. Claire tries to identify the area.

Steaming tea, four large scones, a bowl of whipped cream and a small dish of gooseberry jam are placed in front of the honeymooners.

'Thank yee, sir … ma'am,' chants a petite waitress as she toddles off, adjusting table settings as she goes.

'This is *so* lovely,' says Claire. She catches sight of two distinguished young women sipping tea near a front window. One is dressed in a white cotton gown with lilac stripes and a light blue silk hat, the other in a grey crepe dress, matching hat and blue shawl.

Claire smiles warmly at Geoff. Leaning forward, she whispers. 'I love you my husband, this is all so very exciting.'

He looks into her eyes. 'If I were King,' he says with a smile, and a touch of comedy, 'you, my Queen, would want for nothing.' He musters an important look. 'We would take tea here, you in your finest gown. We would care for the poor. All men would be equal. 'And I,' he hesitates … 'fair and noble. You my lady, kind and beautiful as you are would not have to change.'

'Oh Geoffrey, that sounds like your story of Camelot, Geoffrey … I have you, I do not need to be a Queen.' Claire smiles and gazes out the window at the busy road and pedestrian traffic.

'Ello.'

A small pale face looks up at Geoff from under a short reddish fringe. The small girl is about four years old. Her thin arms poke out of a tailored, white cotton dress, dotted twice at the bottom by two tiny red shoes. Around her neck hangs a matching bonnet. Her green eyes are poignant. She holds her dolly tightly around its neck, with a strong, determined little arm.

Quickly plucking a pink rose from the table setting, Geoffrey hands it to the little one. She accepts the flower with a soft, 'Ta,' a sound, which echoes her vacant expression.

'What is your name, love?' Geoffrey asks.

With her eyes fixed on the couple, the little girl buries her small nose in the petals. Her expression changes from sombre to curious.

'What's your name little one?' Geoffrey coaxes softly again.

'Chrissie.'

'Hello, Chrissie, I would like you to meet *Mrs* Blake.' Chrissie holds forward her dolly. She stands for a moment soaking up the warmth radiating from the happy couple.

And then she is gone.

Claire and Geoffrey spend over an hour watching the passing parade.

*   *   *

Late 18th century London still awakes to the continuous crowing of roosters. Each cock is allotted its own time to crow. Dogs barking and yaps overlap.

These ancient sounds stir a sleeping population. The innocence of sleep is pushed away by the strengthening rays of the rising sun.

Claire and Geoffrey awake apart, but are soon in one another's arms. They take some time together before the outside world places its daily demands on each of them.

The cold autumn morning sun, after losing its dawn's pristine meekness, streams through the window onto the physically exhausted lovers. They lay white, naked, dishevelled and, it would seem, at the bottom of life's ladder for the day. Claire silently tries to lift her mood. Geoffrey's mind wanders. Work duties will focus a mind inclined to delve too deeply.

*   *   *

He's like a cute, big teddy-bear. Jane is thinking as she looks at the interesting, well-dressed gentleman sitting in the window seat next to Margaret. *He seems wise and friendly with those big brown eyes. His voice sounds like Peter Ustinov's, warm and articulate. He's a tad like him actually, unusual looking, but very distinguished.* This fellow traveller on flight 1033 to Australia has connected with her.

'You like him don't you?' Jane's quiet reflection is interrupted by Margaret's comment.

'Who, Margaret?'

'Him.' Margaret indicates with a side nod in the direction of the contented face near the window.

'I hardly know the man,' whispers Jane. 'Find out what he does.'

'You ask him,' replies Margaret.

'He must be bursting, he hasn't moved out of his seat since we left London. He's alright, isn't he?' Jane smiles.

'Of course, look, his tie's going up and down,' Margaret points.

In the next second his eyes open. He has a terrified look on his face.

'I've *got to* go! I've got to go!' he says frantically.

The other passengers look around. Margaret and Jane stand up and move out of the way as he shuffles sideways past them. On reaching the aisle, he stops, tips an imaginary hat, smiles, and thanks the two women kindly. He then calmly proceeds to the rest rooms.

Margaret and Jane reseat themselves feeling a little silly. Jane manages to smile.

The gentleman returns as turbulence begins to shake the aircraft. He seats himself unperturbed. Jane looks down at her clasped hands. This flight is so important to her. *How sad it would be for my life to end now before I have a chance to see Michael again. God, let me please arrive safely and then you can do with me what you will.* Jane's mind makes a childlike deal.

Travelling at five hundred and seventy miles per hour, thirty-eight thousand feet above the earth and crossing two time zones, Jane's mind can't settle.

Her ex-lover Greg's last words to her were. *'You'll never find anyone who'll love you as much as I do.' Does his comment show his lack of love? Was he subtly threatening me? Or was that an expression of his deepest feelings — maybe a little of each? I can't really tell. Maybe what he said is true.*

CHAPTER SEVEN

The back door of the Blake's modest Elizabethan residence opens into a small, formal garden. Two walls, one smooth, the other with large dollops of slag protruding, border the side and the back of the property. Dogwood trees and dense privet complete the rest of a very private boundary.

Well-manicured border plants follow the edges of two gravel paths which circle around each side of the garden. They join at the rear with a central walkway that returns to the house. Visitors, especially at this time of year, would have to imagine pretty annuals, which are sown in the neatly dug-over fallow areas, in the springtime.

Two swallows have claimed the garden for themselves. They have chosen a position high on the side brick wall for their nest. They fly as one, in and around the garden, but lack vitality, as do the plants. Samhuinn is the ancient name for this time of the year; it's the period of the dark moon … autumn is well under way.

The garden responds to Claire's touch. She is convinced her voice also encourages the plants. In the process of creating her small retreat, she is careful to try and spare any worm, beetle or snail from becoming a casualty. However, one particular plant, a hydrangea, has to go. She clears an area of approximately two square yards, digging out the obstructing plant.

At precisely midday, when the sun is at its highest, a gap between the two walls allows a ray of sun to shine directly onto her cleared patch. This is exactly what she planned for. Each year, and every year, at midday, the sun will light this exact position.

All is complete. The tools are all stored in the garden shed. Claire stands contented, admiring her handiwork. It is twelve noon. She met Geoffrey twelve months ago on this very hour, and now celebrates this special October day.

By one o'clock she is ready. With a prepared list of necessities, and two very special items in her mind, she closes the front door and walks to the shops.

The novelty of visiting the bakery with all its tempting pastries, fresh rolls and hot bread, never diminishes. Fresh mackerel, cockles and mussels are piled high on the fishmonger's stall, the familiar smells reminding her of Cornwall. Claire chooses some vegetables and meat for the evening meal. The stores excite her, she always feels Sundays to be a little boring when the merchants close.

'Good afternoon to you, Mrs Blake.' An old, experienced tradesman greets her.

His wise, smiling, dusty face and blistered hands give a clue to the meticulous but rugged nature of his occupation. Claire hands him a piece of paper. He reads it carefully, asks her four specific questions, one being her address, another if the approximate cost is agreeable. 'I have given all this a great deal of thought since we last met … we should be ready next Tuesday week, Ma'am,' he confirms, tucking the order into the top pocket of his leather apron and wiping his brow with a coarse chalky cloth.

'Thank you, sir, thank you very much,' she says politely.

She has one more call to make before returning home.

Approaching the drapery store she discovers the dress she was going to purchase has gone from the front window. Geoffrey has bought her several dresses since she came to London, but this one is different. 'It's gone!' She stands staring at the empty space, thinking, *if I had come yesterday … it might still have been here.*

Two big eyes look back at Claire from behind the window

display. A beaming smile appears. A hand moves into view, signalling a beckoning motion. Surprise flashes across Claire's face. The hand waves even faster. Both faces experience excited smiles, which then turn to childish laughter. Claire runs to the shop door and enters.

The two faces, still laughing, now meet. The beckoning hand of the assistant points to Claire's dress which is hanging behind the counter.

'Shhh ... Catherine, please.' The stern voice of the proprietor resonates from the back of the premises.

'Shhh, shhh.' They mimic mockingly.

Claire whispers, 'My name is Claire.'

'Are you looking for this?' says Catherine, floating the elusive dress across the counter. 'I've seen you admiring it through the window many times. Would you like to try it on?'

Claire takes the dress. 'Thanks!' and goes to the fitting room.

The line of the dress complements her body. The blue bodice moves in tight over her waist, and the flares and folds fall elegantly to her ankles. As she turns before the mirror, the dress gracefully swirls out, wraps around her legs and straightens. The puffed sleeves highlight her slender arms, which she holds squeezed together in a V at her front. An inch of French lace at the hem completes the picture.

'This is not me!' she says loudly looking at her face in the mirror.

She moves out. Catherine shrieks with excitement.

''Tis you silly, the dress is you ... I wish I could look like that ... it fits you so perfectly.'

'You don't know what I mean Catherine ... The face in the mirror ... it didn't look like mine.'

'Don't be a silly billy, Claire. The dress is new to you, that's all.'

Claire looks again in the mirror … front, side to side, back and front again.

'I will take this dress, thank you, Miss Catherine.'

'Yes, Madam. Madam will be wearing the dress, won't Madam?' Catherine says with another glowing smile welling up.

'Yes, yes of course,' Claire replies and then both their excited smiles turn to happy laughter again.

'You must visit me, Catherine — will you, please?' Claire says after they've settled down.

'I will come, I will … I promise.'

The impatient proprietor seems mollified by Claire's payment for the garment. But then, 'Staff do not fraternise with the customers, *Catherine!*' she exclaims after the door closes.

'Yes, Ma'm … Uh … No Ma'm,' replies Catherine. She has heard all this before, but it still manages to fluster her.

Outside, everything has changed for Claire. She feels beautiful and complete in this new dress. Her attractiveness is confirmed by the admiring looks she receives from people she passes, especially the men.

As she walks along the footpath, it feels to her as though there is another young woman walking out in front, smiling at the passers-by, laughing, and swirling her new dress around. The only indication of the way Claire is actually feeling inside is the slight cheekiness in her step and the clasping and movement of her hands. Psychics or attuned individuals however, would see it all in her sparkling eyes.

*　　*　　*

'I'm home, love.' Geoffrey calls eagerly. Claire has been in his mind all day and he can hardly wait to see and hold his lovely wife.

The evening meal is prepared; the living area is spotless, warm and inviting. Claire takes off her apron and moves towards him. She stops, raises her arms out to each side.

'Do you like my new dress? I was so fortunate to find it,' she explains, as she bends at the waist moving into a provocative pose, her arms clasped in front and her bottom extended out and up.

'You are a picture of loveliness my girl.'

'Do you *really* like it?'

'You are the most beautiful girl in the world and this is the most beautiful dress because you are wearing it,' he says, moving to hold her.

'I knew you'd like it,' she hugs him tightly. 'Now dinner,' she replaces her apron and moves to the stove. 'Vegetable soup and dumplings tonight … I met the most delightful young lady today, she's coming to visit … her name is Catherine.'

'I'm glad you have made a friend. I look forward to meeting her. We have trouble all the way up the coast,' he says. 'It would seem the winds have gone forever. Twelve ships at anchor. I've never seen this before. Nature will run its course I suppose,' unaware he has completely changed the subject.

'Mr Hamsley will be irked about that, I'm sure.'

'If the weather doesn't change the sky will be filled with the stench of rotting cargo.'

Claire sympathises, hugs Geoffrey again and coerces him outside. 'Quickly, before we sit down, look at this. I finished the garden today.'

The cold foggy dusk, by lamplight, sets a haunting scene. Claire points proudly.

'This is … this is very beautiful,' Geoffrey says hesitantly. 'And here?' he points to the cleared area.

'Surprise … you will see next Tuesday.'

'Tell me now,' Geoffrey urges.

'No, Tuesday, I'm going to *surprise* you.' Claire smiles firmly and hugs him again.

'I really adore this new dress,' he whispers as he takes her in his arms, kisses her and runs his hand down her back and across her thigh.

He is edgy. The dress, the new friend, the secret in the garden momentarily confuses him. This independent side of his wife, the very strength in her nature, which draws him ever so close to her, also creates anxiety inside him.

Sometimes I don't understand. Is it me? His mind is racing ahead. I have bought her most things she wants. Why does she need more? Why these secrets? Does she doubt me? he is thinking, as they both move back inside.

CHAPTER EIGHT

Here is a knock.

'Is there anybody at home?'

Unsure, but trusting, Claire opens the door.

'Mrs Blake? I bid you good morning.' Her visitor's clerical collar puts Claire at ease.

'Mrs Blake, I hope I didn't startle you. My name is Wren. I am the assistant cleric to the Reverend Dickenson. I was passing by and thought I might pay you a visit. I am acquainted with your husband Geoffrey. He and I have had many a long discussion ... If it's not convenient ...'

'It is *lovely* to meet you Reverend Wren, please come in. Would you like a cup of tea?'

'Thankyou, I would indeed, Mrs Blake.'

An austere, but handsome man, Reverend Wren walks through the door and sits at the dinning table. Swivelling into position, his knee drags the tablecloth, nearly causing a vase to topple. Straightening the cloth, he pretends it never happened.

'Do you like living here in London, Mrs Blake?'

'Yes, very much so ... I do miss the hills of home sometimes,' replies Claire, sitting on the edge of her chair.

Carefully combed dark hair, trimmed eyebrows, long eyelashes, and friendly penetrating brown eyes interfere with the image of a professional man of God. Religious righteousness circles around him like a flock of flighty doves unsure of a secure place to land. His style would more suit a good doctor.

'Your church, I think Geoffrey said, was at Camelford. How was it? Did you have many parishioners? I've never been to the south-west coast. I would dearly love to go there one day. Would you suggest it a worthy journey?'

The boiling kettle whistles.

She answers from the kitchen. 'I used to go to church each Sunday with my mother and father. I must admit though, I did lose interest as I grew older.'

'Thankyou, Mrs. Blake,' he says as she pours the tea. 'Life's interests tend to challenge the spirit at puberty. Some children in our parish become restless as they develop to young adults. It's quite normal,' he says.

'No, no, there were *other* issues.' Feeling a little confronted, Claire changes the subject. 'I'm sure you would enjoy visiting Cornwall, Reverend,' she says.

'Maybe one day. You said there were other issues?'

Claire's face straightens. Her cheeks flush a little.

He pulls back.

Claire can't help herself. 'I had, and still do have an interest in the Druid culture, Reverend.'

The expression on his face clears away like a carnival that has packed up and is ready to move. He places his tea cup on the table. 'Oh, I see,' he replies.

His voice stiffens. The Reverend Dickenson would like to talk with you and Geoffrey. He is also interested in the southern shires, possibly even more so than myself. Maybe, you and I can take up our discussion some other time … yes, some other time, maybe,' he mumbles.

'Maybe we can,' answers Claire. There is something attractive and challenging about this man.

'Well, I must be going. Good day, Mrs Blake. Please tell your husband I called. I enjoy my talks with him very much. He speaks about you often. What an exquisite garden,' he remarks, catching a glimpse through the rear window as he moves to the front door.

'It's been a pleasure to meet you Reverend.'

'Thankyou for the tea, Mrs Blake.'

He waves and smiles in a boyish fashion as he awkwardly moves sideways down the steps to the footpath.

Claire giggles. *He's basically an interesting, and kind man,* she thinks to herself, watching him puzzle over which direction to walk.

*   *   *

The grinding wheels of a heavily laden dray move slowly but surely down the roadway towards Claire's home. It's Tuesday — special delivery day.

As the cart slows and comes to an uncertain halt, its old frame twists from side to side under the immense weight of the load. The creaking sounds are unnerving.

'Whoa boy! Whoa boy!' calls Mr Whelan.

The huge draft horse, seemingly proud of its accomplishment, lowers its head, snorts sharply through its large nostrils, and does a small shuffle with its front legs. A pat on the snout from Mr Whelan rewards the horse's ritualistic performance.

A tall, thin man directs two of the helpers.

'Good morning to you all.' Claire greets each of them with individual nods of recognition.

Mr Whelan avoids eye contact. He is a large, reserved, physically strong man.

The men place thick planks into position. The dray twists and straightens as the heavy weight of the crafted consignment is transferred onto the roadway. On wooden rollers, the monster work is carefully manoeuvred through the narrow side-entrance towards the rear garden. Claire is ecstatic as the timeless piece is placed onto her prepared space.

The job now complete, the workers, detached from their

achievement, prepare to leave. After receiving payment, Mr Whelan bids Claire farewell. He starts to walk away, then hesitates and looks back for a moment. The feelings aroused by this delivery are different for him; most of his work finds its place at the cemetery. He is mystified, but enjoys the change. He smiles kindly at her, tips his beret, 'Ma'm,' and leaves.

Standing seven feet in height, and fashioned from granite, the newly inserted stone statue has a base of five smooth sides, which form two-thirds of the design. The top section resembles two hands twisted at the wrists, with interlocked fingers reaching upward.

Claire runs her hands slowly down over the stone's surface in a pressing, weaving manner. The intense feelings she is experiencing, centred in the middle of her chest, take her mind back to the cliffs and the shoreline of Cornwall, where she roamed as a child.

'It's here, and it is just what I wanted,' she squeals softly to herself. 'Oh dear, dinner,' she remembers, her dreaming has to be put aside for now.

Proud of her achievement, she moves indoors. Her excitement is continually stoked as she glances at her stone through the kitchen window.

*　　*　　*

Geoffrey returns home, as usual, he is eager to see Claire. Hugging her close he sees the statue — over her shoulder — in the garden.

'What in the heavens is *that?*'

'This is my surprise … do you like it?'

She follows him outside. 'My stone is a symbol of love and my life with you, strong, and forever lasting.' Sensing a problem, the ring of confidence in her voice is fading.

He stands staring. 'Can we afford to pay out hard-earned money for this piece of rock?' he says crassly, though part of him sees the beauty in the work.

Claire light-heartedly says, 'I don't think the gentleman will take it back ... do you?'

'Well I suppose it will have to stay there won't it?' he says, his tone softening.

There is no doubt about that in Claire's mind.

'I'm ever so grateful you understand. Lets have some supper, a special supper. How has your day been?' she says, changing the subject.

CHAPTER NINE

In the mythical world of Camelot, men would win the honour and hearts of women through chivalry and combat. Men set the laws and justified their actions with a conflicting mixture of reverence, manliness, and self-indulgence.

Eighteenth century Britain still reflects that myth. Men are still the conquerors and women the prizes. The church, with a hierarchy of males, sanctifies relationships through Christian marriage. Hypocrisy, especially amongst leading citizens and royalty, is mostly overlooked by the church.

Reverend Dickenson, with his curate Peter Wren, has invited himself to visit Geoffrey and Claire on a Friday evening at eight.

The Blake's are not ardent churchgoers, but Geoff's unconventional convictions, together with his wife's attachment to pagan ways, have drawn the Christian crusaders to their home.

Claire has invited her friend Catherine. She is first to arrive looking very smart, but a little overdone, in a mauve full-length cotton dress with lace sleeves. A small hat covers her curly, blondish hair. Her scent is also overwhelming, but her lovely smile and the tone of her voice redeem any of these drawbacks.

'Sorry I'm early. I was so thrilled about comin'. It's good to see ye again Geoffrey, and you Claire.' She gives Claire a tight hug.

'I am so, so pleased you could come,' Claire whispers excitedly in Catherine's ear.

There's another knock and Claire opens the door, a little hesitantly this time.

'Good evening, Mrs Blake,' is about the only comment

Reverend Wren would make for at least the next fifteen minutes. He steps back to one side, as the short, distinguished Reverend Dickenson moves portentously through the doorway … as a King might walk into the royal kitchens.

Ministers seem to be either narrow in the face, or round and chubby. He is the latter, but projects thin and narrow in his manner. If viewed through half-closed eyes his moon face directly matches his belly and his rear end.

'Good evening to you, Geoffrey my son … Mrs Blake.' Like a clockwork figure he performs a rigid bow from the hip up, at the same time handing his hat and coat to Claire.

'Your hospitality is greatly appreciated, Mrs Blake.'

He moves to the fireplace, parts the back of his jacket and warms his rear end. He has placed himself in the most strategic position in the room. Standing too close to the fire, he hobbles forward to cool his overheating posterior.

'*Well!* Who have we here, young lady? Have we met at church?' He fidgets with some urgency as his bum burns. The hurried, superfluous words of his enquiry to Catharine are really only replacing the simple exclamation of *ouch!*

'Catherine Robinson, sir,' she replies as she attempts a small curtsy.

The invisible cleric appears like a rabbit out of a magician's hat and introduces himself, before returning to a position of stuffiness. It appears he knows his place.

'It is so kind of you to bless our happy home with a visit, sir.'

'Think nothing of it, Geoffrey my son. I must admit that I come this night with a hidden agenda,' he says, winking at Claire.

Without thinking, Claire winks back. The reverend is shocked.

Catherine, the only other person in the room to see Claire's wink, starts to giggle. The reverend, who is only five foot one inch in height, seems to shrink another two inches.

Catherine opens her mouth to explain her mirth, but cannot. Claire supports the Reverend by remaining objective and light-hearted. Her distracting playfulness however, is at the expense of poor Catherine, whose persistent laughing finally comes to an awkward halt. For a moment Claire has the upper hand but she does not hold the advantage for very long, nor had this been her intention. The reverend rallies, his religious training giving him a decisive advantage, even over kindness.

Claire and Catherine prepare tea and cake.

As if prearranged, Geoffrey and Reverend Dickenson move towards the back door and then outside.

'I have heard reports about, as some have put it, your pilgrimage to the south. I would very much like to hear your impressions of Cornwall … My goodness! My son, we have got a problem here, where did this monstrosity hail from?' he says, knowing the answer to his question before he finished it.

'Claire had it delivered.'

'Claire commissioned it?' questions the reverend with absolute astonishment. 'It's not Christian my boy … it reeks of blasphemy.'

'Claire says the stone is a symbol of our life and her love for me.' Geoffrey supports Claire, but without full conviction.

'Blasphemy, blasphemy, thou shalt not worship heathen idols,' says the reverend, heartlessly.

'The church too has idols and symbols, *sir*,' Claire counters as she and Catherine walk out of the rear entrance with refreshments. She is angry and surprised to overhear the reverend's comments.

'*My* child, watch your tongue … do you realise what you have just said?' He knows where Claire is coming from.

'I'm not a *child*, sir!'

Ignoring her protest, he continues. 'Is this your design my girl … or did you purchase the work completed?'

Catherine moves forward and stands beside Claire.

Reverend Dickenson's inference stirs vivid memories from Claire's past.

Back home, our minister, The Reverend Michaels of our Camelford church chastised my mother in a similar way. I stood there as he belittled her. 'Are the words you speak about the mother of Christ your own or are they hastened by the cider, Mrs. Etheridge?' he said.

Mother replied firmly. 'My words did come forth on the strength of a little alcohol, sir. But still, cannot the greatest of men, Christ, be born of a woman in the normal way … I ask you? These words I now speak come from my heart … I care to say no more on this subject, sir.'

Reverend Michaels replied to both of us. 'The Scriptures clearly describe the mother of Christ to be a virgin.'

Mother let sleeping dogs lie on that day eighteen years ago. 'What more can I say, sir,' she said 'Come, Claire, we have supper to prepare.'

I won't let this go as mother did, I can't, Claire says to herself as they all move back inside the house.

'Reverend Dickenson, my love and faith runs deeper than my love expressed through my marriage in Church, sir,' Claire tries to explain. 'My stone is a symbol of the deeper part of myself, and my love for my husband.'

'How can this be?' Reverend Dickenson is offended. He states. 'The love of Jesus Christ is the purest of love … and the love between a man and woman, sanctified in church, is the most holy of love.'

Reverend Wren, stunned by the exchange, wants to contribute, but tries to hold his tongue. Catherine cannot believe her ears … she has never seen this side of Claire. She is looking for an opening.

She loves to stir the pot, and intuitively understanding what Claire is on about and, with Wren in her sights, she impulsively proposes her one and only question. 'Reverend Wren,' she enquires with a one-eyed pert look. 'Do you think men are equal to women in the eyes of God?'

'*I* … I can't be sure,' wavering, he gives Reverend Dickenson a submissive glance.

'Do you think men and women are equal in the eyes of God, Geoffrey?' Reverend Wren repeats Catherine's question with a hint of mischief in his tone. Reverend Dickenson is far from pleased, but he would like to hear Geoffrey's reply.

'As I feel men are equal in the eyes of God … men and women too are equal in the eyes of God.' He says this with intense conviction.

'I hear what you are trying to say my husband, but reality cannot be ignored … women are not treated as equals within the Church, women cannot vote or hold a position in Government … double standards run right throughout our society.'

'Double standards?' questions Reverend Wren. Reverend Dickenson gives him a look fit to kill, but it is too late.

'To this very day men fail to respect women.'

'Double standards?' mumbles Reverend Dickenson.

'*Yes*, the downright arrogance and indulgence of our kings throughout history clearly shows the mistreatment of women. Maidens taken for king's pleasures … families honoured to provide daughters for royal rape.'

'Mrs Blake, you cannot speak this way.' Wren gets nervous and really regrets his probing. 'If those words were to be heard outside this house …'

'That is exactly right, Reverend Wren, and this is precisely what I am speaking about, why can't I speak … Why?' Claire is getting more upset.

Catherine has her hand across her mouth. The Reverend Dickenson is temporarily speechless. His anger towards Reverend Wren is only lessened by his overriding resentment of Claire's behaviour.

Claire now speaks to everybody. 'I am born of simple parents, I have only a basic education, but what I am speaking about is so clear. The future will pay for the hypocrisies of our time.'

'Mrs Blake, the Druids were unusual, to say the least, were they not?' Reverend Dickenson gets straight to the point, Claire's stone foremost in his mind.

'*Unusual*, Reverend?' Claire's deepest beliefs are now being challenged.

'Human sacrifices, torture and depravity,' he replies with almost lust in his tone, 'were an integral part of the Druid culture, were they not?'

'No civilisation is perfect. The crusades, sir, could be viewed as human sacrifice and torture,' Claire replies quietly and calmly. 'Cannibalism was a practice of our noble invaders, was it not? I have read that the Arab states modelled their barbaric habits on our crusading forces. Slavery, *sir*, exists in our lifetime. Men and women from Africa are being taken against their will and sold like *animals* in other lands.'

Catherine is amazed at Claire's outburst.

'Did you know, sir,' continues Claire, that women were held in high esteem in ancient times? Women attained positions as priestesses within the Druid and Celtic organisations. They were respected, feared and revered. Women hold no position within the Christian church, sir! And furthermore it would seem that Christianity invented monogamy and preserves it hypocritically,' Claire declares.

Leaving words like blasphemy and irreverence behind, Reverend Dickenson responds vigorously.

'Mrs Blake, have you any idea what would happen if there was no structure? Family life would crumble. The basis of our society is founded on the family. Most civilised communities have a monogamous family structure.'

'Christian communities, sir?' asks Claire respectfully.

'Yes Christian,' he replies. 'We have learnt that the non-Christian communities of the Pacific Islands swap their women and murder children at birth to prevent overpopulation. In Asia, female babies are done away with and a son is worth seven times that of a baby girl. These are pagan acts of the most despicable and brutal type. Christianity will eventually spread through these lands and free people, showing them the love of God through Jesus Christ.'

Catherine is fascinated with the interchange.

Claire looks to her husband for support. Geoffrey has never realised Claire felt so strongly.

Reverend Wren, caught between the church and his conscience, puts forward a compromising comment.

'Isn't our society progressing? Are not things improving day by day?' His statement, disguised as a question, just hangs in the air.

'I don't understand,' Geoffrey is distraught and irrational. 'Is my love in question … I love my wife so deeply … more than I can explain.' Tears come to his eyes. 'I love you so much; I would do anything for you, Claire.'

'Is there more Geoffrey could do for you, Mrs Blake?' Reverend Wren asks cautiously.

'No there is no more you can give me, Geoffrey … no more anybody can give.' Claire says calmly. 'Last night I had a dream,' she says to everyone, an owl sat on my shoulder. It was very fluffy, very wise, and very cuddly. It looked at me with its large brown eyes. I saw myself in its eyes. I felt complete and warm … it rested its head close to my neck — it loved me very much … Geoffrey came and it flew away.'

Catherine begins to cry. 'That is a lovely dream … I've never had a dream like that.'

'It's only a dream … Dreams are whims of the mind are they not?' comments Reverend Wren.

'Dreams can be the work of the Devil. Dreams are fruitless.' The Reverend Dickenson is now getting quite annoyed and tries to pull rank. He gets up to leave.

Wren is now sitting silently with his mouth wide open. He is quite pale.

Suddenly, there is a huge explosion out in the garden. Everybody is shocked by the noise, which equals the full report of a small cannon.

Geoffrey, Reverend Wren, and Catherine run outside. Claire's stone is smouldering in the cold night air; a chunk, one third of the stone's size, has split off and is laying ten feet away, also smouldering.

Claire and the Reverend Dickenson arrive as Geoffrey and Reverend Wren are trying to work out the cause of such a powerful explosion. There is a warm earthly smell in the air.

Geoffrey is speechless and confused.

'Lightning, gunpowder?' suggests Wren, 'Maybe a lightning bolt has struck the stone.'

Reverend Dickenson surveys the situation, but remains silent. He knows about unexplained phenomena.

Claire's emotions are spinning. *Why can't they understand, why?* A deep feeling of aloneness engulfs her. Her love for Geoff, strong as it is, has been stretched. Her stone lies shattered.

Everybody is speaking and speculating, but Claire is in another place in her mind.

Am I selfish? she thinks. *Am I being unreasonable? I should speak … no, I cannot, I cannot.*

She stands alone, amongst the group, staring at her stone. *I need my husband*, part of her is crying out.

'This broken stone is a sign from God,' Catherine says quietly.

CHAPTER TEN

One week later

n the distance, sounds of music can be heard getting closer and closer. When Claire is certain the musicians are near, she opens her window shutters. The minstrels stop, and forming a half circle, begin to play a bewitching melody.

Every now and then the group experiences an encounter such as this. Using their musical skills they tease and momentarily flirt with her spirit. Claire's mind lifts and soars with the magic of the music and all problems of her world temporarily vanish.

The group plays three pieces and prepares to leave. Claire offers to pay, but they do not accept. As quickly as they appeared they are gone, their musical notes following them down the road.

She goes out into her garden, still listening to the music as it fades into the distance.

It is near twelve noon, her broken stone is lit by a stream of sunlight. This is what she has so carefully prepared for. For twelve minutes the stone will glow.

As a young girl, Claire grew up with the stones of the Druids. She would spend hours on the Cornish cliffs sitting on and around these keepers of time. The early mornings were haunted by their presence. Throughout the day they would seem to change in size and colour. They would be dwarfed by grey storm clouds, highlighted in the golden late afternoon sun.

They would be lost in ocean fogs, and scoured by hail. After the hot summer sun heated the stones, Claire would press her body against them and feel their continuing warmth long after the onset of cold westerly changes.

The stones were always there. They were giving her a link with the past and the future.

Focusing on her lighted stone, time begins to expand. She can see and feel the varying nature of time … one minute can last forever. She feels part of the stone; it is the lighthouse in her life.

Claire steps back. What is that? She cannot believe her eyes. An image … Somebody is standing next to the rock. She squints … It looks like me. She moves further back, crouches down and still the other image remains. She stands, and the shimmering outline moves towards her, hand outstretched. *What am I seeing? Who is this?* It is moving closer. She puts out her hand, and the fingers of the vaporous apparition touch each of hers. *Is this somebody from the past … maybe a sign of the future?* A feeling of wellbeing moves through her whole body as the look-alike figure disappears. 'Well I'll be,' she says, trying to fathom what has just occurred.

The stream of sunlight moves away from her stone. The light will shine in another place and another time. Nothing seems to matter, but all does matter intensely. She deeply understands this contradiction. She thinks back. *I was hopping-mad with bossy menfolk as I grew up, and I know mother was. I was sure London would be different, but it's unbearable. I thought my husband would understand.*

Claire's clasps her abdomen gently with her two hands. At this disquieting time in her life, when there are so many things to consider … 'I am expecting a child,' she finally admits to herself.

'Yoo hoo … yoo hoo, is anybody home?' The sound of a happy voice pulls Claire's mind back into the immediate present.

'Yes, come in! Come in! I know who that be.'

Catherine appears at the front door with a beautiful bunch of flowers, and a smile to match.

'It's so good to see you again, Claire.'

'You too,' replies Claire. Looking away suddenly, she begins to set the winter blooms in a vase.

'There's a difference about you Claire … such a difference.'

'Did you hear the minstrels? Their music was beautiful Catherine.'

'Claire, you're changing the subject.'

'I didn't think it showed,' Claire teases, wrapping her dress tightly around her waist.

'What shows?' Catherine looks back at Claire with a piercing, but kindly stare and tight smile.

'I can't say as yet.'

'You are with child … no?' Catherine's eyes demand an answer.

'*No* … eh, well… I can't tell you,' replies Claire '*Ah*, that is … I can't tell you first,' she says more softly.

'You are … I know it … aren't you?'

'Yes, yes, I am. … Please don't tell a soul, *promise?*' Claire pleads.

A mischievous look flashes across Catherine's face as she moves across to the open window. 'Guess what everybody! Claire is …' She turns jumping up and down, and laughing.

As much as she wants to, Claire cannot share her friend's joy. She clasps her fingers nervously together and fear comes to her eyes.

'What's wrong girl, what's wrong?' Has this got somethin' to do with them … that Reverend Dickenson, and Reverend Wren … last week … has it? You're not happy are you, love?' She puts her arm around her friend.

'I could not have anymore than I have. My husband is a fine man'.

'Yes, he certainly be that.'

'And he loves me so. London is exciting, I have my health, you are my friend Catherine and, I have my baby.' Tears are now streaming down her cheeks. 'Come to the garden.' Claire leads, stooped forward and walking quickly, her hands partly covering her eyes. 'I can't, I can't … I must be free Catherine.'

Claire leans against her broken stone. It's half-past one and the sun's rays have moved past the stone and onto the wall behind.

Catherine holds Claire tightly. 'There, there, me dearest, there, let it be. Everything will be just fine. Nothin' matters as much as this. You know that.'

'Everything matters as much as this, life itself matters as much as this. I see it all so clearly, Catherine. My baby girl knows it too. I feel so alone, so desperate.'

'Now, now, no you don't, don't be a silly Milly. She, that is if a little girl is to be, will be God innocent when she is born. Innocent as a baby deer on the meadow. How would she know anything?'

Catherine is way out of her depth. She is strained and hurt.

'It's passed on Catherine, from generation to generation, male control, it's passed on. I cannot be free … but, I must … of that there is no question. My love must be free to love Geoff. He has my love completely … oh God why don't they understand?'

Even at this point, as stressed and resigned as Claire is, she puts out her arms and tries to hold Catherine above the consuming waters of her depression and sadness.

One of the two resident swallows flashes through the ray of light moving up the wall. It lands on a bare twig seemingly looking for its mate. The male swallow sits silently for several seconds and then flies straight upward. After a short pause it is caught by a sudden gust and, without any control, flies south in a direct straight line.

The two women move inside.

'The garden doesn't look real from the window, does it?' says Catherine as she pours their second cup of tea. 'It looks creepy.'

'No … no it doesn't,' replies Claire softly.

Claire considers telling Catherine about the mystery figure in the garden … *No I won't, I can't tell anybody about that.*

'Mrs Thomlinson did it again. I knows I talk too much, but I keep workin' while I talk, I think it's good for the shop. The customers are all my friends. When I talk to them they buy things. Mind you that's not the reason I do it. Anyway, yesterday Mrs Sears was talking to me and we was having a good natter, there was a hell … Oh dear! I should not have said that … There was a big crash in the storeroom. Mrs Thomlinson fell off the ladder … she was at 'er shoe box again.'

'*Shoe box?*' Claire enquires with a giggle.

'That's where she keeps 'er extra dosh, 'er ill-gotten gains,' Catherine explains. 'I knows it's there, I've known for ages. *Anyway,* she screams at me, 'it's your fault Catherine.' Mrs Sears gathered up her packages and left embarrassed like, then it started. My talking were blamed for 'er toppling off the steps! She was real angry, she was. All of a sudden, in the middle of another small scream, 'er voice just went.'

'Went? What do you mean, *went?*' asks Claire, now becoming temporarily distracted from her own problems.

'It went, out the window, gone never to be heard again. She can't say a ruddy word now. Ooh, I've sworn again. She has ta write me notes, and needs me more than ever. I'm the manager now; I speaks to the merchants and the most important custom-ers. I even go to the bank. God works in mysterious ways don't you think, Claire?'

By now Catherine has forgotten the original intention of her story was to cheer Claire and has become completely absorbed in her own distraction.

'Does you think God works in mysterious ways, Claire?'

'What I think, Catherine, is that is an extremely funny story and Mrs Thomlinson deserves all she gets. She will probably never be able to speak again.' She laughs, patting her friend's arm with excitement and support.

Catherine now realises in her efforts to help her friend she has become completely sidetracked and, under cover of their laughing, she returns to the seriousness of Claire's situation.

'Now that takes care of 'er, what are we going to do with you, Claire?' says Catherine, her now serious look slightly out of place.

'All is done Cathy … let it be done. Tonight I will prepare dinner, Geoffrey and I will sit by the fire and we will talk, possibly read, and then we will retire to bed.'

'Tomorrow is anotha day … eh?' nods Catherine with a wise and thoughtful look. She is sure she has helped Claire solve her problem.

'Yes my dear friend, tomorrow is just another day. The world goes on, and each day the faults of men and women are partly reckoned and paid for. New seeds are sown for future days and the seeds grow in accordance with our intentions. Mistakes produce bad fruits, different to those of deception and repeated errors — they make fruit of poison. Goodness sown produces fruits of nourishment and fine taste. The laws of sow and reap are true and fair. There are many times however, where we have to pay not knowing who the sowers are. These are the big mistakes sown deeply in the past.' Claire is babbling now.

Catherine too is struggling. 'Well Mrs Thomlinson is payin' and I know what seeds she's sown. Once more I am enjoying every moment of it, anyway. Is that how it works? Is that how it works, Claire?'

Claire can't do much but smile. She understands she has stressed and disorientated her loyal friend, but that now seems all beyond her control.

'Yes my dearest Cathy, I'm sure that's how it works, it's all too clear to me, and I feel I cannot change any of it.'

CHAPTER ELEVEN

The small female swallow struggles, a cat has a firm grip on its wing and is in full control.

Detached, Claire watches the cat torment the small bird, tearing away body part by body part. The swallow is still alive to the very last moment, its soft red breast stained a deeper scarlet with the colour of blood.

The cat's eye catches a glimpse of another small creature moving near the rear of the property. It leaves the swallow in a fluffy, bloody mess on the cold gravel path and then proceeds, machine-like, to attack again.

Claire, still in a deeply reflective frame of mind, picks up the dead bird ever so gently and takes it to her stone. Near a small flat broken section, she places the little creature and kneels down in deep silence. As she does there is a small movement from within her womb — she is sure her baby is stirring.

Claire reflects with sorrow and then relaxes. Her mind is made up.

She will poison her body. She can no longer live in, and bring her baby into, a cruel, hypocritical, unchangeable world. A world she feels represses and dehumanises women.

*　　*　　*

Across all times, there are common threads that run through human lives. Babies are born, grow to men and women, make choices, experience happiness, sadness, and die. Every now and then predictable patterns are broken, and time as we know it, can change and alter in its nature.

The experiences of an upbringing, the consequences of mistaken decisions, and luck, have gone on in advance, as they do, and await the stick of the blind man.

Smoke from the evening fires rises straight up from chimney pots into an unsettled sky. Geoffrey Blake feels uneasy as he steps from his cab. The erratic clattering of the horse's hooves on the hard cobblestone roadway, synchronise as the cab begins to move off slowly into the cold foggy night.

Geoffrey's hand reaches for the door latch with the urgency and paralysed restraint a dreamer understands. He opens the door; everything appears to be in place.

'I'm home love,' he calls in his usual manner. He hesitates. There is no answer.

'Claire!' he screams, His wife is lying on the floor her new dress stretched tightly around her pregnant form.

'What bloody monster?' he cries out frantically, moving to her side.

With a trembling hand he feels her pulse. Her heart has stopped. Lifting her gently, holding her tenderly, he reaches for their five-month unborn child.

'My baby has gone too.' A feeling of helplessness screams through his whole body. Standing up, he looks down at her in disbelief. Placing a moist cloth on her forehead, again he listens at her chest, she is still not breathing.

'Claire, Claire, don't leave me.' He shakes her, almost violently.

*　　*　　*

In the month of May, in the year 1967, two swallows complete their nest in the gardens of the Royal Chelsea Hospital, London.

Baby Jane Turner, seven and three-quarter pounds, is born. Jane shares the same birth date, and the identical birth time as Claire Etheridge, one hundred and seventy-seven years earlier.

Several days after the birth, Jane's mother and her sister Jocelyn, watch baby Jane — fascinated.

'She's been here before?' jokes Jocelyn.

CHAPTER TWELVE

London, September 1789

The sounds of creaking and the splashing of oars break the misty dawn's silence. A putrid stench wafts out to meet the long boat as it approaches the prison ship anchored on the Thames near Woolwich. Geoffrey Blake and five other prisoners are being transferred from the overcrowded Newgate Prison, to the hulk of *Censor* one of many disbanded navy ships acting as temporary floating jails.

As the lighter draws closer to the hulk, Geoffrey's mind is taken over by a recent powerful dream.

… Loud roars and howls from behind two huge oak doors stop me in my tracks. I am curious, my chest is tightening, my heart is beginning to pound. I must look inside. Pressing my fingers between the two massive doors, I steadily push until they begin to open.

A splash of water across Geoffrey's face brings him out of his dream back into his present reality. He looks into the fiendish eyes of the offending oarsman as another skimming oar sends an even larger splash across the entire rear section of the lighter.

'That be taken as an accident, sailor,' the guard gives the oarsman a warning.

In my dream all is silent as I slide open the warehouse doors. I'm scared, but I must go in. Before me, a narrow cobble stone path disappears into the musky dinginess of the old building. I move inside, the doors close by themselves leaving me temporarily blinded.

From my right comes an excruciating, trumpeting screeching sound, which echoes around the whole building. I stand — I can't move — my heart is racing. Then out of the gloom I'm hit by a massive blow to my mid section. I buckle over. A second blow throws me to the floor. A small, elephant-like animal with long, curled, thin ivory tusks, swipes at me for the third time, but a restraining chain holds the angry animal back. Another agonising cry cuts though the air as the longhaired elephant's huge tusks catch my leg and spin me around on the stone floor.

It's not too late, I can still go back … no, I say to myself, I must go on. I have no choice; I must see what is inside.

Suddenly from a stone pen on my left, a massive crocodile attacks with open jaws. I roll away as an iron grate stops this evil reptile's assault.

I feel if I keep in the centre of the path I will be safe. If I move too far either way, I will be done for.

Covered in animal excreta, mud and rancid water, I crawl on my hands and knees.

Bats and pigeons flutter about in the half-light. Huge pythons lie on rocks, and hang motionless only inches away from me. Apes and monkeys are swinging and screeching, the larger animals menacing the small. A usually harmless, long-armed sloth comes threateningly close to me, curls its upper lip, stares, and hisses at me.

Seals and penguins hideously packed into a small rock-pool enclosure are all trying to survive together in putrid conditions. A fairy penguin lies crushed by a frustrated, snorting bull sea lion.

I stand and move on past these dismal pens of aggravated and hopeless creatures. Stopping, I see a pathetic figure approaching, unrestrained, out of the gloom. As it gets closer, I know it's a male. He's stooped and walking side on. He takes a full step with his left foot and a half with the right; his uneven gait makes him look frightening. But I have no fear. I refrain from moving closer for I sense he is territorial. This creature in my dream is powerful, but has no pride. He seems ashamed of his own existence. As he crosses my path he glances quickly at me — he knows me. Slowly this grotesque, sad figure moves away into the gloom on his predetermined journey.

I need to go no further.

Preoccupied and accustomed to his presence, the poorly, pathetic animals of the menagerie ignore him as he makes his way out.

His mind has produced a character, the ancient man, to show him an aspect of himself, as dreams do. However, he believes this powerful dream has no purpose and the players exist only by chance.

The dream continues. *Outside a small, silent, lifeless crowd is filing along a meandering walkway towards a wooden pavilion, on a hill, in the distance. I join the queue of these characterless, expressionless people.*

The longboat moves alongside the prison ship's gangway. Geoffrey's dream recollection is interrupted. He finds his arm being gripped by a younger man next to him, the lad's brown eyes reflecting fear and desperation.

'Break it up, move it on,' orders the officer as he prods Geoffrey in the back with his baton. The apprehensive group shuffle from the rocking boat onto the more secure gangway of the stinking hulk.

'I'm not going!' screams a man.

'Brother, I'm right with you,' reassures a voice from behind.

A wave of groans and vile comments waft up from deep within the grotesque floating prison.

'Come on, Henry,' urges another man. 'One step at a time … one step at a time.'

Geoffrey again tries to help, but is goaded by another officer's baton.

As he waits to be registered, Geoffrey's dream flashes compulsively back into his mind, now more vivid than ever.

Inside the wooden pavilion on the hill, I can see a large square open area. An ancient man crouching in a locked steel cage. From all sides he is being viciously ridiculed and harangued by a crowd. They jab and aggravate the ancient man with sticks and iron bars. The saliva of children drips from the body hair of the wretched creature. His head is swaying back and forth, his questioning eyes sheltered by one hand, the other making futile attempts to fend off the attacks.

There is an overwhelming atmosphere of hate and fear as I climb a wooden staircase to a balcony overlooking the whole painful scene. The tormented caged man looks up at me, our eyes lock in a mutual stare. He cannot contain his anguish any longer and lets out two shrilled screams which echo around and around the pavilion. The crowd freezes and is instantly silent. Tears stream from my eyes. God, I can feel the condemnation of the crowd, I know that lonely feeling, I feel like that hairy ugly creature.

After his venting screams, the ancient man relaxes — the crowd vanishes.

The pitiless reality aboard the foul-smelling hulk now pushes all else aside in Geoffrey's mind. He has entered hell. As his group is taken below deck, responses from the resident prisoners range from silent empathy to straight-out abuse.

In the dim light of his allocated quarters, he can just make out a line of cubed wooden sleeping units. Geoffrey is cheered by the smell of freshly bailed straw stacked in one corner.

The overall stench gradually becomes less offensive to his senses, although it has not actually dissipated. Arms crossed, shoulders twisted forward, he only allows the warm thick fetid air to penetrate the upper parts of his lungs.

Prisoners well enough to work have already been rooted out of the early-morning darkness and allotted a day's labour at the dockyards. The sick, the dying and the pretenders remain motionless, barely discernible from the piles of prison blankets and straw. For many of them hard labour would be a better alternative to their downward-spiralling condition.

If there is a hell on earth, the prison ship must be it. At church, as a boy, Geoffrey learned of a hell in the hereafter. Even then, he thought, hell was a fairy tale, and that it only existed as a tortured state of mind, a reality in this life only.

'You won't be here long my lad.'

'Sir?'

'You won't be here long my boy,' repeats a physically defeated man nearby.

'If you are speaking to me, and if that were to be true, I'm not sure that be good or bad news,' Geoffrey replies trying to humour the old man.

'Did you go down that rope my boy?'

'What do you mean ... *down the rope?*'

'Are you guilty?' the man asks.

'*Guilty?*' Geoffrey is becoming agitated.

The rough but kindly face of the man stares straight at him.

'No! No! I am not! Why should I answer you anyway? Who the hell are you?'

'Everything will be alright then, eh?'

The old convict reclines back into the darkness of his bedding area.

Geoffrey doesn't have the energy to go into this any further. He makes himself as comfortable as he can in his allocated bunk and manages to take a small nap.

* * *

Geoffrey is awakened suddenly by a rough voice.

'What have we here lads, a fuckin' fancy boy?'

Shocked and groggy he opens his eyes to see a motley mob that looks like something out of a skull and crossbones saga.

The four inmates, sent back prematurely from a daily work gang, grab Geoffrey.

'Bring him here,' calls the burly one. Geoffrey is pinned against a wall near a lamp with a thin arm wrapped tightly around his throat. The burly character clenches his huge hand firmly in the centre of Geoffrey's groin.

'*Whatta* ya got, whatta ya got?'

Overcome by fear and confusion Geoffrey stares straight ahead in silence. As his assailant pulls his other fist back, Geoffrey turns his head to one side.

'Found it! Found it 'ere, Moose!' calls one of the other two.

Moose's fist comes down hard on Geoffrey's right cheek.

Geoffrey's belongings are spread across the under decking; edibles and any valuables disappear like water on a dry sandy surface.

Moose viciously throws Geoffrey to the floor.

The sounds of batons smashing against the iron isolation gate send all his attackers, except the leader, scattering. Three armed guards appear, and the ring-leader retreats defiantly into the surrounding darkness, like a jackal frightened away from a carcass.

Geoffrey is manhandled and thrown forward onto his bunk by two guards. 'Welcome aboard sailor.' They laugh as they leave.

Shock is surging through Geoffrey's whole body. If there was any doubt about the gravity of his situation, it is now gone. He remembers his father's dictum that intelligence is the ability to adjust to change.

His anger and fears eventually give way to sleep, and he slumbers for six hours without incident.

On waking, he makes his way to the tubs, which are provided for the relieving of body wastes. It is first in first served for the limited amount of fresh washing water in containers near the exit.

The violence Geoffrey experienced on the first day is never repeated. In the three months he spends on the prison ship, he makes no lasting friendships.

Miraculously he escapes sickness. Most prisoners become ill, some slightly, some critically and many perish. The old grey-haired philosopher dies not long after speaking to him.

He gets himself through the ordeal by keeping his days quiet and consistently disciplined. He views the penal labour at the dockyards as exercise, and makes the most of simple foods available.

CHAPTER THIRTEEN

On the tenth of November 1789, Geoffrey Blake is handed a summons. The fearful rumours of another transportation fleet to Australia, sweeping through the prison systems have become a reality for him. From the ease and affluence of his previous lifestyle, to an existence of servitude and suffering aboard the prison hulk, *Censor*, yet another journey is about to begin for Geoffrey. He will be shipped to Port Jackson, Australia on the Second Fleet.

The news of his transportation whips up mixed feelings amongst his fellow prisoners on the hulk. Many who did not communicate with Geoffrey now find an excuse to come forward. It would seem envy; fear, sympathy and mateship now find a common chord. Even the man who assaulted him on arrival emerges as a long lost friend, wishing him luck and returning some of Geoffrey's personal items they stole from him.

Geoffrey is touched by the obvious feelings of loss aroused by his departure amongst his fellow prisoners. Throughout his experiences on the prison ship, apart from his initial violent initiation, the convicts basically let him be. Most of the time he was treated with the same respect he gave to the men.

As the transfer boat pulls away from the prison ship, a line of convicts bids him farewell.

'Good luck, *Geoffey boy!*' Moose calls out.

Geoffrey waves back. He is relieved to be leaving, and feels sadness for the men who are left to endure the unrelenting conditions aboard the hulk.

*   *   *

The harbour water is speckled with the lights of several ships waiting in the dark. The *Neptune* will sail soon on the first leg of the voyage from Plymouth to Portsmouth.

Forty-three Marines, some with wives, have been aboard the HMAS *Neptune* for over a week now. Prisoners from city and country goals from all over England have been coming aboard progressively. Geoffrey and two other prisoners from the *Censor* now join them.

An early morning crowd has gathered on the wharf. Calls of good tidings and 'You get what you bloody deserve, the lot of you!' lift above the murmurings and the cry of a baby.

Some of the well-to-do prisoners are allowed visitors. Last-minute petitions have been hurriedly circulated trying to influence politicians and prison authorities to reconsider their fates.

The three-mastered *Neptune*, 809 tons, largest of the ships in the second fleet, is ready. She sits majestically in the still waters

Geoffrey was employed by a shipping company so it's not the first time he has been aboard a sailing ship. He looks up through the rigging at the towering masts and massive bundles of canvas. *'Did you go down that rope? Are you guilty?'* Geoff recalls the words of the old man on the *Censor*.

'What bloody rope? No … no, I'm not.' He remembers his own words.

He is still unsure why the old man spoke to him in this way.

Terror, fear and a kind of hope does a slow dance through the early morning air. The prisoners below are relatively silent.

Our small, chained group for some unknown reason is being held on deck probably as an example to the crowd Geoffrey thinks, but he cannot be sure.

Through an almost spiritual silence, again comes the cry of a baby. Geoff turns and looks at the wharf but the woman with the little one has gone. The baby's crying continues, but this time it is coming from within the *Neptune*.

An unidentified figure stands alone on the quay at Plymouth. Jamie, Claire's childhood friend from Cornwall knows Geoffrey. He met him at the wedding. Letters Claire had sent to Jamie told him many times about her loving husband Geoffrey. Jamie knew of Geoff's intense love for Claire, but he also knew about her deep sadness.

Jamie has waited fourteen hours. He has not left the ship's side. Challenged several times for loitering, he is finally let be. The authorities judge him as queer, but harmless. He learnt of Geoffrey's predicament from the Reverend Wren. Patiently he waits, hoping he will be able to catch a glimpse, or maybe talk to Geoffrey before the *Neptune* sails.

As the *Neptune* drops her moorings for Portsmouth, Jamie waves. Later Geoff is to overhear some sailors and marines joking about the looney on the wharf. He would never find out it was Jamie.

In her letters Claire had told Jamie, several times, about her stone, he knew how important it was to her.

With some help from the Reverend Peter Wren and assistance from the shipping company that employed Geoffrey, Claire's repaired stone would accompany Jamie back to Port Isaacs by sea.

Jamie would spend the next three years of his life working to pay for the transportation of Claire's broken stone to its final resting place, between Port Isaacs and Tintagel Castle, high above the ocean on the Cornwall cliffs. This is where Jamie and Claire dreamed and roamed as children. This is where, unbeknown to Claire, he loved her as a man.

CHAPTER FOURTEEN

At a Portsmouth quay the gangplanks of the *Neptune* are becoming less steep as the 810-ton vessel rises with the incoming tide. The decks are temporarily littered with steaming animal manure as panic-stricken livestock are being moved aboard in the final hour. The crew is preparing for departure.

Captain Thomas Gilbert appears on the quarter-deck from time to time. Some of his contemplations are probably similar to those of the crew and the prisoners, but he alone knows what is ahead. Gilbert commanded the HMAS *Charlotte* on the First Fleet to Australia.

Camden, Calvert and King are the new contracting agents responsible for transporting the convicts to the new penal colony. The use of contractors instead of government operated and funded expeditions is a new approach, an approach that will lead to ruthless, profit-motivated cost cutting during the voyage.

Captain Gilbert, a strong but compassionate man is about to personally experience the realities of this new government policy. Before the *Neptune* leaves England, he is to be replaced by Donald Trail, a Scot and a former Navy Captain, who had previously been employed by the same contractors as a master on several of their African slave ships.

Compassion and economics rarely make good bedfellows. Throughout the voyage, Captain Trail's benevolence will be measured in pounds, shillings and pence.

In mid December 1789, the HMAS *Scarborough*, and the *Surprise*, rendezvous with the *Neptune* and its new Captain at

Portsmouth. The supply ship *Lady Julian* and its cargo of female prisoners has set sail at an earlier date. Another small ship the *Justinian*, a late-comer, will also accompany the fleet.

The crew are moving more about the deck. Geoffrey feels the vessel stir in a way which is different. The hull eases mysteriously up, down and around in a giddy motion. A gathering of momentum can be felt through the thick timbers. The ship is underway; the might of a powerful England again begins to silently, forge forward.

*   *   *

After two hours, huge seas and head winds force the *Neptune* back to quieter waters. The temperature below decks begins to rise steadily and agitation amongst the prisoners is building. The forward motion of the vessel and the commencement of the journey, although threatening, had acted as a panacea. Now the mood has changed.

Captain Trail decides to allow groups of eight prisoners on deck for ten-minute periods. This decision lifts the men's morale instantly. Two hours and ten minutes later, it is Geoff's turn to move up on deck. Although shackled, for a few brief moments his mind is able to lift away from the ship and bid farewell to his England. The operation of the vessel and even the presence of the Captain on the quarterdeck is only background to his overwhelming grief and retrospection. Claire is in his mind constantly.

CHAPTER FIFTEEN

The first scheduled port of call for the *Neptune* is Tenerife, situated on one of thirteen islands within the Canary Island group, 820 miles south-west of Spain. Captain Trail's radical plan, which he is keeping confidential, is a non-stop voyage directly to the Cape of Good Hope.

In contrast to the stormy weather during the first night, the dawn brings fresh north-westerly winds, which push the *Neptune* firmly on through light choppy seas. The general feeling amongst the convicts is still optimistic despite the harsh conditions.

The Orlop deck where the convicts are confined is three levels down. It is seventy-five feet long by thirty-six feet wide and seven high below the beams. The men sleep in bunks or hammocks in four main rows. They are chained at the wrists or the ankles and in many cases two men are shackled together.

After only a couple of days the voyage has gone from a nightmare to hell. The stench and damp, the groans, the darkness and the continual rolling of the vessel, are unrelenting. Some of the horrors of Geoff's menagerie dream seem to be coming true.

From days spent at sea during his employment in the shipping industry, Geoffrey is familiar with the smell of lamps and oil of tar, the taste of salt air, the creaking of timbers, the sounds of tightening and easing ropes. *I can't believe I am here chained like an animal,* he thinks to himself.

Smells constantly emanate from the men's unwashed skin, hair, clothing and body orifices. Vomit from sea-sickness along with human waste fills buckets long overdue for emptying. Salt water and sea air flush out the most permanent odours, but this is only early days.

Feelings of hope, denial and anger are moving around the Orlop deck like the restless waves of the ocean around the *Neptune*.

*   *   *

Jane Turner and her psychic friend, Margret Lakes, are aboard British Airways flight 1033 to Australia. It is Tuesday, May 10, 2000. Jane awakes feeling unusually claustrophobic.

Most of the other passengers are also awake and all the toilets are engaged. Jane pushes her feet forward and arches her back. She feels like screaming.

The toilet light goes off. She makes her move, only to be thwarted by smiling hostess with a food trolley.

'Here we are Ma'm.' The flight attendant has unintentionally trapped Jane.

As a tray is placed in front of her she feels like climbing the cabin walls

Jane calculates. *The passengers are expecting refreshments.* The toilet light shows vacant. *If I follow close behind the attendant's trolley, I will be first there.* She makes her move again. The trolley rattles slowly up the aisle with Jane close behind.

'Made it,' she says to herself.

A quick glance in the toilet mirror reveals her green eyes dulled, her dark hair lifeless, face drawn and lips a little blue. 'I look lousy, very lousy indeed,' she says to herself as she pops a small pimple.

'Now look at what I've done.' The bright fluoro highlights a major blotch on her cheek.

The friendly man next to Margaret is smiling as Jane returns.

Margaret is obviously feeling chatty.

'Tell me about you Jane,' Margaret enquires with a yawn as Jane sits down.

'There isn't very much to tell.'

She and her crystal ball probably know all about me anyway, Jane is thinking. *Well … I'm not going to find out now — she's falling asleep. She asks about the most special person in the world — me, and then dozes off.* Jane has a lump in her chest; her life's story has been stirred up and there is nobody to tell it to.

Margaret is dead to the world.

Jane smiles at the gent in the window seat and then looks at Margaret. *I think she has had a few worries in her life. She seems prematurely wrinkled for her age. Look at the worry lines across her forehead and between her cheeks and nose. Her hair is coloured. Facelifts? Jane can't tell for sure, but Margaret's nose may have been altered. She has a kind and friendly face though*, thinks Jane.

Jane is unsure about her assessments of Margaret, for she has judged others before and been very, very wrong.

Margaret's arms are relaxed and folded below a largish pair of breasts. She is wearing a long flowing, slightly, outlandish dress. Her gold earrings match a gold chain around her neck. A linked bracelet and a large, deep blue sapphire ring complete her jewellery. Her watch is Gucci. *That must have cost a pretty penny*, Jane guesses.

The time on Margaret's watch is 7.45 pm, London time.

We've only been in the air for four and a quarter hours … It seems much longer. Jane's mind begins to wobble, she is still very tired, her eyes flicker to a close and she slips into another sleep.

*   *   *

Throughout the night on the *Neptune*, there are disturbances on the upper decks. Verbal and physical confrontations are not the prerogative of the prisoners. Other disagreements are originating right at the top of command and will persist for at least half the voyage. These conflicts will affect everyone on the ship.

During the first leg of the voyage from Plymouth to Portsmouth a duel had taken place between the original Captain Gilbert and Mr John Macarthur, a young free settler travelling with his wife Elizabeth, their five year-old-son and maid.

A military man, young Macarthur had sided against Gilbert with the ship's Captain of Marines Nicholas Nepean, on the question of direct responsibility and control of the convicts. Macarthur's other dispute with the captain was about the size, accessibility and location of his and Mrs Macarthur's onboard accommodation. These two disagreements ultimately lead to the duel with Gilbert at the Fountain Tavern, Plymouth. Both men faced each other, discharged their weapons, and missed. The matter was then put aside.

But not long after the duelling incident Captain Gilbert was replaced by Captain Trail. The Marines gained no authority over the convicts and Macarthur remained dissatisfied with his family's accommodation until they were finally moved to another vessel later in the voyage.

*　　*　　*

'He'll do! Him, the fair-haired one,' says the Chief Mate, Ellington, pointing at Geoffrey.

It looks random, but Ellington has plans for him.

He is unchained and briefed on his duties. He will be responsible for the needs of fourteen prisoners. There is silent approval from the men who will be in Geoff's group.

Geoffrey is now free to move about the ship, and is allowed to choose a lad to assist him. A mess leader's official duties include collecting the rations and preparation of the daily meals. At meal times, communal boilers are set up on the upper deck where he will, with the unenthusiastic help of his new assistant Horace, prepare a basic stew made from salted meat, some potatoes, flour and water. Porridge and flatbread they will cook in separate pans. Geoff and Horace are also responsible for the issuing of water rations.

Large tubs are used for toileting. Depending on the weather, ship politics, closeness to ports and the whims of the Captain, prisoners may be released from chains to use the toilet tubs. If not, pots are to be supplied to the incarcerated men, another task Geoff and Horace are expected to carry out.

His second night consists of some sleep, talk, water-fetching, a little nursing, and the toilet pots.

His young assistant Horace who, for now, is required to be chained when not on duty, sleeps soundly.

CHAPTER SIXTEEN

The second day on board the *Neptune* begins. Within an overwhelming atmosphere of confusion and sadness, the human spirit manages to appear as pockets of chatter spread rapidly across the whole deck. It is not long before most of the men, apart from the sick and dying, are bustling with momentary hope.

The poor health of the convicts, the inadequate rations and the cold conditions has already resulted in sickness and death. Death comes slowly. The eyes die first. Then all anyone can do is to offer comfort. Geoff has learnt this already. Fifteen convicts die before the ship leaves English waters.

Geoff and Horace are escorted by a marine and Ellington up through the hatch to prepare breakfast for the men in their mess. On deck the air is fresh; the morning sun is shining in contrast to the foul odours, darkness and death below.

Reflected sunlight across the water hurts Geoff and Horace's eyes, they haven't seen the natural light of day for forty-eight hours. A brisk breeze is blowing and the vessel is making steady progress. The occasional squeal of piglets, the mooing of a cow, the disoriented crow of a rooster all seems quite out of place on the high seas — but reassuring.

On deck the officers strut like peacocks in their fine regalia.

Aloft is the domain of the sailors, also confident of their mastery.

The marines, the soldiers, the guards make up a second group. The politicians decided prior to departure that the marines would have no authority over the prisoners whatsoever. The captain of the marines, Nicholas Nepean, does not hold a set of keys to the convict quarters, nor can he make any decisions about the chaining of prisoners or their movements about the ship. The marines have no official billets; the forty-three of them bunk down wherever possible. Their lack of authority reflects in an absence of motivation and their shabby attire.

The female convicts form a third group. They are unchained and free to move about the main and quarterdeck whilst at sea. As on land, the females, even the plain and pregnant, hold a powerful influence over the men. The relative freedom Captain Trail has allowed the women prisoners increase their ability to influence even more. Though he insists the women be treated with respect, he classes the single women as prostitutes.

In contrast to the *Lady Julian*, a sister ship in the fleet, the female prisoners of the *Neptune* are strictly forbidden to co-habitat with the crew and the officers. This leads to immense dissatisfaction amongst the sailors, who vehemently claim Captain Trail promised otherwise before the voyage commenced.

The free settlers keep to themselves. They are organized and polite and like most onboard, choose to ignore the plight of the convicts.

Although absorbed in preparing porridge for his men, Geoff takes in the whole scene. The deck of the ship seems to him a stage where a play is unfolding. A play, with no audience, no critics … only actors.

Horace, Geoff's assistant, taps him on the shoulder and points.

'Ello' a quiet voice comes from behind. 'Ello mister.'

Geoff turns. He recognises the small child as the one from the Northumberland tearooms at Charing Cross. She is older now. Her hair is still the same red, her green eyes still very sad. She holds in her thin arms, not a doll as before, but a tabby kitten.

'Hello little one,' says Geoff and places his hand lightly on her shoulder as he crouches down and gives her a small hug. 'Where's your mummy, is she here?'

The little one points to the other side of the ship. Reminded now of where she should be, she runs off. Geoff tries to remember her name.

The appearance of the young one takes his mind back to Charing Cross, the tearooms and Claire. *The last time I saw that child Claire was with me*, he thinks. Pain and happiness churn around inside him as he mixes the huge vat of porridge with increased intent.

'Get on with it will yah!' calls another mess leader waiting to use the boilers.

*　　*　　*

'Hello, is anybody home?' sings Margaret.

'No … nobody home,' says Jane, touching her left ear.

'Something wrong with your auditory apparatus, dear?'

'My what?' Jane is distracted from her thoughts.

'Your ear, silly,' Margaret jokes.

Jane's other companion is sleeping soundly. Irregular snoring seesaws between his nose and his mouth.

'Tell me about you Jane, last time I asked you, you fell asleep,' says Margaret.

'Did I?' Jane hesitates. *I don't think so, Margaret*, she thinks. 'Well … I was born and educated in London. I have a sister Anne, three years younger than me. My father works for Lloyds of London and my mother is currently a medical secretary. I am thirty-two years old, love men, play tennis, and ride horses. I am honest, sensitive and adore children. Billy Connelly and I could be great friends, and I can't stand Celine Dione. My favourite colour is blue and my best number is six.'

She takes a breath, and becomes a little more serious. 'Really my life has been blessed. As a kid I travelled with my parents. Whatever I wanted I usually received … I don't think I'm spoilt though. I always loved Christmas-time. She taps her middle-finger on the armrest and then gently moves it back as if using it to focus. 'I can remember one Christmas in particular — it was so special, so magical. I received, among stacks of presents, a tiny, miniature doll from Santa — it was complete in every detail. I made a bed for her in a matchbox where she would be cosy and safe. I carried her everywhere. If I didn't take her with me I would hide her in the attic until I returned. I would become that excited at Christmas I would get headaches. Everyone thinks that *Janey* is a tad too sensitive. I know I am. My teenage years were fun and hell all rolled into one. I have no need to go back there again. After university I worked as a school counsellor, and then with single parent families … God knows how I helped them, I had enough trouble helping myself. I then worked my way around Europe — Paris, Amsterdam, and Italy. Nearly married Fulvio, an Italian boy, when I was twenty-eight. Then I met Greg. He was forty-six … he made a huge impact on my life. He was fifty-one when we split up — his age didn't make a great deal of difference though.'

'Didn't it?' Margaret enquires. 'He was good for you then?'

'He was *so* good. My mum was very domineering and I went the other way. My sister Anne is like mum. I found I kept giving too much to others. My parents loved me, but they, especially mum, didn't demonstrate it … never hugged much and things like that, you know. Greg was affectionate and assertive. I'm afraid I took him for granted, he *was* so good to me.' Jane pauses; her cheeks drop and her lips open slightly as time winds further back in her mind. 'One day, when I was only eight, I found myself staring at my goldfish and thinking, you *poor* thing, you swim around and around, get nowhere and then die. I wondered what's the use of living and growing up if all we do is one day die?'

'Did you ever find an answer to that question, love?'

'No, I don't think I have.'

'And Australia could be the answer for you?'

'Something is telling me yes. I have to take a few chances, Margaret.'

Half an hour later, coffee has been served and Jane's other companion is full of beans. 'Ladies would you like to hear a joke?' he asks.

'We don't know anything about you, *Mr Smith*.' Margaret says jokingly.

He shuffles around, finds his wallet, and hands them both a card. Again, the women are surprised.

'"Office of the United Nations. High commissioner for human rights. Gordon Nesbeth-Smith, special rapporteur for religions and beliefs" … well,' says Jane. *I have an excuse, a thought rockets through her mind. I'm normal but Margaret should have known how important he is. I suppose some things just slip through that psychic net of hers.*

'Now ladies, may I tell you my yarn?'

Both the women agree.

'My name is Jane,' she says, nodding.

'And mine is Margaret.'

'Gordon Nesbeth-Smith, I'm very pleased to know you both.' He commences.

My God, I've probably got Sir Richard Attenborough sitting across the isle. How did Margaret know his name is Smith or was that just a coincidence? thinks Jane, missing the start of his joke.

'Sorry I missed that, could you please repeat it?' she asks.

'Oh yes,' he replies and then continues: 'Sister Caroline calls from the window …'

'No, I'm sorry, I missed all of it.'

'Well, it goes like this.' With genuine patience and confidence he starts again.

'Sister Caroline is taking a shower. The rest of the nuns are at market-day. A man finds himself at the door of the convent. He knocks. From the bathroom window on the first floor, she asks who it is. *The blind man from the village,* he replies. All the washing is out to dry and the Sister cannot find a towel. *If the man is blind, I won't need to wear any clothing.* She runs down the stairs and opens the door. *Can I help you?* she asks him. Looking very surprised and a little excited, the man informs Sister Caroline he has come to measure for the blinds.'

Jane and Margaret laugh.

'I know several more,' he adds.

'I bet you do.' Jane gives him a warm smile and relaxes.

I'm very lucky to be sitting next to two such accomplished individuals, she thinks to herself.

CHAPTER SEVENTEEN

hunderous waves, lightning and wind gusts exceeding seventy miles per hour, focus everybody's thoughts on survival. The events that are taking place in the Bay of Biscay, off the coast of France and Spain, will never be forgotten by anybody on board the *Neptune*.

The ship is lifted from bow to stern and rolls heavily from starboard, simultaneously. Still chained, the convicts on the lower bunks attempt to stand, their footing threatened by two feet of surging, wintry cold seawater. The condition of the sick and dying is further aggravated and they are moved to the upper bunks.

There are very few screams or cries for help. Most of the convicts just quietly suffer and try to keep warm.

With storm sails straining, the Captain holds the ship head on into the mountainous waves, many of which break over the entire front section of the ship before surging down across the deck towards the stern.

A man is washed overboard during the night and there are many stories of how God saved others.

Throughout the following day, conditions are not much better. The decks are still awash. The crew, with extreme difficulty, is able to move about, carrying out repairs to ropes and sails. Deck cooking for the convicts is out of the question and the galley will only cater for the crew, marines and free passengers.

However the galley cooks, with authority from the Captain, agree with the mess leaders to prepare enough hot broth to satisfy the needs of the sick convict men, women and children. Geoff is involved in the preparation.

The huge concoction of beef stock, water, barley, corn-flour and a small amount of potatoes is prepared precariously over the galley stove.

Finally, the broth is ready for serving. The large boiler is lifted to the deck. For his efforts, Geoff's men will be served first. Everybody's attention is focused on the huge vat. Suddenly, without any warning one side of the galley bursts into flames and smoke begins to billow out onto the deck. The pitching of the ship has overturned a container of hot cooking fat and it has ignited with a severe *whooshing* sound.

'Fire! Fire! … Fire! Fire!' The alarm spreads around the ship within minutes.

The heat, but mainly the dense smoke forces everybody out of the galley leaving it to the mercy of the flames. Three marines with ropes attached to buckets attempt to hoist water from the ocean. The heavy seas and gale force winds push them both back from the side of the heaving ship, and their buckets are lost in the powerful wash. Several more attempt the same manoeuvre, but only one is successful. The fire is out of control.

Geoff empties his food pail of broth on the flames and manages to scoop up three more, but this has no effect on the fire.

The galley being only small, with a confined entrance, makes it virtually inaccessible to fire fighters. For this reason, bags and blankets cannot be used to extinguish the blaze. The ship is burning ferociously from the inside. More containers of cooking fats and alcoholic substances ignite and explode, adding to the fire's intensity.

Geoff remembers seeing a long boat with a torn storm cover. He pushes through the mesmerised crowd.

He thrusts his arm through the tarpaulin. *'There's water here!*

Over here!' he screams. As a mountainous wave thrashes across the deck threatening his footing, he tears back the cover and fills his buckets from the storm-flooded deck-boat.

'There's water there! ... *plenty!* ... *over there!*' He screams out, returning to the galley with his pail full.

Buckets are no longer the problem, one dozen men and two women now have them. With a virtually unlimited water supply close to the fire, and under directions from Geoff, it is only a matter of ten minutes before the fire is being contained.

Discovering the source of water gives Geoff some control of the situation. It does not even enter his mind for a second that he is ordering the crew. His instructions at one point even override those of the Chief Mate, second in charge of the ship.

Though the fire has been intense it is no match for the determination of men and women fighting for their lives. The fire's last dying act is to surround the deck in thick greyish, fetid smoke, which then disperses, swirling in the wind like a bad genie.

The Captain calls, 'Well done!' And there is spontaneous applause and cheering as the last buckets are emptied onto the smouldering timbers.

The rough weather took second place during the fire emergency. But now the huge seas and winds again become the major concern, and there is still rigging damage. The intensity of the storm, however, has tempered.

Three hours later the storm is over; the sun is shining, and repairs to the storm-battered ship and fire-damaged galley are underway.

Apart from the congratulations from the vast majority of prisoners on the Orlop deck, Geoff receives very little recognition for his actions from the rest of the passengers and crew. A notable exception is the congratulations he receives from one of the free passengers, the impressive Mr John Macarthur.

Foremost in Geoff's mind are the needs of the men in his

group, especially the ill. The calm conditions again allow the setting up of cooking coppers on deck, and the mess leaders rally. The re-lighting of fires concerns Geoff and everybody else, but their worries are, out of necessity, quickly put aside.

*　　*　　*

'We are just passing over Southern Turkey,' reports the co-pilot. He wishes all the passengers a comfortable journey and indicates arrival time in Singapore will be in approximately seven hours and fifteen minutes.

After Gordon Nesbeth-Smith's credentials have been made clear to Jane, the penny drops. In her life she has learnt, on two other serious occasions that a book should not be judged by its cover. This may just be her final lesson. Professor Gordon Nesbeth-Smith was on the short list for the Nobel Peace Prize, is a professor of history and a high-ranking official of the United Nations.

'My dear, I must make this apology, there again I don't feel fully to blame. It is impossible to sit in such close proximity to you and not overhear everything in minute detail, whether I want to or not.' The Professor says genuinely.

'That's not a problem Mr G … not a problem at all. Believe me, on this flight, sitting here with you and Margaret, my life is an open book.' Jane smiles convincingly.

'By the way,' he says. 'I would be so pleased if you would continue to call me Mr G … I like that very much.'

God I would like so much to give him a big hug, he is so cuddly, thinks Jane.

'Mr G,' Jane emphasises and then lowers her voice to a whisper. 'Can I ask you a personal question?' He nods expectantly. 'Why do you travel back here in Siberia and not in business class?'

'That's a good question Jane … it's a philosophical thing.

Sometimes I hobnob it, but usually I try to save my organisation some money. The world with all its excesses worries me at times.'

'Well I'm certainly glad you did this time.' She takes a chance, and when nobody is looking, gives him a quick hug.

Margaret is fascinated by the view from the window. She's in a world of her own.

'Everything looks so beautiful and innocent from up here, it's the view the angels get I suppose. The distance we have covered in hours would have taken the early Crusaders months,' she muses.

'Four to five months to be precise Margaret,' adds the professor with authority. 'They had to stop and plunder along the way. That all took time you know.'

Margaret's ears prick up. 'I thought the Crusaders only attacked the land of the infidels?' she says, still looking out of the window.

'The one hundred thousand strong forces of English, French, Italian, German and other Christian countries came from all over Europe. If they couldn't obtain what they wanted to survive by barter or fair means, they literally just took it by force from Christian and Arab towns alike.' Mr G continues. 'In one known case the holy forces pillaged an area three hundred miles north of Jerusalem and were even guilty of cannibalism — boiling pagan adults in cooking pots, impaling children on spits and eating them grilled.'

'Well I'll be.' Margaret is amazed, she had never heard of that before.

'What went on in the name of God and religion has been smoothed over through the centuries. Yes, the crusaders also pillaged Christian towns. The psyche of men and women can be a molten fury just under their thin outer layer. Like the planet earth we live on, the human psyche can erupt and spew out molten lava of hate and destruction at any time — we see it every day. By the way, we are not just talking about the distant past. Sadam Hussein recently attacked the Kurdish people in the north of Iraq with chemical weapons. But do you both know, in the 1920s, whenever there was the slightest resistance to their occupation in Iraq the English bombed and obliterated many Kurdish villages using the newly invented aeroplane. When the villagers heard the planes approaching they would flee, so the English dropped time delayed bombs to explode when the Kurds returned. It just goes on and on.'

*   *   *

'Geoffrey Blake, an envelope from Captain Trail.' Chief Mate Ellington says, with an expressionless look on his face. He turns and walks off without another word.

> *Geoffrey Blake Esquire,*
> *On behalf of Camden, Calvert and King, I and all aboard the Neptune would like to indeed thank you for your courageous effort and initiative, which was instrumental in leading to the containment of the galley fire, two days ago.*
>
> *Your actions are listed in the ship's log. It has been decided by me, to grant you some concessions and requests of your own choosing.*
>
> *Your food rations have been revised. You already have privileges of freedom aboard the Neptune, as a mess leader. Those privileges are now extended to equal those of the female convicts.*
>
> *An invitation is extended to you to attend dinner at the captain's table three days hence, on Wednesday.*
> *C.J. Trail*

Geoff accepts the captain's invitation and puts forward a modest request for pen, ink and paper. Within an hour all the writing implements and paper he asked for are hand delivered back to him by the Chief Mate.

Geoff has the urge to write, to keep a diary and log daily events. As a child however, he wrote short stories and won a school prize for a poem.

From Newgate Prison he corresponded with Catherine twice and she wrote back to him. Her letters were quite formal and did not broach the subject of his innocence or guilt. The undertones in her communications were very friendly, sympathetic to his situation and conveyed extreme sadness about losing her best friend Claire.

*   *   *

Geoff's mess assistant Horace, is thoroughly enjoying his increased popularity by association. The saving of the ship and all aboard, by his friend Geoff, as he puts it, has gained him unbridled attention amongst the convicts. Not all the attention is positive, but it's attention and that's what counts. Even a whack across the back of the head means something to dogs and boys like Horace who have never experienced very much attention from others, let alone love.

Horace's face is a little piggish looking. With half-closed puffy eyes and drawn back ears, he more resembles a small scavenger shark, than a boy of that era. Horace is a seventeen-year-old, convicted petty thief. Like many underprivileged lads in trouble with the law, many of Horace's problems result from his upbringing and environment. The odds are stacked against them from the day they are born.

Horace is skinny, determined, and cunning. He is a survivor -– all he needs is a chance.

'Horace, have you been raving again?' Geoff asks with a half smile.

'Na, Mr Geoff, what do ya mean? I be sayin good thins.' Horace's smile tells all, he knows exactly what Geoff is on about.

'That lot will understand about me after we have dinner wif the Captain. I told em … the lot of em.'

'Horace, you will not be meeting the captain, only me … do you understand?'

Horace's disappointment only lasts for a second; it was only a pipe dream anyway.

'We have a job to do with these men …'

'I only want ta cheer 'em …' replies Horace.

'Be that as it may. Just keep your mouth shut and we will go about our duties. Do you hear me … Do you?'

Horace nods, but Geoff knows this will not be the last of it. The boy is feeling good about himself; it has to come out somewhere.

'Mr Geoff, I'm gunna steer this ship one day,' Horace rehearses his fantasises as he climbs in a cocky manner, up the companion ladder to the upper deck.

From a distance, the *Neptune* is a picture of elegance and peace as it cuts across the blue waters of the south-eastern Atlantic basin.

CHAPTER EIGHTEEN

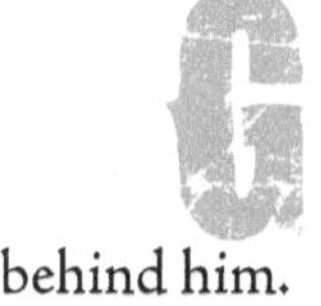eoffrey is standing on deck at the cooking coppers preparing the late afternoon meal for his mess, when he becomes aware of a woman standing behind him.

'My daughter has a hero for a friend.'

He turns.

'Mr Blake, Sarah Parkinson is my name. I believe you know my Christie?'

'That's her name … Oh, excuse me, I've been trying to remember the little girl's name for days now. She's your daughter?'

'Yes, she is.'

'Geoffrey Blake, pleased to meet you, Sarah. I met Christie at the Northumberland Tea-rooms in London.'

This brief communication with Christie's mother has already attracted the attention of several men. Geoff feels the weight of their focus.

It is not difficult to understand why she attracts attention. Even in a convict smock she stands out. She has the complexion of a fine crafted porcelain doll and the face of a goddess. Her hair is red, shoulder length and curly. Her shape is neither skinny nor large. Her abdomen is out of proportion with her medium build indicating she is with child. Her green eyes reveal both strength and vulnerability, but her manner is very independent.

'Are you enjoying the voyage, Mr Blake?' she says, light-heartedly.

'Yes, I always wanted to make a journey such as this.' he replies, flicking some porridge from his fingers and wiping his brow with his sleeve.

'You're allowed on deck Miss, but there will be no talking, especially to them lot. Do you hear?' calls one of the Marine Sergeants.

'I was with company in the tea rooms,' she says, ignoring the Sergeant. 'I saw you give Christie that rose … Was that your wife you were with? The slender one with the dark hair?'

'Do you hear me Miss? *Move back with the other women!*' The marine's voice is sterner.

Geoffrey politely asks the sergeant if he may continue his conversation with Sarah for a little longer. Ever since the fire Geoff has had some clout and respect, but he does not want to push his luck. For lack of response from the sergeant he assumes it is alright to go on.

'You're the talk of the ship, sir, I'm glad we had a connection before the fire … before you became famous,' she says in a flirtatious manner.' Her eyes glance quickly across the deck. The Chief Mate Ellington has appeared. 'I must go.' She waves as she walks away.

My god, how beautiful is she? Geoff's mind is bemused. The image of the women — mother and daughter, mother with child — strikes a very deep chord within him. *The woman is so damned attractive*, he thinks.

*   *   *

'Tell me about you Gordon,' asks Margaret.

'Right,' he replies. 'Now let me see, do you want to hear about the UN, my part-time lecturing at Queens College, the editorial work for the Sun newspaper, or my family?'

'Your family, tell me about your family.' says Margaret.

Jane thinks to herself, *I would love to hear about his work with the UN.*

'You can ask him about that later, dear,' Margaret directs a reply at Jane without even looking at her.

Jane feels that familiar attack from nowhere again land right in her lap.

Gordon raises an eyebrow before responding to Margaret's question.

'I have six children from three marriages and I have done quite a substantial amount of marriage counselling,' he says, deadpan.

'Oh, lovely, marriage counselling.' Margaret thinks about that and then … 'You're a bit of a kidder,' she says, in two minds about his humour. 'Now then, how many children do you really have Gordon?'

'I have four, three girls and a boy. My boy is from my first marriage, and he has a son. One of my girls is still at school, one at university, and the other is a journalist. I've only been married twice.'

'So you're a grandfather,' says Jane.

'I certainly am,' he replies proudly. 'Where are you bound for, Margaret?'

When he talks to, or questions a person, he has the knack of being able to make a person feel like he or she is the most important individual in the world.

'I'm spending some time in Sydney with a girlfriend I haven't seen in twelve years. I'm looking forward to that so much. We spent some of our childhood together after my parents moved to England from America.'

'So your parents are American like mine?'

'No, wait for this, my mother is a Russian Jewess and my father is Canadian. We are quite a mix, our family.'

'Does your friend share your interests in the paranormal and psychic area?' He leans closer.

'No she's always been a tad sceptical. A little like *Jane* … but so much has happened over the years she has had to accept something is going on. She's seen it *all*,' says Margaret with a pretentious sigh.

Without any warning a tray of food is whisked past Jane's nose, over Margaret's shoulder and on to Gordon's table. As Margaret's tray is placed in front of her a small container of sweets consisting of sticky date pudding and custard, topples into her lap, landing upside-down.

Wow, that will teach her. Smarty-bum, an impish thought slips out of Jane's mind.

'I'm so sorry Ma'am,' says the hostess.

'That's all right, my dear,' replies Margaret, holding her composure.

Jane's tray makes a three point, perfect landing.

How is Margaret going to get to the toilet with sticky date pudding in her crotch? Jane struggles to hold back a giggle.

'How would you like that to happen to *you*, Jane?' mutters Margaret, pondering over how she is going to clean herself.

She wasn't reading my mind that was just a fluke, thinks Jane.

'Yes, just a *fluke* accident, I suppose,' says Margaret to herself.

'Would you like me to help you clean up, Margaret?' offers Gordon wielding a dessert-spoon.

'No, certainly not!' says Margaret, annoyed with everybody.

Her involuntary feminine reaction to Gordon's purely innocent advance results in the closing of her legs and squashing the date pudding beyond all recognition.

CHAPTER NINETEEN

'W if a side-glance a … g … g … guarded heart, sa proud she stood …' A voice wafts erratically up the companion ladder.

Horace attempts to read on, but then stops and laughs a high-pitched shallow laugh. Apart from the name Claire, he hasn't got much of an idea what the words mean. He pauses as his native cunning alerts his defences.

Geoff, returning from the top deck, has overheard Horace.

'My boy, where did you find those papers and pencil? Where …?'

'In yer bunk, Geoff,' replies Horace, his audacity now converting to fear. Geoff realises immediately that there is no use in reasoning with, or chastising Horace, he just does not understand.

'I didn't know you could read Horace?'

'I can't really Mr Geoff … I thinks what you wrote about Miss Claire is very beautiful too.'

The mixed messages are making Geoff feel very uneasy.

'You know we are speaking about my wife, don't you?'

'Yes,' replies Horace, practically standing to attention. 'Mick read it ta me.'

'*What!*' shouts Geoff, his shout echoing around the gangway and out onto the Orlop deck.

'You showed my writing to *Mick*?!' Geoff is dumbfounded.

'Yea.' Horace again straightens up, but then slumps. His eyes are staring straight at Geoff but his focus seems to be twenty feet past him.

'I only showed 'im a bit and snatched it back. He wanted ta

see more, but I wouldn't let 'im. I won't touch any of ya kit again Geoff, I promise I won't.'

Horace puts out his hand prematurely to shake Geoff's. For a moment Geoff is about to take his apology until he sees the ink all over Horace's fingers.

'You've been into all my things.' Geoff's mind is in flux. Shock, embarrassment, forgiveness, his feelings are out of control. The lad begins to laugh which ends quickly with a lost look reflecting the old, sad and confused Horace. He means sorry, but he is unable to say a word.

Geoff hasn't the heart to push the lad any further and softens his tone. 'Mick didn't see much, did he'?

'Na, Geoff, I snatched it back quick, I … I told ya that.'

'Be off with you lad, you have work to do. Let me be, I want to sit here for a while.'

'Are you gunna be alright Geoff?'

'Yes lad, just go.'

Geoff sits on the steps in the isolation of the companionway.

From the jumbled feelings and words moving around in his mind, and with tears running down his cheeks, he begins to write: *When a new world seems to close, the squawking self in the nest screams for more, the owl in the night is silent. 'Where did she go?' calls the child I cannot see. Through the mist comes a golden glowing light. I will always be here, she whispers, the voice that never goes away.*

'Claire, I miss you so much.' Geoff says softly.

CHAPTER TWENTY

Two large ships cut through the blue; headwinds making the going a little difficult. All aboard feel secure. Stars above are clear, setting the direction. The sun is about to rise in the east as it has for millions of years. The captains of the two craft check their bearings and make slight adjustments to their courses.

The soft morning sun shines through the window onto Gordon's face.

Jane has awoken. She sits so quietly the bodily urges of nature would not dare disturb her translucent mood. She watches the sun spread its rays across the top of the clouds. Sunrise at near forty thousand feet is different to that at ground level, but it is always a precious moment.

*   *   *

The only indication of morning on the Orlop deck is a single ray of light which sometimes streams down the companion stairway as the ship temporarily changes direction. The ray of light is a blinding luxury for some of the convict men; it's their only link with the outside world for there are no portholes.

Geoff has managed four hours sleep. The men have been restless throughout the night, and many are ill. The lack of exercise and sufficient food, especially green vegetables and fruit, is paving the way for scurvy and other illnesses.

'They're not giv'n us enough to eat, look at this.' Maurie, one of the men in Geoff's care, carefully holds out his meagre meal. 'This is not enough to feed a dog, Geoff.'

Transportation of slaves was handled differently by Trail. The condition of the slaves had to be at its best on arrival; their fitness and appearance determined their value at auction. Under the new English contract transportation system a convict's passage is paid for whether they arrive at their destination dead or alive. By saving on provisions he has it in the back of his mind to open a general store at Sydney Cove and sell off the surpluses. As a result, conditions on the Orlop deck are deteriorating faster than the captain has realised.

*   *   *

The flight attendants are collecting blankets and the cabin lights are now on. The hustle and bustle replaces the colour of the sunrise and the mystique of the new day. There is the smell of breakfast.

In contrast to her reticent mood when the journey commenced, Jane can hardly wait to jump into discussion again with Margaret and the Professor.

The professor's move into the new day is signalled by a cup of black coffee.

'Good morning! This is your chief flight attendant speaking. I refer you to the aircrafts navigational map. We are now flying over Istanbul. Our arrival in Singapore will be in approximately six and a quarter hours. We are running a little behind the scheduled time due to head winds. We trust your flight is comfortable. Thank you.'

'Constantinople is where it all started!' announces Gordon.

Margaret and Jane look at him with surprise.

Where did that come from? thinks Jane to herself. *Did I miss something?* She remembers that as a child, the first big word she ever learnt to spell was Con-stan-tin-ople.

He looks at the two women with eyes wide open like *Felix the Cat*. There seems to be a big question mark suspended over his head. It was as if the word Constantinople just slipped out.

'Constantinople!' bursts from the two women's mouths simultaneously. He has got them.

Only on an aeroplane, at sunrise, before breakfast, between relative strangers could such a discussion occur.

'The *bottom* line, ladies, is the Arab races are not very happy with us.' Jane and Margaret look at each other. 'It's not too difficult to see why. Nine hundred years ago Constantinople was the headquarters of the Christian Empire. The Turks, newly converted to Islam, were constantly invaded by the big C. The king asked the Pope in Rome, for help. What followed was one of the most amazing and destructive set of circumstances in the history of the planet to that time. Will I go on?'

Margaret and Jane nod in unison; they both appear fascinated. In any case what else is there to do? Gordon's credibility however, is still on the line.

'Just as our friend Hitler used the Jewish people to manipulate the German population, Pope Gregory, in the year 1078 AD, used the rebel Turks. Harnessing the anger and discontent at the Islamic Turks, the Pope was able to mobilise the largest army the world had ever seen. 'It's only a sin to kill Christians,' he said. 'Brandishing your swords against the infidel eastern Islamics is the only warfare that is righteous.'

The professor pauses for a moment, looks at Jane and Margaret, and continues his own small crusade.

'One hundred thousand Christians from all over Europe then progressively moved towards Jerusalem and began to slaughter, and were slaughtered, in the name of their Christian God … do you know the port of Acre near today's Tel Aviv?' he asks.

Margaret says, 'yes.' Jane is all ears.

'Richard the Lionheart led the third Crusading force, a very large well-equipped army, in ships across the Mediterranean. The aim, using the cream of European and English knights, was to liberate Jerusalem from Muslim control.'

Mr G is a born storyteller and his zeal is attracting attention from the other passengers.

'How in the name of Christianity and God, can over three thousand captive women, children and soldiers be put to death, I can't comprehend.' The professor looks moved. 'In 1191 AD, Richard the Lionheart requested a ransom from the Arab leader. Four days passed and there was no response from Saladin, so the crusaders systematically beheaded the entire population, including the children. During these four days of horror, blood ran so freely it poured down the drains into the harbour of Acre.'

Margaret feels for him. 'You seem to take this personally, Gordon?'

'I suppose … my wife and children are Arabian. That probably influences the way I feel.

'What's her name?' asks Jane gently.

'Hasina,' says Gordon, softly. 'She's from Tiberius.'

'You do take all this to heart don't you?' Jane says sympathetically.

He nods slowly. 'I do, Jane.'

'All those things happened a long time ago, but one does not have to be Nostradamus to predict the ramifications from such horrific actions,' says Margaret.

'Nostradamus made these predictions in such striking detail, didn't he?' says Jane.

'*Yes*, he did,' says Gordon. 'And he predicted that Islamic aggression would move throughout Europe around the year 2000 as indeed it has. He foretold the levelling of Rome, the demise of Switzerland, and blasts that would boil the English Channel. The New City he refers to, which many claim is New York, would experience a massive fireball in the sky at right angles to the ground. He said Russia and America would become allies and they have. He said they would split again and then come together to defeat the extremist Islamics. But, mind you, he also made it clear that we all as individuals, communities and cultures have the ability to change the outcome of his predictions if we really want to. Whether he meant that the western world should become passive, more aggressive, or be more understanding I just don't know.'

'Only when we have learnt the lessons of pain and suffering will there be peace and harmony.' Jane declares.

'For some reason we focus on the negatives, you only have to look at the news reports.' Gordon shrugs. 'We know conflict is all around us but, on the less dramatic and non-reported level, every day is full of kind and beautiful actions from those unsung heroes, the ordinary people of the planet. We tend to forget that … we must not forget that,' he emphasises, as if trying to remind himself as much as anyone.

The three sit silently as their modern rocket, the best in human technology, cruises effortlessly over the earth on the borders of outer space.

CHAPTER TWENTY ONE

eoff looks out across the sea and then up at the clouded night sky. The conditions on the Orlop deck are weighing heavily on his mind. He hasn't seen Christie or Sarah for eight days. He wonders how they are.

Dinner with Captain Trail is this evening. Geoff thinks about the meeting with a combination of cautiousness and excitement. He plans to speak with the captain about the condition of the convicts.

At seven o'clock he is ready. The Chief Mate Ellington escorts Geoff to the Captain's cabin. A single knock on the Captain's door is followed by a request to enter.

The two men greet each other with outward respect, but the gap between Geoff's unassuming nature and Captain Trail's bombastic persona is as wide as the ocean the *Neptune* is traversing.

Trail's strong and burly physique seems to focus in his handshake. His grip knows no half measures — it's like a vice.

Trail's big face is proportionate to his large, thickset body. He has a smile, which goes one way, and eyes that go another. Geoff can see Trail is a troubled man. Trail's instinctive first impression of Geoff is predominately: troublemaker. They're competitors, these two, as well as being curious. Trail has ruddy cheeks and dark sideburns that blend into a small grey beard. An arch of hair moves up under his small nose linking up with his whiskers on the other side. His neatly manicured facial hair partly covers a lined face, and a determined chin beneath up to a stiff lower lip. His eyes resemble those of an expressionless, unpredictable old bear.

Mrs Trail stands to one side. There is an indescribable something that makes a woman attractive. Those indefinable's can be physical or come from within. Mrs Trail lacks both. She is of medium height also, thickset with silky auburn hair. Her reticent eyes move in a similar way to her husbands; they avoid assertive contact. Any attractive feminine charms she may possess are hidden under a shapeless brown dress. She appears strong, and would need to be to hold her own with the captain.

The Captain and his wife mimic each other, speak in unison, and finish one another's sentences. *I think I'm dealing with a two-headed dragon, though the wife may have more of a conscience than her husband,* Geoff concludes.

'On behalf of the owners, Camden, Calvert and King, and everybody on board, I would like to thank you Mr Blake, for your brave and quick action,' says the Captain.

'… We know we speak for everybody on board the *Neptune*,' Mrs. Trail adds.

At this point Ellington leaves.

'Only doing my duty, sir,' says Geoff. 'And thankyou, sir, for the pen, paper and ink … I have put them to good use.'

'No *doubt* you have, Mr Blake,' replies the captain.

Geoff feels a little uneasy. *Why does part of me like this monster of a man?* he thinks.

He treads carefully; the Captain is a bag of snakes.

'Take a seat, Mr Blake.'

Seating himself, Geoff reaches for a glass of wine and looks around soaking up the relative luxury of the captain's cabin. Trail has poor taste, but some of his personal items are extremely interesting. There are two paintings, one of Africa, and another of London. A small gruesome roman statuette sits secured on a shelf. A vase of artificial flowers and a small statue of a ballerina show Mrs Trail's feminine influence.

Home away from home is the first thing that comes to Geoff's mind.

It might feel claustrophobic to a landlubber. To a seafarer, like Geoff it feels like a secure retreat. Trail's cruel spirit hovering around the polished timbers of the cabin, however, interferes with his fantasy. What would those who crafted those timbers think of the man who now inhabits this cabin?

'If I may, sir, I have two requests directly related to my work on the Orlop deck.' Geoff prepares to get down to business.

He is interrupted by a knock on the cabin door and the serving of the meal.

'Over here thank you, Miss,' directs Captain Trail.

Geoff takes a second glance. *It couldn't be … Sarah?*

A mischievous look appears on Captain Trail's face. Geoff is aware Sarah's appearance is no coincidence. He takes the initiative and greets her by name.

'You know this young lady, Mr. Blake?' says the captain, like a cat tormenting a mouse.

'Yes, sir, we have met.' Sarah intervenes with a slight waver in her voice. 'Mr Blake knew my daughter back in London, sir.' She is petrified of this man and the presence of his wife does not ease this feeling.

Geoff throws Sarah a comforting look, which Mrs Trail notices.

'So you knew each other before the voyage, did you?' asks the Captain.

'No, sir.'

There is a quiet pause. The Captain looks ready to pounce.

Sarah does not dare to look around. She serves the salted beef with potatoes and gravy and moves quickly away.

There is awkwardness in the air as the first course is completed. Mrs Trail leaves.

With a nod from the Captain, Geoff returns to business.

'The soup for the sick during the storm, sir, was undoubtedly authorised by you. The men appreciated it very much.'

'Get on with it! Get to the point!'

Geoff pauses. 'The marines, if I could say, with respect sir, spend a great deal of their time sitting around and getting into tomfoolery. Could they not be put to better use?'

This comment stands like a shag on a rock. Geoff braces himself for a reaction.

'What do you propose, Mr Blake,' asks Trial without the slightest trace of irritation.

'Increase their guard duty by giving the prisoners more time on deck, sir.' Very few on the vessel could make a comment such as this, and get away with it.

The captain thinks a while and then agrees to consider this suggestion. They are both aware that there is trouble with the soldiers and their indolence is disruptive. The advantages might outweigh the disadvantages.

Mrs Trail returns. She is preoccupied.

The three talk generally about the voyage so far and what lies ahead. The prisoners and that part of the ship are not mentioned again. It is as if the Orlop deck does not exist in Mr and Mrs Trail's minds.

There is another knock at the door and the ship's cabin boy enters, with dessert.

Mrs Trail's looks a shade embarrassed.

'Young Sarah?' asks the captain in a soft creepy tone, looking at Geoff. 'Where is Miss Sarah?' he asks his wife.

'She's gon back Captain, back to the women's place,' says the boy. He places the stewed fruit and pudding on the table and leaves.

Trail hesitates for a moment, and then gets back to Geoff.

'I find it difficult to understand why a young man like you ends up in the hull of the *Neptune*.

'Sir, I loved my wife Claire with all my being … why would I harm her?'

'So you are innocent?' presses Trail.

'Yes, sir, I am innocent of the crime, but I feel guilty. I know in my soul I contributed to my wife's death, but how, I don't know. This lives with me each day.'

Trail's hands lift slightly from the table. Mrs Trail looks momentarily saddened, and touched. They are both unaccountably moved. Geoff's admission and personal dilemma has affected them both. Raw honesty and genuine human feelings can affect the hardest of human personalities.

'Your other request, Mr Blake?'

'The rations for the men, sir,' he quickly responds.

'I won't discuss the rations. Your rations Mr Blake have been increased … leave it there my boy.' He shuts down the discussion.

As he shakes Geoff's hand, he considers implicating him in stoogery on the Orlop deck. He sneaks a considering look at Geoff.

'*Na,*' he decides.

The genuineness within an individual's character will protect it, without words sometimes from invading complicity.

Back on deck, it is another world. The *Neptune* is ploughing through an ocean that is as unwavering as the will of the men sailing the ship. Geoff moves back across the main deck. It's only a short walk from the peace of the captain's cabin to the hell of the Orlop.

The men know he has been with the captain.

'How's our white-aired boy!' Blurts out one called Maurie, partly delirious with fever.

Geoff, full of his own thoughts, ignores him.

CHAPTER TWENTY TWO

'Ladies and gentlemen, we regret to announce ...'

Jane lets out a loud gasp.

The chief flight attendant continues ... 'due to upper atmospheric head-winds, our arrival time in Singapore will be delayed. There is the possibility of an unscheduled stop at Bahrain. We will keep you advised.'

All eyes are on Jane, who is surprised at her outburst. 'I thought there was a major problem,' she says, giving a sheepish look.

'It's all right, Daddy's here,' says Mr G, for which he is awarded a solid thump on the arm.

'I think conditions on a slave ship would be better than this.' Jane shuffles around in her seat, still feeling confined and a little irritated.

'What would you like to know about slave ships, ladies?' asks Gordon imitating the rowing action of a slave, with a sore arm.

'Nothing!' both the women reply in unison.

*   *   *

Horace nudges Geoff and points through the smoke of the cooking coppers. Sarah and Christie appear from behind the main mast. Christie comes skipping across the deck. Sarah's hair and dress are blown back in the wind revealing a belly the size of a medium pumpkin. Her breasts are also swollen. Stalking behind them is an intoxicated marine offering unneeded assistance. Sarah says, 'Oh, *do* go away.'

'It is lovely to see you again, Mr Blake,' says Sarah, her eyes alight.

Christie just stands staring at Geoff.

Geoffrey reaches into his pocket and takes out several pieces of folded paper. He hands two of them to Christie. She opens them cautiously at first, but is delighted on seeing the contents.

Horace sneaks a look, and sniggers.

Although Geoff cannot draw very well, it is obvious he has put a great deal of time and effort into creating the illustrations. Several types of birds, ships, trees, funny faces, houses, country scenes, a merry-go-round, and different types of fruit, all make up his amateurish collage. The largest drawing of all is of a cat, a friendly cat with long whiskers, big paws and two large eyes.

The drawing of the cat takes the shine out of Christie's smile and Geoff feels responsible. It would seem Geoff has put his foot in it.

'Christie's cat died,' Sarah tells him. 'She's fine. Puss has been gone for a week now. One of the crew takes missy here down to the animal pens each day. She has lost a kitten, but has now gained six pigs, two cows, three roosters, twenty hens, and scores of small chickens. I wouldn't worry too much about the cat.'

Sarah then says. 'It's really good to see you.' He is about to ask how she has been, when …

'*Sarah! You will have ta com, eer!*' One of the female convicts calls from across the deck.

Sarah quickly goes to her. One hour later, the cry of a newborn baby is heard around the ship. Sarah has assisted the ship's surgeon with the second delivery since the *Neptune* left England.

*   *   *

'Mr G,' Jane whispers. 'You remind me of somebody I know.'

'Do I, Jane?' he says. 'Somebody kind, understanding, intelligent and extremely good-looking, I hope … is he from England?'

'Yes, all of the last,' she replies, laughing.

'You're so much like him. He always said humour is very important. That's something I'm not good at. I can't even tell a joke without getting embarrassed.'

'Did you hear the one about the …'

'Mr G, you are incorrigible, you really are.'

Jane sits back, frozen in her seat with an imitation childish pout, which in no time changes into a beautiful smile.

Margaret, between them, seems lost in her book.

Jane takes a deep breath and continues. 'I met Dr Raynor at a lecture he was giving on comparative religions. He talked about the deeper and broader approaches to life. He believed achieving inner development is found in acceptance of oneself, others, and within the life of opposites we live … that the striving for individuality is the most important thing. I was fortunate to be associated with him,' Jane goes on. 'And, he said that humour, Mr G,' she emphasises, 'is the bow with which to tie it all up. We mustn't become too serious, must we Mr G? That's where I fail dismally. And you,' she pokes his shoulder affectionately with her finger, 'and you have such a great sense of humour … maybe I can learn from you?' she says with a wistful look.

'Sure,' smiles Mr G.

'What do you think about women developing their individuality?' she asks him confidently.

He does not hesitate. 'They should be kept pregnant and in the kitchen.'

Is this man for real? Jane wonders. *He must be joking.* She looks at him baffled.

Margaret pricks up her ears.

'Jane,' he answers, 'we are living in turbulent times. This aircraft we are now flying on wasn't even dreamt about one hundred years ago. It is only one example of the huge changes taking place in our world at this time. We are in a period of transition which is impacting on us and will for several more generations to come. Technology is the key and the cause of our confusions and it is here to stay. Technology is a fact and is with us forever. It is driving our inner evolution. I feel the difference between male and female is basically physical. Technology is empowering women and giving them the opportunity to perform equally alongside men. We are so preoccupied with our culture, no thought is given to the impact that the equalising of the sexes is having on the Islamic and Asian populations. It's huge. The western world, due to its perceived evil permissiveness could be blamed and used as a scapegoat for other cultures who find it difficult to recognise the rights of women. We're in for a stormy time.'

Margaret nods, 'Suspect you're right.'

'Let you both into a secret. The flight we're on is captained by a friend of mine, a woman. What do you think of that?' He grabs the armrests with each hand and feigns a panic attack.

*　　*　　*

As the *Neptune* is sailing non-stop to South Africa, there'll be no fresh supplies for weeks. The prisoners and several of the marines and crew are beginning to suffer from scurvy. Young Horace has some telltale signs including bad breath, skin irritations, anaemia and slight bleeding of the gums. What skerricks of vegetables, fruit peel and cheese Geoff can lay his hands on, he feeds to Horace. He also puts aside some of his rations for Christie and Sarah.

The convicts are frustrated enough without having short

rations and disease to cope with. There is mutinous talk and the situation is becoming explosive. Captain Trail knows that if he gives these men half a chance, he is gone.

'Are ya with us?' Geoff is frequently asked.

The men talking mutiny are taking big chances, for they know Geoff has a relationship with Trail. But he has the freedom of the ship and access to keys. They will take this chance.

Geoff cannot reason with the men. But he thinks if he were in their position, he might feel the same way.

He is temporarily prepared to overlook extra food gained by the convicts propping up the dead to secure extra rations. He is prepared to get extra supplies for his mess at great risk to himself. He is also prepared to nurse the men, counsel and take the weight of their miseries. Mutiny, however, he considers to be contrary to hope and good sense, an act of desperation, which invariably fails. He will not support it.

CHAPTER TWENTY THREE

The sea is dead flat and there is no hint of a breeze. The sky is black. There is no moon, but the stars sparkle like diamonds. It is the early hours of the morning and most aboard the *Neptune* are asleep. In the distance, the lights on board the becalmed sister ships, *Scarborough* and the *Surprise*, blend with the stars on the horizon. It is seldom that ships of the fleet are sighted. The salty smell of the sea hangs heavy in the air. The yard creaks as it moves listlessly from side to side and there is a constant smacking of ripples on the hull and the occasional splashing of fish. The moans and groans of the sick convicts on the Orlop deck can't be heard.

Geoff, with permission, sits in a small alcove on deck. The candle flame beside him burns straight up and unwavering. His growing feelings towards Sarah are acting on his brain, but his Claire, ever-present in his mind, dwarfs and blankets any fantasy which struggles to grow.

He looks at the night sky and feels he can almost touch the stars. He reflects about life on earth and the possibility of life on other planets. *There must be other civilisations out there more advanced than ours*, he is thinking. Away to his right, the brightest of the stars, which has a pink tinge about it, is pulsating softly.

Geoff, my love, he hears it say.

*   *   *

'That's *fine* Jane,' Margaret gets serious. 'It's one thing to say the negative things in life must be welcomed, accepted and understood. But when it hits the fan, really hits the fan, it takes somebody like Jesus Christ, for instance, to take the pain and not cry out.'

The confines of the aeroplane have done it again and another deep and meaningful is in full swing.

Wow, I can't believe Margaret's comment about Jesus, thinks Jane. Her eyes are animated. 'I see it like this,' she replies. 'There is no such thing as perfection. We only truly develop as a result of making mistakes. We cannot know the positives in life without experiencing the negatives.'

Gordon, silent, hangs on every word.

'Jesus *did* cry out,' Jane replies passionately. '"Father, Father, why hast thou forsaken me …" were his words, on the cross, according to the scriptures. Jesus did have feelings like you and me. It seems he did temporarily lose faith. We all do at times,' she continues. 'But he also said, "Forgive them Father, for they know not what they do."' Jane is not actually crying, but she has tears running down her cheeks. Gordon touches her hand and says nothing.

'Margaret, I didn't say we should welcome pain and suffering. It comes along all by itself whether we want it or not. What I am saying is when it comes we should understand there are reasons for the pain. In most cases, reasons we — our family, or our brothers and sisters, past and present — have set in motion. Our country has done some fine things, but it has also wronged the world many times. England is now paying the price for the negative actions of the past. It's not hard to see, it's happening as we speak. It's not wrong to fail and make mistakes; this is all normal and human. It's how we come back and put into action what we have learnt from our mistakes, that's the important thing.'

Jane sits back in her seat, and then sits forward again.

'What I'm really saying is, free will is of the utmost importance. If we believe that, then mistakes must be part of the deal.

A life of perfection stagnates without contrast. Each individual has free will. We all have it. It's what we do with it that's important.'

'Wow, young lady where did all that come from?' Mr G is visibly impressed. 'Could you repeat that?'

'No … no, I don't think I could,' Jane gives him a foxy smile and sits back. 'I *don't* know where all that came from, she says quietly, I *really* don't know where.'

Margaret just smiles.

*   *   *

From the Cornish cliffs, far above the sea, Claire's rock faces to the south. A British Airways jetliner, cruising high over the deserts of the Middle East, edges south-eastward. The *Neptune*, becalmed, is waiting for the next winds to take her south around the southern tip of Africa, then to Australia.

CHAPTER TWENTY FOUR

'This is your Captain speaking ...'

'You were right Mr G, the Captain is a woman,' Jane is impressed.

'Shhhh,' says Margaret, listening intently.

'... the stop in Bahrein we previously referred to has now been confirmed. Don't be alarmed. We will touch down in approximately forty minutes. Please follow the normal seat-belt and no smoking signs.'

Jane has already had two mini panic attacks on this flight. She's determined not to have another. 'What does this mean, Margaret?' she asks, hoping Margaret's psychic abilities will prove reassuring.

'I don't know, Jane, I just don't know. But I don't like it very much at all.'

Mr G seems unperturbed.

The aircraft banks to the right slightly and then levels out. It's obvious a new course has been set.

The lofty discussions between Jane, Margaret and Mr G have ceased. Most of the passengers are sitting quietly.

Margaret scrutinizes the faces of the flight attendants.

Flight 1033 begins its slow descent into Bahrain.

Even Mr G has fallen quiet. That adds to Jane's apprehension.

'How about a joke, Mr G.' Jane gives him a small nudge.

'Attention passengers. This is the chief flight attendant speaking. We have commenced our descent and will land at Bahrain Airport in thirty-five minutes. Thank you.'

'Well I'm sure there is nothing to concern ourselves about, ladies. We'll land and then be on our way in no time.'

'Have you been to Bahrain, Mr G?' Margaret asks.

'Yes, twice before, once for several days and another time for a stopover during a flight.'

'I've no idea what to expect,' says Jane.

'There's part of it,' he points through the window. 'Bahrain is an island in the Arabian gulf, eighteen miles off the coast of Saudi Arabia. The Portuguese ruled for eighty years in the 1500s. We pressured Bahrain into a treaty in 1820. In 1860 Britain took over this country, as Britain did with many countries around the world. The first oil on the Arabian Peninsular was discovered here in the 1930s, and we were hoisted out. Bahrain has one of the largest refineries in the Middle East. I think its population is about five hundred thousand.' The professor excels himself once again.

'Would you like the window seat, Jane?' asks Gordon. Jane accepts with alacrity.

With her nose practically glued to the glass, she watches as an alien world appears out of the desert. Even from 2000 feet, Bahrain is different from anything she might have expected. Her ideas of Arabian landscapes never included a view from above. There is a contrast between the yellow of the desert and the aqua of the sea. As the plane descends further she can make out the pastel colours of buildings in yellow, light blue, dusky pink and white, which all blend with the desert. The houses are flat topped and arranged in very neat rectangular and square blocks. There is very little greenery. *It is immensely different to England,* she thinks.

The aircraft touches down smoothly and Jane turns to Mr G, relieved. The friendly jet engines ease into reverse thrust, the huge wing flaps are fully extended up to hold the massive flying machine securely on the ground — slowing it also. There is a particular point in an aeroplane landing where tension amongst most on board is replaced by a feeling of ground security.

The concern of everybody on British Airways flight 1033 now turns to what is going to happen next.

The huge machine slows and turns to commence the long taxi to the terminal. Everybody on board is shuffling about in readiness for what, nobody is sure.

'This is your Captain, Rhonda Stroud speaking. We have landed at Bahrain International Airport. It will take us approximately ten minutes to position the aircraft. I will update you shortly.'

The aircraft is not proceeding to the main terminal. Along with all the other passengers, even Gordon is becoming apprehensive. Where it finally stops will tell him a great deal. However, with all his experience, even he has not an inkling of what is about to happen. Uneasy chatter breaks out. Anticipation and fear bounces off and around the passengers like a shower of out-of-control ping-pong balls. Something is wrong.

The dreaded next announcement cuts through the air like a sharp knife.

'This is your Captain speaking. I'm now able to give you an update on circumstances leading to our stopover at Bahrain. Three aircraft leaving Heathrow airport have been involved in a bomb threat. Your flight is one of those. We ask all passengers to remain calm and follow instructions. We have a security problem, and we are in Bahrain, so please be prepared for culture and procedures that are very different to what you would experience in a western country. Bahrain police will board our aircraft before we disembark. They will be in national or military dress, and possibly be carrying automatic weapons. But don't be alarmed. They are the official police, and friendly. Please stay seated in your allocated seats until you are told to leave. Please leave the aircraft in an orderly and relaxed manner. After leaving the aircraft, all passengers will be escorted to the terminal. Bahrain International Airport is one of the most modern in the world. Thank you.'

Pulse rates quicken. Everybody remains silent. One passenger, zonked on sleeping tablets is oblivious to the drama.

'Would you like one of these Margaret?' Gordon whispers.

'No *thankyou*, I have *never* taken drugs in my life.' Margaret is offended.

He turns the container around.

'*They're only* Tictacs!' Jane calls out, belatedly putting her hand over her mouth.

The other passengers look daggers at her. What right has she to joke at a time like this?

The aircraft, now in tow, is turned 180 degrees and comes to a stop. The flight director is now on the blower. 'Please remain seated, but pack your immediate valuables. No hand luggage is to be taken off the aircraft and the overhead luggage compartments are not to be opened. Women's handbags, which will be searched, are the only exception. We need to evacuate the aircraft without any delays. Thank you.'

'Well, what do we do now?' says Margaret as Jane swaps back to her allocated seat.

'Not very much, Margaret. All we can do is wait.'

Gordon is resigned. As he feared, the aircraft has been kept well away from the terminal buildings.

The two women pack their handbags.

'Jane, I'm going to have my hands full, would you put my toiletry bag in your handbag please … I may need my medication and may need to shave at the airport.'

'Certainly, Mr G.'

'Would cabin crew please disarm the exits,' instructs the co-pilot.

Passengers with window seats have nothing to report. The aircraft is probably being approached directly from the front or the rear.

From business class there are some alarming murmurs, and a child screams.

'Can you see anything, Jane?'

The first class curtain opens and one of the hostesses is followed by …

'*My God,*' whispers Margaret.

Four Arab males appear magnificently dressed, two in galabeas and two in police uniforms. Three are brandishing automatic weapons. The flight attendant stops next to Jane, and consults with the head man.

'Mr Nesbeth-Smith?' he enquires, checking the seat number.

'Yes … that's me,' Gordon replies, with a surprised look on his face.

'May I see your passport, sir?' asks the official.

Jane gets the courage to look up. The senior man is a straight-faced handsome dark man, with slick black hair and a moustache to match. The second thickset man is very serious. The third is enjoying waving his weapon at petrified Westerners.

'Would you please come with us Mr Nesbeth-Smith, thank you,' requests the officer in charge.

Just then, the man in the seat opposite Jane stirs and wakes from his sleeping tablet induced sleep. To awake from a deep sleep and be confronted by four Arabs, three brandishing automatic weapons absolutely panics and petrifies the man.

Jane and Margaret stare. The passengers next to him try to explain, but the man's eyes are way ahead of their words.

'*Can't anybody do something!*' he screams out.

'It's all right. Truly it's all right,' Jane tries to reassure him.

The third policeman turns around and glares, staring straight down the barrel of his gun. Jane can only imagine how waking up to this situation would feel.

Mr G stands. Jane and Margaret squeeze back into their seats, with anxious looks on their faces. Gordon turns and smiles.

'This is no joke ladies,' he says. 'I'll see you both soon.'

Further to the rear, another man is also being removed from the aircraft under armed guard.

As the police leave there is a buzz of excited chatter.

'What do they want with Gordon?' says Margaret, in some panic.

'God only knows,' says Jane's rubbing her shaky legs.

'This is your captain speaking … We are sorry for the inconvenience and the intrusions. When indicated would you please disembark promptly through the front of the aircraft. We will return to our flight as soon as it has been cleared. I repeat again, male passengers are only permitted to carry personal items in their hand. Female passengers are permitted one personal handbag, which will need to be ready for inspection. We are sorry for this inconvenience. You may now commence leaving the aircraft.'

As Jane moves through the exit doors, she is hit in the face by a wall of very hot dry air, not unlike opening a hot oven door. Her second impression is of a local muskiness; a very different, not unpleasant smell, which mixes with the fumes of burnt avgas.

Hot, barren and scary are her immediate thoughts as she walks across the tarmac. She does not speak to Margaret or anybody else.

Before she enters the building, she stops and looks back at the aircraft. 'Oh!' she jumps as Margaret taps her on the shoulder.

The passengers file up a stairway towards the customs area.

'I hope Mr G is all right,' Jane whispers to Margaret.

Margaret nods. She looks hot and confused. The women wait

patiently as their bags are manually checked. 'I must look like death,' she whispers to Jane. 'I'd kill for a cuppa.'

A senior customs officer is called in when Gordon's toiletry satchel containing a battery-operated razor, a mobile phone and transformer is discovered in Jane's bag. The two officers consult for a couple of minutes.

'Please come this way, Mrs Sinclair.'

Jane looks at Margaret. Margaret moves forward to join Jane, but is abruptly told to move on with the other passengers. *This is all I need,* Jane thinks to herself.'

The blankness of the customs interrogation area is clinical and bare. Jane sits uncomfortably in a plastic chair at a steel table staring at an off-white wall with no windows. She only wishes that Margaret was with her.

Finally. 'My name is Fatima,' says a young Arab officer. 'We are sorry for detaining you,' she says in a high-pitched monotone voice. 'The toilet bag you had in your handbag was not your own. It contained an electrical razor and many batteries. This catches our attention, but the matters have been resolved. Mr Nesbeth-Smith realised this to be a problem for you and alerted us. His name is on the inside of the case. The contents have been checked, and we have no problem. We apologize to you for this inconvenience.'

The woman points to Jane's bag on a table and indicates the way out. 'Thank you Mrs Sinclair.'

'I'm *not* Mrs …' Jane begins, *oh what the …* she decides.

Jane passes through the customs exit door into another world. Looking further a field she can see Margaret with several other female passengers sipping cocktails.

'Have a cocktail Jane, they're free … Gordon will be here soon. One of the flight attendants is keeping us informed. You know, they took him in for questioning in spite of assurances from Captain Stroud.'

Jane grabs a cocktail and downs it. The stress is getting to her. Despite the Arabs in local dress, the whole scene is unexpectedly very western.

'We've got one and a half hours to wait, Janey.' Margaret has had a couple too many and Jane does not really blame her.

Jane has another drink.

CHAPTER TWENTY FIVE

eoff and Sarah are standing close together on the main deck talking, while Christie is playing nearby.

Mr Ellington, the Chief Mate, can't help himself. 'If you wanted *her*, ya couldn't afford her Blake,' he says loudly as he walks up to them.

Sarah takes hold of Geoffrey's arm.

Several marines and three mess leaders overhear the Chief Mate's comment. Geoff stays calm. The onlookers are silent. Ellington moves further away, turns and calls out.

'The murderer and a whore!'

Sarah screams. 'No! … you men are all the same … I know the likes of all of you.' She gives a prolonged growling shriek.

Many, including free settlers, convict women and crew have now been exposed to Ellington's malicious, cowardly accusations. He calculates and lets fly again.

'There's only one thing more despicable than a man who has committed a bad crime and that is a self-righteous man driven by guilt.'

He looks Geoff straight in the eyes.

Ellington, like many others, has underestimated Geoff. Geoff stands his ground, emotionally wounded, but strong. He is stirred deeply. His soul groans within.

Sarah is devastated. These demons have danced before. Her feelings are frozen and locked securely in a trunk on the ocean floor of her mind.

'I'll kill him,' mutters Horace. 'He's got no rights, no rights to talk about you, Mr Geoff and Miss Sarah, like that. He's a *bad* man, that's what he be.'

CHAPTER TWENTY SIX

Back aboard Flight 1033, Margaret and Jane are seated ready for departure, but there is still no sign of the professor.

As Jane is served tea she takes the opportunity to ask the attendant, 'When are we taking off? Do you know anything about Mr Nesbeth-Smith? Was there a bomb on board?'

'We'll be leaving in fifteen minutes. Your friend, that nice man, is with Captain Stroud now. No, we didn't have a bomb, but a suspicious device was located aboard,' says the hostess mischievously. Margaret and Jane listen intently.

'A *vibrator*,' she whispers, 'somehow switched itself on when our Kenneth, from business class opened a bag for inspection. You should have seen the look on his face. *That* caused a big stir.'

'Did they go through all the bags?' Jane asks, blushing a little.

'Yes they did,' replies the hostess giving Jane a wink as she walks off.

Several passengers come and ask Margaret and Jane about Gordon. They are interrupted by the sounds of cheers and clapping.

'What now?' Jane stands to see. 'It's *Mr G!*' she calls out excitedly.

Gordon walks down the aisle, half embarrassed and half enjoying the attention. His protracted smile and his awkward wave have worn themselves out by the time he reaches Jane and Margaret.

'*Mr G* … What happened to you?'

'I've been speaking to the pilot, she's a friend of mine, you know. I actually knew her in primary school,' he says shuffling past the women. '*Little* Rhonda Stroud … And now she's flying 747s,' he says with a sigh, sitting down. The ordeal has taken its toll — Gordon is exhausted.

'Strictly between us, Rhonda was telling me about the search on board. This is confidential and so funny. The flight attendant found a vibrator buzzing away merrily in a bag, and then they found … 'He stops and has a giggle. 'I'll leave that one be.'

'Maybe you should,' says Jane.

'What actually happened to you, Gordon?' Margaret persists.

'Well,' he begins, as their aircraft commences taxiing. 'As you know, there were three aeroplanes involved in the bomb scare. One of them was sent to Cairo, we and the other aircraft were directed here to Bahrain. After they arrested me, I was whisked away to the other end of the airport. That was scary.'

'We haven't heard any news about the other aircraft,' Jane cuts in.

'No, no you haven't, not yet anyway.' Gordon continues. 'Just as my interrogation commenced, there was an explosion, not a large explosion, more like a huge thumping sound. Well, that didn't do much for my situation I can assure you. I was immediately locked in the interrogation room. On returning they put me through the wringer. Being completely pre-occupied with the explosion they wouldn't listen to reason. It took me another half-hour to convince them of who I was and even then they weren't buying it completely. They tried to check me out through the UN, but our rigid security temporarily foiled that. Eventually Rhonda, the Captain, finally talked some sense into them. One minute I'm the bad guy, and the next their confidant. "Mr Nesbeth-Smith, please follow us," they said. 'They took me to a viewing window and what I saw is what we are coming up to right now.' He points out of the aircraft window.

'My God,' is all Margaret can say.

Jane is speechless.

Another buzz of chatter fills the cabin and a small boy cries out. '*Look Mummy*, that airplane has smoke coming out of it!'

At a safe distance, fire fighters, ambulances, police, and service vehicles have it surrounded.

'That could have been us!' says Margaret.

'That could have been us,' repeats Jane.

Smoke is still pouring out of the crippled aircraft's rear exit.

'The threat of fire and another explosion is still a possibility,' explains Gordon.

'It's a nasty piece of work. The device must have been timed to go off halfway between Heathrow and Bangkok. The airport police were searching the business class area when the rear section exploded. Luckily all the doors were open which lessened the impact. There are several people injured, but no fatalities.'

A sickly smell of smoke has worked its way through the aircraft's air conditioning system. It will stay with them until long after take off.

'Why were you singled out and detained?' inquires Margaret still persistent.

'I'll give you two guesses, Margaret.'

Jane couldn't miss this opportunity. 'Because you look a little *dodgy.*'

'Maybe,' replies Mr G, with a big grin.

'Because you have an Arabian family,' guesses Margaret.

'Yes, they did mention my wife. I have made, you might say, some controversial statements in the past. Where they dug that information up from I don't know. *Well,* these things happen I suppose. By the way have you noticed the other man taken for questioning is not in his seat?'

Gordon is interrupted by, 'Champagne, sir, with the compliments of the Captain?' says a flight attendant, placing a glass in front of each of them.

'Thank you very much, *French champagne*! Just what the doctor ordered.'

Through the window, Margaret watches the sands of the desert and the whole terrorist incident fade into the distance. Flight 1033 climbs into the middle-eastern skies. Again they have moved into another world and time.

CHAPTER TWENTY SEVEN

'What's *that?*'

A small silver dot, high in the cloudless sky trailing a line of smoke, is moving from west to east.

Horace looks up. 'I can't see nothing, Mr Geoff.'

'Over there, look, look at that.' Geoff points as the strange object moves quickly out of sight.

'Tis people from the stars,' laughs Horace.

Just then, out to starboard, a whale breaks through the choppy whitecaps. A pod of four including a calf is moving in and along with the ship.

'Go and tell Christie and Miss Sarah about them would you please, Horace?'

'Wow!' calls Horace, looking over his shoulder as he runs tangle-footed to the women's quarters. Soon after, Sarah, Christie and the other women move excitedly out on deck.

These are the first whales sighted on the voyage. For ten minutes the spectacle of nature holds all on board the *Neptune* spellbound. For ten minutes, class, rank and other divisions separating these humans from each other are put aside. For ten minutes, the psyche of the child takes over; a common bond amongst all on board has surfaced with the whales.

Sarah and Christie are standing close to Geoff.

As if courting the ship, the huge mammals alter their direction and come closer.

Geoff holds Christie's arm as she leans over the side. 'I can see a big green eye. He's looking at me. There's a baby one, mummy, look.'

'Yes I can see …' Sarah begins to weep.

Geoff has only seen Sarah show emotion once before. He puts his hand on her shoulder. She looks at Christie and then at Geoffrey putting an arm around each of them.

For several minutes the whales cavort with their captive audience. Then as if bored with this clumsy, inflexible floating structure, one of the pod waves its tail out of the water and rolls effortlessly down into another world.

Edging slightly away, Sarah takes her arm from around Geoff.

Several remain on deck trying to hold onto that feeling of childhood wonder, still mesmerised long after the last whale disappears into the depths.

Horace is still excited. He runs off, tripping and slipping across the deck. 'I'm gunna tell the men about *this*!' But his enthusiasm is halted by the guards.

Sarah, Geoff and Christie stretch the moment as long as they can. The Captain and his wife have left the Quarterdeck.

'Back to work you *scrawny* lot!' calls the sailing master.

The canvass is re-trimmed, the course is corrected and the *Neptune* again hooks into the wind.

CHAPTER TWENTY EIGHT

ane is missing Michael, and at the same time her mind flashes back to Greg.

'You love him, don't you,' whispers Margaret as if they are having a conversation.

'Yes, I do, I really do,' replies Jane caught unawares. 'Now come on Margaret, who are we talking about … who was I just thinking about?' Jane can't help herself. She still wants proof of Margaret's psychic abilities.

'Geoff, of course,' Margaret replies without any hesitation.

'You mean Greg, don't you?' quizzes Jane.

'Oh, Greg … that's right … yes Greg.' Margaret looks confused. 'You haven't said much about Greg, have you? He was the fifty-two year old, wasn't he?'

'Yes, Greg showed me the world. I think he came into my life for very good reasons.'

As usual, Margaret doesn't pull any punches. 'Do you think Greg was a father figure?'

'Yes, I often thought about that. I suppose he was. I have probably sought several father figures in my life,' Jane goes on. 'I can't see why though, my father was very rounded, and a good man. I couldn't have asked for more.'

'Maybe your inner self required more than *your* father could give you,' Margaret says.

*　　*　　*

'Ya still love yer missus, don't ya, Mr Geoff?' Horace talks of love but he does not comprehend the feelings. 'I heards you call out to someone called Claire in your sleep last night.'

'Did I?' Geoff is not surprised.

'What is love, Mr Geoff?'

'Well we're good friends Horace, aren't we?'

Horace nods.

'You could say I have love for you.'

Horace gets a little agitated. 'Well, I wouldn't say that.' He fluctuates between joking and deep seriousness. 'Na … that's not right! I'm not a fancy boy ya know. Mick says I am, but I'm not ya know. I not.' His serious side now overtakes any humour. 'Ya dain't think I'm queer do ya, Mr Geoff?'

'Do you think Anne is special?' says Geoff, referring to one of the young convict girls he knows Horace idolises from a distance.

'*Yeh*, I do.'

'Well you're not a fancy boy then, are you?'

'No, naa. I'm not, am I Mr Geoff, I not?'

'Now, how much do you like me, Horace? Are we good friends?'

'Oh *yeh*, Mr Geoff, you knows that, very much.'

'Well, Horace, that's how people in families love one another. You loved your sisters?'

Horace had to think about that.

'Are we a family, Mr Geoff?' asks Horace with his head tilted and one eye screwed closed.

'You could say that my boy, you could say that. *Now*, guess what our next job is?'

Horace straightens his head, closes both eyes, and quickly pinches his nose.

'Not the *lavatory* tubs, no not *dem*, Geoff!' He knows the roster.

Below deck, large tubs are used both as lavatories and receptacles for pots and wash basins. Weather permitting, as the tubs fill they are carried up top and emptied over the side.

This is not Horace's favourite task, but he accepts it.

'Oh 'ell Geoff, it stinks. Dis would be a good job for shithead Mick. It's so heavy.' He groans as they lift the unwieldy tub. 'Dah, it's on me shirt!'

'Horace do I have to remind you what happened last time your mouth was wide open and we were carrying a full one of these?'

'Oh buggar!' Horace's facial muscles tighten. His mouth then closes like a steel trap.

It wasn't long however, before the steel trap prised itself open.

'First mate said ya killed your wife,' Horace says dispassionately as the contents of the tub empties over the side.

'Did he, where did he say that?' says Geoff as the tub balances on the gunnels.

'*Oh pooh…* on deck he said it,' splutters Horace, now perplexed. '*Na*, he didn't exactly say *that*.'

'Who else have you been speaking to?' Geoff stares at him.

'Oh yeh, it was Maurie,' says Horace, 'he said you killed your wife … 'ee did. I knows this not be true … 'ow could Mr Geoff kill somebody he loves?'

They place the empty tub on the deck. 'I want you to believe that Horace, because that is the truth.'

'You still love your wife, Mrs Blake, don't you Mr Geoff?'

'Very much Horace, she is still real to me as if she hasn't died at all.'

*   *   *

The new settlement at Port Jackson, Sydney Harbour, Australia is running short on supplies. Huge expectations are being placed on the promised arrival of the *Neptune* and the other Second Fleet ships, which are still over four months away.

Shortages of cloth, seed, hospital supplies, oats, barley, hardware, rum, and livestock will lead to quarter rations before the Second Fleet sails through the Heads.

Huge expectations are placed on the arrival.

CHAPTER TWENTY NINE

The marines' discontent is still a major problem aboard the *Neptune*. Control of the convicts was officially taken away from them at the beginning of the voyage and their resentment at this decision has not gone away.

As Geoff pointed out to the captain, they are military men and have no tasks or responsibilities. His prediction of trouble has long become a reality. From day one the marines have been drinking and lounging about, and more recently they have taken to accosting the females, both convicts and free passengers alike.

The Captain has prudently decided that the male prisoners, under the supervision of the marines, will spend more time on deck.

*   *   *

The new responsibilities, which includes control of the keys to the male convict quarters, is appeasing the marines. As a result there is an immediate improvement in their attitude. They clean and polish their weapons and their uniforms are washed and trim. Their interests in the females, that previously manifested in blatant innuendos and sometimes direct physical advances, have converted to male pageantry.

Geoff's mess is the third group on deck. Like the men before them, they are a sorry bunch. Most have not seen the sky for over two months. They are weak, pitiful to observe, but their spirit has been rekindled. The result of their harsh confinement and squalid conditions is now, mostly on a nightly basis, paraded for all to see. No longer is their misery buried on the Orlop deck, deep in the hull of the ship.

*   *   *

A misty, salty air hangs over the ship as a small group of convicts are for the first time allowed to attend a burial at sea. The ocean is calm as the Captain reads from the Book of Common Prayer. He has only done this once before on the voyage.

Eight chained men from the Orlop deck witness two of their fellow prisoners slide slowly down tilting planks to their final freedom. Overlapping splashes are heard as the weighted bodies slip into the dark depths.

Through the stillness and mist some willowy notes drift from a recorder played by a young sailor. Like fragile doves fluttering timidly around their loft, the musical notes stay close to the ship as if fearing they will be lost over the vast ocean.

Like a long deep note squeezing out of the recorder one of the convicts slowly begins to move, lifting his chained hands into the air in a graceful arc. A marine moves to intervene but is ordered back by his superior. The convict's hands lower, he lifts one leg high and bending it pivots like an ailing ballet dancer. Nobody interferes as he moves further along the deck. They all watch spellbound as the man dances below the sails, through and around the rigging. The young sailor follows the dancer with his music. The pied piper is the dancer.

The convict captures everyone's attention for several minutes. Even the Captain watches for a while.

Below, Geoff is attending another dying man. Horace whispers in Geoff's ear.

'Maurie's gon mad … He's dancin around the deck.'

'Dancing, you say?' Geoff thinks for a moment, and then smiles.

'Yes, Mr Geoff, he's off his cart.'

The dying man in Geoff's care also manages a smile. 'Maurice … he's free for now, eh?'

Geoff replies, mostly to himself. 'Yes … he's free, as free as any of us can be.'

CHAPTER THIRTY

ritish Airways Flight 1033, is thirty-eight thousand feet above India, five hours from its Singapore stopover and fifteen hours from its final destination, Australia. The aeroplane seems relentless; unlike its passengers, it does not tire.

Margaret and Jane are having a cuppa.

'I'm tired of looking at the back of this seat,' Jane says clipping at it with her finger tips. '*And* the aircraft food is giving me the irrates.' Not only is she tired of the food, the cramped conditions, the stale air; she is also tired of the movies, which roll on relentlessly like tumbleweeds across an American desert plain.

'I feel grotty and washed out. I would kill for a hot bath. Margaret,' she says changing the subject in hope her quibbles will disappear, 'how can you see the things you see?'

'What are you talking about, love?'

'You know, all this psychic stuff.'

'Lets see … I see it this way. A cord of common consciousness links everybody.'

'You think so?' Jane's eyes widen.

'The same cord also links communities, states and countries. Some think it links the whole universe. This very same cord connects the past and the present. Along this continuum travels the positive and negative evolved characteristics of individuals, families, whole communities and nations. Sometimes, through meditation, dreams, when the time is just right, it may be possible for any individual to link into this slipstream of past and present knowledge. Attuned people, such as psychics,' Margaret straightens up, 'soothsayers, witchdoctors, mystics and gifted individuals from all religions, appear to have the ability to link into segments of this cord of higher consciousness and access the past, present and the future. Is this all making sense to you?'

Jane nods again. Gordon listens. Margaret continues.

'Most people potentially possess these psychic abilities, but have to be content with having isolated experiences. Many times these phenomena are written off as coincidences, fantasies, or just dreams. However, most of us believe these magical, special things do actually occur … *Don't* we *love?* Gordon, looking straight ahead, nods. 'Not *you*.' Margaret gives him a nudge and continues. That miracles can occur is officially recognised by the Catholic Church. Sainthoods are bestowed upon some of its leaders and followers, who are said to have mystical powers. The church's most basic mystical events such as the resurrection of Christ, the prophecies of the Bible, the healing abilities of Jesus and modern-day sainthoods are put forward as the cornerstones of the Christian religion. Yet the church is quick to deny a belief in the supernatural. The Christian church, although allowing this unusual contradiction within its own ranks, shows little tolerance to mystical happenings, or the beliefs of mystics and other religions. For Christ to be resurrected from death is believable to the Christian church, but the idea of reincarnation is out of the question.'

Jane sits amazed, thinking, *the way Margaret puts it, it's all quite feasible.* 'That will take me a while to digest, but it was really good Margaret.'

'Do we think alike, love?'

'We do Margaret, we do.'

'*Well*, stop fighting it Jane'

* * *

'*Yes you killed her lad*,' says Maurie. '*Sure as I'm sitting here, you killed her.*'

Now Claire is speaking to Geoff. 'Sorry my husband, for I did the best I possibly could. You know that. It is you I love, but something inside pulls me away so strongly. Our baby girl could not come into this world of double standards. You tried and I know you love me so much. At another time …'

Geoff awakes from his dream. He needs to talk. It is three-thirty am, and most of the men on the Orlop are asleep. Geoff shakes Maurice.

'Oh, *oh*, Geoffy boy, what's wrong, what's wrong?' Maurie tries to wake up.

'Maurie, I've just had a dream — you said I killed Claire.'

'It's only a dream Geoff … 'tis only a dream.'

'But you told Horace, just the other day, I killed Claire, didn't you?'

'Dats what I hear. I was only sayin' what I hear. Now go back to sleep lad. Go'rn, back to sleep with yuh.' Still drowsy, Geoff follows Maurie's advice.

*   *   *

'Jane, may I say something?' Margaret has a distant look about her.

'Certainly,' says Jane.

'I can see a ship …' Margaret hesitates.

'Yes, go on,' Jane urges, though she really isn't in the mood.

'There is fighting in the streets of Paris. There is trouble on board the ship. There is mutiny in their minds.'

'Paris? … Whose minds Margaret?'

'The men in the dark below. He must be careful Jane, for your sake …' Margaret closes her eyes and falls into a trance.

'Careful … for my sake? What does she mean, Mr G?'

'I don't know Jane, I don't know. However, I do know we all need some shuteye, don't you think. You haven't had very much at all.'

Against a background of bomb threats, changing time zones, high altitude flying and aircraft food, the modern travellers try to settle back to rest.

*　　*　　*

The next day on the *Neptune* begins with the usual routine. It's been eighty days since they left England and it's only a few more days before the ship will anchor in the harbour of False Bay at the southern tip of Africa.

At midday, some frightening screams begin to echo around the ship. The slap of the lash is partly muffled by parting and bleeding flesh. Each time it is pulled back the trail of blood along the deck increases. Droplets are also flicked into the air as the leathers change direction and come down again on the back of the tortured convict. Captain Trail has ordered this diabolical flogging at the Chief Mate, Ellington's request.

'Damn you, were you not out of your irons last night?' asks Ellington.

'No, sir ... how, sir?' whines the convict.

The order is given to check his wrist irons. The armourer reports the irons were too tightly riveted for a man to slip out of them.

The chief mate is not satisfied.

'Come here and hold out your hands,' he calls out to the terri-fied prisoner.

Ellington tries to pull the irons off the man's wrists, without success.

'*Please don't use me ill, sir*, please don't hurt me anymore,' pleads the man.

The chief mate then places his foot against the convict's chest and pulls the irons with great force. The screams of the poor soul can be heard around the ship as one of his hands pulls away at the wrist. Lashed again to the bow of a long boat, the convict's punishment is continued. Once released, he collapses on deck calling out, 'It's the last day I will live!'

He begs for water and drinks it in great gulps. He dies three hours later in the same place, unattended in the tropical heat. The ship's surgeon is forbidden to treat or comfort the man and all others were kept away at gunpoint. Many of the crewmembers, years later in court, will voice their horror over the treatment of this man and others on the *Neptune*.

Apart from the overwhelming brutality of the morning which sickened Geoff to the core, his dream from the preceding night plays on his mind. Claire's expression of love for him, and the deep-down feeling that he in some way was responsible for her death, taunts him.

'What's wrong with you, Mr Geoff?' Horace has never seen Geoff like this before.

Geoff would prefer not to talk, but for Horace's sake he says, 'This has been a terrible day, Horace, and for me it still is, but tomorrow will be different.'

Horace then does something which surprises himself. He places his hand on Geoff's shoulder and holds it there. Tears begin to run down Geoff's cheeks.

'I knows you are very sad, Mr Geoff, I knows that.'

Predictably, the men in chains below are extremely agitated by the thrashing to death of one of their own, but say nothing. The women prisoners — who are allowed to get away with much more than the men, let rip at the crew and the chief mate.

*   *   *

The last meal before touchdown in Singapore is being served.

'You know Margaret; whenever I think about Michael I get goose bumps. I don't understand why he has such an effect on me. I've never loved anybody so much.'

'Well Jane, I don't know either. The only things I get worked up about these days are a good film and my next gourmet meal — neither of which are likely on this trip.' Margaret points at the tray of food in front of her. 'Where was I? Oh yes and my trips overseas and my cat Jellybean, *they* can get me going.'

'You have no man in your life then?'

'No, not at the moment. I was divorced a couple of years ago and then went out with a couple of men, but I tended to find they were more trouble than they are worth, and I'm *sure* they probably felt the same way about me.'

Jane glances at the Sidney Sheldon novel Margaret has in her lap. 'We just can't do without men and their ways, can we Margaret? It's as if God made men and women totally different just to keep us all confused and on our toes.' She pauses for a moment. 'I must say though, whenever I blame a man for something, if I'm honest, many times, I can see that same fault in myself.'

'That doesn't happen for me at all,' Margaret says quickly, 'what do you mean, Jane?'

'What Jane means is that it takes one to know one,' says Gordon.

'No, that's not what I mean,' rebukes Jane. 'What I'm saying is there seems to be a male side of my character that understands and sympathises with men.'

'It takes one to know one. You have just confirmed my point,' smiles Mr G.

'So you have a female side, do you Gordon?' asks Margaret.

'Yes, I do, and I even have a name for her, Lucy … I listen to what she has to say. She is sometimes catty; sometimes off with the fairies, sometimes wise, but what she has taught me most is how to feel.'

Jane and Margaret can't argue with that.

'How does she communicate with you?' asks Jane seriously.

'She talks to me. It's like another voice. When she is being devious, I have to be very careful because she does it in such a way I don't notice until it's too late. When she is kind and influencing me, I also have to be careful. People do misunderstand feminine kindness in a male sometimes, you know. *I think it is healthy to have male and female attributes, it's helped me so much in my work.'

'So, if your theory is correct Gordon I can blame my male side for my aggressiveness, manipulation by placation and flattery, and exploitation of people's weaknesses by making them feel guilty.'

'Well Margaret, if they're all aspects of you — and I would *never* believe that for a moment — it's best to blame your male side, don't you think?'

Margaret can't argue with that either.

'I'm so glad to find somebody that agrees with me,' says Jane.

*　　*　　*

The funeral of the convict flogged to death takes place on the *Neptune*. Captain Trail petulantly reads from the Old Testament.

I will utter my judgements against them concerning all their wickedness because they have forsaken me. Therefore prepare yourself and arise and speak to them all that I command you …

The proceedings are short.

For a split second Geoff looks into Trail's eyes. Momentarily his mind fills with horror.

CHAPTER THIRTY ONE

'That bitch, with her nose in the air, ain't got no feelings. Typical.' One of the convict women is referring to Mrs Macarthur, John Macarthur's wife in the makeshift cabin next door.

'She thinks her *shit* dain't stink. An as for 'im, well, whata smart arse he be,' calls another female convict, loud enough that the Macarthur's might overhear through the thinly partitioned wall.

Mrs Macarthur writes in her journal:

On two sides we — my husband, child and maid — are surrounded by wretches, whose dreadful imprecations ever ring in my distracted ears. These wretches triumph, and pleasure seems to consist in aggravating my distress. Our access to the upper deck was nailed up. We are now compelled to share a passageway with the convict women and their filthy toilet buckets and tubs.

Is it the refinements of the Macarthurs which provoke the convict women, or the convict women's base coarseness which infuriates the Macarthurs, or both? Since coming aboard, John Macarthur has sided with the marines. Disgruntled, the captain has manipulated the Macarthur family into an intolerable situation by placing some of the convict women in close quarters alongside them. Trail uses discord between groups and individuals to his advantage constantly.

Sarah's belly is now the size of a medium pumpkin and Christie is so proud of her expectant mother. They are among the group of women convicts sharing the overcrowded cabin next door to the Macarthurs. Sarah tries constantly to quell the abusive and crude behaviour of the women, but to no avail.

Amidst the squabbles, swearing and screaming, a knock at the women's quarters' door is barely noticeable.

'Who da hell is that?'

'It's me … Horace!' his voice quavering.

'Go away ya little slime!' calls one of the women.

'Wha you want?' calls another.

'I have somethin for Miss Sarah and Christie. Somethin from Mr Geoff!'

The door is opened quickly. 'Give it here,' says one of the young women, trying to snatch the parcel without success.

'I *gotta* give it to *Miss Sarah*,' pleads Horace.

Horace hands Sarah a small hand-made wooden box covered in scratched waxed brown paper and tied with some hemp.

'Thank you, Horace, that's very kind of you.'

'It's not from *me* Miss, it's from *Mr Geoff*.' Horace is embarrassed.

'Do thank Mr Blake for me, Horace,' says Sarah, smiling.

Horace stands still when he should be going. Very few men get a chance to see into the women's quarters. The softness, the colours, the relative tidiness and cleanliness confuse him. *It smells different in there*, he thinks. Memories of his mother and sisters stream into his mind. But beyond all that, these are females and his male hormones are pumping, resulting in a lumpy feeling just at the bottom of his ribcage, a feeling that, if given a little extra encouragement, would probably manifest itself between his legs.

This is nothing new to the women. They see it every day on the ship. Men lose themselves and gawk, sometimes consciously but often like Horace, they are just mesmerised. Even the plainest of the women have this effect on the men and they know it.

A young convict girl at the back of the quarters lifts up her dress and opens her legs displaying her anything-but-clean undergarments. She has obviously done this before.

Horace, completely innocent to this point, is actually shocked. He turns and moves off. Only later would he revel in the provocative behaviour of that young girl. He will be itching to deliver messages to the women's quarters in the future.

Sarah moves Christie onto their bunk, thinking, *they can open the package in private,* but the women crowd around them silently trying to peer over their shoulders. A parcel is very unusual on a sailing ship and the women want to see what is in this covered, wooden box. Sarah finally gives in and turns around. All eyes are on Sarah's hands. The parcel sits crossways in her lap. She begins to undo the hemp tie. Ten pairs of eyes are all fixated on the box.

Sarah slowly undoes the tie and folds back the brown paper.

'Whatcha going so slow for girlie?'

'Yeah, come on Sar, hurry it up.'

'This is *my* parcel,' she says with some irritation in her voice … '*I* will open it as *I* wish.' Sarah stops for a second to compose herself.

Christie lifts the lid off the box. At the top is the most beautiful bunch of flowers containing two roses, one pink and the other a soft yellow, a stem of lilac and three sprigs of foxglove, all backed with green fern.

Christie starts to giggle.

'That's ridiculous,' laughs one of the women.

Christie stops giggling. Her eyes look up and she touches Sarah's arm gently.

'I think it's so beautiful,' says one of the other women with a sigh.

As Christie knows, Geoff is not much of an artist, but he is improving. The flowers, with the assistance of one of his fellow convicts, are drawn and painted in marine paint. One of the younger women playfully puts forward a cup as a vase. Sarah smiles as she attaches the drawing of the flowers to a protruding nail above her and Christie's bunk.

'There's more, mummy,' Christie is excited.

Toffee, boiled sweets and crude shortbread biscuits, enough for all to try. Sarah generously shares her gift with the delighted women.

Since the fire the cooks in the galley are friendly with Geoff and over a period of two weeks they have saved some handmade off-cuts from toffees destined for the officers' table. The crude shortbreads were baked specially the night before.

Silence in the cabin is broken by muffled mutterings from half-filled mouths expressing delight and satisfaction.

*   *   *

Groups of convict men are now allowed to move about the main deck under the strict supervision of the marines. As Captain Trail expected, there have been positive and negative consequences of the more liberal treatment of the male prisoners.

The marines are definitely more motivated and less troublesome as a result of their new responsibilities. As Captain Trail had predicted, the improvement in the morale of the convicts has resulted in an outcry over the rations. Now the men are exercising they need more food. Punishments over breaches of conduct by the convicts are on the increase. Again, the talk of mutiny amongst the men in chains is commonplace. Horace parrots all this to Geoff who warns him about the dangers of such talk. Indirect and direct pressure to join mutinous groups is being placed on all the mess leaders. Because of their access to weapons and keys their involvement would be vital to any successful mutiny.

*   *   *

Jane and Mr G's meals are running late. Margaret receives hers first. Despite what she thinks about airline food she devours into the roast beef and baked potatoes.

Jane's tray comes at last.

'Well, somebody's spoilt, aren't they?' comments Margaret.

Jane just sits and stares. 'Isn't that lovely,' she says. In the centre of her tray there are three fresh roses, one yellow and two pink.

'Do they have a perfume?' says Mr G.

'I hope you like them, I sneaked them from business class,' says attendant Bruce, learning across the back of the seat in front.

'They're truly lovely, that's so nice of you,' says Jane, smelling the yellow rose.

'You're welcome,' says Bruce.

'He's the guy who searched the bags.' Jane whispers.

I don't know how flowers survive this trip. How can I keep them? Jane wonders.

Mr G takes over. He carefully wraps the stems of the roses in a paper hand towel, wets it thoroughly and then puts them in a small plastic bag and tin foil from the meal tray. He then places the bunch in the pouch at the back of the seat in front of Jane.

'There we are,' he says proudly.

'That's so sweet, thank you Mr G.' Jane gives him a kiss on the cheek.

'Margie?'

'Yes Janie?'

'What was all that back there about the men below in the dark, and he will have to be careful for my sake, and … and mutiny on the ship?'

'It sounds a bit grim I know but this unusual ability I possess, or possesses me, has proven itself to be true time and time again. This stuff has to come out and there are intense feelings involved. I just can't control it, it is so strong.'

'Yes, I think I understand,' replies Jane. 'But it is difficult when it involves me.

'Listen to me Jane. The flowers you have just received … well, they don't mean what you think they do. They have a more beautiful meaning. If I was to tell you they came from another place, another time, you would think I had gone around the twist, wouldn't you?'

'No, no, I wouldn't.'

'*Wouldn't you?*' Well, that's good. Can we leave it there for now?'

'I'd sooner you didn't.'

'I have to Jane, for now, I just have to.'

The weary passengers are given thirty minutes to prepare for landing and change of aircraft at Changi Airport, Singapore.

'Do you think we will be in the same seats on the next flight?' says Margaret.

'Don't worry, I have already asked if that can be arranged.' says Gordon.

*   *   *

'*Land to the port bow!*' hollers the crows-nest. This is the first mainland sighting since the *Neptune* left England eighty-six days ago.

Captain Trail's accuracy in navigation has resulted in his ship being positioned directly outside the entrance to their South African harbour. The crew is more than impressed.

Against the majestic mountains in the background, the calm clear waters of False Bay provide a welcome relief from the unrelenting ocean swell. White sandy beaches bordering the bay sift through the palms to the edge of the lush mountainous rain forests.

A fresh north-easterly breeze cools the hot deck and a special sail has been rigged to direct fresh air down the hatch to cool the incarcerated men below. Everybody has been warned against swimming. Man-eating monster white sharks are common in these waters. To the right of the ship a rocky island is home to over five hundred slippery, shiny, barking seals — the white sharks favourite meal. Even the sounds of Dutch civilisation echoing across the water seem reassuring. The *Neptune* answers with the abusive rattling sound of its anchor chain.

The crew and marines are ecstatic about the stopover at False Bay — fantasies abound. The older sea dogs have very few illusions. They know from experience that unless they have contacts, are exceptionally good looking, or have money to pay for the services of women, alcohol will be their only consolation.

The free passengers are looking forward to fresh fruits and vegetables, a chance to purchase a bargain at the markets, finding their land legs, to warm baths, to forest walks, and to sampling of locally cooked meals.

The freedom of the prisoners on the other hand has been completely curtailed and, of the mess leaders, only Geoff and two other leaders will stay unchained. Horace is distraught as he is re-shackled. The usual ribbing he continually receives from the men now, in most cases, turns to support.

'Now you know how it feels you little *bastard!*' yells a voice from the next section.

'*Shut your gob*, yells one of Horace's supporters.

While female prisoners are also to remain below decks Trail allows them on deck to briefly view the foreign land.

The convicts are aware of their legal rights to fresh food when the ship docks, but knowing Trail, expectations only rise marginally. Despite Trail's Scrooge-like administration, fresh vegetables, fruit and meat will reach them.

A third of the soldiers and the crew have signs of scurvy. The increased supply of vegetables, and the new supplies for the remainder of the voyage, will curb the outbreak. William Grey, the ship's surgeon, continues to pressure the Captain to provide extra greens for the prisoners.

On the thirteenth of April, 1790, the *Neptune* dropped anchor in the harbour of False Bay, twenty miles from Cape Town. It has consigned the bodies of forty-five male convicts and one woman to the sea. The deaths on board the *Neptune*, to now, are ten times greater than any ship of the first government-operated fleet.

*　　*　　*

The landing wheels of Flight 1033 spin from zero to two hundred and eighty miles per hour in a split second. Two small puffs of bluish-grey, rubberised smoke appear and hang in the windless, humid air at Changi Airport.

The mighty 747, as if exhausted by its journey, makes its way slowly to the terminal. Like Gulliver, it will be tied to the ground by fuel lines and passenger walkway fingers. Restrained, little people will walk all over and under the aircraft, prodding it, and inspecting it.

The *Neptune*, in False Bay, a Gulliver of its day, is also under control, covered in ropes, anchored, with little people moving all over her from bow to stern. She lies motionless for sixteen days.

On the twenty-ninth of April 1790, the *Neptune* and her sister ships move out on the final leg of the voyage to Australia. The Macarthurs, disgusted, have moved to a sister ship to complete their journey.

CHAPTER THIRTY TWO

I n the early hours of the morning, Sarah, in the corner of her bunk, recalls the first night she sold her body in London.

He arrived at eight-thirty. Night covering his tracks he gives a single knock at the door.

'Mr Smithers?'

He answers, 'Yes,' with a slight nod.

'My name is Stacey, please come in.'

'Would you like refreshments, sir?'

'Yes thankyou, a brandy and water,'

'I'm not used to mixing drinks. I only jist started 'ere — they've been real good to me, oops,' she misjudges the amount of brandy.

Without delay she leads him up a darkened staircase. They enter one of the many rooms on the first floor.

'I'll take your money then.'

He pays.

She undresses and lies down beside him. Small nipples nestle on top of her small breasts. Big hazel eyes look at him momentarily from under a red fringe of hair. She makes her move.

'That's not necessary,' he whispers, lifting her hand and drawing it to his chest. With one arm around her skinny shoulders and the other around her small torso, he caresses her back and she falls into a hypnotic half sleep. Awakening with a start, she says, 'Me father would kill me if he knew what I was doing.' She is vulnerable. She is his to do with whatever he wishes. For an hour and a quarter, although tempted to do otherwise, he embraces and caresses her only.

When his time is up, the small window to her mind closes. She dresses herself, leaving him fumbling in the half-light for his shoes and socks. She leads the way down the stairs to the front door. With eyes looking down she hugs him, and bids him 'goodnight.'

Sarah had failed at most things in life and now she feels she has failed yet again. The kindness of her first client only confused her. Little did she know the compassion he showed to her would be the first and the last. She was not to be confused by kindness again. No part of her body would be sacred or left untouched. Men growing old would suck and fondle her youth as if in some strange way trying to steal her years, her attractiveness, her innocence and even her strength. Young men, restricted by a society fumbling for decency, cast any considerations for her feelings aside as the long frustrations of their short lifetimes were vented.

It never stops; the ghosts of each of my clients still visit me. They suck at my soul, she thinks as she curls into a ball in the corner of her bunk on the *Neptune.* She refuses to cuddle Christie for fear the demons within, the demons she must face alone, may in some way transfer and impact on the innocence of her daughter.

Part of Sarah wants to like men; another part of her hates them. The beauty she once flaunted has now worn thinner than skin deep. Day in, day out, the vulturous males aboard the *Neptune* pick at her wounded swan, which can't fly away.

At False Bay, two of Sarah's female convict friends are taken away in the middle of the night. Somewhere in that South African town, men, probably men of high ranking, will take advantage of these imprudent women. Sarah has seen it all before.

*   *   *

'Room for *another?* Penny for your *thoughts* Geoffrey,' Sarah seats herself abruptly, her pregnancy and the rolling motion of the ship hindering her judgement. Geoff is taking a break outside the galley.

'I … was just thinking about home, and Claire.'

'You loved her very much, didn't you?' Sarah asks.

'As God is my witness, I didn't harm her.'

'You *did* love her then?'

'With all my being. Her death was the biggest shock of my life. To this very day I still don't understand what happened.'

'Was Claire happy, Geoff?'

'Our baby was coming, we had everything. But Claire wanted something more.'

'And that was?' Sarah urges.

'I'm not sure. We had most things. She had her stone.'

'Her *stone* …?'

'*Yes*, she had it sculpted … she worshiped it. She said it was a symbol of her love for me. I know it meant more. It seemed she wanted more than *I* could give her,' he replies staring at the deck.

'She wanted more than *you* could give, or more than anybody could give her?' Sarah tries to understand.

'It's a feeling I can't explain, I don't know, Sarah. Her *stone* represented *everything* to her.' He is disorientated and has not taken in what Sarah has just said.

Christie returns from the animal compound and cuddles in between Geoff and Sarah.

'The wind has come up. It's quite cold.' Sarah can't cope with these complexities. 'It's time for Christie to bed down.'

Geoff helps Sarah to her feet and carries Christie to the women's quarters.

*　　*　　*

Jane looks across the wing at the fluffy white clouds. They remind her of mashed potatoes. She hated mashed potatoes as a child, so focusing on these clouds will not lift her spirits. Her mind rests instead on warm thoughts of Michael and his daughter Becky. *It won't be long,* she thinks to herself.

Singapore is now far behind them and the aircraft is heading south towards Australia.

'He's not going to find what he is looking for and neither are you, until you both start looking in the right place,' says Margaret in a dreamlike voice.

Here we go again, thinks Jane. 'Margaret, I hope you can back up that comment or I am going to be very cross with you.'

'I honestly don't know what it means … truly.'

Jane looks to Mr G.

'Don't look at me, lass. That goes way over my head,' he quickly replies.

'Just a moment and …' says Margaret.

Jane sits still, mesmerised. Margaret's deep concentrating state ends five minutes later.

'Claire,' she says talking directly to Jane, 'his name is Geoff. Does that name mean anything to you?'

'What are you talking about? My name's not Claire and I have no idea who Geoff is. Do you mean *Greg?*' asks Jane, very puzzled.

'He may be Greg to you, but he's blonde-haired Geoff to me. When I said Claire, I meant you. Is your second name Claire?'

'Greg has dark hair,' Jane mutters to herself. 'Claire must be my guardian angel,' she laughs. 'What else Margaret, did you see anything else?'

'Ocean, no land, and again the sadness. And a small girl,' replies Margaret. 'And … the *Neptune* … the *Neptune.*'

Jane looks at Gordon. '*Neptune,* what does that mean Mr G?'

'I don't know Jane. King Neptune? The planet Neptune is the fourth largest planet in the solar system. In Roman Mythology, Neptune is God of the Sea and Son of the god, Saturn.' He pauses. 'The *Neptune, of course* was the largest convict-carrying ship in the Second Fleet from England to Australia.'

Jane sits back as dinner is served. She removes the lid from her main course.

'Golly!' she says. 'It would be mashed potatoes!' She takes a mouthful and pulls a face then gets back to Gordon. 'I've heard about the First Fleet to Australia but not much is said about the Second Fleet.'

She looks across at Margaret who is sitting watching her with a, *it will be alright smile,* on her face.

'What's this all about Margaret? Where am I heading into?'

'I thought you knew love,' replies Margaret enigmatically.

CHAPTER THIRTY THREE

For a powerful, intelligent nation such as England not to learn from its previous expansionary errors, is an indication that mistakes were and are nothing but continuing premeditated actions.

The use of contractors on the Second Fleet was a deliberate decision by the English government. Captain Trail was chosen for his record, a record that suited a less compassionate thrust. The Government would later publicly scorn Trail's approach, the very person they sooled onto the task.

Many men and women have been chosen to drive the Empirical machine and later, once the task is completed, condemned for driving too hard.

Captain Trail was a slave-trading captain, and the new contractors for the second fleet — Camden, Calvert and King — had previously operated slave-trading vessels. All this was on record when the British government made their decisions.

Geoff is aware of the fleet contractor's slave transportation history, but he is unaware of Captain Trail's past record as a slave-transporting captain.

*   *   *

'MURDER' The World newspaper, London on November 3 1791, headlined. Warrant is being sought for the arrest of Donald Trail, Master of the *Neptune* and his Chief Mate Ellington, accusing them of the murder of the ship's Portuguese cook, John Joseph.

It goes on to say they were accused of causing excessive mortality among the ship's convicts, through neglect and mistreatment on the voyage to Australia. Days later, in the same newspaper, Ellington, the chief mate is accused of a barbarous murder. He beat an unnamed convict to death.'

*　　*　　*

'Have you been to Australia Mr G?' Jane asks.

'No I haven't, but I have friends there. We've all heard of kangaroos. I have eaten kangaroo steaks in London. Geographically, Australia is cut off from the rest of the world. It's lucky like that. Europe with its density of population and mix of cultures has always been a troubled area. Australia up until the mid 1950s has been a staunch supporter of the English monarchy. But American influence, a developing independence and the expansion of the European Common Market has seen Australia pull away from England in the last forty years.'

'Koala bears are the cuddliest little creatures, aren't they?' says Margaret.

'Actually Margaret, koalas are not bears, they are large marsupials and can be very aggressive little characters if disturbed.'

'*Oh*,' says Margaret, squashed.

Gordon continues, 'Most Aussies live on the rich, narrow coastal strip situated between the Pacific Ocean and the Great Dividing Range which runs up its eastern coast.'

'So what takes you to Australia, Gordon?' Margaret asks.

'I'm involved in negotiations with the Australian Government. You could say I'm the man in the middle. The Aboriginal people have spiritual relationships with specific areas of land and have instigated further land right claims. They've made submissions both to the UN and the Australian government. I can hopefully act as a go-between.'

'We made a bit of a mess, didn't we?' Jane ponders out loud.

'Who Jane, who are you on about?' asks Mr G.

'The Empire … the British Empire.' says Jane. 'Look what we did in Africa, India, America, China, the Middle-east and Australia.

'Empire building is a messy business at the best of times,' says Gordon. 'Hitler was an empire builder.'

'Yes, but he was different. Are you serious, Gordon?' says Margaret.

'There have been many empire builders. It's all relative you know,' he replies.

'Relative to *what*? Are you *really* serious?' Margaret is getting extremely agitated.

'Which empire came first Margaret?' he asks. He has nothing to lose now. This issue has already upset her.

'This is not a chicken and the egg thing you know. Hitler was evil,' asserts Margaret.

'I can see what he is saying, Margaret. It depends on the perceptions of individuals and the outlook of cultures. Isn't that why we still have trouble in the world today?' says Jane.

Margaret stops and thinks. Her English upbringing is battling with her inner fair judgement.

'That is a *tad* idealistic Jane. Anyway, I suppose I'm outnumbered,' Margaret seems to yield.

'That's a cop-out Margaret,' replies Jane calmly, looking her right in the eyes.

'I know it is. But you're not saying Hitler's actions are forgivable are you?'

Gordon and Jane both look at her blankly.

'No … *no* … I didn't mean that.' Margaret still looks uncomfortable but shrugs her shoulders and settles back in her chair.

'Well,' she continues, 'we've discussed so much, it seems like we've been travelling for a lifetime. So now that we have solved the world's problems, where do we go from here?'

'I don't know about you fine people, but I am going to get some shut-eye,' says Gordon quietly as he closes the window sunshade.

As Jane settles to sleep, Michael is on her mind.

eoffrey, you know I love you and I know you love me. Love moves through time and all barriers. Love and time is the key to change, it's just we sometimes do not see the change in our own lifetime.

Geoff sits bolt upright. 'Claire!' he calls. He feels around in the dark at the end of his bunk.

She looked like Claire. She spoke like Claire, but her clothing was different — thoughts are flashing through his mind. 'I can't see, where did she go?' he says aloud. Struggling to wake up he stumbles to his feet, climbs the companion ladder to the top deck and calls the guard.

'Mr Blake … is there a problem?'

'No,' replies Geoff, 'I need to go on deck.' He moves past the confused guard.

The woman appears again near the foremast. She stands, looks at him for a second only and then is gone. He runs to the front of the ship. His heart is pounding. The power of this encounter leaves him breathless and a warm feeling rinses through his chest and arms. 'That *was* Claire. I'm sure,' he says to himself looking over the side into the black, surging ocean. She has vanished.

'You look like you've seen a ghost, Mr Blake,' says Sergeant Thomas, who has been alerted by the other guard about Geoff's strange behaviour.

'I'm not well at all, Thomas,' replies Geoff.

'You'll catch your death up here. Go lie quiet till you feel yourself again,' replies Thomas as Geoff moves back down the hatch.

'I'll do that Thomas. *Yes I will,*' Geoff calls, as he returns again to the rank atmosphere of the prison deck.

The two marines are temporarily left spellbound. They decide to make no report about his strange movements on deck.

Morning finds the sun rising over the bow of the *Neptune*. Winds are blowing from the south-west. A huge ocean swell lifts, lowers and rolls the ship.

Horace wakes Geoff. 'Mr Geoff, *Mr Geoff,* Christie wants you.'

'Where? *Where?*' Geoff looks around, rubbing his eyes.

'On deck, Mr Geoff.'

'Shut up you lot,' calls a sick man on an adjoining bunk. Horace moves to pacify him.

'Mummy's sick, Mr Geoff, she's bin sayin' funny things.' Christie looks ragged and tired when Geoff reaches her.

In the women's quarters one of the more responsible convict women reassures them. 'She's not ta bad, just a bit a fever, she looked afta me, I'll take care of er, Geoffy.'

With that, he is ushered out of the women's area. As if an invisible string hoists her arm, Sarah gives a frail wave as he goes. Then the cabin door is pushed shut in his face. He wraps Christie in his coat and wipes her face and hands. She stares at him with tired eyes as he carries her to the galley.

The cooks are friendly and find some porridge for them both.

'Mummy is fine and she'll get better.' Geoff assures Christie. She smiles back and nods trustingly.

*   *   *

Even without land and trees it is apparent autumn has arrived. The ocean temperature has dropped. It smells different and the water is taking on an icy-looking hue of blue. The skies are clear. The air is crisper and the days are becoming shorter.

Within two days, Sarah is out of her bunk and back on deck. She is very pregnant, and looks anaemic and tired.

The ship is making slow, steady progress, enabling the crew to relax and contemplate fishing the large schools of tuna that appear around the ship. Poles, cord, red rag and hooks are all that is required to lure the large fish. Motivated by the need for fresh food and some excitement, the crew are given permission to begin the sport. Eight sailors and two marines have their strength tested as thirty-five fish, including six barracuda, each weighing in excess of twenty pounds, are landed on the deck. .

The dying, bleeding fish flap frantically on the blood stained deck. Many of the children, standing at a safe distance, watch fascinated. Christie and two of the older boys edge towards the pulsating creatures. They poke at the smooth slippery flesh and glassy eyes of the suffering fish.

Chief Mate Ellington voices his concern for the children, warning them away from the barracuda. 'The teeth of these long, ferocious fish are still able to bite and inflict deep wounds, even out of the water,' he explains. Ellington's concerns are scoffed at by all. After his barbarous fatal abuse of the chained convict four weeks prior, people are dubious about him offering kindly advice to children. Everyone, without exception, moves away from him whenever he appears.

Christie leaves the other children and returns to where Geoff and Sarah are standing. Geoff takes a rag from his pocket and begins to wipe her slimy, bloody hands.

'*I'll do that Geoff*,' says Sarah abruptly, taking the cloth away from him.

Geoff has seen the oceans and weather change quickly. Sarah's abruptness has swept in like a rain-squall out of nowhere. Only minutes before she was enjoying the fishing and laughing and joking along with everybody else. Geoff guesses it's the pregnancy making her moody. He moves to comfort her but is rebuked. Christie tries to intervene but Sarah pulls her away and walks off with her. The child is in tears.

'That's a woman for you,' laughs one of the marines, harm-lessly.

'She's a handful that one,' calls another one.

For the next two days the fishing becomes a daily event aboard the *Neptune.* Everybody eats fresh fish and benefits from the much needed fish oil. Empty barrels previously containing beef are now filled to the brim with salted fish fillets and steaks

That night, the dream of the menagerie streams back into Geoff's mind as he settles down to sleep. It continues to confuse him. He recalls the hell and torment it predicted for him, and the Neanderthal-man, who passed him at the crossed paths in the old warehouse.

What became of that tortured, pitiful creature? he wonders. *What did the old warehouse mean? Why did I open those doors? What did the pens of suffering animals mean, and what was that light in the distance? This all must mean something. That dream did come out of my mind.*

Lost in a world of his own, Geoff is oblivious to the mass of smelly, suffering humanity around him on the Orlop deck. He falls asleep.

CHAPTER THIRTY FIVE

s the *Neptune* and her sister ships move steadily towards the Australian continent, food in the colony at Port Jackson is getting more and more scarce.

An over reliance on the promised Second Fleet, the inhospitable New South Wales countryside, the ambivalent, but growing hostility from the local Aboriginal tribes, are factors placing heavy pressures on the fledgling colony.

The initial fantasies of the new settlers are waning. Provisions sent with the First Fleet are near depleted. Basic equipment such as shovels, saws and building supplies are too few and of poor quality. The semi-tropical climate with its extreme heat, high humidity and torrential rain, is proving very difficult for the British-born to cope with. Crops are failing due to poor soil conditions in the immediate vicinity of the new settlement.

*   *   *

Ellington has discovered the convicts have been covering up the deaths of their fellows to obtain their food rations. Seven hasty, unceremonious convict burials in one day and a further reduction in rations is Trail's cold-hearted reaction. This only increases the despair and deep-seated anger amongst the men. They plot revenge.

The captain, aware of troublemakers amongst the convicts agrees to meet with Geoff again.

'I feel I owe you once more Mr Blake, but hear me loud and

clear, after this meeting we are squared. Now state your case, young man.'

'The men are hungry, sir.'

'My God! Is that all?' Trail moves to dismiss him.

A galley cook serving hot chocolate milk with warm griddle-cakes and maple syrup interrupts the meeting. Geoff uses the small amount of credit he has with the captain and presses him harder.

'The good condition of the men is in everybody's interest, sir.'

'You don't understand do you, Mr Blake. Your type never would. How would you operate this vessel? … you wouldn't last a week. They would have you over the side, the women would be ravaged. Then the idiots would roam the seas causing havoc. I have personal commendations from Lord Nelson. I've operated merchant vessels from Africa to the Americas. How do you think I have done this successfully? I can assure you it was not by making it a pleasure cruise for the scum I was consigned to carry.'

Only now does Geoff finally understand how futile it is to reason with the Captain. He realises it would be a mistake to push this man any further, that things are probably going to get worse, and appealing to Trail's good side is a lost cause.

*　　*　　*

'Margaret.'

'What's wrong love?'

'I feel spooked and I don't know why.'

Margaret thinks for a moment.

'Look at me Jane, I'll show you something that might help.'

Margaret lifts her hand across her forehead. The position of her hand resembling the act of shading one's eyes from the sun.

'She and I think you're strange Margaret,' says Gordon.

'Who?' Margaret looks around.

'The flight assistant who just walked past.'

'I didn't see anything,' says Margaret.

'How could you silly? You had your eyes covered up.'

Jane begins to giggle. 'We haven't started yet and I feel good already. Now I get it. To cure my fear, all I have to do is to sit here like a *nut-case* and the thought of doing *this* will really give me something to worry about,' says Jane laughing. 'Is that how it works?'

'When you're ready smarty pants, we'll continue.'

Deep down Jane understands something special is happening. She concentrates and quietens.

'All we are doing is a mind-focusing exercise. Now listen to what I have to say and follow me. Close your eyes and relax.'

Jane settles. 'I can see a blue light,' she whispers in wonderment.

'Don't speak love; go into your blue light, we will speak about this later. Relax Jane … *just*, relax.'

Jane has succeeded in entering a very deep state of relaxation and Margaret leaves her there for ten minutes.

'Now on the count of three, I want you to open your eyes, be wide awake, take a deep breath and remember all we have done.'

Jane sits for a moment as she readjusts.

'What's wrong, Jane,' says Mr G, returning from stretching his legs at the rear of the aircraft. 'You look like you've seen a ghost … a kind ghost.'

Jane is unable to answer. She just sits, wanting to go back there, wherever there was. She is totally relaxed.

*   *   *

Christie has been helping Geoff and Horace with the cooking duties.

'You *will* see mummy today,' she says, squeezing the words out as she lifts a huge ladle of broth.

At twelve noon, Sarah comes out on deck. She is weak and still unwell.

Like a jackal, one of the crew walks up close to her. He stands just staring and smiling into her drawn, expressionless face. Another approaches feigning assistance, but when she refuses his hand, he calls her, 'Whore!'

'Geoff!' Horace points.

Geoff up to now, busy with the cooking, has been unaware of the disturbance. Seeing it is Sarah being abused, he is furious. He pushes the young offending sailor across the deck. Another moves towards him, but is restrained by two marines. Sarah is shocked further by all this and faints into Geoff's arms. Geoff and Christie assist Sarah. They move her away and sit her down.

'Is there anything I can do?' Geoff says as he holds her. She is unable to answer. Nothing more is said.

Captain Trail comes on deck. He and Geoff make eye contact but Geoff takes no solace from this exchange as he may have previously. Under Trail's gaze he assists Sarah back to her quarters.

The unremitting miseries on the voyage are also taking their toll on Geoff. The never-ending ocean reflects back his sadness and loneliness. The ship is stark and cold. The crew are selfish and cruel. The marines lost and tin-soldier like. Today the sun, although shining brightly, has, for him, lost its warmth.

Horace stands at the top of the companion ladder as Geoff returns to the deck. The voyage is changing Horace. He is learning to care and trust. He would do anything for his friend Geoff. They return together to the stench and horror of the Orlop deck.

CHAPTER THIRTY SIX

ehind the Sydney Opera House I can see a vast forest of trees. To my right is the harbour, a glassy pristine waterway stretching west towards some bluish mountains far in the distance. The fading sunlight is mixing with the smoke making a lovely golden hue …

Jane is in a deep relaxed state. *It seems to be a beautiful combination of the past and the present. Bricked buildings at the waterside — in some ways it looks like home. There's an old sailing ship by the quay. There's another. Tents with chimneys and cottages constructed from roughly hewn timber dot the hillside.*

There's no bridge, no Sydney Harbour Bridge, she thinks. She pauses. *Where did all that come from? I didn't know I had such an imagination. I wonder if this has something to do with Margaret and the technique she showed me.*

'Mr G?'

'Yes, Jane.'

'What's Sydney like?'

Sydney? I'm not really sure, I've never been there, but I have been assured by several Australians, that it's *bloody terrific, mate,*' he says, thoroughly enjoying the Aussie expression. 'Why?' he asks.

'Oh … nothing.'

∗　　∗　　∗

Sarah arranges to meet Geoff. She moves awkwardly towards him through the light and shade made by the sails.

'Geoffrey,' she says, in an uneasy tone, sitting down, '*please* don't get me wrong … you're nothing like them lot on this ship, but some of your ways hurt me so,' she stops for a breath. You have done the very best you can. You can't help being you. I just don't understand.' Her voice is breaking up. 'I don't understand your kindness, I never experienced that before. Christie understands and that makes me so envious, so envious I can't explain. Will you take care of her?'

'I will take care of both …'

'Geoffrey,' she interrupts. 'I know I've come from a darkened past and you accept and show care for me. But that hurts me, can't you understand? You are kind, you give me things, support me and I know you love Christie, but can't you see what has happened?' She stands, looks at him despairingly, and then looks down. 'I am in love with you Geoffrey.'

He looks up at her in disbelief. 'You love *me*? I don't understand.' She takes half a step forward and stops. Her hands clasp in front of her, release and slowly lower to her side. She looks at him, 'I could never replace your Claire, I know that.'

Confused he looks at Sarah with near- tears in his eyes. He can't deny her conclusion. 'What more can I do?' he asks.

'Geoffrey, *please* don't do any more for me! You have shown me many things. I have changed because of you. With all my faults and misjudgements I have *tried* to be a special person too.'

She takes his hand with both of hers and holds it tightly. She then gives him a soft kiss, and moves off crying. 'I *hate* my life. I can't bare this floating hell!' she calls. The men on this ship *repulse* and terrify me. I can't *bear* it!'

'*Sarah! Sarah!*' he calls out, but she continues to walk.

✳   ✳   ✳

An electrical storm is moving from the east, across the path of the *Neptune* as Christie comes on deck. 'I want to stay with you Geoff,' she says and holds onto him.

'You can't, love your mummy needs you very much. Let's go back to her. How about I help you with the animals tomorrow … eh?'

Christie nods.

On a calm night the pains of Sarah's childbirth would probably echo around the ship for all to hear. But rough seas and a small storm cover any audible signs of baby Jonathan's birth. He is born just before midnight.

✳   ✳   ✳

In the early hours of the morning Horace, with a marine escort, wakes Geoff in his bunk. Christie is sitting at the top of the companionway.

'What are you doing *here?*' Geoff calls to her.

He sees the look on the face of Horace and the marines. He knows something is amiss.

'What's wrong love, what's wrong?' he calls to her again.

'*Mummy has gone!*' she calls out. My little baby brother is ere, but mummy is *gone.*' Her little red eyes are streaming.

Geoff can't grasp what's happened. He has to deal with the news of the birth of Sarah's baby, Christie's appearance on the Orlop deck and Sarah's seeming disappearance. His mind is spinning.

'What's going on, Horace?'

'Nobody knows, Mr Geoff. Nobody knows where Miss Sarah went.' Horace is visibly upset.

Geoff scoops Christie up as he heads for the top deck and makes his way to Sarah's quarters. Several women convicts are looking over the starboard side of the ship as he passes. He catches glimpses of some of the crew smiling, others in groups with their faces turned away. He sees the Captain on the Quarter Deck and detects some concern in his manner.

He knows something is up and doesn't want to admit it anymore than Christie does.

'Mummy is playing hide and seek with me, just like she did when I was, a little girl.'

Putting Christie down, he thumps the door to Sarah's quarters. It opens and without thinking he rushes through.

'It's no use Geoffrey, she's gone. *That* Ellington's *bin* here and told us. She's gone,' says Val, in a voice mixed with sadness and anger. She takes Christie from Geoff and holds her close.

Geoff moves to Sarah's bunk. In the centre there are two neat bundles, one containing all of Sarah's belongings and the other a swaddled newborn baby boy, waiting warm and secure for his mother to return.

'Dat's baby Jonathan, Geoffrey. Sarah told us his name, she did … didn't she Christie?' says Mary, another women. She is trying to be cheerful for Christie.

'Yes, she did and mummy will be back soon to play with him, back when she has finished her walk,' says Christie in a very matter-of-fact way.

Geoff reaches out hesitantly. 'Can I pick him up?'

'Corse you can luv, he's more yours than anybody's in the world,' says one of the older women.

He holds Jonathan close to him and watches his small sucking lips. As if a switch is turned on in his brain, he places the baby down and rushes out on deck.

'Captain! Captain! Where is she?' he screams. 'I want to speak to the Captain.'

The Captain is nowhere to be seen. The chief mate ignores him.

'Where is she?' he calls out to a group of sailors.

'She went over the side Geoffy-boy, into the drink.' The

informer begins to laugh. Another member of the group finds enough compassion to push the taunter firmly in the chest.

Geoff stops for a moment and looks out across the never-ending, grey sea. His friend Sergeant Thomas moves beside him.

'It seems she went early this morning. The baby was born just before midnight and she disappeared between five and six thirty. She was seen on deck briefly. I'm sorry Geoffrey.'

'Has all the ship been searched?'

'It has, from stern to bow.'

Christie catches up with them.

'Where's Mummy, where's my mummy?' It's as if she already knows.

'Mummy can't be found, love … She is nowhere to be found.' Geoff, in shock, has blurted out the truth.

'She might be down with the animals. She might be with the cooks, or with the other ladies.' Christie tries to reassure herself.

Geoff has a compulsive need to search for Sarah and instinctively he knows Christie should do this with him. Taking his freedom to move around the ship for granted, he commences, knowing it will probably be a fruitless search. Nobody stands in his way.

The sadness of Geoff and Christie searching for Sarah touches the hearts of nearly all on board. The roughest and hardest are struck speechless at the sight of this little girl looking, and continually calling out for her mummy.

The more Geoff and Christie search, the more silent she becomes. By the end of morning her lips will be sealed and she will speak very few words in the coming days.

Geoff's last act of denial, although sure he would not find Sarah, is to unwrap two convict bodies he had personally prepared for burial at sea. As he anticipated, neither was Sarah.

*   *   *

Geoff stands staring back at the horizon. He has not accepted Sarah's disappearance. *No amount of worrying is going to help*, he thinks. 'In the end all any of us can do is trust, accept, and hold on like hell,' he says quietly to himself.

*   *   *

Feelings aboard the *Neptune* about Sarah's demise are mixed. Some care a little. Some care more, and some couldn't care less.

A baby stops crying.

Mary, the other lactating convict mother, is feeding baby Jonathan.

ane practising what Margaret has taught her has entered a deep state of hypnosis. As her childhood flashes through her mind, she can see her old school playground.

There's my bicycle near the trees. I feel nice and warm here against the school wall. There's Lois with her tartan skirt and hanky pinned to her red jumper … The incinerators smell funny … The boys are playing ball against the lavatory wall.

Sally is sad, I'm sad sometimes. We are not allowed to pick the flowers in the school garden.

There's John over there by himself. I like him, but he never sits with me. I wish he would. He brings animals and things in boxes to school. He doesn't fight like the other boys, he thinks he's scared — I know he's not. He knows more than all of them. When he gets bigger, he will go all around the world. People don't understand him … they will try to hurt him, but they can't.

Jane's insights flash forward in time. Her childhood soul-mate, John, now appears differently.

Geoffrey, talk to me Geoffrey … what hurts you so?

'Geoffrey, did I say Geoffrey?' she says aloud, snapping out of her deep state. 'Who is this Geoffrey, Margaret? You were talking about a *Geoffrey.*'

Then Jane realises how stupid she must look. *Just as well Mr G's not here,* she thinks.

Margaret is not fazed. She's aware of what's happening to Jane. 'He's out there love.'

'What on *earth* do you mean, Margaret?' asks Jane, bewildered.

*　　*　　*

Word has circulated amongst the convicts about Sarah's disappearance.

'I knows who it be, Geoff,' says Maurie.

'What do you mean Maurice?'

'I know the bastards who were causing offences to Miss Sarah … It were 'im … *Yates*. Billy Yates and that mob,' replies Maurice, fiercely.

'Who told you that?' Geoff asks.

'Horace told us. He sees 'im, he knows.'

'Horace opens his mouth too damn much. You'll have to let it be, Maurice.'

'The men are angry, Geoff, real angry. The stories about you, Christie and Miss Sarah gives the men and me all some 'ope. The ones of us who have seen Christie think she's a lovely little thing.'

'I appreciate your concern and your feelings, but we must leave this behind us, Maurice.'

The incident with Sarah has turned out to be the last straw. The men in Geoff's mess are furious and nothing Geoff can say or do can alter this.

'They chain *us* like *animals* and feed us *shit* nothing,' Maurie says angrily. 'They taunted Miss Sarah and those bastards drove her over the side. *The bastards!*' he screams, throwing his meagre rations against the wall.

There are cries of support from all over the convict deck.

*　　*　　*

The next day there's a shout from the Captain of the Marines.
'Stop that man! How did he get up here?'

The men laugh. Entertainment aboard the *Neptune* is hard to come by. In any case, this poor wretch is harmless. Free from his main shackle Maurie is dancing around the main deck. Everybody is, for the second time, temporarily mesmerised by the gracefulness of this man in filthy convict clothes.

'Stop that man immediately!' the Marine Captain orders.

The soldiers move to grab Maurie.

Billy Yates is laughing with some other sailors when Maurie suddenly breaks from his dance and charges. He screams across the deck, singling out Billy. He head butts him in the chest and with raised wrists he wraps his hand chain around Billy's throat. Billy strikes the gunnels and Maurie follows up with a push, which flips Billy over the side. The sailor bawls out as he falls to the water. Maurie climbs up and stands like a crazed ape on the side of the ship.

'That's for Miss Sarah, ya rotten piece of scum!' he stops, then turns and glares at the crew and the marines defiantly. 'I hope ya all burn in hell, the lot of ya, you pack a gutless bastards!' Narrowly escaping capture, Maurie throws himself over the side.

The Captain appears and instructs the Chief Mate to order the ship about. The ship tacks several times but the two men are nowhere to be seen. Captain Trail immediately orders an investigation and a tightening of security.

This act of revenge does nothing to pacify the men below. Their sporadic jeering can be heard as far as the upper deck.

CHAPTER THIRTY EIGHT

The *Neptune* is taking advantage of the prevailing westerlies and ploughing steadily across the Indian Ocean. Geoff can't stop thinking of Sarah, left behind in an inhospitable ocean as vast as her sadness.

*　　*　　*

Flight 1033 is sailing through the upper atmosphere and will, within minutes, be over the vast Australian continent.

It is early morning in their current time zone, and most passengers are sound asleep. Jane sinks herself again into another hypnotic dream state, her mind flashing back through time. The schoolyard seems to be her access point into the past. *Her playmate John is getting upset as the other boys are persistently teasing and pushing him. Jane wishes she could help him.*

Abruptly her mind switches from a schoolyard to the deck of an eighteenth century sailing ship. *A young man, Geoff, is sitting at the front of the vessel staring out to sea. Jane finds herself moving towards him. As she puts out her hand to touch his hair, his neck and his shoulder energy streams through her. He straightens and turns his head to look at a disturbance on board. Then he stands, his face only inches from hers.* She will never forget that face strong and true and those eyes so kind, so sure, but at the same time sad and searching. *She moves closer until they are both touching. She seems to melt into him and for just a few seconds they are one.*

Soldiers and sailors are assembling. Geoff moves to investigate.

Jane awakes screaming. Margaret and Mr G grab her hands.

'Are you all right love? Did you have a bad dream?' Gordon looks at Margaret, puzzled.

Jane throws her arms around Margaret. 'I've seen him again. I *touched* him!' I don't understand.' She is beside herself. She gets up to walk.

God what have I started? wonders Margaret.

'How do I look, Margaret?'

'Absolutely terrible, love. Here, take your bag. Go and freshen up.'

'I need Michael,' says Jane.

*　　*　　*

The investigation is underway on the *Neptune* to establish how Maurice escaped. Although the padlock device must have been unlocked and there are only two men among the convicts who could do this, they are eliminated as suspects on the evidence of their mess leaders.

During the course of the investigation, a report has been given to the captain showing that Geoffrey Blake incited Maurice and released him. Chief Mate Ellington has used extra rations as bribery to subtly concoct evidence connecting Geoff to Maurice's actions.

'Horace, did you have anything to do with the release of Maurie?' Geoff asks, well out of the earshot of anybody. He knows Horace, and is aware his young friend is terrified of the investigation.

Horace cannot lie to Geoff. 'I did it, Geoff.' Horace whispers, half in a triumphant tone and half absolutely petrified. The boy had not thought this through and Maurie is a con from way back.

'What the hell are we going to do?' says Geoff, looking around. 'Listen to me, lad. If they find out it was you, they will hang you from the yardarm. Do you understand? Whatever happens, keep your mouth shut.'

Horace nods uneasily, only now is he beginning to understand all the implications of his actions.

Meantime Ellington has decided somebody is going to pay for the murder of Billy Yates, and that person is Geoff.

* * *

'Mr Blake, have you any idea who released Maurice Owens? The Captain has hauled him in for interrogation.'

'Sir, as you are aware, I have no keys during daylight hours. I can only say the chain locking device must have been insecurely latched.'

He hesitates as a thought flashes into his mind. *Maurice was released to go to the lavatory by Marine Cuthbert, and, under his supervision, Horace relocked Maurice.*

'Something else, Blake?' The Captain hones in on Geoff's hesitation.

'No, sir.'

'By the way Blake, I was saddened by the loss of Miss Sarah.'

'I think I know that, sir,' Geoff replies, looking him in the eyes. It's one thing to receive some sentiment from Trail, quite another to highlight it with prolonged eye contact.

Trail begins to pace, his hands clasped behind him.

'We have a serious problem here, Blake. There are witnesses, one from your group and two others, confirming a plot. Maurice was in your mess and it would appear you had a motive to incite him. You hated Yates, didn't you?'

'There was no plot, sir. I had no motive to incite that man, sir.'

'I'm afraid the evidence shows otherwise. You have three days to come up with some answers, Mr Blake.

Geoff is dismissed and returned to the Orlop.

'What did the Captain say, Geoff? Will things be settled up now? You're his friend, Geoff. You know the Captain don't ya?'

'I'm responsible for what happens in our section, Horace.'

'Maurie done it and he paid. That should be it.' Horace temporarily cheers himself, but he knows they haven't heard the last of this matter.

Horace may be young and inexperienced, but he knows right from wrong. He knows Geoff is in trouble and he won't let anything happen to him on his account. He considers if he comes clean and tells the truth, the Captain and Ellington might forgive his mistake. This belief would prove to be one of Horace's worst misjudgements.

*　*　*

Days later, the day-to-day routine on board is interrupted by an official assembly and announcement. Geoff runs to the middle of the ship to discover Horace tied to the rigging, his young back bared and about to feel the weight of English justice.

The Chief Mate reads out the findings and judgements. That Horace Browning contributed to the death of William Yates by leaving Maurice Owens, the perpetrator of the murder, unsecured.

Geoff screams 'No!' He is restrained by two marines.

Horace turns his head and smiles a naïve, defiant look at Geoff. As the cat spreads across Horace's back, Geoff watches Horace's expression turn from teenage bravado to sheer horror. The second and third lashes wrap around his skinny mid-section, cutting into his side. Twenty bloody lashes later the boy is losing consciousness. At that point Geoff breaks free of the men restraining him and throws himself screaming across the lad. This is the opportunity Ellington has been waiting for.

He orders Geoff pulled to his feet and restrained, then despite a belated interjection from the Captain, is kicked and punched unconscious by a furious Ellington. As Geoff is left on the deck unconscious Horace receives another five lashes.

Horace escapes the death sentence only because his admission is considered to be concocted. Conned by Maurice, he did leave the shackles unlocked in spite of the guards being present.

The sight of the bruised, battered, and bleeding bodies of Geoff and Horace sprawled across the deck sickens most of the witnesses. The Captain orders Ellington to his quarters and permits the ship's surgeon to attend their wounds.

Horace and Maurie have paid the price. Justice has been done. The pressure has been temporarily taken off the Orlop deck. Rations are back to normal and there is talk of increasing the deck walks for the male prisoners.

CHAPTER THIRTY NINE

The pages of sorrow, sadness and the consequences of life are piling high for Geoff, each new page temporarily masking the distress and the repercussions of the proceeding. Yet, at the same time, respect, love and some happiness, circles around him.

He feels like he has lost all that has meant anything to him. And yet new inner strengths are stirring within him.

Captain Trail's previous slave trading activities represent part of a page in history. Cruelty to convicts currently being transported to Australia aboard his ship the *Neptune* is another addition to this saga.

Empire building, on the surface, probably appeared romantic and the norm to the many countries and individuals who practised it, but many mistakes were made.

When the First Fleet entered Botany Bay, comments put forward by a military man, Captain Watkin Tench, highlighted yet another English mistake. There were basic miscalculations made by Captain Cook's original expedition to Australia regarding the density and the distribution of the Aboriginal tribes.

Tench wrote: *We found the natives more than numerous as we sailed into the harbour. Later expeditions showed us without any doubt, Australia is not just populated on the coast, but well into the interior.*

The basic misconception put forward by Cook that the natives only sparsely inhabited the periphery of the Australian continent directly influenced decisions made by politicians in

London. They assumed and wanted to believe Australia was basically uninhabited and theirs for the taking.

Based on Cook's reports and recommendations, England fast-tracked another of its expansionary moves.

Two years after colonisation the inappropriateness of the land at Sydney Cove to support a colony is more than clear. The settlers live in fear of starvation and have become very dependent on the arrival of the promised Second Fleet. They have dropped their guard and this has undermined their resolve. The human mistake to take for granted what is available and rely on what is pending has subtly swept across the colony. By the time the ships of the Second Fleet finally arrive, the colonists will have whipped themselves into a state of desperation.

*　　*　　*

Geoff has been laid up below deck since his beating and it has not been possible for Christie to see him. She misses him a lot, but her little brother Jonathan has been keeping her occupied. The reassurances she kept repeating to her baby brother that Mummy will be back soon, no longer fall on his tiny ears.

It would be six days before Sergeant Thomas could slip Christie from her daily waiting place near the main mast to see Geoff, who is still laid up with two broken ribs and a fractured jaw. He carries Christie, clutching a carved figurine, down the stairs to the Orlop.

Like her mother, Christie has a strong side. Geoff's vicious wounds and bruising around the face distract her for only a moment.

'How are you *love*? How is your baby brother, Jonathan?' Geoff's voice is strained with pain.

She shows him the intricate carving of a lady made for her

by one of the crew. 'This is Jonathan's mummy,' she assures him, holding it carefully.

'What a special and beautiful lady.' Geoff reaches out awkwardly and touches the carving.

She nods extending the figure closer to him.

'Jonathon, he is getting bigger and bigger,' she gestures with one hand. 'He cries *all* the night long.' She moves closer and gives Geoff a big hug.

'Miss Mary feeds both bubs, both of 'em together sometimes.' Christie takes a sharp breath and puts her hand over her mouth, smiling sheepishly from under her fringe. 'It smells *real bad* down here,' she says screwing up her nose. Christie's voice switches from the rawness of childish chatter to a more adult tone. 'I saw what they did to you and Horrie. Why do they do these things, Geoff?'

'There are reasons for most things love … It's really good to see you, but you must go back to Jonathan.' Geoff pauses, thinks and gives her a hurry-on hug.

'Thanks for bringing her to me, Thomas. Would you take her back? It's not the place for a little girl.'

'Sure Geoff, *sure*.'

'I'm not little anymore, Geoff.'

Geoff smiles a fractured-jaw smile. 'I'll see you soon. Take care of your little brother.'

Reassured, Christie leaves.

*　　*　　*

'Michael is probably getting ready to go to the airport.' Jane is more or less talking to herself, thinking ahead to Sydney now only a matter of hours away.

'Yes, Jane,' replies Mr G, preoccupied with some writing. Margaret just smiles.

'It's all right for you two. You don't know how it feels.' Jane is caught up in apprehension about what lies ahead. A new country and will it work out with Michael?

'Don't we?' Margaret replies. 'Love, don't place too much importance on your reunion with Michael …'

Jane swings her head around, her eyes wide. 'What do you mean, Margaret? Don't place too much importance?'

'What I mean is don't put all your happiness and security completely in the hands of another.'

'Is that what you *really* mean, Margaret?'

But before she can answer there is an announcement.

'This is your Captain Bret MacDonald speaking …'

Jane, Margaret and Mr G look at each other, the announcement bringing back scary memories from the previous flight.

'Passengers on the left of the aircraft,' the captain continues, 'will be able to see Ayres Rock. We are approximately two and quarter hours from Sydney. We trust you are enjoying your flight. Thank you.'

CHAPTER FORTY

'**I**s your friend meeting you at the airport, Margaret?' Jane asks.

'Her son, Phillip, is picking me up love. Are you being met, Gordon?'

'Yes, Margaret, we always get *well* looked after.'

Now close to the end, Jane casts her mind back over the flight. It all seems like a fairy story. She is amazed at the in-depth discussions she has had, and where her new-learnt skill at meditation has been taking her.

Can any of this really be true? she wonders. *It feels real.* She can't help herself. The first chance she gets, under the cover of napping, she lets go and returns to her schoolyard. It appears on cue as if it is running in direct parallel to her current day. Again, she feels the warmth of the sun. Again, she feels the little fears and excitements of daily school life surging through her chest.

The boys are nowhere to be seen, so Jane decides to search. She finds herself at the rear of the schoolyard. Water appears out of the blue and the gravelled playground turns into the timbered decking of a ship. The dry grassy, smokey smell of the schoolyard has given way to a salty, wooden, canvas, air. She sees what appears to be her school-friend John sitting by himself. She moves towards him and sits herself down beside him. One second he is a young boy, the next a grown man.

In response to her questioning look his blue eyes look into hers. 'My name's Geoff,' he says.

'Geoff, I have always been with you,' she finds herself saying.

He moves his hand along the bench and their fingers touch.

As his strength surrounds her, she kisses him softly on the cheek, then still in her eight-year-old guise, she gets up and walks away.

Jane awakes from what appears a short nap. *Maybe I'm loosing my marbles,* she thinks. *If there is any possibility I have communicated with this striking guy, I don't want to mess up the experience by trying to put it into words.* She now has an inkling of why Margaret is apprehensive about discussing her experiences.

Just a dream, a beautiful dream, she thinks to herself. *My old mystic friend, they say he was a mystic; Dr Raynor assured me that infatuation is the best parts of oneself imagined in another person. That's all, just my deepest imaginings.* But wow, how special. And then her mind rushes back to Michael.

Gordon is picking up on Jane's vibes and places his arm across her shoulders, which is the exact way her father would have comforted her after she awoke, as a child. She understands his intentions.

It doesn't take long before Jane's mind starts to whirl again. 'Hope to see you at the airport,' were the words Michael said to Jane in their last phone call. *It was all so rushed when I left home,* she remembers.

That word *hope* is going round and round in her mind.

'Margaret … Michael said he *hoped* to see me at the airport. What do you make of that?'

'It sounds like he is a busy man.' Gordon answers for Margaret. Didn't you say he was preparing an exhibition?'

The more Jane thinks about it, the word 'hope' takes on a changed meaning for her. It now feels hollow, far away and sad. She remembers standing in the classroom with her friends enthusiastically reciting aloud a small rhyme that one of the older girls had made up. It was about their teacher, Miss Hope, a strange cold lady. She laughs to herself as she recalls the words.

Miss Hope is a dope with a belly full of soap, she had sung, swinging her bottom to and fro. Halfway through the second, very boisterous repeat of the ditty, Jane had been lifted off the ground by a swift, surprising whack to her bum. Miss Hope had been standing right behind her. Jane remembers to this very day the power of that smack.

*   *   *

From time to time the crew and the marines on the upper deck entertain themselves with singing and dancing. What a stark contrast to the lot of the poor wretches below on the Orlop deck where the men are dying like dogs.

The contrast makes Geoff appreciate his freedom even more as he considers how he would feel if he was still chained like an animal, unable to move about the ship and experience the satisfaction of friendships he has made.

Horace has grown up. A man has sprung from a boy in a matter of months. Christie is changing too. Understanding Geoff and Horace are still physically hurting she has been helping them with the meals. Some youngsters on board only go through the motions of helping, but Christie makes a substantial contribution. She also has other responsibilities now, with a small brother to help look after. She is a proper, responsible young lady.

The familiar cry of a baby causes Geoff to look back over his shoulder. He is touched. With her eyes glued on him and Horace, Christie is carefully struggling along the pitching deck carrying baby Jonathan, closely followed by two of the female convicts. Geoff now has a number of supporters among the convict women. Christie hands a whimpering Jonathan proudly but awkwardly to Geoff. As he watches Jonathan settle in his arms, he is sure he can see Sarah in him. His mind again remembers the tearooms at Charing Cross. 'I could never have imagined any of this, little man,' he says to Jonathan.

'I never had a brover,' says Horace squeezing one of Jonathan's big toes.

'Nobody would want *you* for a brother,' teases Christie, pushing him so he nearly falls into one of the cooking coppers.

'*Watchit* ya little *brat*,' he scorns.

The *Neptune* is thirty days from the western coastline of Australia.

'*Geoff?*' asks Christie.

'Yes love.'

'Where would my mummy be now?'

CHAPTER FORTY ONE

'I don't know about dat. I do knows you expects too much from Miss Sarah.'

Geoff is stunned by Horace's remark. He has just finished light-heartedly telling Horace about a dream.

'The dream tells ya painted her golden.' Horace goes on. 'Any fool can see dat's not normal, Mr Geoff. You don't really paint people gold, do ya?'

'How do you know the dream's about Miss Sarah, Horace?'

'If it's not about 'er, who else would ya have painted gold, eh? Not me,' Horace shrugs.

Geoff, snared by Horace's piece of casual wisdom stands smiling a shallow smile as his mind looks from another place.

* * *

The acquisition of Australia by England was to be humane, but the darker side of the coin would prevail in the new southern land, just as it did in North America, Africa, India, China, the Middle East and a host of small countries throughout the world. Exploitation of people, natural resources and acquisition of their lands is again the common denominator.

On board the *Neptune* a microcosm of hypocrisy is taking place.

If cruelty could be measured, the treatment of the convicts on the Orlop would rank high on the list of human savagery. The *Neptune* is a horror ship.

Captain William Hill, Sydney Cove, July 26, 1790 wrote:

The slave trade is merciful compared with what I have seen in the second fleet. My feelings never have been so wounded as in this voyage, so much so, that I shall never recover my accustomed vivacity and spirits.

This army officer, who could not speak until after the event, had a reaction of rage and despair. He indicated that evil had been done. He singled out Captain Trail 'as being guilty of villainy, oppression, and shameful peculation', describing him as 'a lowlife, barbarous master.'

*   *   *

One hour from Kingsford Smith Airport, Sydney, everyone, both passengers and flight attendants, are shuffling around in preparation for the arrival in Sydney. A visit to the toilet now has an urgency nobody seemed to think about twenty minutes before.

Jane is going to miss her two friends. Although Mr G is only staying in Sydney for two days and then flying on to Canberra and Margaret's accommodation is out in the western suburbs they, all agree to keep in touch by phone.

It's only forty-five minutes until I see Michael, Jane thinks, as streams of adrenalin begin to run through her body. It feels like a triple shot of rum she had once. With her hand on her chest she visualises Michael and Beckie at the airport. *She sees herself run to him. She feels his strong arms hold her tightly. She bends down to hug Beckie. Beckie likes me, she is sure. She watches the three of them walk through the exit doors into a new world.*

The schoolyard visualisation is again tugging at Jane and in spite of all the developing excitement around her she slips easily into her hypnotic state, opening yet another box.

'Jane,' a gentle voice speaks. 'Jane,' the voice comes again and she goes with its flow. *She sees the young man Geoff lying on a bunk, surrounded by thick wooden walls. The energy is electric.* Jane opens her eyes, still partly tranced; she finds a pen and writes.

All has changed beyond forever.

Pulsating, spiralling through the unison of a galaxy known to a few.

Parallel stars streak into the blue of tomorrow.

Arms holding a newborn compares to spirit circling spirit.

Poised breathlessness, halves become whole, as one.

You head, I lead, the motionless white light speeds to a new dawn.

'Margaret, look at this.'

'That's beautiful, Jane, did you just make that up?'

'I don't know where it came from,' replies Jane perplexed.

The constant powerful operation of the aircraft changes as flight 1033 begins its decent to Sydney airport.

Jane is trapped in her dream state, staring at the writing in front of her. She has never written anything like this before in her life. As the aircraft drops into a fine layer of cloud, it trembles all over from nose to tail. The sun disappears temporarily. The seat belt sign chimes and Jane is jolted back into reality. She holds her writing folded tightly in her hand. Mr G insists Jane take his window seat as they drop below the clouds.

'Beaches, beaches, all I can see are beaches and ocean. Look at all the red roofs, swimming pools, and trees. Look Margaret! *Wow,* that is so beautiful,' Jane is glued to the window. *I'm probably flying over Michael's house right now,* she thinks.

The huge jet adjusts to its final approach, heading south.

'What area of Sydney does Michael come from, Jane?' asks Mr G, trying also to peer out of the window.

'Manly,' she replies.

An Australian accent pipes up from across the isle. 'That's Manly coming up over there.'

'This is your Captain speaking. We should touch down at

Sydney International Airport in thirteen minutes at 1.45 pm local time. It's twenty-eight degrees with a south-easterly breeze. A cool change is expected in the evening, with scattered showers. On the left of the aircraft, in approximately three minutes, you will see the Olympic city, Sydney. We trust you have enjoyed your flight and look forward to you travelling with us again on British Airways.'

'Over and out!' says Jane to the laughter of Mr G, Margaret and the people in the row across the aisle.

A surge of chatter and pointing heralds the appearance of the Sydney Harbour Bridge, the Opera House and yachts on the harbour. *This is Michael's and Becky's city*, thinks Jane.

The jet engines quieten as the aeroplane seems to glide over the city area. It's a magic moment, but Jane's mind is reluctant to stay in the present. As the city moves past, a grinding, thumping sound interrupts her thoughts while the jet's undercarriage is lowered and locked into position ready for landing. Jane is again pulled back to reality. She takes a deep breath as the tension is building. *Michael*, she thinks to herself, *I can hardly wait to hold you.*

As the aircraft touches down, loud cheers and clapping erupts from the rear as a group of Australians spontaneously show their excitement about being home.

The taxiing from the tarmac to the terminal seems to take forever. Then, as if on cue, everybody stirs in their seats and pulls all their belongings together. The aircraft comes to a stop and everyone crowds the aisle as if there is prize for getting off first. Eagerness, feelings of fatigue, excitement to see loved ones or just plain 'follow the leader' prematurely fill the aisles with people going nowhere.

Jane, Margaret and Gordon, by mutual consent, continue to sit. Then the queue begins to file past. Margaret stands. Gordon begins to remove all their gear from the overheads. 'Remember this?' he jokes, holding up his toiletry bag. Jane smiles. 'Jane,' he goes on, 'I may need to have a shave in the airport. Could you carry this for me?' Remembering Bahrain they all laugh. With her hands already full Jane takes the strap of Mr G's accessory bag between her teeth, picks up her luggage and expertly heads down the aisle. She exits the aircraft and only then hands Gordon's bag back to him.

Jane is first to the customs counter. She slides her documents in front of the young processing officer. *I'm nearly free,* she thinks to herself, *I want to see Michael.*

After being processed, they make their way to the baggage pick-up and final custom's clearance.

The three re-group and Jane readies herself for the big moment.

CHAPTER FORTY TWO

here is a large crowd in arrivals. Jane looks good in spite of her twenty-two hour flight. She waves excitedly to a little girl but it's not Beckie. Gordon and Margaret look at each other. Gordon engulfs Jane with one of his big fatherly hugs. He is lost for words, so gives them each one more hug and moves away.

'*Phone me! Don't forget me!*' he calls as he waves over his shoulder, and is gone.

Jane stands on her tiptoes looking for Michael.

'Well,' points Jane at a young man holding a white card with Margaret's name printed neatly across it, 'that's the two of you taken care of.'

'*Phillip!*' Margaret calls. 'The last time I saw him, he was only a little tike!'

'Hi Aunty *Margar–*' His welcoming words are crushed by Margaret's bear-hug.

'Phillip, I'd like you to meet Jane. Could we wait a moment? Jane may need a lift.'

He takes a breath. 'Pleased to meet you, Jane. Of course we can.'

'Thankyou, Phillip,' she smiles warmly, 'but no Margaret, Michael will be here soon. He's probably had trouble parking. You go on. It's been a long trip. Go, truly, I'll be fine.'

Margaret hesitates.

'Off with you, I'll give you a call.'

After another long hug, Margaret begins to leave reluctantly, but then stops and whispers in Jane's ear. 'Look out for yourself young lady. Where the rocks meet the sea is where he will be.' She gives Jane a 'not of this world look', and leaves.

'Where the rocks meet the sea …?' Jane repeats. *My god, Margaret.*'

Jane's fantasy about Sydney Airport has faded. Standing amongst all the happy reunions she feels completely alone.

'*Well it's all rather sad,*' she thinks. '*He said he hoped to be at the airport, and he's not. Maybe he's come through the other entrance. Maybe Beckie is unwell or Michael has had an accident. The flight was delayed in Bahrain. Maybe he's not coming at all.* Her mind empties itself of all the possibilities and then settles to wait.

Each time the sliding-doors open her heart skips a beat.

'Well I'm not alone. That guy's waiting for somebody as well. 'Misery loves company, how true is that,' she whispers.

She watches the second hand do fifteen slow circles around the clock- face. Fifteen minutes was the deal in her mind. She then dials Michael's mobile. It's switched off. She thinks about what Margaret said as they flew across Indonesia. How could she have known Michael wouldn't be here to meet me?

Something has gone drastically wrong, she confidently considers. She checks out the availability of cabs.

'*Sorry I'm late.*' She'd only taken her eyes off the entrance for a second. To her dismay she watches as the newcomer embraces the other guy.

'Hope your buddy is here soon!' he calls as the two men kiss and head for the doors.

So do I, says Jane to herself. She waves.

After an hour she's had enough. She rings Michael's mobile and home number for the third time then she picks up her hand luggage and wheels her trolley through those foreboding automatic doors. She feels washed out and sad. The Sydney Olympic Games finished twelve months ago and the beautifully renovated airport feels deserted just as she does.

It seems the taxi only knows two speeds, stationary and very fast. Memories of the taxi drivers in Rome flash through Jane's mind. The driver takes off as if he's in the one hundred metre dash. Appearing to be half-asleep he screams along the freeway, in and out of the traffic. She has never seen such precision and madness before. Soon they are approaching the city centre.

'When will we see the harbour I've heard so much about?' she says. 'I've been looking forward to seeing it from the bridge.'

'We're travelling under it right now,' says the driver with an Indian rhythm in his voice and a proud Aussie smile on his face.

So much for the harbour, she says under her breath.

'My name is Rasheed.' He turns to shake Jane's hand.

'Jane, my name is Jane!' she calls out, tapping him on the shoulder and pointing to the front.

Through the rear window she can now see the huge coat-hanger Bridge, the harbour and the city skyline beyond. Colourful, bustling shopping centres, people and traffic stream past her as they travel in an easterly direction along the north side of the harbour. She keeps thinking about what Margaret said, she can't get it out of her mind. *She did know, she tried to tell me, but I didn't listen*, she thinks to herself, crossing her fingers in the hope she is wrong. Then the freshness, the brightness and vitality of this new country jabs through her depression. *It's so beautiful here*, she thinks.

After careering past some of the most expensive properties in Sydney, the cab driver looks through his rear vision mirror and announces 'We are in *Manly*, this is *Manly*.' He makes Manly sound like a town in India. He stops, checks his directory and zips along the beachfront esplanade. Jane looks at the street names.

'That's the street ... look,' she points out.

'Oh, very good,' he says.

'There it is — number seven. We're here.' He smiles proudly.

Before Jane can say 'Rasheed' he has all her luggage unloaded onto the hot pavement. She pays him and he is gone.

Michael's house is just one block back from the main beach area in a quiet tree-lined old-world area. She can smell the sea-air. She is relaxing and her excitement returns as she struggles with her bags through the front gate.

All her affection for Michael and everything about him comes surging back. She places her bags in the shade of a flowering gum tree behind a high brick wall which separates the house from the street. *I must look like something the cat dragged in*, she thinks, stopping to adjust her hair and apply some lip-gloss. *He may not be home*, flashes through her mind. She moves apprehensively to the front door and knocks. She knocks again, but there is no answer.

The heat of the day, which was a novelty at first, is now distressing her. That, together with the constant sound of cicadas surging all around her, is driving her nuts. She suddenly feels tired, lost, a little faint, and very thirsty. She sits on the porch, jet lag clouding her mind. The warmth of the day, the special feeling of being close to the sea, the exhilaration of arriving in a new country should all have added to her excitement, instead everything seems a symbol of her hurt.

'Well, I'm not going to sit here and mope. Besides, I'm dying of thirst,' she tells herself. She decides to walk to the beach. There a cool sea breeze relieves the heat and the ocean is blue, big, crystal-clear and thunderous. The huge breakers continually pounding the yellowish, white sand fascinates her. 'There are no rocks here Margaret,' she says aloud.

She is distracted for a moment, but reality then surges back into her exhausted mind. 'I feel like crap,' she says. 'What the hell am I doing here?'

Hesitantly she dials Michael's number again. It now rings to message bank and she can hear Michael's voice. 'Please leave your name and number and I will get back to you at my earliest convenience.' She hangs up without leaving a message. '*My earliest convenience …*' she says. From a water fountain she quenches her thirst then she dials again.

'Hello, hello Jane, is that you?' Michael answers. 'Where are you love? I'm sorry, I'm running late.'

The sound of his voice helps.

'I'm at your house in Manly, Michael.'

'Christ, how did you get there? 'It's good to hear your voice love … I was just about to head for the airport. What time did your flight come in? I must have got the times mixed — sorry. Beckie is with me. We should be home in about half an hour. Make yourself comfortable, there's a key under the Chinese jade plant, near the side gate. I've put drinks and snacks in the fridge. I'm just approaching the bridge, the traffic is chaotic … see you soon … love you.' He hangs up.

'I love you too, Michael.' Jane says gently to herself.

Excited to hear his voice, she decides to shelve the contradictory feelings of love and denial still whirling about inside her, until she is rested.

Hurrying back to the house, she locates the key and slowly opens the front door. Every home has its own particular scent. Michael's house has a clean masculine air about it. The interior seems familiar to her, but then he has often spoken to her about the house. Two bedrooms, a study, a large living area, bathroom and kitchen make up the floor plan with an open fireplace, polished parquet floors, high ceilings with chunky cornices providing a pleasant ambience. The kitchen has all the mod cons. It's obvious Michael likes to cook. It's a man's kitchen, but Beckie has left her mark, with toy magnets claiming the refrigerator door.

He likes his garden, she thinks as she looks through the rear window to a landscaped outdoor area that includes a pool and a green and leafy garden.

Michael's furniture consists of a black leather sofa and chairs, a pinkish marble-topped dining setting and matching sideboard. A large flat screen TV and sound system takes one wall completely. Several kids' videos are scattered on the coffee table.

Michael's professional works hang around the walls, and they are excellent. He excels at action pieces and portraits. An abstract painting of bodies wrapped erotically around each other tells more than it probably should, although its subtlety could leave an onlooker unsure exactly of the theme and possibly a little guilty for maybe placing a wrong interpretation on it. *It's probably my vivid imagination*, thinks Jane trying to shrug off her doubts. 'No … no, it's naughty all right,' she says aloud.

She peeps into Beckie's bedroom. In contrast to the rest of the house's décor, Beckie's room is full of bright colours but, for a child, it is unusually neat. Her walls are shelved and amassed with toys, books, fluffy things and games. Mobiles of different shapes hang from the ceiling. Her wardrobe contains the cutest little dresses, blouses, shorts, jumpers and shoes. The doona cover matches the curtains and next to the window hangs two original Disney animation frames.

Next door is Michael's room. Jane feels like an intruder as she pushes open the half-closed door. His room is simple, stylish and also colourful. Greens, navy blues, and egg yolk yellow with touches of orange is the basic colour mix. Jane feels strange and out of place in Michael's bedroom. The curtains are drawn completely, she is tempted to throw them open and let in some light.

The whole house is meticulously clean and trim. The garden is well kept and the pool is sparkling. Jane adores the palm trees and she can identify several English flowers and plants. Three flowering hydrangea shrubs — Jane's favourite plant — flourish against the side fence.

Jetlag is having its insidious effect and she has lost track of time. *I must get tidied up,* she realises. But before she can do much about that there is a click at the front door and a voice calls out …

'We're home, where are you?'

Just as well the next room for inspection is the bathroom. Without thinking, she brushes her hair and, readies herself as Michael and Beckie come through the front door, carrying her luggage.

'How do I look … how will he look? she thinks and checks the mirror, assuming Michael will understand she has been travelling for twenty-four hours and probably looks and smells that way too. She makes an impulsive decision, closes the bathroom door and turns on the shower.

'I'll be out soon, won't be long!' she calls out, quickly stripping off. She had made the right decision; a quick sniff under an armpit proves that. *In any case he kept me waiting,* she thinks. It will do him good.

She enjoys her wash and gathers herself. As she turns off the shower, Michael calls out. 'You have twenty seconds and we are coming in!'

'God, that's all I need.' she says breathing in, her composure in tatters. She can hear them counting.

'Seventeen, sixteen, fifteen, fourteen.'

She grabs some blusher and lippy from her bag.

'Ten, nine, eight, seven, six.'

Her face is reasonable, a spray of fragrance and on with Michael's dressing gown as…

'Three, two, one, coming ready or not.'

The door opens slowly, a little blonde head cautiously peeps through. Beckie nods at Michael and he throws the door wide open. Jane hesitates and then they fly into each other's arms.

'Oh … it's good to hold you gal. You look gorgeous and smell so good.'

She is speechless. She is now having the embrace she was hoping for at the airport. His strong arms engulf her and pull her close. The intimacy of the embrace relaxes as Michael scoops Beckie up and they all hug together.

'I've missed you so much Michael.' She lifts her shoulders, smiles warmly and gives him another kiss.

'And Beckie, I've been waiting so long to meet you. Here you are.' She frames Beckie's small face in her hands and kisses her on the cheek.

*   *   *

The *Neptune* now heads due east. When it approaches the east coast, it will sail south around the southern tip of Tasmania, a long and tedious journey.

Horace can now stand on deck with Geoff and Christie. The crew's feelings towards him have now mellowed. As they stand looking at the new land in the distance, a convict woman brings Jonathan to them.

Plans of mutiny among the male convicts have disappeared. Trail's strategy has worked. The mistreatment of the men has knocked the stuffing out of them, more and more are dying. Any remaining rebellious impulses have been converted to plain survival. Geoff and Horace have worked hard for the men, but their efforts have been undermined by lack of food, medical supplies and medical attention. The Orlop is a constant nightmare, a seething, stinking mess of defeated men.

The flute player aboard is softly piping out a jig. At the bow of the ship two sailors, one young and another middle-aged are dancing. Christie starts to wobble in time to the music, patting at Horace in a cheeky, provocative fashion.

'*Don't Chrissy,*' he shrugs away impatiently and turns his back on her. But Christie wants to dance. Against a background of misery and sorrow, the human spirit still wants to dance. Several other children join Christie and the small ragamuffin group of hope dance and shuffle on the deck, mostly unaware of the horrors that surround and lie ahead of them. They are a beacon of hope for the anxious and suffering adults.

Geoff looks at Horace and the two children who have just naturally fallen into his charge, cementing in his mind an obligation to care for them, in the future, as much as he possibly can.

He slides his arm around Horace to comfort him. Christie is absorbed with her jigging, but soon joins in the embrace. Geoff and Christie move in time to the music and Horace tries to move with them. The three of them jig gently together as the *Neptune* peels through a flat, deep blue sea.

Jonathon is sound asleep in Geoff's arms oblivious to all but his little dreams.

CHAPTER FORTY THREE

eckie doesn't speak much at all. Her slender little frame is the average height for a six year old. A mop of shiny straight blonde hair, in a bob cut, surrounds a small face with eyes that want to sparkle. Her complexion is pallid, and just below a small upturned nose are two lips held tightly closed together by more than just the muscles of the face and jaws. Jane knows very little about Beckie's mother, but she is sure Beckie must look very much like her for she bears little resemblance to Michael.

Michael is very good looking, a little taller than Jane, with a slight olive complexion and short, black hair. He speaks with an excited but soft tone. He works out regularly as shown by a well developed upper body which tapers to a small waist, with a sexy butt which Jane is sorely tempted to fondle. If she were to choose three things she likes about Michael, apart from his face, they'd be the back of his neck, his butt and his long-fingered hands.

There isn't much wrong with Michael as far as Jane can see. Love can do that. He's now making up for all the disappointments at the airport. After Beckie goes to bed, he prepares a late dinner for them both, whilst Jane sits back and relaxes, sipping a glass of good Aussie white wine. She watches his tight black trousers move around the kitchen, her sexual appetite increasing with each sip of love nectar she takes.

The stress of the trip, her four weeks of celibacy, the wine, Michael's sexy posterior, the intimate setting, more wine, the blue roses he bought for her, the ocean, the music, more wine, the back of his neck and the kiss he gives her as he serves the rack of lamb and roast vegies has her softly grinding her knees together and tightening her pelvic muscles. Jane is intoxicated and as sexy as hell.

Michael is an excellent cook and he knows it. Through the meal Jane catches up on all of his most recent accomplishments, including his forthcoming solo exhibition.

'Does Beckie get excited about your stuff?' Jane inquires.

'Yes, she does. She is such a good kid and does so much for me.' Michael replies. 'I love her so much. I would be lost without her.' Jane detects pensiveness in his manner. He moves around to Jane. 'How was your flight?' he whispers in her ear, nibbling it at the same time.

'It was *so* interesting, but a tiring flight. We had a bomb scare! … *ooh Michael* … we were diverted to Bahrain … I made two very good friends … *they* …' Michael now has Jane's earring and earlobe between his lips, sucking them gently. Jane quivers all over as he kisses the back of her neck. With his mouth and nose he zigzags slowly through her parting hairline. She drops her head forward and relaxes as his hands run over her shoulders, down the neck of her blouse onto her warm breasts. He lifts Jane off her chair and carries her across the room, kissing her at the same time. With her bare feet, he nudges open Beckie's door to check she is settled and asleep. Her bedside light, which stays on all night, softly illuminates her face.

'Goodnight, Beckie,' they both whisper together.

With his elbow, he switches off the hall light and places Jane gently on the end of his bed. The streetlight through the window softly lights her body as he undresses her slowly. Closing the door he strips down in front of her. His body, silhouetted against the window, reminds her of a roman god, near perfect in all proportions. *Just what I have been waiting for*, she thinks and turns slowly onto her side taking his hand. He begins to softly kiss every part of her from the tips of her toes to the very top of her head. He then slides alongside her. This night is completely theirs.

*　　*　　*

The early morning light slowly illuminates the bedroom. Through the quietness and stillness of the morning the constant roar of the ocean dominates all sounds with the exception of the occasional morning-quiet motorcar.

Michael is up and showering. Jane would love a cuddle, but that may not happen. She would like to bathe in the feeling that everything is just perfect but she holds this feeling at arm's length. She can smell coffee brewing and hears Michael operating the toaster.

He appears at the bedroom door with a bright orange towel around his waist, a tray, a blue rose, two cups, a coffee pot, toast and marmalade.

I'd love a cup of tea, she thinks to herself.

No sooner had she thought this, the towel around Michael's waist loosens and drops. He tries to grab it with one hand, but the tray tilts and the coffee, toast and rose fall to the floor.

It's definitely not a towel rack this morning, thinks Jane, but laughs aloud. 'Let me help Michael.'

'I can manage … It's not funny love,' he whinges, bending over to pick up the broken mess.

'My God, that's not your best angle Michael,' she attempts a loving joke, but it misfires.

Indignantly he grabs the towel. He picks up the bent and limp rose.

'That was the last of the coffee, I will have to make some tea,' he growls.

He turns to walk out and the towel drops again.

Bugger it, he mumbles.

Michael returns with a pot of tea, plain toast and a pair of teddy bear boxer shorts.

Beckie comes through the door quietly after him. Holding her favourite dolly she runs over to Michael and gives him a hug. She then sits on the bed next to Jane. She whispers, 'Daddy had no pants on.'

Jane laughs.

'What are you two guys up to?'

Jane tells Michael. They all laugh.

'What are you going to do with yourself today?' he asks Jane, matter-of-factly.

Jane sits, absolutely stunned, thinking they would be together. Her laughter slips quickly away from behind a stayed expression. Michael's inability to empathise with Jane's disappointments scares her immensely, her stressing at the airport streams back into her mind unchecked.

'The space for my exhibition only became available yesterday. I have only days to prepare. I'm not sure we're going to be able to meet the deadline. You understand, don't you, Jane? You will be on your own today. Do you mind taking Beckie to school?'

'Certainly, Michael. We can take care of that, can't we Beck?' says Jane, privately wondering why she should understand. She looks down at Beckie's doll which has been pushed towards her. Jane takes a second look. The dolly has a sad face — extremely sad. Jane has never seen a face on a doll like that before.

'I can tell this is a very special dolly,' says Jane softly, adjusting the doll's hair and dress. 'What's her name?' she asks, handing the doll back to Beckie.

'Emily,' says Michael.

Beckie lifts Emily and sits her next to Jane in the bed, while Michael gets dressed. Jane sits up in bed with Emily and begins to drink her tea.

'If you get two cups Beck, Emily can have one too, can't she?'

Beckie runs to the kitchen.

'Call you later.' Michael gives Jane a hug and passionate kiss, patting her back as he does so. 'Thanks for understanding, I knew you would.'

Standing back from the window she watches his black Porsche pull out from the driveway. A vacuum centres in her chest, seeming to suck the energy right out of her, leaving her weak and breathless. She turns to see Beckie silently watching her.

It's only ten past seven. Beckie starts school at eight-thirty. In their dressing gowns, Beckie and Jane go out into the garden leaving Emily on the table near the window. Next to the pool and Michael's vegetable patch are Beckie's two fairy statues surrounded by rings of white pebbles and yesterday's freshly-picked flowers. While Beckie gets absorbed in her own little world, Jane checks out the rest of the garden.

After leaving Beckie at the school gate at eight-thirty, with a kiss and a hug, Jane decides to go on and explore Manly, eventually finding herself in the main local shopping centre. Over a cup of coffee she ponders how she will fill in her day. *God, Michael,* she mouths the words, *I don't understand. Things will be fine it's all just bad timing I'm sure.* Her mind oscillates. *I could ring Michael. I could go and help him with the exhibition,* she considers. *I'd probably be in the way, and, at the moment, I really don't feel inclined.*

She walks out along the Manly wharf and watches the jet cat ferry as it streaks across the busy harbour to the Sydney CBD far in the distance. The main shopping centre is situated on an isthmus of land separating the ocean from an inner harbour. A mixture of modern and old stores line a long pedestrian mall, named The Corso, which connects the ocean beaches with the picturesque, historic harbour area. Locals and some day-trippers are already out enjoying the hot sunny morning.

Jane enters what she is convinced must be the largest

newsagency in the world and sorts through some Aussie souvenirs to send home.

Walking towards the ocean, just off the main thoroughfare, she sees an unusual dress in the window of a small boutique. She stands fascinated by the long, blue, lace hemmed garment. *It's very old world … but I love it,* she thinks. She begins to walk on, stops, and looks back. *No it's not me.*

The hot sun is the right angle above the water to produce a beautiful, silver reflection. The whole ocean appears like a huge sheet of shimmering, moving silver paper. Walking along the seawall she feels the sea spray on her face. The pounding magnificence of the waves and the smell of the sea stir a myriad of feelings within her — a small rush of adrenalin fans out through her body. *To live near this ocean, swim in it and bask in this sunshine, must reflect in the personality, physique and health of those who do it,* she is thinking. *This is what Mr G referred to, the much talked about Aussie character.* Michael flashes in and out of her mind. 'Mr G, I must give him a call,' she says to herself.

The wind abates and there is a temporary silence, broken only by the crackling and thumping of the huge breakers. Tubes of rolling, glistening surf swish across the flat sand, have their moment of glory, slide back into the ocean to begin again. *That's life,* she thinks. Jane's mind turns to her imaginary friend, somewhere out on that ocean of time.

Part of her enjoys being by herself. In spite of life's ups and downs and her current disappointments, for a magical moment she feels complete within. She moves on. She sees in a split second the good that is trying so hard to break out of each and every person that passes her by. She is in the midst of one of her relaxed states and everything around her is detailed and appears remarkably clear. She sits down and watches several small children playing on the sand. Her mind relaxes even further and she sees everything appear to gain momentum, to speed up faster and faster. She sees the children grow up, grow older, and die. She feels the intense pains and sorrows, the happiness and elations of life. For a very brief moment her mind touches a multitude of answers, answers she now knows she can touch again. The beach scene becomes a swirling, shimmering, sunny glow, and then all returns to normal.

She looks ahead. 'Rocks,' she says, smiling to herself.

At the south end of the main beach is a very pretty, private cove, sheltered by a rocky outcrop. She walks down onto the hot sand. Encouraged by several topless young mothers, young children without bathing costumes, the absence of males, the very hot sun and the inviting crystal-clear water she forgets herself and strips off to her underpants. Arms folded in front she walks to the water. Paddling for a moment she studies the clear water moving vigorously back and forth around her legs. *Will I or won't I?* she asks herself. *Yes, I will.* Closing her eyes, tensing all over she takes the plunge. Compared to English waters, the Manly Sea is warm but still a shock to her system.

The natural rocky breakwater deflects the large ocean swell causing small waves to hook around into the cove. Relaxed and now adjusted to the water temperature, she floats on her back. She can feel the Pacific Ocean waters swirling through her hair, across her white belly and between her legs. She feels magical. The dress in the boutique moves in and out of her mind as she floats up and down.

'I will spoil myself, I must have that dress,' she calls, then holding her nose she stands and dives to the sandy bottom where she retrieves two shells, one a cowrie. It doesn't take long for her to start shivering. Refreshed, proud of herself, but a little self-conscious, she washes her shells and makes a beeline to the security of her clothing, thinking if only she had a towel and brush. She intends to repeat this swimming experience as soon as possible, but next time, wearing a bathing costume.

I'll save skinny dipping for Michael's pool, she thinks.

The sun and hot breeze soon dries her as she makes her way back along the beach.

*　　*　　*

The *Neptune* is in rough seas. After rounding the most southern tip of Van Diemen's Land, she pulls into a northerly direction and commences the last leg of her voyage up the east coast of Australia. A northerly headwind is forcing the *Neptune* to tack. This monotonous zigzag course will continue until they reach the southern coast of the main Australian continent.

Possible political ramifications are forcing Trail to moderate his approach towards the convicts. His calculations have shown him the surplus of rations is too high. He is aware the statistics of the First Fleet will bear no resemblance to the low survival rate of the convicts on his voyage. Pressure is put on the mess leaders, the ship's surgeon and the crew to clean up and improve the conditions of the male convicts. But it is too late; five months of deprivation cannot be turned around in a matter of weeks.

Even Horace understands what is going on.

'It's too late Geoff, most of the men are buggered,' he says.

'We can only do our best,' says Geoff as he has the chains released, and pulls a blanket over the face of another poor soul.

*　　*　　*

As a boy, Geoff had seen mystical sketches of faraway lands. Not even the loftiest artistic imaginings can compare with what he is now looking at, the rugged, spectacular Australian coastline. From the southern tip of Van Diemen's Land to the south-east coast of the main continent, where the *Neptune* is currently located, the islands, cliffs, the mountains are both inspiring and scary — they are from a world he has not known before.

The seas off the furthest most southern point of the mainland are dotted with huge granite boulder islands which rise up out of the ocean like massive tortoise shells, smooth and beautifully barren. On the tree-covered shores, cloud-touched pristine mountains meet the ocean. Where there are no rocks, strips of pure white sand greet the rolling surf.

As he looks at this unique, mysterious landscape, the following words flash into his consciousness.

'Do you like my dress?'

'Do you like my dress?' The words come again.

As if only yesterday in his mind he can see Claire in a cheeky pose. Her bottom slightly pushed out, and her hands clasped down in front of her.

'You are a picture of loveliness, my girl,' he says. 'You are the most beautiful girl in the world.'

No … my God, why did I say that to her in such a way? He can now clearly see his remarks and attitude were condescending and trite.

Again, another pertinent phrase flashes to his consciousness.

'What the hell is that?'

He recalls what he said when he first saw Claire's stone. He graphically remembers her answer.

'This is my surprise. Do you like it?' she said softly and a little apprehensively. 'My stone is a symbol of my life, and my love for you, strong and forever lasting.'

He painfully remembers as if it were only minutes away, how he rebuffed this loving and innocent statement from his well-meaning wife.

Then without pause, Claire's owl dream flashes before him.

An owl was on her shoulder, he remembers. *She said it was very fluffy, very wise, and very cuddly. It looked at her with its large brown eyes. She said she saw herself in its eyes. She felt complete and warm as it rested its head close to her neck. It loved her very much …*

'My God!' he says, closing his eyes.

Geoff, she said, *you came and scared my owl away.*

His jaw trembles as he only now recognises the despondent look on her face. He can now see how saddened she was as her feelings for him and life symbolised by her stone, were rejected by him. He can now clearly see Claire's face as she recounted her dream which mirrored her innermost feelings.

The words and the memories don't stop there.

Mrs Blake. More words come from within. He tries to block out these revelations, but another part of him is holding him ruthlessly accountable. *The Druids were unusual to say the least.* He can clearly hear the voice of the Reverend Dickenson in his mind. *Human sacrifice and torture was an integral part of Druid culture, was it not, Mrs Blake?* The Reverend's comments were sparked by Claire's pagan stone.

I agreed with you Claire. I admired the strength the Druid women possessed and the respect they received from all within their community, he thinks. *I could see the Christian church's negative attitude towards women, but I said nothing. I stood by and allowed the church to stifle your spirit. I am as guilty as they.* 'I didn't support my wife!' he screams at the never-ending, relentless waves moving past the front of the ship. 'I should have, my love!'

Horace comes looking for Geoff. Finding him, he can see something is drastically wrong. He moves to do what he can.

'Horace, I've done wrong,' Geoff cries out loud.

'Mr Geoff, you're a good man, I know na better.'

'I killed my Claire, Horace.'

'Nah, you could not. I know that. Come on Mr Geoff, pull yourself together … don't let the *scum* on this ship see yuh like this, eh.'

Christie, who is never far away, moves in alongside Geoff. Her unquestioning arms wrap themselves tightly around his neck. As Geoff picks up Christie, Horace moves closer to them both.

Did you go down that rope? The words of the grey-haired, old man from the hulk, now attacks Geoff's mind.

He closes his eyes and holds Christie tightly. He now knows what that comment was about.

Yes, I did go down that rope, he thinks, drooping his head … *I am responsible for what happened to my lovely Claire … and our baby.*

Christie holds onto him tightly.

CHAPTER FORTY FOUR

As she returns to Michael's place that day, Jane is beginning to realise that in her whole life she has never been so disappointed with day-to-day happenings and yet so strong and contented within herself. This is a complete turnaround and she can only wonder how it's occurred in Manly, Australia, on the other side of the world from her home. On reflection, she can see this process really began back home. Thinking about it further she realises all this change has been developing over a long period of time. She is now beginning to understand everything that has taken place in her life has all been for a reason. She wonders if her new strength, her ability to feel good inside whilst her world is seemingly falling down around her, is only temporary. But something deep down tells her it's here for keeps. This doesn't, however, stop her feeling disappointed with Michael.

She hurries through a shower, has a quick bite to eat and is off to The Corso, thinking, *if I'm quick I will be able to buy my dress before I pick up Beckie.*

Approaching the boutique, she finds the dress has gone from the window. With her hand up to the side of her face she peers through the glass. A young shop assistant beckons her in.

'Are you looking for this?' The assistant holds up the dress. 'I saw you looking at it in the window this morning. It will fit you I'm sure. We were just about to send it to another store of ours, but if you say you want it, it's yours. Try it on.'

'What price is it?' Jane asks hesitantly.

'Three hundred and ninety dollars,' says the assistant without batting an eyelid.

Jane quickly converts to English pounds. 'That's a bargain,' she says, tongue in cheek.

When a garment feels right, it usually is. Jane looks in the mirror and could not be more pleased with the dress though she's not really sure why. The dress hugs her trim figure. Blue is not her usual choice, but it makes for a special change, she thinks. *I've always loved lace.* She smiles as she lifts the hem to look at her flat shoes. 'What am I doing? *What* am I doing here? What am I doing in *Australia?*' she says, in a forced, quick whisper. She shrugs, *fun can take place in unchartered waters,* she thinks with a determined, pert smile.

'May I use a credit card?'

She pays for the dress and heads off to pick up Beckie.

Thoughts of the dress swinging in its carry-bag give her a free and warm feeling. Her hair is ruffled, she has no makeup on, and she couldn't give a damn. Several young men give her the once over and she couldn't give a damn about that either. She feels as if she is the main character in a movie. She imagines the mood-music intensifying as the camera pulls back from a close-up and lifts into the air. Everything in her scene centres around and compliments Jane — the star. Elation such as this is only fleeting, so she soaks it up.

*　　*　　*

The personal revelations Geoff experienced at the bow of the ship were only the first of many. For days afterwards he sinks into depression, his past surging up from the inner catacombs of his mind and engulfing his consciousness with layers and layers of guilt.

What has also become painfully obvious to him is the truth

of the comment screamed at him across the deck by Ellington that, 'there's only one thing more despicable than a man who has committed a crime and that's a self-righteous man driven by guilt'.

Horace is keeping a close eye on Geoff. He has seen, on the *Neptune*, how a man can lose hope.

'Do ya member when I spilt ink all over your bunk, Mr Geoff?' Horace nudges him. 'Remember the fire? I thought we all be goners that day.' For a moment he looks serious. 'Why did ya throw yourself across me as they were whipping the shit out of *me*, Geoff? Why did you do that?' Horace is near tears.

'Because I care for you, Horace,' Geoff answers croakily, his moodiness is making him very candid.

'Why do ya care so much about me?' The word *care* seems to stick in Horace's throat like a dry lump of bread.

'Do you know what, Horace?' says Geoff smiling, looking him right in the eyes. 'I *really* don't know.' A tear runs down Geoff's cheek as he gives Horace a hug.

Horace has succeeded in cheering Geoff, but is still confused himself.

'Geoff, you keep telling me that everybody in the end is 'sponsible for themselves. Do you really believe da? I dunno Geoff. But if it were me, I'd be real pissed off with Miss Claire, I would.'

'Yes Horace, I do believe grown-up and level-headed people are mostly responsible for their own fate.'

'Was Miss Claire grown up and head level?' asks Horace.

Geoff doesn't know whether to laugh or cry. Even though Horace has gotten his words mixed up, he has made his point.

'You know, Horace, I have been that busy blaming *myself*, I …'

The trauma of Geoff's personal problems, for the next five days will be matched and exceeded only by the torrid weather. Huge seas, pelting rain and sweeping gales stretch the sails, the masts, the ropes and the ability of the crew to the absolute limit.

The ship creaks and strains as its rides up the monstrous waves, stalls most times at the top, then either drops into temporary weightlessness or slips alarmingly into the troughs, flooding the bow.

Again, the stuffing is knocked out of the prisoners. Now it's the turn of the cold Tasman Sea to wash over the ship and through the decks. Seasickness is now added to the plight of the men chained below. Dark by day and darker by night, their chamber of horrors becomes awash with vomit, effluent and battered hopes. The stench and cold, although extreme, is dwarfed by desperateness and fear.

Geoff, tired and hurting from his own personal dilemmas and the strain of tending to the men, has developed a severe bronchial infection.

'They're doing fine, Geoff.' Horace has just visited Christie and Jonathan. 'They're dry and warm, but real scared, Geoff. The wind is screaming out there and the night is as black as pitch. The women gave me this for ya. It's a cup a rum.' He smells it and turns up his nose. 'They said to gargle with this shit and *swallow* it.' His revolted expression changes as he remembers it's a man's drink. 'I've had it before,' he assures Geoff, who at this point couldn't care less. Sickness brings with it its own depression. Coupled with his already solemn state, Geoff's lot now feels totally unbearable. His ability to be rational is completely stretched. He downs the rum.

*　　*　　*

'What's in the bag?' gestures Beckie, excitedly.

'This is *mine*,' says Jane, playing the child.

They both burst out laughing.

'*Now*,' says Jane dramatically, 'for you'. She reaches into her carry bag and produces a small wrapped parcel.

Tearing it open, Beckie finds a box with a see-through plastic front.

'Oh', Beckie begins to flush with excitement. Then, as if a switch is thrown off in her mind, she refuses to look at what is in the box — a dolly with the beautiful happy smile. Nevertheless she holds the box tightly to her chest as they both walk off silently for home.

'What's your new dolly's name?' Jane asks as they open the front door. Beckie doesn't answer and runs quickly to her bedroom, followed by Jane. Beckie places her new doll, still in the box, next to Emily. Beckie stands for a moment looking at both dolls, then she picks up Emily and turns to Jane.

'Let's make a smoothie, shall we?' suggests Jane.

As they are getting ready the phone rings. 'How does dinner out sound?' Michael whispers in a sexy voice.

'I'll wear my new dress,' says Jane.

'I'm really sorry I'm so busy Jane. I'll make it up to you. I'll be home at five and we can all go for a walk along the beach. Our dinner reservation is for seven-fifteen. Could you give Nola a call? Her number is in the teledex.

Jane rings the sitter to find she has another appointment.

Michael arrives home at four-thirty with an exquisite bunch of red roses. He seems ecstatic to see Jane. She smells the flowers.

'Nola isn't available.'

'Damn, this happens from time to time.' he says, flipping over the yellow pages. 'Now, let me see, that's them, they never let me down.'

It's a commercial agency that will look after Beckie and it appears to Jane that this may have happened many times before. Jane just can't understand how blatant and mechanical Michael is in certain situations. It's as if he is not aware.

He pats Beckie on the bottom. 'Let's all go for that walk, it's a lovely afternoon,'

Beckie is so excited. Dad's home early and it would seem the walk is a regular event. Beckie fetches her roller blades.

Their late afternoon walk along the promenade starts on a positive note, but it is not long before Michael drifts into a world of his own. Beckie is left to race about on her rollerblades. Michael speaks about his exhibition, his gym, his personal trainer, his car and the attributes of Manly.

'Beckie doesn't speak very much, does she?'

'No, the doctors say the trauma of her mother dying when she was two is the main factor. Linda had been having lots of headaches and on this particular day went to bed with a really severe headache. She had rung her mother and asked her to come over and take care of Beck. We don't know exactly when Linda died, but by the time Linda's mother got there, she found Linda dead and Beck on the bed beside her. It was a blood clot to the brain. Since then Beck tends to stay in a world of her own. I'm all she has.'

They walk on.

He is not paying attention to her. 'How was your day?' he asks, watching a fisherman on the beach. Jane tells him about her new dress, her swim in the ocean and Beckie's new doll.

'I'm glad you had a good day and we will top it off with a *fantastic* night.' he says, squeezing her hand.

'Look at that!' He points to three large pelicans using the warm evening breeze to circle effortlessly overhead. Jane looks up and Michael kisses her softly on the lips. She kisses him back.

Everybody's different, she thinks to herself and takes a quick glance at him. For a split second she sees something very special in him. He looks at her with a gorgeous smile on his face. *He's so cute,* she confirms in her mind.

'What are you going to have for dinner tonight,' she says, giving him another cuddle.

'Oysters and steak, I feel like a nice juicy steak, he replies and with an imitation growl as he playfully bites her on the back of the neck.

*   *   *

Bouncing seas lap and smack at the hull of the *Neptune* as it forges onward. The northerly wind, which has been persistent, has given way to a southerly change resulting in ambivalent waves which churn up the surface.

These conditions bring fish up from the depths and the crew are quick to take advantage of the bubbling, jumping schools. In no time, ten yellow fin tuna and thirty barracuda are hauled aboard.

The difference in Captain Trail's attitude sickens Geoff and Horace. It would seem most on board don't see it, or don't want to see it. Trail can't turn things around. Horace was correct when he said to Geoff, 'It's too late for many of the men in chains.'

In a desperate effort to improve the health of the convict men, Captain Trail orders deck exercise. He personally observes the first group of ten men move pathetically around the top deck, their hunched, limping bodies of skin and bone a disgusting tribute to his previous mismanagement of them. What he has set in motion will only intensify the men's plight and create one of history's most horrific scenes when the *Neptune* berths at the new settlement and disgorges its emaciated human cargo.

Despite the obvious horror of these parades, Trail persists.

Geoff is still not well. His lung infection worsens and he is coughing up phlegm continually. Lying in his bunk he has more and more time to reflect. His hallucinating mind returns to his dream of the menagerie and he remembers the frightened ape-man crouched in his steel pen fending off the angry, aggravating crowd. He remembers the stare of this dejected creature in the dream. He feels himself staring back. He sees the creature's questioning horror, looking to him for help.

'Part of me couldn't help the poor creature, I couldn't help the pathetic thing,' he says aloud. Horace, who stays close to Geoff all the time now puts his hand on Geoff's shoulder and gives him a sip of water.

Geoff thinks of Claire, her caresses and her strength.

She did love me, she did. And I love her,' he moans quietly.

Horace squeezes Geoff's arm. He doesn't know what else he can do.

*   *   *

The food and atmosphere at Michael's favourite restaurant is excellent and he even manages to talk to Jane about her family, the flight and her new country Australia, but something is wrong, drastically wrong and Jane can't put her finger on it. She didn't wear her new dress. It didn't seem appropriate especially when Michael seemed to have forgotten she'd told him about buying it.

Out of the blue, Jane hears a voice. She looks around.

'Did you hear anything Michael?'

'How could I, I was speaking.'

Everything seems perfect as far as Michael is concerned, although he seems to sense at some level Jane is preoccupied 'Are you happy?' he asks, putting his hand on hers.

'Let's get some air, let's go for a walk.' Jane shifts her chair back abruptly and Michael jumps to his feet.

Outside he holds her almost too tightly as they look out across the dark ocean. The smell of kelp and large areas of beach exposed by the low tide combined with the humid air and lack of any breeze creates a pungent stench.

Michael begins to caress Jane, but tonight she makes no

response. She is preoccupied with projecting her mind out to sea.

'It feels you're not even with me, Jane. It feels like you are oceans away. *What's wrong, honey?*' he asks her.

Michael, who are you to ask that, she thinks to herself angrily, but says, 'I'm just thinking isn't it lovely to be near the ocean.'

'What about me. Where do I fit into all this?' he asks.

Jane is again prepared to put her needs aside. It has only been a couple of days. But his continuing unawareness of her feelings is flipping her out. *Maybe it's my fault,* she thinks. *He's possibly nervous. His exhibition is preoccupying him, I know that. Fear of commitment could be worrying him, who knows. Love is patient, they say.*

One second she is in control, but the next she finds herself spewing out her feelings.

'Michael, you've done nothing but think and talk about yourself ever since I arrived.' She pauses, but she can't hold it. 'Michael I don't expect much … how *you* can say I'm not there for you. God! You didn't meet me at the airport or give me the slightest explanation why. You've spent very few daylight hours with me.' Jane's upset is building and building. 'It just seems you want to talk about you, get me drunk and screw me. I just don't understand. *I really don't.*'

Michael is absolutely stunned and speechless after hearing Jane's revelations.

Maybe I'm not the first woman to have done this to him, her mind is spinning. *Passion must be as strong as life itself,* she is thinking. *Michael just doesn't have it. Fight back Michael, fight back please … He's just standing there. For God sake Michael say something. He just hasn't got it, he doesn't have it for me,* she squirms with this conclusion inside her. How these basic kinks in his behaviour didn't reveal themselves when she met him in London, she can only but speculate. *It couldn't be, surely not, I've travelled*

all this distance, left everything behind me, including Greg, and ...
Michael is unwittingly taking advantage of me, or is there something
or somebody else?

Michael says nothing.

Jane's mind seems to lift and hover in front of her, then sweep out over the breaking waves and zoom up into the dark night sky. She is soaring. She looks back as she climbs, seeing herself and Michael on the seawall. Like a rocket, she boosts higher and higher, watching the lights of Manly clustered together and become a small part of the overall.

Somewhere in the upper areas of her psyche, she knows there must be somebody who can give her the same as she is capable of giving, or is she only searching for an impossible dream? Is she only fighting the windmills of her mind or will she actually find her special reflection in another? Michael is already slipping away.

She hears a voice in the upper areas of her mind saying, 'I love you, I need you ... I love you.'

Without another word said, Michael and Jane return home and see out the baby-sitter.

From Michael's bed Jane can hear a southerly change whipping up the surf. *Maybe it's not Michael, maybe it's me,* she thinks. *Margaret said ...* She falls asleep.

CHAPTER FORTY FIVE

ust past nine am and Beckie is at school. Jane stands again on the ocean seawall. Already the temperature is twenty-eight degrees; a slight onshore sea breeze makes it just perfect. The tide is in. Despite the events of the previous night being very stressful for both her and Michael, she feels good inside.

Although Jane has spoken her mind, she prays that the man she has always been looking for, Michael, will snap out of his insensitivity and miraculously reappear as the lover she met in London. But part of her is now convinced that will not happen.

*　　*　　*

Geoff's health has improved. The congestion in his chest has dissipated to an annoying tickle. Nurse Christie and Doctor Horace, as Geoff refers to them, are proud of their patient's recovery.

As the *Neptune* moves steadily up the eastern coastline of Australia, Geoff for the first time is beginning to accept his life's situation.

*　　*　　*

Michael has offered to drive from Sydney to Manly and take Jane to the exhibition, but they both have decided that it would be better if he stayed with his clients and Jane take the ferry and meet him there.

Jane feels awkward about going to Michael's exhibition. She wishes it was different. She wanders aimlessly around the house looking at each room as if in one of them she may find the answer to her predicament. Sometimes looking at the belongings of a person can give a clue, some inspiration, or just comfort. But none of this is working. The part of her that wanted so much to consolidate this relationship has stalled. She is falling out of love.

I'll try on my new dress, she thinks.

It feels as if a light of a very different colour is switched on as she opens the closet and impatiently slips the dress out of its plastic covering. The smell and feel of the fabric more than satisfies her. She adores the soft sound of the dress crinkling as it slides over her body.

Is this me, or is it not me? she thinks looking into the mirror intently.

'She loves the dress, she loves it not. I love the dress, I loves it not,' she sings to herself as she dances a cheeky, strange dance around the bedroom.

'Oh my *God!* What's the time? *Shit!* It's a quarter to ten. My eyebrows, I was going to wax.'

She slips out of the dress. 'What will I wear? I wish I had more time.'

*   *   *

The Jet cat ferry streaks towards Sydney. It lifts and sinks as it cuts precisely through the large ocean swell entering the Harbour between the heads. North and South Heads form a magnificent entrance to Sydney Harbour. Romance can combine with a location and form a mad mystical set of feelings, but not, in this case, for Jane.

North Head, a short distance from Manly, is a continuous line of sheer rock cliffs that rise majestically out of the ocean.

I must go there, she thinks, as she considers giving Michael a call.

The Cat leans into a powerful right hand turn and lines up for the straight run along the main harbour.

In the distance, Sydney Harbour Bridge, the *coat hanger* as it is affectionately called, joins North Sydney with the main CBD. Jane, seeing the impressive Opera House, Sydney Tower, the tall buildings, expensive homes along the waterfront and the hot balmy weather is aroused to romantic feelings again, but she holds them firmly at arm's length.

What a damn shame, she thinks, her mind going back to the aeroplane and her trip over. She remembers those magic feelings she had for Michael, feelings that still persist. She also remembers those strange and lifelike fantasies of the schoolyard, the sailing ship and the eyes of that intriguing young man on board the …

'Well … look at that,' she says aloud.

'Are you talking about the *Bounty?*' asks a Mr G type man, standing several feet away from Jane.

'I'm sorry,' says Jane. 'I was speaking to myself.'

'That's the *Bounty* replica, it does day trips for tourists around the harbour.'

'It looks very realistic,' says Jane with interest.

'You're from England?'

'Yes,' replies Jane.

'You should sail on her. You'd love it. By the way, I don't wish to be personal, but I think you've lost an earring.'

'So I have, thankyou,' she says, her mind on other things.

She can now see Michael, waving with one hand and a mobile phone in the other.

Thoughts buzz through her mind. *Hairy legs, my eyebrows, one earring gone and I was going to put my hair up. The dreadeds are circling and I don't have any tampons. Michael will be ashamed of me. Do I expect too much of him?* Part of Jane still desperately wants to reconcile with Michael.

Convinced that Michael is waving to her, a wishful-thinking gorgeous woman, standing to Jane's left, waves back at him.

What's your number, I might give him to you, lovey. Jane thinks sadly to herself as she waves alongside the other woman.

If numbers are anything to go by, the exhibition is an outstanding success. Jane counts over forty-five people including, as it happens, the gorgeous young woman who waved to Michael from the ferry.

Jane loves Michael's work, some of the pieces stir her deeply and in them she can see the side of Michael she fell in love with. *The gap between his aspirations and the reality of his character is life-times too wide,* she thinks. When she briefly speaks to him, she considers suggesting afternoon-tea, but lets him off the hook. He is surrounded by well wishers and prospective buyers.

'See you tonight?' he calls. *I'm sorry, but what can I do,* he gestures, with a boyish, lost expression on his face.

Jane takes one of the mid-afternoon ferries back to Manly. From the top-deck she can see the rock cliffs of the North Head peninsular.

I must give Margaret a call, she thinks.

At the school-gate, Beckie is really excited to see Jane. Her excitement says it all. *My mummy is picking me up too — isn't she beautiful? I'm going home now with my mummy,* thinks Beck. Jane gives her the biggest hug and kiss.

'Should we buy an ice cream on the way home?' Jane whispers. Beckie quivers with excitement. She decides on three colours. The ice cream lady looks hesitant as she piles the triple delight onto the cone. Jane wonders if Beckie will be able to hold the huge cone with her little hand, but hold it she does. The next problem however is the angle and the ever-increasing drips. Beckie is determined not to miss one of them. Jane looks down to check on Beckie's progress to find she is gone. Looking back, she discovers Beckie has wandered off to the other side of the mall. With ice cream dripping out of control in the hot afternoon sun, she stands staring into a toyshop window. As Jane approaches she can see what has caught Beckie's attention.

An angel, holding a glittering wand is smiling through the window at Beckie. The strawberry layer of ice cream slides off the cone and falls to the ground but Beckie is oblivious to everything except the happy, magical little figure in the window.

'Will we take that angel home to meet Emily?' Jane asks quietly.

A slow, happy, nod and then Beckie rediscovers her ice cream, minus the strawberry bit.

The second happy dolly is purchased and securely placed in a colourful carry bag, and they all head for home.

CHAPTER FORTY SIX

'Could I speak with Margaret please? This is Jane, Jane Turner.'

Margaret comes to the phone. '*Hello love. I've missed you,*' says Margaret warmly.

Jane chokes up and is temporarily speechless, thinking it's good to know somebody misses her.

'Things aren't the best, are they love?'

Jane hesitates, she is not sure how to answer Margaret's question.

'Jane, listen to me. It's admirable to be strong and sure, but there are two sides to everything. Do you want to talk?' Margaret treads lightly.

'Yes Margaret, I need somebody to talk to. I'm sick and tired of talking to myself.'

'How do you feel love?'

'Michael says I feel good to him ... all over,' jokes Jane.

'There's not much wrong with you,' says Margaret.

'Have you spoken to Gordon since the flight?' Jane asks

'No I haven't as yet ... *you're* changing the subject. Now, back to feelings, young lady.'

'I should have listened to you Margaret, things here could not be worse.'

'It's that bad is it? You sound sad, if I may say so.'

'Well, it's hard to explain. I'm sad, but so secure and happy — it's creepy, Margaret. I feel right at home here in Manly, but that's got nothing to do with Michael ... Well, less and less to do with Michael.'

Jane fills Margaret in on her attachment to Beckie.

'I've got a mental picture of Beckie,' Margaret says cheekily.

'You've seen her photograph on the plane, you *impostor*.'

They both laugh and then Jane runs through all her experiences, and Margaret fills Jane in on a bush walk in the Blue Mountains and a visit to the Jenolan caves.

'What about your dress?' Margaret asks.

'Oh, I forgot about that.' Jane goes on to describe all about the dress. *That clinches it*, Jane thinks. She finally and wholeheartedly now is convinced of Margaret's psychic abilities. *There is no way she could have known about the dress*, she tells herself.

'That dress makes me feel complete. But it's not *me*. I just hang it in the closet and look at it. I snuck it on yesterday, but I haven't worn it out as yet.'

'You *will*. Tell me Jane, how do you *really* feel, love?'

Jane thinks for a moment. 'Times I'm very sad and very angry, Margaret.'

'If you could locate these feelings in your body, where would they be?'

Jane thinks again. 'I'm sad in my chest … sad in my heart.'

'And the anger, where do you feel that?' asks Margaret.

'In my stomach and shoulders,' Jane replies thoughtfully. 'Why?'

'It's extremely helpful to identify feelings and then relate them to an area of the body.'

'What about my feelings of security and strength?'

'What about them? They are coming straight from your solar plexus area, aren't they?' says Margaret.

Jane thinks for a moment. 'That's *damn* right Margaret, and it feels so good.'

'Build on those feelings love, just let it flow. Identify the negative ones and then let them go … like a sad movie on a television screen. Anchor onto the positive stuff. It sounds like you're doing that anyway. I'll give Gordon a call in a couple of days. I'll ring you after that.'

'Thank you so much Margaret, I don't know what I would do without you.'

'You're doing just fine. Remember Jane, enjoy the journey, arrival at life's ultimate destination is only a momentary experience, it's the climb that's the fun part.'

'Is that *right*? Just keep telling me that won't you Margaret? Part of me knows exactly what you are saying and another part of me is just trying to survive the day-by-day experiences in life. But, it hurts Margaret, it hurts *so* much.' Jane begins to cry.

*　　*　　*

The settlers at Sydney Cove are still awaiting the arrival of the Second Fleet. Expectations have lifted and lowered so many times now that the excitement of anticipation and the misery of hopes dampened are levelling out to a general feeling of acceptance. Looking out to sea expectantly torments those who keep doing it. But even the most stoic are losing hope; the fleet is well overdue and the consensus of opinion is that the ships have perished.

The increasing harshness of punishments for stealing food seems to reflect the desperation in the colony. The theft of two pounds of potatoes from a private garden earned a convict one hundred lashes and his flour rations were stopped for six months. For the theft of six cabbages, another man received one hundred and twenty-five lashes.

Governor Phillip makes his personal supplies available to the colonists. It's claimed his private kitchen serves nothing more than what is available from the public store.

A small expedition rows up the centre of the harbour noting and mapping all the small coves and extensions to the waterway.

In the distance, North Head looms majestically up from its rocky base. The Aborigines can be seen fishing and bathing along the rocky shoreline, their daily routines converting to silence and stares as the long boat makes its way towards the open ocean.

*　*　*

There is more hope aboard the *Neptune* than there is at Sydney Cove. Although the seas are rough, the prospect of the journey's end encourages all on board.

The authority of the Marine Captain will return when his unit reaches the settlement and are out of the official clutches of Captain Trail. The marines have never been at home on the high seas.

The free settlers stand for long periods, staring at the new coastline. The fears of the voyage are now subsiding but are being replaced by new trepidations, lesser fears, to which their minds will now give just as much credence. Talk of an excruciatingly hot climate, savage natives, snakes and sharks, is now circulating.

For several sailors accompanied by their wives, this will be a one-way trip for they will settle at Sydney Cove.

Ellington, the chief mate, has mellowed. His health has not been good. Sickness can level a man.

*　*　*

'Hello Jane, it's good to catch up again. Margaret said you have run into a sticky situation. I'm sure it will work out.'

Jane is glad to hear Gordon's voice. *But he never seems to talks about feelings,* she thinks. *I wonder if that's his man thing, his wisdom, his absolute confidence in me, or that he really doesn't want to get involved?*

'How's your work, Mr G?'

'Always seem to be the bunny in the middle, but that's my job I suppose.'

'Have you gotten over your embarrassment about what happened in Bahrain? God when the police came onto the plane with guns ...'

'How do you think I felt when they marched me off? I was annoyed Jane. But, all's well that ends well. You have my phone number love. Do give me a ring whenever you want. I hope things turn out well for you; they will you know you deserve it. You're very special.'

*   *   *

Geoff is now feeling the invigorating effects of his personal exorcism. The lifting of guilt that for so long burdened him now leaves him a little off balance and curiously liberated. The wounds in his life are now cleansing and beginning to heal.

'How will it be Geoff, do you think, in our new land?' Horace asks excitedly. Christie, beside him is all ears.

'I've read about a man called Mr Joseph Banks, who studied plants and animals on Captain Cook's voyage. He wrote that the Aboriginal people are very friendly, and there are special creatures in Australia, which can't be found anywhere else in the world. Dog-like animals called dingoes came right up to Captain Cook's camp areas when he first landed at Botany Bay.

Christie's eyes nearly pop as Geoff continues.

'Large animals, like *giant* mice, called kangaroos hop around on their back feet. Some stand six feet tall and can rip out a man's belly with one downward kick from their large powerful feet. The skies are full of beautiful and unusual birds. White, black and multi coloured parrots live together with cuddly koala bears in the tall eucalyptus trees. The bears eat gum leaves.'

'What do the parrots eat?' asks Christie.

'Koala bears,' Geoff answer, looking very serious.

'I don't believe you,' says Christie hitting out at Horace who is laughing at her.

Geoff holds her hand and continues. 'The sea and rivers are full of fish and the shores are of fine golden sand. Like those over there.' Geoff points to several white sandy beaches way in the distance. 'It can get icy-cold or very hot.' Christie's mouth drops wide open as she stares at the coastline.

*   *   *

Jane sets off for the beach hoping a paddle or a swim might clear her head.

When Michael's exhibition closes in two days he is going to take a short holiday. Only a few days ago she would have been excited about the prospect of them spending some time together, but now …

She sits down on the sand. It's a lovely day and there is not a soul nearby. Small stones and clumps of seaweed roll around in the waves flashing across the sand banks like silver veils on their way to nowhere. She watches the water spread quickly across the beach until there is a point where it actually stops. What was once a huge breaker soaks into the beach and disappears. *Life is just like that,* she thinks to herself.

Deciding it's too rough for a swim she stands and as she meanders along the water's edge, her mind moves out across the ocean and she recalls her fantasy about the young man on the sailing ship. She tries to visualise the ships from those early days sailing up and down this very coastline. She remembers the young man's kind, but stressed face. She recalls a feeling of strife and horror aboard his ship. For some unexplainable reason she is taking solace and strength from her vivid fantasies. *Geoff … where did that name come from?* she wonders. 'My mother always said I had a vivid imagination,' she says aloud as she looks down at the sand. Thoughts of her special friendship with Margaret and Mr G stream back into her mind. *Maybe I will write a book about all this one day … maybe I won't,* she thinks as a usually powerful wave sweeps across the sand and washes up her legs.

Despite her wet shorts she decides to walk the length of the beach. She hasn't exercised for ages.

*   *   *

Mary Cochran, the convict woman who is breast-feeding Jonathan, in the course of seeing Geoff on a daily basis has become attached to him and begins to make advances. Part of him is attracted to the woman but to take advantage of her would only complicate his situation and definitely not help hers. Despite this, he gives Mary support and part of his rations.

Geoff has a vision, deep inside himself, of his perfect mate. All through his life, that image of his five-year-old childhood, fantasy friend has set the physical outline of his ideal female. Only in his dreams or imaginings can he find another like Claire.

He remembers how beautiful Claire looked in her new blue dress the night before she died. He remembers his vivid dream when she, at least he assumes it was Claire, visited him below the decks on this very ship. It felt so good. He remembers the unusual clothing she wore in the dream, and the reassuring feeling she left with him. 'Trousers, and a man's shirt, open at the front. Women don't dress like that,' he says to himself.

CHAPTER FORTY SEVEN

eckie lets go of Jane's hand and runs on ahead. She can hardly wait to get home. Like an excited puppy she scuttles through the open front door and heads for her bedroom. Jane remembers how exciting it was to arrive home from school and play with her dolls and toys when she was young. She knows where Beckie is at.

'Angel told me this dolly is *Jane*,' Beckie startles Jane. She is taking the smiling doll, Jane purchased for her, out of its box.

Jane is touched.

'That is so nice, would you thank Angel for me?' she says as Beckie disappears back into her bedroom.

A few minutes later Jane surprises Beckie out of her secret world with the tinkling of glasses and the crackling of plastic wrap as she places two large chocolate-coated biscuits on the table in her bedroom. Beckie takes both biscuits and puts them on her plate. Jane indicates *no* with her finger and breaks one biscuit in half, putting the half on her own plate.

'That's *mine*,' says Jane with a laugh at which Beckie goes to the cupboard bringing back three extra plates. She then fetches Emily, Jane Junior and Angel for afternoon tea.

Michael comes in soon afterwards and surveys the happy scene. 'Well, Jane and Beck, I have the next three days off. Who's coming to the beach?'

'*Me!*' Beckie calls out knocking over one of her dolls. '*Me! me!*' she calls.

'I'll clean up here and catch you up,' says Jane, feeling Beckie should spend some time alone with her father.

Jane thought she knew where Michael and Beckie would go. She's wrong. Today they must have gone in another direction or onto the sand. She can't see them anywhere.

The late afternoon sun has dropped behind the tall Norfolk Island pines at the back of the beach. As the sun sinks further into the western sky the tree's shadows can almost be seen moving across the sand toward the water's edge. Apart for two joggers working up a sweat, the gulls, the people, even the lazy surf seems to be in late afternoon mode.

Jane walks to the southern end of the beach where she finds a road leading up to the old monastery overlooking Manly Beach and the northern coastline. She passes the old building and the Manly hospital experiencing a twitch of excitement as she walks under a quaint stone archway. She has entered an old military base which is open to the public. She asks a young man in uniform where the road leads.

'To North Head,' he replies.

'How far is it to the lookout?' she asks.

'Three and a half kilometres ... maybe four, but I wouldn't go out there, it's getting dark.'

'Thank you. I'll only walk a short way,' she replies.

The evening is beautifully still. The straight road takes her past several houses which were part of the original military complex. She then moves onto North Head Reserve proper. Small black birds with white and yellow wings flash silently in, out and around the low-growing Tea tree and Banksia bushes. The sky is a late afternoon bluey mauve.

She feels relaxed. She can't see the ocean to the east, but she can smell the pungent saltiness a rocky coastline can produce. She has glimpses of the harbour shoreline to the west and can just make out Sydney, in the distance, through a fine layer of smog.

That would be two and a half miles to the lookout and two and a half miles back, she calculates. *It would be dark coming back and there are no streetlights.*

Her idea to continue just a tad further is changed instantaneously by two carloads of screaming youths speeding recklessly along the road.

'Come with us you sexy *slut!*' calls a youth from one of the slowing vehicles. The other car has the bared backside of another larrikin protruding out of its window.

Jane does an about turn. North Head attracts all types by the looks of it. The vastness and the pristine nature of the area soon soaks up the noisy interruption, but her heart is still thumping. She will continue this escapade to North Head another day.

* * *

Geoff has been wondering whether Trail has developed a conscience over what he has done to the convicts, or if his new attitude is a cunning ploy to gain the backup of potentially influential people on board. He has seen him discreetly lobbying the free settlers and the marines for the past three weeks.

'*Mr Blake!* Can we speak?' The captain breaks into Geoff's thoughts as he stands at the deck rail and ushers him to one side. 'I would like to inform you that your efforts and service aboard the *Neptune* will not go unnoticed. I will be passing my recommendations regarding you to Governor Phillip on our arrival.'

Geoff is surprised; he did not expect anything like this support from the Captain. He wonders if this is another tactic coming from a man under pressure trying to balance the ledger.

'I'm not revered by many, Mr Blake.' Trail lowers his voice and looks around. 'And I'm not revered by you. This I know, but you don't give up on a man, do you? You're either a fool, a smart man or one of a kind. The part of me that searches for something special in this Godforsaken world has decided to place a small amount of faith in you. *Not much, mind you,* just a miniscule. Now excuse me please, I have tasks to attend. We won't speak again.'

Trail closes the discussion with a flash of eye contact. Only once before has Geoff seen this look in Captain Trail's eyes. Again he sees it briefly — eyes searching for a glimmer of light from somewhere, or from somebody — a spark to link with his own inner spark within.

*   *   *

Jane returns from North Head. Michael is angry. 'Where have you been?' he demands. 'I couldn't find you anywhere. I've tried, Jane,' he says. 'What's wrong with you? I have so much to offer you. You get on so well with Beck … I care deeply for you, oh … *what's* the use?'

For a brief moment, Jane again doubts herself. Beckie comes from her bedroom carrying her three dolls. She moves towards Michael, but walks past him and stands next to Jane.

Nothing more is said.

Miffed and unsettled Jane decides to go out for the evening.

*   *   *

The ship's bell sounds 5 pm. Geoff has a short break from attending to the evening meals. He sits at the front of the ship considering Captain Trail's supposed recommendation of him. He distrusts it.

Then he falls into thinking about relationships in the colony. He is aware of the scarcity of women in the new land and while Mary's a good woman, the thought of a relationship with her does not enthuse him. He considers Christie's, Horace's and his own future, and then Claire moves back into his mind.

He sits deep in thought, watching the sunset over the new land and the never-ending waves swelling towards the beaches in the distance.

*   *   *

The sun has now dropped behind the city's skyline as Jane makes her way to the Manly Pacific Hotel Resort. She has a dinner reservation for one at a window table. Just below is the beach where she was standing with Michael when everything came to a head. She watches the thundering breakers roll in. *Each wave, she thinks, is washing away all the hurt.*

That's a Margaret visualisation! Why does Margaret keep popping into my head? Jane wonders, as she absent-mindedly consumes a delicious prawn cocktail. *How the hell did she know about Michael? She knew he wouldn't be at the airport, she thinks. Not once did she show any enthusiasm for him.*

On the strength of a vodka and lemon, Jane starts to make excuses for Michael. She constructs a mental list of all his good and not so good points.

He's kind and caring … no he's not. He tries so hard, or does he? He loves Beck, he really does, but it's such a strange love. He's successful and good-looking, but this seems only to make him more self-centred. Greg was never like that. He cares for me — or, he thinks he does.

Jane's mind goes on and on. Margaret's words are all around her. 'Why bother love. How long is it going to take before you understand? Michael is doing the best he can and learning lessons as he goes. You, my love are further along life's path, you can't change him. He has to learn for himself. Do you need all that? Lift your sights, girl.'

Jane looks away from the beach and out to sea as the combination of her empty stomach and the vodka begins to take effect. Part of Jane mischievously considers never having anything to do with men again. *Maybe I could become a lesbian?* she thinks. *Then, no, I got close to that once before. That was nice, but not for me. I even fantasised with the idea of suicide once.*

A strange feeling comes over her. *It's all about respect and strength,* she thinks. She looks across at the monastery on the hill in the distance. *That's a towering monument to male domination from the past,* her tipsy but unusually clear mind thinks. She sips her second drink. *The church has lots to answer for. Most denominations still limit the involvement of women in their hierarchy, but that's changing. If I can change, it will change men, women and children around me — my God, I am changing. I know I am, but I can't see it clearly. How long is all this going to take? I want it all in this lifetime — I want to be done with it this time around.*

Margaret again flashes into her mind.

Having another sip of her drink, Jane considers how she would have to adjust her behaviour to co-exist with Michael — I could do it. Maybe he can change.

'No *ruddy* way!' she says aloud. Several people at adjoining tables momentarily look at her in some astonishment and then resume their meals. She feels good inside, so good she feels like dancing. She has made up her mind. She hasn't been with him long, but she knows Michael is not for her. She hungrily finishes her main course.

Leaving the restaurant, she hears the inviting sound of recorded music and moves into another area of the resort. She settles herself down in a huge comfy chair and closes her eyes. Twenty minutes later she awakens to the magical sounds of a live band readying itself to play.

Why not, she thinks, and orders a champagne cocktail. She sits back to enjoy the scene. Several young women and one guy are dancing. Jane feels an irresistible urge to join them. She moves onto the dance floor. For the first time since she was a child, she doesn't care what anybody else thinks.

Maybe it's the alcohol, she thinks, *I feel so good. I've never felt like this before.*

The coloured lights, the music, and her mood all spontaneously blend. She feels she is dancing amongst the stars for herself and herself alone. And it could go on forever. She is confident, provocative and sexy. She needs nobody and yet, she needs everybody.

Her personal demons are cast aside.

What the hell was in that drink? she thinks and smiles.

She is dancing with her own reflected self, which is weaving in and out of her body with the music. Everybody has left the floor; she is dancing alone. From her finger-tips, feelings and emotions are cast in swirls and circles as her hands move in ways they have never moved before. She is encouraged by the musicians, who every now and then encounter experiences such as this. They inspire her and she inspires them.

'Can I hold this feeling?' she asks herself.

Yes, you can, replies a voice. *It has been there all the time. You know that Jane.*

'*Margaret,* is that you?' Jane is confused. Her dance has slowed to a hypnotic snake like sway.

Take care of him, Jane. He is a good man, he really is.

'Who, who are you talking about? Who …?' Jane stops in the middle of the floor. She sinks to her knees. The female vocalist leaves the stage and gives Jane a hug.

'Are you okay?' the singer asks.

'Yes, I am fine, really I am. I have never felt better in my whole life,' says Jane.

Go to him Jane, go to him, the familiar voice speaks in her mind again.

'Go to *who?*' asks Jane, as she begins to sob. '*Who are you, please tell me?*' There is no answer.

Standing, Jane seems to leave part of herself kneeling in the centre of the dance floor, and moves outside into the cool night air.

Arriving at Michael's house she finds another vehicle, with female belongings on the front seat, in the driveway. 'Maybe it's his sister, maybe it's his friend, maybe this or maybe that, I really don't care and I really don't need any of this,' she says quietly to herself. '*Poor Beck.*'

She makes her way back to enquire about accommodation at the resort where she hopes to continue her magic evening with herself and herself alone.

'If they're booked out I'II sleep on the beach,' she giggles. 'I can do whatever I want.'

CHAPTER FORTY EIGHT

What motivates a nation to move away from its own shores to explore and colonise? This very spirit of adventure and dreams of conquering a virgin unknown is evident in the history of many races, both ancient and modern. Tribes moved and explored down onto the great southern land and settled Australia as far back as one hundred thousand years ago, before the continent was geographically split off from Asia.

Geoff has read about the treatment of the American Indians. He has been repulsed by the slavery of the African people and, from a crew-member, has now learnt about Captain Trail's involvement in slave transportation. Looking at the new coastline he speculates about the extent of the Australian Indian population.

Through a field glass, offered by Sergeant Thomas, Geoff scans the beaches and the rocky outcrops trying again to observe the local native presence. Not a sign of life is visible. *How must this vessel appear to these Aboriginal people?* he thinks. *A modern ship like the Neptune must seem like a craft from another planet. Has England learned from its previous mistakes? Maybe the colonisation of Australia will be different.* He has a sinking feeling as he wonders what the natives of Australia would think if they could see into the hull of this ship with its pitiful cargo of sick and tortured men?

My God, he thinks to himself. *The history of this colony is already scarred.*

The *Neptune* is three days and two nights from the completion of its long voyage. To Geoff, this magnificent vessel appears detached from the horrors which have taken place and still exist in its womb.

* * *

Beckie looks up at a helicopter hovering very low over Manly. She is frightened by its roar, which is amplified by the low cloud cover. She holds her father's hand tightly. Michael is taking Beckie to school.

'When is Jane coming home, Daddy?'

'I'm not sure, honey.'

'Mommy didn't come back, did she?' she says, releasing his hand.

Michael doesn't answer. He has never really talked about her mother's death. Besides they're running late.

Beckie looks ahead at the school gate where Jane usually drops her off. Much to her surprise, Jane is waiting there.

Beckie jumps up and down.

'Jane's back, Daddy!' She stands looking at Jane with an awkward smile.

'I'll see you after school sweetheart.' Jane gives Beckie a tight cuddle and waves her off.

'We should talk,' says Michael.

'I'm not sure there is much to talk about Michael,' says Jane, quite detached.

What's the use? He couldn't change, even if he wanted to, she thinks. She feels sorry for him, but taking care of herself has become a priority.

'I could help mind Beckie,' she offers. Michael's eyes flash to one side, body language Jane already knows all too well. Within a split second he has weighed it all up. He agrees.

One second she feels fine about leaving him, the next, the

momentum of her love, which has been steadily increasing since the day they met, is edging back into her mind.

She has to go.

*　　*　　*

Within four days, Jane has moved into a duplex unit two blocks away from Beckie and Michael. She has agreed to take Beckie to school three mornings a week and take care of her three afternoons after school. She has also offered to be with her on a Saturday or Sunday every second weekend. Any plans, however, will be conditional upon her obtaining a work permit and an extension of her visa.

Although this decision to move away from Michael seems justified to Jane, the part of her that travelled to the other side of the globe to be with him is still hurting. She can still remember the feeling of elation that swirled around in her mind and her chest when the aeroplane touched down in Sydney. Now part of her feels empty.

'It's a *horrible*, horrible shame!' she calls out.

A quick call to Mum and Dad might help, she decides impulsively.

'I have a new address for you, Mum.'

'How are Michael and Beckie, love. We both miss you so much.'

After filling Mum in, she expected a big *I told you so.* That doesn't happen.

Hanging up, Jane settles down for the night. She can hear the ocean in the distance. *I should ring Margaret tomorrow,* she thinks. She is asleep in minutes. In the early hours of the morning, she partly awakes to a screaming sound. She lies spread-eagled in bed, unable to move. She has been in the midst of a dream and can't throw it off. The howling wind outside sounds like a 747 aeroplane trying to take off. The rain is pelting against her unit's window. In the dream she is looking out of the window of a jet flying through a storm, trying to take off. She can see the ground, buildings, and mountains.

'*It's not high enough!*' she cries out. She can feel herself trying to lift the whole aeroplane. The huge jet is thrusting with full power, but getting no higher off the ground. Suddenly, in the same half-sleep state, she is in a light aircraft, on a calm day, floating way above the clouds. Again, she feels unsafe, but now very high in the sky. Her small aeroplane has an underpowered engine which is misfiring. She is floating all over the sky.

Jane is now fully awake. Fears of uncertainty and loneliness begin to loom but they don't take hold. Her silent prayer has been for some time that she would retain her positive feelings about herself. The negative feelings fall away as she heads for the bathroom.

The whole duplex is ringing with a quiet roar as heavy rain strikes the corrugated metal roof.

*   *   *

Fair weather overtakes the *Neptune* from the south. If the Captain's calculations are correct, midday will have the ship in Sydney Harbour.

'I wish there was more I could do, John. I feel so helpless,' says Geoff to one of the convicts.

'You've done well Geoffy. And him too,' John lifts his scabby, chained hand and points to Horace. 'He be a good kid.'

Nearly a third of the male convicts have perished so far and most of those remaining are only excuses for men. They are all aware the voyage is nearly over, but only a handful of them can raise any enthusiasm.

'That bastard Trail, he's done a good job on us, asn't he Geoff?' says John hanging his head.

Geoff agrees, but keeps his feelings to himself; he doesn't want to upset the men any further.

'Don't insult what intelligence we have left by saying everything will be all right, cos it won't be all right, will it Geoff?'

Geoff pauses. 'All I can say John, is it will be better for some than others. Soon we will all have fresh food and our feet will feel dry land again.

Several of the men who are silently listening slowly nod their heads.

Within twelve hours the *Neptune* will dock in Port Jackson. The disembarking of the prisoners will prove to be one of the saddest scenes in Britain's colonial history.

CHAPTER FORTY NINE

'I've moved, Margaret.'

'*Oh … what does that mean Jane?*'

'It means I have left Michael. Michael and I are through.'

'Well I never,' said Margaret. 'What are you doing today, love?'

'Is that it?' Jane is stunned.

'Yes, that's it. There's not much more to be said, is there?'

'Margaret, you're one of a kind.'

'Yes love, you have to be kind to be cruel.'

It takes Jane several seconds to work that one out. *It's obvious Margaret doesn't have the emotional handicaps I have at the moment,* she thinks. *Actually, I don't think she has ever had an emotional handicap in her whole life.*

'Today is going to be one of the most important days of your life, Jane,' Margaret goes on.

'Yes, yes,' says Jane, looking out of her window at the partially flooded road. 'Every new day is the start of a new life — isn't that right *Margie?*'

Margaret laughs.

'Give me a call; I'll be home tonight and tomorrow. Have to fly.' Margaret hangs up.

'Thanks a lot, friend,' Jane continues to speak. 'I'm sad, lonely, depressed, angry and frustrated, but Margaret, you don't want to know about that. You never did. By the way, I feel damn good. Speak to you soon … *mate.*'

Jane watches as the morning current affairs program converts to Humphrey B Bear.

That's a load of poppy-cock Margaret, I should have said, she thinks. *I'm looking after Beck tomorrow, so today I should do something for me, after all today is going to be the best day of my life, or so Margaret says.*

'Before I do anything, I should tidy up,' she tells herself. Picking up her clothes from the chair, she opens the closet. *There's the new dress.* Throwing her slacks across the bed, she takes the dress off its hanger, looks at it and slips it on.

'All I need now is a pumpkin carriage.' She smiles, admiring herself in the mirror. 'Not bad, not bad at all.'

She feels a compulsion to go outside, but thinks, *that's out of the question because it's pouring rain and it would look absolutely ridiculous walking along the Corso dressed like this. My weird friends Nicki and Susan went out starkers in London one night with only coats on. Will I or won't I?* She rummages through one of her cases and slips on a see-through plastic raincoat over her dress.

Looking in the mirror, she laughs a defiant laugh. Outside the rain has eased. 'I *will* go out,' she decides.

It seems all Manly is deserted as she splashes through a large puddle scaring a group of seagulls sitting on the seawall. Hoping to be fed, the last thing the gulls expected was to be harassed. They take off, squawking, and resettle well out of range of this wacky, unpredictable human. She moves onto the beach.

Her dress feels so comfortable, so sexy and so perfect. *But out of place here,* she acknowledges to herself.

'How silly,' she mutters. *Here I am on the other side of the world walking along a beach in the rain, in a dress I shouldn't be wearing and … a transparent raincoat. How nutty is that?* She giggles as she picks up a piece of wet sea sponge and begins to sing to it.

'I was all right for a while … (No, I wasn't.)

I could smile for a while … (Sometimes, I suppose.)

But I saw you last night, you held my hand so tight, as you stopped to say *goodbye.*' She laughs out loud.

'Oh, I *wished to hell*, but you couldn't tell, that I'd been, crying, crying over you … you damn, *damn* sod.'

She flings the sponge into the ocean.

In the south, the sun is breaking through the rain clouds and the whole area has a fresh golden colour about it. Up on the hill the old monastery bathed in the unusual light catches her attention.

North Head, she remembers. North Head, *that's* where *I'm* going today … that's where I'm going *right* now, she says. Then suddenly she stops and thinks, *but I can't go out there dressed like this.* 'Yes, I *can*,' she assures herself. Then she starts walking again.

'Lovely day,' says the shopkeeper of a small mixed business where Jane stops to purchase two bottles of water, a salad roll, a muesli bar and a small chocolate.

'Going to the beach?' the shopkeeper says jovially.

'I've already been to the beach. I'm now off to North Head.' Jane replies with a smile and a wink.

The storekeeper returns the smile as he looks out of the window at the weather. 'E*h* … oh. That will be exciting, have a good day. Watch your step out there won't you?'

Today is the first day of my new life, Jane light-heartedly laughs to herself. '*Isn't it Margie!*' she calls aloud as she moves off.

*   *   *

Mary is preparing herself and her own child as well as Jonathan for the arrival at Port Jackson. Apart from her relief and excitement, she has a secret, another reason to feel secure and optimistic. The marines and the free settlers cannot hide their happiness and relief about going ashore either. The crew are becoming more animated. The sound of two sailors clapping echoes down from the crow's nest. Captain and Mrs Trail come on deck. They are also relieved that the voyage is coming to an end.

Christie is not the little girl she was at the beginning of the voyage. She is much older now in many ways. She is talking to a group of passengers, every now and then confidently looking back at Geoff and Horace.

Horace too has caught some of the excitement as he talks to Geoff. 'I 'ave heard dem say, the Captain's men, we will be sailing up the harbour by twelve noon. They pointed to some mountains of rocks. They won't take Christie and me away from you, will they Mr Geoff?'

'You have to understand Horace I'm not your official guardian. I'm not sure what's going to happen lad, but it will all work out. I've had assurances from Captain Trail,' he says placing both hands on the rail.

'I dain't trust 'im.' Horace gives Trail a side-glance. He's feeling insecure. 'Ee doesn't do anything fa *me … nothin* at all. Geoff, some of the men below say they dain't wanta leave the ship. They seem to be used of it. I don't understand why he done this to them.' He glares at the Captain again.

Geoff gives him a nudge. 'I don't understand either, Horace.' He places his hand on the boy's shoulder. 'Prepare yourself, for I feel the worst is yet to come for our men in chains.'

*   *   *

The second time around, a journey rarely seems as long. This time Jane moves quickly up the road past the old monastery. If she could see herself, she would probably have kittens. There is something quite special about somebody walking along a road, after the rain, dressed in an old-world dress, a see-through raincoat, rain hat and carrying a plastic bag. The only item missing to complete this wondrous spectacle is a pair of gumboots. If God could be influenced by the determination and humour of this unusual scene, Jane would probably get the maximum amount of brownie points. She chuckles to herself. 'I feel like a giant walking condom.'

As she walks, she can smell the rain amongst the bush. The sun begins to shine and the birds become livelier — darting back and forth, chirping intensely. She can't resist picking a Banksia flower that is glistening with raindrops. She holds the gold flaxen flower as she walks further out onto the peninsular that seems of another world.

There is not a soul to be seen as she approaches the deserted bus and car park area.

'Who else would be silly enough to come out here, on a day like this?' she calls out defiantly. 'It's *so* beautiful and I have it *all* to myself!'

Standing at the cliff top, another woman looks out to sea, her white blouse and crimson scarf ruffling in the gusty, southerly wind. She turns with her back to the ocean, her hair blowing across her face.

Jane looks down at the Banksia flower she is holding. Its golden bottlebrush, made up of thousands of small stamens, fascinates her. The wind intensifies as she moves closer to the cliff edge. The low-growing Tea tree and coastal Banksia bushes remind her of an English maze. She panics a little — as a child she was once lost in a maze. She takes off her coat, rolls it with her plastic-bag and places it under a bush.

The path widens. Jane stops. Somebody else is at North Head. A motionless figure stands on the edge of the cliff as if frozen solid by the chilly ocean wind.

'*Are you okay?*' Jane calls out. There is no reply.

The wind eases, but the clouds are moving faster and faster. A small section of cliff top breaks silently away and falls to the ocean below. And then another. Jane can't take her eyes off the woman.

The trees and grasses are shaking strangely from side to side.

The Banksia flower in Jane's hand dies, shrivels, goes to seed and then to dust. Everything brightens to a yellow glow and then in a blinding flash returns to normal. Another chunk of earth and rock next to the woman cracks away and subsides but she remains motionless and unaffected

'*Can I help you? Are you cold?*' Jane calls out, again.

'No thank you, Jane.'

Jane gets nervous, thinking, *how the hell does this woman know my name? It's impossible.*

Moving closer, Jane becomes completely mesmerised by the resemblance of the woman to herself. She has identical hair, only longer. Her eyes are the same blue-green. She is slightly shorter. Her smile is warm and projects an inner kindness. *Even the small gap between her front teeth is the same as mine*, thinks Jane. *It's as if I am looking into a mirror.*

'How do you know my name? Where do you come from?' Jane asks.

'Where do any of us come from?' the woman replies.

Well, I suppose that answer is no more out there, than the dress I'm wearing, thinks Jane.

'Your dress is wonderful,' the woman comments.

'You must be as batty as I am,' says Jane looking down the front of her dress.

'Batty?' the woman asks, then laughs as she realises what Jane means.' I once had a dress just like yours.'

'At this very moment I am unsure of three things,' Jane confides. 'Why did I ever purchase this dress? Why did I wear it here? And why I am standing here talking to you? It's all so strange and not me.'

'Only strange to you, Jane,' says the woman

'Are you from London too?' asks Jane.

'Yes.'

'Are you holidaying here, working?'

'You know the answer to that question, Jane. We are both here for the same reason.'

Jane breathes in sharply. '*Margie*'.

'We don't need Margaret,' says the woman.

'You must be cold. I'll find my coat for you.' Jane looks around.

'It can't be there, Jane.'

'It must be.' Jane knows exactly where she left it. 'There are no tracks, where have the paths gone? And my coat?' Jane looks confused.

'I'm not cold, Jane, are you?'

'No … no, I'm not at all.'

The weather has moderated and the wind has changed.

'Take my hand Jane. I have something to show you'

'I've heard that one before, but it always comes from a male, well … nearly always.' Jane gives a singular laugh.

The woman looks at Jane with a questioning smile as they take each other's hand and move closer to the edge of the cliff.

'Margaret said this day would be very different for me.'

'I think Margaret could be right. Look, way into the distance, Jane.'

Jane thinks of the warning from the shopkeeper. She looks down. She is only inches away from a three hundred foot drop, but she feels safe holding this women's hand.

'I can't see anything,' she says, squinting.

'Further south, over there, closer to the coast.' The woman points.

Jane can just make out a tiny white speck.

'Oh, oh yes, it's a sailing ship,' says Jane and then turns back to the women. 'What is your name?'

'My name is Claire.'

* * *

A cry from the lookout indicates the Heads are approximately three miles due north. Everybody on deck watches as the *Neptune* rides across the last of the ocean's swell on a direct course for Port Jackson and the new settlement.

The coastline is now a continuous series of small beaches with rocky promontories reaching varying distances out to sea. The steep and sometimes sheer cliffs are topped by never-ending plateaus, vegetated mostly with low scrub. Ahead are the massive rock portals standing either side of the entrance to Port Jackson. North and South Heads. Most on board are rather disappointed with this area comparing it to the rich forests, mountains, valleys and rivers they saw further south.

'Jonathon will miss mummy at this place,' says Christie to Horace. It's the first time she's talked to either Horace or Geoff about her mother.

Horace, who knows how it feels to be parentless, moves closer to Christie and distracts her by pointing out a small cove and pretty beach. Next minute Christie is chasing Horace around the deck. He joins in the fun in spite of the sad conversation they have had only minutes before.

Several orders are shouted out and a sharp adjustment to starboard is made to the ship's course to avoid striking a semi-submerged offshore reef. The children run to the front of the ship and walk slowly back to watch the huge rock reef, skirted in kelp, which appears to move by like a pod of whales, splashing, surfacing, and subsiding beneath the large swell.

For the first time Geoff has caught sight of Australia's Aboriginal population. They stand like stick figures, blending with the rocks, the scrub and trees. Some young native children run along the beach trying to keep up with the ship, but they are left far behind.

Geoff hands the field glass he has borrowed, back to another crewmember.

'Look at the savages.' The crew are bunched along the port side of the ship. In spite of information from Cook's voyage regarding the lack of sexual prowess of the Australian Aboriginal women compared to that of the Pacific islanders, it does not stop the fantasies of the crew.

*   *   *

'Who are you, Claire?'

'I am *you*, Jane,' she replies.

Jane looks at Claire amazed, she can see they resemble each other but, *that's ridiculous*, she thinks.

'Why do I look like you? Why am I standing here with you looking at a ship in the distance?'

'It is me that looks like you Jane. All will be very clear to you soon.' Claire looks at her with a smile and then out to sea again.

'It's a sailing ship,' says Jane, her mind still trying to sort everything out. 'It must be the replica of the *Bounty* doing a tour.'

'No, Jane, that is not a replica. It's the *Neptune* and he is aboard.'

'Who is aboard?'

'Geoff, of course.'

Jane recalls the dream she experienced on the flight from London. *That was the Neptune!* she thinks. *And his name was Geoff.*

'My God!' Jane exclaims.

'Do you want me to pinch you, Jane?' Claire smiles as if she knows exactly what is in Jane's mind.

Jane pinches herself and smiles. 'So, I've pinched myself in a dream?'

'Just go with it, Jane.' Claire reassures her.

'Last time I heard those words, I became pregnant. I just don't understand.'

'You will. Trust me.'

Jane looks across the harbour to the city centre. *There are no buildings, no ferries,* she thinks in some amazement.

The two women move closer together as the *Neptune* ploughs through a choppy sea.

'You say his name is *Geoff* and he is on *that* ship?'

CHAPTER FIFTY

Geoff is not about to die, but his whole life seems to be streaming before his eyes.

My new life here in New South Wales, he thinks, *will be like a re-birth.*

He feels he has both accomplished a great deal and made many mistakes on the voyage. He still feels sure he could have done more for Sarah. But, as Horace so maturely reminded him, using Geoff's very own words, each person is responsible for their own actions. He can see Horace talking and bantering with some of the crewmen, and thinks, *he's a good lad.* Nothing can ever take away the experience we have both had together on this voyage of misery.

Geoff looks at the crew individually. He sees men who, mostly, love the sea and adventure. He sees bravado which is rooted in loneliness and fear. He sees men paying for their past deeds and their future dreams with blood, sweat, and repression of conscience. His mind switches quickly to thinking about Trail. *Why do I see any good in that bastard?* 'My God!' he says aloud, 'in some ways I'm like *Trail* myself!'

*   *   *

Jane is fighting what is happening to her, but as the *Neptune* draws closer, she can't help feeling intrigued.

Margaret said this would be one of the most important days of my life, she tells herself again.

Claire is smiling at her.

*   *   *

Salt spray from small choppy waves flings past Geoff, occasionally wetting his face. Looking into the water from the front of the ship, reminds him of the first day he met Claire on the seawall — her face, her frustration, and the mackerel she threw into his arms. He remembers the pain of her temporary disappearance and the joy when they re-met at Tintagel. He thinks with sadness and regret of the wonderful days in London and the terrifying sadness of her death. The truth about his relationship with Claire, and himself, continues to untangle itself.

'I loved her so much, why could she not stay? Why did she have to take her life?' he says quietly across the waves.

*   *   *

Holding Claire's hand tightly, Jane can now feel a physical connection with the ship and Geoff.

It was all too much, Geoff, Claire thinks to herself. *It was all too much.* 'I love you Geoff,' she calls aloud to the *Neptune.*

Jane puts her arm around Claire's shoulder.

'Jane, I can *still* feel the pain,' Claire says. 'I remember the agonising moments after I took the poison. I remember when I first met Geoff … how he swept me off my feet and made me so angry at the same time. He's a good man and *much* more,' she sighs. 'And the day we re-met at Tintagel, the beautiful day we were married, my garden and stone, my special dress …' She touches Jane's dress. 'Why *couldn't* he *understand*'?

Jane stands dumbfounded.

'My stone meant *everything* to me. It just split in two. Why, Jane … *why?*'

Jane has no answer. She feels strange. Everything is beyond her control, but somehow all right. The warmth she feels for Claire and Geoff is overwhelming. *The answer to this whole thing, up here on the cliffs, is possibly aboard that ship, down there,* she thinks.

The *Neptune* is drawing closer. The direction of the wind will cause the ship to sail very close to North Head before coming about to position itself for the final home run up the harbour to the new colony.

*　　*　　*

The views from the deck of the *Neptune,* are spectacular. For a moment the captain's navigation skills again flash into Geoff's mind. Then thoughts of the men below and the bodies of their dead compatriots spread across the oceans of the world, sicken him. Trail is a talented, but barbarous, man.

The sheer cliffs of North Head loom closer and closer. Huge waves surge and smash at the dark base of the age-old sandstone cliffs causing a crackling, echoing, hollow-thundering sound.

The *Neptune* finishes its run and will soon begin to come about. Geoff's eyes follow one of two large white birds circling high around the cliff tops. He can't believe what he sees.

'Look up there, *Horace, Christie*! There are two ladies at the top of the cliff.'

'Where, Geoff? … probably *savages*,' says Horace.

A group gathers around them.

'It looks like my Claire waving to me!'

'There's nothin' up there but rocks and scrub, Geoff.' Horace wrinkles his forehead, squinting intensely.

'That's wishful thinking,' says one of the crew. The rest begin to laugh.

'*He's bin at sea too long!*' another calls and they laugh again.

'Here, take this you may want to have a closer look, Geoff,' says Sergeant Thomas. He hands Geoff his field glass, hoping to get his friend off the hook.

'*Yes! See!* … there they are. There *are* two women.'

The crew cheer.

'Look up there.' He focuses the glass. It's Claire and, Horace, it's … They both look exactly the same.'

'*Wow!*' the onlookers exclaim in unison.

Horace looks scared.

Geoff then stops, realising what he has said. His surprise and excitement to see Claire and her friend is momentarily crushed by the disbelieving crowd.

Horace is hoping he will be able to confirm Geoff's sighting as he scans the cliff tops through the field glass that Geoff has pushed into his hands.

'Nah, I can see nothin,' Geoff. You're joking with us.'

'Can I look too?' asks Christie. She attempts to hold the glass correctly. '*I can* … I can see two fine ladies,' she says, unconvincingly, then turns away and begins to cry.

There is a momentary hush.

She takes Geoff's hand and her look asks him to stop this make-believe.

∗　　∗　　∗

'There're so many people Claire, is that Geoff! Near the lifeboat?'

'*Yes. Yes* that's my husband! *Yes, yes,* that's Geoff! Oh my *goodness!* That's him, that is him! *Geoff!*'

Jane finds herself waving just as frantically as Claire. The *Neptune* turns slowly.

∗　　∗　　∗

Geoff quickly moves to the other side of the ship. The crew who are not busy with manoeuvres follow him, some supporting him, some preying on his disposition, and some actually caught up in this fascinating fantasy. Most on board are convinced Geoff has lost his mind. The first mate Ellington does not know what to think.

'There she is,' jokes another crewmember. And there's *a mermaid* down on the rocks.' They all laugh again.

By now most on deck, including the Captain, are staring up at the cliffs. As the ship begins to pull away, Geoff quietly watches and waves to Claire and her companion.

Nobody else can see them. What the hell is going on? It feels like only yesterday I found my wife at Tintagel. And now I have the same kind of feelings I had then. Is all this a dream? Am I going mad? he wonders.

'Horace,' he says, as his young friend appears next to him.

'Yes, Mr Geoff?'

'You can see them, can't you?' Geoff whispers.

'Mr Geoff this has bin a bad voyage,' he talks into Geoff's ear. 'You show'd me, and I seen how a man can 'magine things. The men down below need us Geoff, lets put all this dreaming aside and be with them, eh? What do you think?'

Geoff now seriously begins to doubt his own sanity. *I can still see them, what the hell is going on?* he thinks. Still able to make out two distinct figures on the cliff top, he gives them a final wave. *Maybe our arrival in the new land and that nightmare of a voyage has just been too much for me,* he wonders.

In one last attempt to prove to himself it is Claire, he thrusts two hands into the air as he did the day he found her again at Tintagel.

'He's waving Jane, look he's waving again.' Claire raises her two hands.

If this is an hallucination, it's an amazing one, Geoff thinks to himself.

Most of the crew imitate him and begin waving with two

hands. It's the joke of the voyage. The *Neptune* begins to sail into the entrance of Sydney Harbour.

'Take another look Horace, just above that large protruding rock shelf, a little back to the left.' Geoff quietly urges.

'I can't see anything Geoff, honest, Geoff, I can't.' Horace whispers. He is disappointed for his friend.

Christie, upset, scared and confused returns to the women's quarters. Horace and Geoff climb down the companion ladder to the Orlop Deck, where tension rather than lessoning amongst the convicts, as could be expected, is in fact, building.

*　　*　　*

'The ships will moor somewhere way over there. That's where our Geoff will be, Jane.'

Jane stares at Claire with astonishment. She is now convinced that the sailing ships are authentic. She watches the other ship follow the *Neptune* into the harbour. The modern city of Sydney is not where it should be and Manly is not visible from where she is standing.

'Claire, we must talk about Geoff. I …'

'We have all the time in the world, Jane,' says Claire, giving her the warmest of hugs. 'I can't *believe* I've seen him again.'

Jane wonders about Michael. Has all this been affecting my relationship with him? 'Don't leave me Claire, will you?' Jane is feeling quite disorientated and fragile.

'How can I leave you if I have been with you all along?' Claire half whispers.

'God, you're beginning to sound more and more like Margaret. Where are you staying Claire?'

'It's not as simple as that, Jane. You still really don't understand, do you?'

'No I don't understand, Claire.'

'For a short time you've had a glimpse into the past and I've had a brief journey into the future,' says Claire. 'I've seen Geoff again and now I know he is safe. And soon I will be gone'.

'Where are you going to, Claire?'

'Back from where I came, I suppose, where we all come from. You see I was responsible for what happened to Geoff, but I've seen him again and I know he will be fine.'

'Please come with me Claire, I can't lose you now I just found you. We can go to my house and talk, we …' Jane coaxes. Claire appears to think for a moment, moves two steps towards her, but then stops.

'Damn! Where is that coat of mine?' cries Jane.

A mist is rolling in from the east. The sandy tracks begin to harden and then turn to asphalt. The air warms to a summer temperature. The mist develops a golden sheen and again the vegetation begins to pulsate.

'Here it is; I've found my coat. Claire, look!' Jane turns. 'Where's she gone? I've *lost* her, I've lost her!' she cries. She edges carefully back through the mist watching her footing. 'Claire, where are you? Where are you? *Don't go,* I've just found you. *Claire! Claire!* Please don't go away from me. *Claire I need you.*' Jane sinks to her knees and puts out her hand. 'Don't go Claire,' she cries. 'Don't leave me in this world.'

'I will always be with you, Jane,' whispers a voice through the mist.

'Where are you, I'll come with you Claire.' Jane stands and moves to the very edge of the cliff.

'*No!* no! Go back, Jane, go back! It's too dangerous for you here.'

Beside a large stone, which protrudes out over the edge of the cliff face, Jane finds Claire pale and vague. She takes her by the hand.

'There is more for both of us, Claire. You can't go away, not now.'

'Jane, please take this.' Claire hands her the crimson silk scarf from around her neck. For a moment their eyes stare at each other.

'I've seen him Jane,' says Claire. She thought it had all been settled, but now she is the one who is confused.

'Claire, stay with me.' Jane sees hesitation in Claire's eyes. With the scarf knotted around her hand she binds the other end to Claire's wrist.

The wind builds to gale force then drops back to a breeze. Through the clearing mist Jane can see the modern skyline of Sydney, its suburbs and Sydney tower. The harbour is dotted with small motor craft, modern yachts and ferries. A jet streaks overhead.

'Claire, Claire that is Sydney.' Jane points, but when she turns around Claire has gone. The scarf that was binding their hands is still stretched out and weighted.

'I can feel you there, but I can't see you Claire.'

'I'm with you Jane.'

'Where, where are you?'

'Please trust yourself, Jane.'

The scarf goes limp.

*　　*　　*

On 28 June 1790, the *Neptune* enters the harbour. Convicts are still dying in its hold as it approaches the new settlement. Bodies are ordered to be dumped overboard and are later found washed up on the shores of the harbour.

Geoff and Horace are preoccupied with a new and unexpected decline in the condition of the convicts. It was thought the convicts' morale would improve with their imminent arrival. This generally is not the case. The men have been below for so long that their bodies and most of their minds cannot conceive things can be any different. Shock and disillusionment has taken over the Orlop deck.

'A man would have ta be well and strong to start again. We *are* all buggered, Geoff,' was the sad sentiment of one of the men in chains.

The full horror of what had taken place on the voyage becomes apparent when the disembarkation of the convicts begins.

The Reverend Richard Johnson, who was the chaplain on the First Fleet, witnessed the terrible scene and wrote:

The landing of those people was truly affecting and shocking. Great numbers were not able to walk or to move hand or foot. Such were slung over the ship's side in the same manner they would a cask, a box or anything of that nature. Upon them being brought up to the open air, some fainted, some died upon the deck, and others in boats before they reached the shore. When come on shore, many of them were not able to walk, to stand, or stir themselves in the least, hence some were led by others. Some creeped upon their hands and knees, and some were carried on the backs of others.

CHAPTER FIFTY ONE

ane has never felt so alone in her life. For an hour she sits huddled at the edge of the cliff, Claire's scarf still tied to her wrist.

I don't understand what is happening to me. Is Claire something my mind has created, or is she real? She looks down at Claire's scarf. *Just when I meet somebody really special she is taken away from me.* She puts the scarf to her cheek. 'Claire *please* come back. *Don't go!*' she agonisingly calls out over the cliff-top.

Fifteen minutes pass and the same questions are spinning around and around in her mind. *She said she was from London? How can that be? Geoff, is he her husband? Why did she appear to me, and how? Where do I fit in? Well here am I looking stupid in my fabulous dress, stuck out here at the heads.* Oh god it's getting hot.

She checks again. Evidence of modern Sydney is now everywhere to be seen. It is raining in the distance and there is not a soul around. Trying to brush the dirty, grey sand off her dress she prepares to walk back to Manly. 'Oh God it's hot,' she says to herself. Picking up her raincoat she takes a drink from the bottle in her plastic bag. Looking back over her shoulder she half-heartedly begins to walk away.

'It's a taxi! A taxi out here?' She is relieved.

The driver slows and indicates he will pick her up after dropping off his fare. She spreads her raincoat on the ground in the shade of a Banksia bush and sits down. *Just as well that cab came along,* she thinks nibbling on her melting chocolate bar. *Imagine the sight of me walking through the main street of Manly dressed like this, heaven forbid. I can't believe what just happened.* 'I just can't believe it,' she repeats to herself.

The taxi returns, pulling Jane abruptly back to reality with an over-loud blast from its horn.

'You look like you've been through the wringer. Great party, eh?' The cab driver comments off-handedly.

'So good I feel like I've come out of another century,' Jane replies.

'That's the way it looks,' he says. He has seen it all before.

The taxi weaves through the reserve and down past the old monastery into Manly.

'Over there, the cream duplex.' Jane points, handing the cabbie a twenty-dollar note.

She climbs out of the taxi, her mind still in two worlds. *Thank God nobody saw me. I must ring Margaret,* she thinks.

Sitting down on the sofa, she has four sips of her tea, puts the cup down, and falls into a deep sleep.

*　　*　　*

It is the fourth of July 1790. The colony has had its hopes lifted and dashed. Just on five hundred sick and dying and limited provisions have been landed from the surviving ships of the Second Fleet.

Due to the many fatalities, a large pit has been dug to be used as a mass grave. With little ceremony, the convict bodies that survived the voyage of hell, but died immediately on arrival, are wrapped in coarse sacking cloth and dropped into the communal grave. Governor Phillip has no option.

The Sydney Cove Chronicle reported on the thirteenth of June, 1790.

DIABOLICAL CONDITION OF THE CONVICTS THEREON

At last, the transports are here, two hundred and seventy eight died on the fearsome journey to Sydney Cove. The landing of those who remained alive despite their misuse upon the recent voyage, could not fail to horrify those who watched. As they came on shore, these wretched people were hardly able to move hand or foot. Such as could not carry themselves upon their legs, crawled upon all fours. Those who, through their afflictions, were not able to move were thrown over the side of the ships as sacks of flour would be thrown, into the small boats. Some expired in the boats, others as they reached the shore. Some fainted and were carried by those who fared better. More had not the opportunity even to leave their ocean prisons for as they came upon the decks, the fresh air only hastened their demise. A sight most outrageous to our eyes were the marks of leg irons upon the convicts, so deep that one could nigh on see their bones.

✳   ✳   ✳

Geoff and Horace are no longer responsible for their men. They sit under a large gum tree on a bed of rushes. Their blankets and tents are still to be unloaded from the hold of the HMAS Justinian.

It is cold. A campfire warms them and twelve other men. The afternoon meal consisted of stewed vegetables, mostly turnips, and fresh berries. The meal was tasty, hot and plentiful. They have been promised some meat.

As the sun sinks into the western sky, Geoff looks out over a rolling countryside covered in an unbroken forest leading to a low mysterious chain of blue mountains on the western horizon.

The dusk is calm and still. The men are joking and one is

playing a harmonica. Horace imitates standing on the rolling deck of a ship — everybody laughs. Most are still feeling similar sensations.

Geoff turns to the north-east, towards the cliffs of North Head. *Was yesterday just my imagination?* In his mind he can still clearly see Claire and the other woman on the cliffs. He decides that from now on he will spare Horace, Christie and everybody else any further comment on that matter.

The birds are settling for the night, but there are animals moving about in the scrub. On the previous night howling dog-like creatures visited the community grave pit, tearing the sack cloths from around the dead and devouring some human flesh.

Geoff finds it difficult to stay positive when there is so much confusion and despair around him. He looks up at the stars, which are mixed with glowing cinders swirling up from the fire. They steady him.

Geoff has read Sir Isaac Newton who wrote about the speed of sound and light. Mr Newton has determined that the distance of the stars from earth is immense and that light from the stars can take millions of years to reach earth. A star could perish but still be visible for many years as its light continues to arrive on earth. *There could be far away stars now in existence but their light has not reached us yet,* Geoff's thinks, his mind flashes back to Claire and the other woman on North Head.

'*What the hell is going on?*' he whispers to himself.

'Are you all right, Geoff? It's all over now.' Horace mumbles, half asleep.

'Yes lad, yes I'm fine.' Geoff turns over and tucks in for the night. While the men have to sleep out in the open, Christie and Jonathan who are with Mary and the women have the luxury of canvas over their heads.

The immediate threats of the voyage, the uncertainty of the actions of Captain Trail and Chief Mate Ellington are now in the past. Geoff and Horace's deck of life's cards are being reshuffled and now other concerns move to the top of their packs.

Throughout the night the camp-fire is the only reason Geoff and Horace don't freeze to death. At one point, Horace has the fire burning so fiercely everybody wakes up.

'I was only trying to *help*,' pleads Horace as the other men, half-asleep, abuse him as they haul themselves back from the raging fire. 'You'll set the whole bloody forest alight, *you bedlamite*,' whinges one man.

Horace just shrugs his shoulders.

The very loud, strident sounds of two large brown and white kookaburras break the dawn silence. In spite of this raucous noise, most sleep on except for Geoff who, though he slept through Horace's fire incident, is first to awake in the half morning light.

Geoff sits and watches as several black men walk through the perimeter of the camp area. *Some harmony does exist, then, between the new settlers and the Aboriginal people*, he thinks. A distinctive youngish Indian, the only one in the group dressed in European clothing, singles Geoff out, stares at him for an extended moment, then goes.

The fledgling colony is waking. Some enthusiastic exclamations break through the overwhelming silence as both men and women ready themselves for the day. The dying, the sick and the freeloaders balance on the edge of despair. The most intense centres of activity are on the ships in the harbour, the Marine Barracks and the hospital.

The men from Geoff and Horace's camp herald the new day by christening the gum trees with urine. Built-up intestinal wind trumpets aloud, varying in length and pitch, to temporarily pollute the freshness of the morning air. Some laugh like schoolboys at their farting, some keep a serious face, some pretend it never happened at all.

The rising of the sun causes an extra chill to the air as the night dampness uses what warmth it can find to convert itself to vapour. At this time the fires are usually stoked, the dancing flames coaxing vulnerable minds away from the tight grip of night fears.

The new day brings with it more mixed feelings about the realities surrounding the arrival of the Second Fleet. The loss of the fleet's supply ship, *Guardian*, off the coast of South Africa, means there is a shortfall in the materials and supplies. The reassurance and moral support the fleet brings from the homeland, is, however very welcome.

* * *

Jane awakes with a start, at 4.30 pm still exhausted. She strips off her dress and tries to resettle. *I must ring Margaret*, she thinks. Having no other person to share these unusual and exciting events with is nearly unbearable. 'I could write a book, I could be famous,' she says to herself. 'Nobody would believe me, I'm sure.'

A comforting fantasy that Claire is asleep in the next room helps her back to sleep. But fifteen minutes later she stirs again. Half awake she sees Claire clearly in her mind and again hears her voice. She fumbles to her feet and looks into the mirror.

'Maybe I did not love Geoff enough?' says Claire.

'Maybe you didn't trust him enough Claire?' says Jane.

'How far do you trust and how long do you wait, Jane?'

Jane can hear Claire's voice crystal clear.

I suppose true love waits forever. Jane can't believe she has just thought that. *How does this apply to Michael and me?* she wonders. *And what about Greg and my other relationships?*

'What determines true love, Claire?' Jane feels fully awake as she talks out loud again. She is concerned about what is happening but the words just keep coming. Her trance-like state continues as she returns to the sofa.

'It's a search,' replies Claire, 'for that inner dream within, a dream that another can reflect back and share with you … the reflection in the water of the clearest, deepest pool in the heart of a remote forest.'

'Is that easy to find?' asks Jane.

'Probably impossible,' replies Claire.

'There's a song Claire, a song written in the last sixty years. I *love* it. Jane begins to sing the song she has not heard since she was five or six years old.

You may not be an angel, cause angels are so few.

But until the day that one comes along, I'll string along with you.

I'm looking for an angel to sing my love song to, and until the day that one comes along, I'll sing my song to you.

For every little fault you have, say I've got three or four, the human faults that you do have, just make me love you more.

'Those words are so lovely, Jane.'

Tears are now running down Jane's cheeks.

'Well … where do we go from here, Claire … what do we do next? I'd really like to talk to you about Geoff.'

'We just take each moment as it comes, I suppose,' says Claire's voice from within.

'Claire, are you *really* there?' Jane picks up Claire's scarf and holds it to the side of her face for reassurance.

* * *

'Hello, hello, Margaret, I don't know where to begin.'

This time Margaret is willing to listen and Jane can at last fill her in completely on the visit to North Head, Claire, Geoff on the *Neptune*, and the Michael saga. 'Don't you think all this is a little strange, Margaret? It really scares me.'

'What I think is strange is how long it takes us to adapt to changing circumstances. But I assure you we all do adapt. I am just adapting a little more quickly than you love.'

'Well, what happens next?'

'Didn't Claire tell you?'

'That's another thing; Claire is still talking to me …'

Margaret interrupts her, 'Go with it Jane, there's nothing wrong with you, this sort of thing has been known to happen,' she assures her.

'Has anything like this ever happened to you?'

'No, but I am experiencing this with you. The weather should be fine for the rest of the week, good picnic weather.

'Again, Margaret, lets not start that.'

'Jane, I don't start anything. All that's going to happen started long ago, hundreds of years ago in fact. I'm here if you need me, love. Speak to you soon.'

Jane is left with the familiar, 'you didn't let me finish feeling,' for Margaret has hung up.

*　　*　　*

'I wonder if we will see Christie and Jonathan today?' says Geoff.

'I dain't think we 'ave any say about that Geoff,' replies Horace, tilting his head to one side. He misses them both as well, but at the same time he is enjoying Geoff's exclusive company.

A group of fit convict men, including Geoff and Horace, are rostered to assist with the unloading of the *Justinian*, the sister ship to the *Neptune*.

CHAPTER FIFTY TWO

awn breaks across Manly. Jane stirs from sleep.

Good morning Jane.

She sits up. *That was Claire's voice,* she thinks.

'Claire is that you?' she calls out, feeling a little stupid.

Do you have any porridge? Geoff and I would have porridge often.

This is ridiculous, Jane thinks. The events of the previous day are now beginning to stagger her. *This past year has not been good. Things haven't improved since I met Michael. Yesterday I dressed up, God only knows why. Met Claire ... did I really? And saw Geoff arrive in Sydney in the year 1790. My God.*

Still half asleep Jane ambles to the kitchen and smiles as she reaches for a pack of porridge.

'What are you smiling at, Jane?'

Jane ignores the voice. *That's impossible, I must be crackers, but it is still nice to hear that voice again,* she thinks.

Trying to put the events of the previous day behind her she decides to have breakfast, shower, spend the morning cleaning house and then some shopping. She is meeting Becky after school at 3.15 pm.

Becky's school was built in the early twentieth century. Its red-brick construction with long vertical cream, segmentally glazed windows and cream trim is a direct telltale sign of Australia's early link with England.

'Ah, there's Becky.' Jane waves excitedly and runs to scoop her up into her arms.

'I miss you lots and lots. When are you coming *home*, Jane?' says Becky sadly.

'I don't know if I will be able to, Beck.'

Jane can't help but notice how Becky accepts the news so readily. *Poor kid*, she thinks.

Jane stays with Becky until 6.15 when a babysitter takes over. Michael will be home late.

*   *   *

Attitudes towards women in the colony, apart from those with husbands, are only marginally better than those exhibited towards female Aborigines. White females are considered prostitutes, unless married.

During the three days Geoff has been in the colony, he has quickly become aware of such things. He has also heard stories of the organised murder of the natives and some raping of their women.

'God only knows what the Aborigines think of us,' he comments to Horace.

'You've gotta agree, Geoff. They *are* useless. What good do they do? What do *we* care what *they* think?'

Geoff is surprised. But sentiment against the Aborigines is running strong in the colony. It's not difficult to see how a lad like Horace can be influenced.

'You know they've bin killin' people. Look at dem lot over there, just standing and looking at you and me with those black faces and shifty eyes. He turns toward them. 'Whatcha ye looking at you *black* bastards!' he yells, then lowers his voice. 'Don't worry Geoff, they don't know what I'm sayin'. They come out of the scrub, spear and bash people's brains out and, *and*, then they pretend it never happened. That cain't go on, we have to guard ourselves, don't we Geoff?'

Geoff, knowing about the history of the colonisation of America can see history repeating itself in Australia.

'I bin talkin' to a freed convict. If a man wants to work 'ere, he can do well.' Horace goes on. 'The government says, after a man has worked hard he can earn his freedom and a bit of free land. A man can then get himself a wife,' he beams.

'They're all *sluts* son, and those, the black ones …!' comes the uninvited comment of a middle-aged convict from another ship who's overheard Horace talking.

'They could be your sisters, or your wife. How can you talk like dat?' replies Horace. 'They're not ya mother dat's for sure. Cause you didn't have one I thinks.'

'Have a bit of that black arse then son if that's the way you feel, they're not my kind.'

'You not be talking about … *them?* He points to a group of Aboriginals. Those ones aren't my kind *either.*' He lifts his fists. Geoff moves to restrain him.

CHAPTER FIFTY THREE

In their small tent situated on a muddy hillside, Geoff and Horace are waiting on a decision by the authorities about Geoff's request to see Christie and Jonathan. It is early evening when two marines come and hand him an envelope. He opens it quickly, paying no attention to the markings on the outside. He cannot believe what he is reading.

'Trail,' he says. 'It's *impossible.*'

'What is it, Geoff? What is it?' says Horace, excitedly staring at the letter he can't read.

'*Trail*, that bastard, has come through!' Geoff says waving the letter up and down. 'The Governor has *waived* my sentence. It says down here.'

> … For your part in saving the *Neptune*, and all lives aboard.
>
> I, Arthur Phillip, Governor of New South Wales, with all powers vested in me, hereby revoke your sentence. A Certificate of *Freedom has been issued.* You are free within Australia, but there are conditions applicable if you decide to return to England.
> Governor Arthur Phillip

Several of the men gather around hooked into Geoff's feelings of excitement, staring intently at his letter.

'We can visit Christie and Jonathan.' But Geoff, completely overwhelmed by this news, has momentarily overlooked one of its implications. On board the *Neptune* wherever Geoff went, so did Horace.

Horace is way ahead of Geoff. He figured out what the letter meant shortly after Geoff commenced reading. As he dashes off through the rain Geoff tries to grab at the lad's shirt, then sets off after him, but quickly loses him.

Where's he gone? Maybe he headed for the bush where two men disappeared last week. The brutal murders of two convicts committed by the Aborigines, flash through his mind. The bushland around the camp is black and wet.

'Who goes there?'

At the southern edge of the settlement two marines, standing guard by a fire, stop Geoff. He asks if they saw Horace go into the scrub.

'He didn't get past here. What are *you* doing out here?' says one of the guards aiming his musket at Geoff's head. 'What's that?' he asks pointing to the folded piece of paper in Geoff's hand.

Geoff shows him. The other guard snatches the letter and pretends to throw it into the fire, but then hands it back.

'We've heard about you.' Their manner softens.

'Now, about your mate — we would have blown his bloody balls off if he'd tried to get past here', said the other, and they laugh, signalling with their guns for Geoff to go back.

Geoff returns to the tent. Horace hasn't returned.

'He be fine. He can't go far that's no doubt,' says one of the men.

'Maybe he's pinched a lighter and set sail for England,' another jokes.

'He'll have to get used of it, Geoff', says John, one of Horace's young mates. 'He'll be Jake.'

As Geoff decides to go out and look for Horace again, there is a ruckus at the bottom of the camp. A man has been flung out of a tent onto the muddy roadway.

'That'll be him!' says Geoff as he runs to where the commotion took place.

He finds Horace lying dejected in a sorry, muddy mess.

'What did you run out for? Talk to me Horace.' Geoff tries to help him up.

'I can git up meself … I can look after meself Geoff. Don't ya know by now,' he says trying to scrape the mud off his hands and clothes. 'I be fine. After all we have been through on dat *bloody* ship, this won't problem me a bit.'

The look in Horace's eyes upsets Geoff. It reminds him of the first time he met the boy.

'Don't be scared for me, Geoff. I be fine.' Horace goes on. 'Ya've teached me Geoff. Ya teached me much.' A combination of fear, determination and strength breaks through the thick layer of mud on his face.

After all he has taught him, Geoff cannot now weaken the lad by showing a lack of confidence in him. The two men look at one another for several long moments and then hug.

'Oh *shit*, you've got mud all over me, you little scruff,' says Geoff with warmth in his tone.

'*Little* eh!' says Horace and laughs as he upends Geoff into the quagmire. Geoff, sitting on his backside in the putrid water, kicks Horace's feet out from under him, bringing him down into the mud for the second time. They both sit there laughing.

'Look Geoff,' Horace points. 'There they are again, dem same blacks. They give me the creeps. What does you think they's looking at?'

'With all that mud on your face, maybe they think you are one of them.'

'Dah! Don't you be stupid Geoff?'

CHAPTER FIFTY FOUR

s news gets around about Geoff's good luck, a handful of men from his mess group on the *Neptune* wish him well. Without exception, they agree (that to quote one), 'that bastard Trail has done the right thing by, Geoff.' He assures them all he won't be far away. He has subsequently been granted permission by the relevant authorities for him to see Christie and Jonathan. He can hardly wait. No such luck for Horace. He puts on a brave front.

Geoff's first walk of freedom is to the women's encampment. Conditions become obvious as he approaches the area. Though it has more amenities compared to the ship: disillusionment and depression has created a squalor all of its own.

Christie bubbles with excitement when she sees Geoff. She runs shrieking to his arms, grabbing and holding him like she will never let go.

'I was *so* scared Mr Geoff so scared I would *never* see you *again*,' she says in a very grown-up manner, looking straight into his eyes.

'I've been worrying about you too. I missed you *so* much, it's good to see you, love,' he says surrounding her skinny little body with his strong arms.

Standing shyly behind Christie is Mary holding baby Jonathan and her boy. Geoff gives Mary a bit of a hug and takes hold of Jonathan's tiny hands. Jonathan smiles and goos; extending his stiffened little legs up and down with excitement.

'He knows me. He's smiling at me! Look Mary.'

'He smiles at *all* the men,' Mary says jokingly. 'He's a happy little fellow. And so ya's a *free* man now Geoffrey?'

He nods. 'It feels real good, Mary.'

'When are we going, Geoff?' says Christie.

Geoff is caught by surprise. He kneels down. 'I can't, I can't take you from here love,' he says, his voice straining. 'Not yet anyway,' he tries to explain. 'The soldiers and the law won't let me.' Mary has already partly prepared Christie, but she still goes quiet.

They all sit down on a bank overlooking the harbour and watch ships of the Second Fleet being unloaded.

'It's cold at night, Mr Geoff,' says Christie spontaneously.

'There aren't enough blankets to go around, Geoff. Some sleep under old canvass from ship's sails,' Mary says, in a resigned tone. 'Christie has *three* little friends, haven't ya love?' balancing the negative as she usually does.

Christie nods and points. Four disillusioned women and three scraggy kids stare at Mary.

'Those *bitches* …' Mary stops, and thinks about what she was going to say. 'Would you be considering marriage then, Geoff?' She comes straight to the point.

'I have nothing to offer anybody at present, Mary.' He looks at her. There is nothing more he can say. They stare at each other for a moment. Mary continues to stare while he turns to Christie and reaches into a calico bag.

'I have bought something for you, Christie.'

'Jonathon and I can come with you *soon*, can't we, Mr Geoff?' says Christie, her mind now fixed on the future.

'Love, I want you to listen to me carefully.' He moves closer to Christie. 'I love you and Jonathan very much, but sometimes we can't always choose what we want. And there's something else I've learnt.' He draws her even closer. 'It is …' he lowers his voice to a whisper, 'that magic things do happen.'

'It wasn't magic what happened to my Mummy, was it?' Christie says earnestly.

'No it wasn't, but look at this little fellow.' He coaxes Jonathan from Mary.

'He's a bit of magic, isn't he?'

Christie looks at her brother and then back at Geoff.

'He's just me brover. He can be such a horror sometimes, he can.'

Geoff looks at Mary and they both can't help but smile.

'I'll come and see you again tomorrow, love. Oh! I nearly forgot.' Sitting Jonathan between his legs on the grass, Geoff takes some sweets and other food items from his bag and passes them to Christie and Mary.

Christie pops a sweet into her mouth, offers one of them to Mary and puts the others into the front of her smock. She gives Geoff a bit of a wink and returns bravely to Mary's side, seemingly resigned.

'I'll get some more supplies to you,' he tells Mary as he says goodbye to her.

She begins to realise marriage with Geoff was ever only a pipe dream. Her situation, however, is not desperate. She has not told Geoff, but she has another suitor.

Geoff looks back over his shoulder and waves. The four of them make a sad, lonely sight, which rips at his heart. He will find a way to help them.

Geoff may be free, but the unpredictable violence of the Aborigines and the harshness of the Australian bush confine the whole settlement.

He now has many new options. An allocation of land is available to him as an emancipated convict. If there is any possibility that Horace can work with him, he will pursue that. Before he can become Christie and Jonathan's official guardian he knows he must have his own dwelling and a wife.

He walks down the settlement's wide muddy main street. Many businesses are beginning to thrive. There is optimism alongside the fear that shows on many faces.

What the hell did I do to deserve this? Why do I have to walk this bloody tight rope? he thinks.

Geoff wants to be alone on his first night of freedom. He takes a chance and finds himself at the edge of the forest climbing into a huge hollowed-out gum tree that he and Horace discovered on the first day they arrived. He sits, intending to settle for a while, kept warm by an old moth-eaten, sea-smelling, marine coat given to him by his friend Thomas. He relishes the freedom. In the safety and warmth of his primeval hide-out he falls asleep.

Wakening at midnight, he is cramped and cold. Several ships' bells ring across the harbour confirming the hour. In spite of his freedom he still feels overwhelmingly pessimistic. He is shaky, homesick and scared and wonders if life's invitation to him, to be happy and content, is nothing but a subtle trap. *What's the use of it all?* he thinks. He searches for something to pin his hopes onto. The night is dark and foreboding. Negative pictures of everybody he loves flashes through his mind — he sees their struggle, he feels their sorrow and pain. The world and all its horrors flash before him. He is appalled at the pain caused by his country's empire building. Claire and he often talked about the ancient struggles of Britain — the invasions of the Picts, the Vikings, the Gauls, the Romans and the Normans. *Why did my country not learn from the horrors of these invasions? Why do they repeat the same?* he thinks. He can feel the distant thrill of these iniquities titillating, massaging and coercing his psyche, but he understands that he is himself the product of all that has gone before him — the positive and the negative. His mythical hero, King Arthur and his quest to rid England of all invading forces and to uphold the dignity of the ordinary man, triumphantly rides into his mind. He imagines Arthur fighting the good fight.

The darkness of the past begins to lighten.

'God, let me see and learn from all these things,' he says quietly, 'and I want to know myself — who am I?' He feels as he did walking the fine line of the cobblestone path in the menagerie dream — forlorn, tired and scared, but resigned to investigate and go on. Without thinking, the Lord's Prayer runs through his mind, his lips following the words.

A brief rustle of leaves is the only warning Geoff has before two spears are thrust at him, one pressed tightly to his throat and the other painfully cutting through his shirt to his belly. His mind reels with shock and fear, but his body remains motionless. He feels a rush of adrenalin as he can just make out, in the half moon-light, three black human figures — one in European dress. Horace, Christie, Jonathan and Claire flash into his mind. Part of him wants to strike out, but he knows it would be no use. They would kill him immediately. The men grunt threateningly and gesture for him to get up, prodding continually with their weapons. He is herded, without sound, into the forest. Although scared, his brain is cranked up, he must survive.

I can, he catches his breath, *I can break away and raise the alarm,* he thinks. *Now, now is my chance.* He makes a run for it, but is immediately clubbed and pushed to the ground. He is dragged to his feet and quietly led off. The Aborigines are experts at moving about in the dark. He has no option but to follow, and follow quickly. They are moving in a south-easterly direction.

After fifteen minutes, three more men join the party. Geoff wonders why they've abducted him rather than killing him outright. He senses the mutterings of his captors are unexpectedly relaxed and non-aggressive.

After approximately half an hour, the group stop and abruptly sit down in silence. In the dark Geoff can just make out the six men. Two have white markings crudely painted over their bodies making them look like carnival skeletons. They all sit staring at Geoff. He has the strangest feeling these men mean him no harm. *One day of freedom and now I'm a prisoner again,* he thinks.

As things settle he can still hear the waves from the harbour. Howls of the native dingo come from nearby. *I can feel the earth soft and cold beneath me. I can feel its chilled dryness as I dig my hands into it. I can smell the eucalyptus from the trees, and these fellows have a musky scent about them. Strangely I feel like part of the forest and, even more unusual, I feel part of them.*

Geoff stands to relieve himself and nobody stirs, they just watch, knowing he can't escape. Two of his captors follow suit. Another also begins to piddle into the soft earth and onto leaves and branches. Geoff never thought he would ever communicate with other human-beings in such a way. But then he remembers the competitions he and other boys had at school about who could pee the highest on the school wall. He can't help but chuckle. Immediately, two of the group mock his chuckle.

The first words come from the youngest member of the group. The words are harsh and Geoff feels they are directed against him. The comments are quickly terminated by a short order from the man in European clothes. This sends the youth running into the bush.

In spite of the thick army coat he is wearing, the longer Geoff sits the colder he becomes. As if on cue, the young tribal member sent away returns carrying a smouldering piece of wood. He hands it to another who quickly coaxes small flames from the glowing ember.

*　　*　　*

'Fish and chips? Geoff and I adored fish and chips.' Claire's voice is again right inside Jane's head.

Jane has just bought lunch and is sitting at a table on the esplanade overlooking the sea.

'Claire if you were here there is so much I could talk about with you. There is something I have to tell you.'

'I know there is Jane, I've known all along.'

Jane finally admits to herself and to Claire. 'There's a secret person I admire and want to know. I have never met him, but I have communicated with and seen him in my dreams. His name is Geoff. This is all so peculiar.'

'I know, I know it is'.

'How do you know, Claire? You cannot possibly know. My heart is relentless with me. I've known several men. I have come all the way to Australia to be with Michael. I was drawn to North Head wearing a dress, which was not me. I meet you and, and … that damn ship sails into the harbour. What is going on, Claire? What the hell is going on?'

'The dress is you, Jane. The love you feel will become real one day. I lost that chance because I lacked patience. Through you I have been given one more chance, a chance to have it all.'

'Claire, I am so confused about what is happening and yet so sure. It all seems real, but unreal. Life seems like a very fine line. I'm still not sure how to stay kind, become stronger and still strive. It's a big ask, but I'm nearly free. Claire, I know I'm nearly there.'

Several teenagers and an elderly couple look at Jane strangely. This temporarily distracts her. She looks up and decides they don't understand, but then, they're not the only ones.

She continues talking to Claire. 'I do try and see things from the point of view of others, but it's not easy. In fact it's damn near impossible. I don't think I'll ever understand men. Perhaps I should live alone and become celibate.' She smiles sadly.

'I want you to meet Geoff, Jane.'

Claire's voice in Jane's head is teasing her senseless. She stands, and begins to walk away. Her half-eaten lunch is quickly swooped on by the persistent, gulls.

CHAPTER FIFTY FIVE

t's 6.45 am. The day is coming to life and the nocturnal creatures and spirits of the night will soon recede beneath a cover of daylight. The ember fetched by the Aboriginal youth is now a hot, reassuring, roaring fire. *It's no different to the fires back home, Geoff thinks. The smell is the same, the colours are the same, and the smoke still follows me no matter where I sit.* He closes his eyes every now and then to take away that familiar sting. Though there is little communication Geoff is relaxed, sensing the basic gentleness and spontaneity of these stone-age men.

Two of the younger members of the group are still sounding aggressive. They address their leader, the man in white mans' clothes, as Colbee. He passes off their concerns.

Despite being studied by these men, and studying them in return, Geoff is feeling safe with them. He's sure the leader, the man Colbee, is the one who singled him out and stared at him back at the settlement.

Colbee is a slender, but muscular man who, though he looks older, may only be thirty. He has a mischievous but sad look about him, which is accentuated by the absence of one front tooth. His face is deeply pock-marked. As if some message he needed to convey with the wearing of European clothes has been achieved, he takes them off. Rolling them into a neat bundle, he sets off, carrying them with him, and everyone including Geoff follows.

Geoff notices that they are travelling east towards the far reaches of the harbour. He wonders why.

After twenty minutes the track opens onto a lake. Concentrating on the men ahead and temporarily distracted by the rising sun filtering through the gums, Geoff is unaware of a gruesome sight until he is practically standing on them. Two men, convicts, are lying on the ground in a state of advanced decomposition. Their skulls have been bashed in. One's chest cavity and stomach have been split open and the dehydrated intestines spill onto the ground. Animals have further mutilated the bodies. Geoff stands, mesmerised, but he does not have time to contemplate their demise for he is quickly ushered on.

Despite the small lake looking lovely in the silvery light of the morning sun, Geoff is spooked. The party move around the perimeter of the pristine waterhole, which is brimming with life and activity. Ducks and waterhen feed industriously. Fish break the water's surface out in the deeper areas. Small birds skim back and forth in and out of morning mist patches. Multi-coloured parrots of many varieties, and cockatoo-type birds with pink breasts and grey wings, meticulously separate grass seed from husk making sounds not unlike those of contented guinea pigs. Two big red kangaroos snatch a cautious drink on the far side of the waterway.

Most of the group stop abruptly and sit down, while two continue on. Out of the bush, a stranger appears with a smouldering piece of wood and prepares another fire like that at the first camp-site. Nearby the screeching of birds is suddenly silenced. The hot coals are glowing as the two men return. One is carrying three dead birds, one of which Geoff recognises as a duck. The other holds a huge ferocious-looking lizard, which he strikes with a rock. Before the reptile is completely dead it is laid out on the coals. The birds are lowered onto the fire next to the goanna. The obnoxious odour of burning feathers dissipates and the aroma of grilling lizard and bird meat begins to smell marginally appealing to a famished Geoff. Breakfast is ready.

When the carcasses are taken off the fire, Geoff's instincts for survival tell him he must eat. Imitating the others he tears off the flesh and discovers the taste of the birds and the lizard palatable. He picks his way around any of the raw meat. When everyone has had their fill, the men move, one by one, to the water's edge, kneel down and drink. Geoff does the same.

They are unlike other men I have known, he thinks to himself. *They obviously have their pride, but they don't play the games the white man plays. If I humble myself in front of them, they do the same. If I am kind to them, they return the kindness. I am as a child with them and them with me, and yet they are so strong.* How much they are mirroring his behaviour is unclear to him, but he's certainly mirroring theirs.

Their nomadic mind-set clicks in and they move off. Geoff scrambles to his feet to keep up.

The sound of the sea is getting closer, the forest floor is becoming sandier and the vegetation is changing. The gums are thinning, giving way to more bushy trees and stunted shrubbery. Banksias and Tea trees are both now abundant separating the foreshore from the bush. A small creek forces its way around the sand dunes to the sea. The party follow animal prints in the sandy bank to a waterhole and take what seems an unnecessary drink. Geoff is urged to do the same by one of the men.

The chocolate colour of the men and the way they move blends naturally with the surroundings. Geoff, experiencing a feeling of freedom and oneness with these men and what they represent, pauses for a moment, puts down his coat and takes off his shirt. The men sense his hesitation and look back. One of the young men smiles. Geoff moves up over the dune and is hit in the face and chest by a cold wind which instantaneously wipes away his romantic ideas. He replaces his shirt and drapes his coat over his shoulders.

In the distance he can see … *'Boree! Boree!'* One of the men is pointing to North Head rising up out of the sea across the heads. On a sand dune, on the east coast of this foreign land, Geoff stands alongside a young man from an ancient world. They are both looking directly at North Head.

Claire and that other woman could be at North Head, just as Claire was at Tintagel castle, Geoff thinks. It only seems like yesterday Claire was swimming in the rock pool below the castle. It seems like yesterday I kissed her there. And who then is the other woman?

Several dingoes are following his captors as they leave the sandy beach. Twenty yards behind them Geoff scrambles over the sand and kelp trying to keep up. Two dingoes stand watching him. They will not venture out onto the rocks.

Sandstone cliffs rise up to their right. Huge slabs of rock which have broken off over the years lie in varying stages of erosion, monuments to the passage of time. Spray from the crashing waves streams into the air. The sound of the breakers and the dampness of the saturated air swirls back off the cliffs. Apart from the natural tang of this rocky seaside expanse there is an unidentifiable pungent stench in the air.

The men stop and sit down as Geoff catches up with them. They stare straight ahead onto a series of rocky platforms and rock pools. Apparently they will go no further.

Colbee points. 'Go, *go* Mr Geoff', he says. Geoff stops and looks at him surprised by his English and his knowing his name. He then places his coat beside the men and walks onto the vast rocky expanse alone, wondering if this is really what Colbee wants him to do.

Thirty yards on the stench is increasing. A bone parched white by the sun seems to be the remains of some poor unfortunate animal. He sees more bones and these appear to be human. He then comes across a skull — a human skull with one front tooth missing. He immediately doubts all of his previous assumptions of why he is here and what these men want of him. With his heart rate increasing rapidly, he looks around quickly for a rock or a piece of wood to protect himself. There is nothing but bones.

They are going to kill me here. This is an area of sacrifice, he thinks. In panic he glances back at the men. They are just staring at him with no signs of aggravation or excitement. *What then?*

As he moves further onto the rocky plateau the stench becomes overwhelming. He discovers more skulls and bones. The further he walks the more bones and remains he sees. Not all the bodies are fully decomposed. The dead are all Aborigines. Near the cliffs an attempt has been made to bury bodies with sand, stone, and grass. 'There's just *too* many,' he says to himself. Hundreds of skulls and a mass of bones cover the rocks and fill the rock pools.

Fear for his personal safety subsides. This is a burial area. And then he remembers talk at the colony about the smallpox epidemic that moved through the local Aboriginal community. *Only a few bodies were found,* he recalls. 'The sick went away to die, so people said.' he whispers to himself. *Maybe,* he considers, *the salt pools were used by these desperate people to try to cool their fevers or to heal and sooth the painful eruptions on their skin.*

In the open cathedral of rock, surrounded by bones and the remains of men, women and children, he lowers his head. The questions as to why and who is to blame scramble through his brain. He looks back at the group.

'They've brought me here to see this?' he asks himself. *The pox marks on Colbee's face, they're caused by the smallpox disease,* he thinks. *Who is this man Colbee? How does he know my name?*

When Geoff again looks back at the men, he sees, with a combination of relief and disappointment that they have vanished.

'They wanted *me* to see this?' he says aloud. *But at the moment I feel nothing, but sadness and shame,* he thinks.

The squawking of a solitary gull distracts him momentarily.

CHAPTER FIFTY SIX

eoff goes back to where his captors were sitting, picks up his coat, and looks for them as he walks along the beach. They are nowhere to be seen. He is completely alone.

Feeling hungry and tired he knows he must return to the settlement as soon as possible. Unable to find his way back through the scrub, his only option is to follow the shoreline of the harbour back to the colony.

But first he needs to rest. He finds a sunny place sheltered from the wind and catches up on some much needed sleep.

Refreshed, he sets off an hour later. In the distance, North Head towers at the entrance to the harbour.

'You'll do.' He finds an empty flagon washed in by the tide and fills it with fresh water from a pool at the base of a cliff. With a rock he breaks open several large oysters and swallows them raw. He coughs to clear the pungent after taste, and spits. *Rough on an empty stomach.*

'Whata you blighters want?' he says to three dingos staring at him inquisitively. One turns its head to the side just like the antics of a domestic dog. He imagines that if he fell down they would probably tear him apart. The fictional character of Robinson Crusoe comes to his mind his mind as he contemplates how he must prepare for the coming night. 'Maybe I will find my man Friday.'

The sun is going and he has no fire. After another gritty meal of rock oysters and some basal leaves from a grass tree, which he saw his Aboriginal friends chewing, he starts to prepare his camp. To ensure the tide will not overtake him during the night, he lines a small rocky cave with generous amounts of dried kelp, seaweed and grass, then barricades the entrance with driftwood and tree branches.

Unable to sleep, he listens to the sounds of the night. Crabs scatter over the rocks, and in the black background the relentless waves swish up the pebbly beach — waves which seem to be getting closer and closer.

The long, cold, uncomfortable night of segmented sleep abruptly ends at dawn with the sound of five gunshots and excited yelling.

'What was that!' he mumbles as he scrambles to his feet. His heart is pumping as he climbs over a huge boulder to where he thinks the ruckus is coming from. There is nothing to be seen at the next cove, but past another small outcrop of rocks he hears agitated English voices. His eyes scan the bush, the sand and the water until he sees that the voices are coming from a longboat, in a cove, close to the shore. He can see several men poking and prodding furiously at something in the calm shallows.

My God, it's a body, an Aboriginal body' What the hell is going on? he wonders.

'I'm over here!' he calls out. '*Over here!*' he shouts, ecstatic he has been rescued.

The men push the floating body away from the boat and begin to row towards him. Geoff wades out through the freezing, clear water which is stained by blood running off the rocks to his right. He discovers two more bodies hardly discernable against the dark brown rocks. One dying man still grasps a spear threateningly.

The long boat moves steadily towards Geoff. Although relieved about his imminent rescue, he makes his way towards the semi-submerged body.

'Over here matey, quick!' calls one of the sailors.

Geoff points to the man in the water and wades on towards him.

'He's off his bloody perch,' calls a marine as the boat is manoeuvred to cut him off.

Geoff reaches the body as the longboat pulls alongside him.

'Get him men, for his own sake.' Three of the men move to one side of the boat, ready to haul him aboard.

'It's Blake! Geoff Blake. What the hell? Get aboard, lad.'

Geoff reaches the floating body but finds the Aboriginal man is dead — shot in the head. He turns, recognising a familiar voice.

'Thomas, how did this happen?' he gasps.

'Get in the boat, Geoff! We'll talk later. Quickly lad!'

Geoff attempts to drag the man towards the rocks but two men in the boat grab at him. In water up to his chest, he can't fight them. A third man takes hold of his shirt and they heave him aboard.

As the long boat pulls away, spears zip into the water behind them. One makes the distance and nicks a sailor's arm before embedding itself deeply in the hull of the boat.

'See em! — 'ere they come on ta the rocks! Look at the bastards! Gimme me gun,' says a marine with a frenzied look in his eyes.

'There will be no more killing!' shouts Thomas. 'Let's get out of here.'

They row out to sea rapidly, leaving the horror-struck Aboriginal men far behind. Geoff sits silently.

'*My coat* — the coat you gave me, Thomas. I left it on the rocks.'

'And that's where it stays, Geoff,' says Thomas.

The boat then heads for the furthermost point of South Head where one of the two men on ship-watch will be rotated. Then several lobster pots are checked, emptied of their catch and re-baited. The boat turns and heads back towards the colony with a seafood bounty for Governor Phillip's and the officer's tables.

Not another word is said about the three dead Aboriginals they left back at the cove.

*　　*　　*

It is the second Saturday of the month, the day Jane has agreed to take care of Beckie.

How awkward. How can I do it? How can I face Michael again? It seems like ages since I last saw Beckie, Jane thinks approaching the house.

"FOR SALE," reads the sign. "IMMEDIATE VACANT POSSESSION."

Michael and Beckie have gone. Jane stares in disbelief. 'What have I done?' she says aloud.

'What do you mean, what have *you* done?' The familiar voice moves in to support Jane.

'Something always gets in the way. I was going to marry Michael. I loved him, Claire. I love Beckie too.'

'He wasn't ready for you Jane. It's not your fault.'

Those words of advice seem odd coming from Claire, thinks Jane.

She stands motionless in front of the empty house.

Did I want too much of Michael? she wonders.

'I know I expected too much of Geoff,' admits Claire. 'You just haven't found the one who is right for you, Jane. I had the best in Geoff and did not realise it.'

Jane stares wistfully at the house. *What will become of Beckie?* she asks herself.

'Becky will be fine, just fine. It all happened too quickly Jane, between you and Beckie. Let's go in.'

Jane opens the front gate gently. *Michael was so gorgeous on our first night. He made dinner for me, carried me off to the bedroom and made love to me for hours. What a sort he was.* But she also remembers the long fruitless, agonising wait at the airport. She remembers Beckie's dolls, the ice creams, the walks, the arguments. She remembers …

'*My God!*' Jane stops. On a front window ledge sits Beckie's smiling dolly. Jane picks the doll up and holds it tightly to her chest as tears begin to run down her cheeks.

'Beckie has left her doll for me,' she whispers sadly.

She stands for several moments then walks to the side entrance, begins to open the gate, then stops, turns and leaves.

Walking back along the foreshore her mind is in a daze.

'Jane, can I tell you about a dream I once had?' Claire's voice comes again.

Jane frowns, for a second then nods.

'An owl sat on my shoulder.'

'That's cute,' Jane laughs.

'I'm serious Jane. I'm not laughing at your dolly, am I?'

'Claire, don't you understand how I feel? I'm sorry, I really am.' Jane is snappy and confused, but it seems there is no way she can stop these strange and powerful conversations.

Claire starts again. 'An owl sat on my shoulder. It was very fluffy, very wise and very cuddly. It looked at me with its big loving brown eyes. I saw myself in its eyes. I felt complete and warm as it rested its head close to my neck. It loved me very much. But Geoff came and scared it away.'

'Oh Claire, that's a lovely dream. I don't know much about dreams, but it seems to me that's a dream about love, don't you think?'

'Yes. Yes it does seem like it.'

'The owl represents your love, your wise and individual self, loving you.'

'Yes, I think you are right Jane. Yes, that's what the owl is.' But she seems confused.

'What I don't understand is how Geoff scared it away. How could anybody take that special part of you away?'

'It's only a dream Jane,' Claire replies defensively. But, then thinking, she agrees. 'I don't suppose anybody can *really*.'

Jane's mind stops dead in its tracks. *Am I so secure?* she thinks. *Am I too hard on others? Too hard on myself?* She looks at Beckie's doll, slowly lifts her head, turns slightly to the right and looks in the direction of North Head.

Claire, don't play games with me.

*   *   *

After an hour's rowing along the centre of the harbour, the long boat approaches the settlement. Nobody has said a word since they left South Head. A gang of convicts in the distance is building a wharf, and closer, another is loading a vessel which, one of the sailors tells Geoff, is bound for Norfolk Island.

'Geoff, there's Horace.' Thomas points to a small barge.

Horace has already spotted Geoff and is waving excitedly. '*Geoff!* Geoff!' That familiar voice carries across the water.

'Horace!' Geoff waves back frantically. Neither of the boats stop, but the two friends continue to wave and shout to each other.

It's obvious Thomas doesn't want to talk to me about the strife with the three Aboriginal men, Geoff thinks.

'It's good to see you again, Geoff. It's good to be free, eh?' It would seem Thomas has purposely left any conversation until the last moment.

'Yes, my friend, it's good to be free.'

'How did you get to the other end of the harbour, Geoff?'

'I walked the whole distance,' Geoff says. 'Went through the scrub.'

Thomas looks at Geoff in disbelief.

'That's the truth,' Geoff assures him. He's decided there's enough trouble between the settlers and the Aborigines without adding his kidnapping to the pot. Nobody would believe the story in any case.

'All I can say is you were *bloody* lucky. You saw what trouble we had with the blacks in that area. You were plain lucky. Why the *hell* would you want to do that?'

'I was tired of being cooped up.'

Thomas gives a couple of thoughtful nods, looks away and prepares to unload the Governor's crab and crayfish delicacies which, every now and then, flap about in the hessian bag in the bottom of the boat. He looks preoccupied.

Geoff thanks the men and Thomas and gets barely a nod in response. He climbs the bank, thanks the men again, waves half-heartedly and moves off.

'Hey, Geoff!' Thomas is running after him. You might need this, my friend.' He hands Geoff a jacket, which renders Geoff speechless. All he can do is shake Thomas's hand warmly by way of thanks.

Geoff finds a public convenience, gets cleaned up and then has a meal. After a good night's sleep he plans to visit Christie and Jonathan the next day. There's no way he's going to report his abduction to the authorities for fear it may provoke reprisals against his Aboriginal friends.

CHAPTER FIFTY SEVEN

Due to the sinking of the supply ship *Guardian*, the Second Fleet arrived with very few supplies and many more mouths to feed. What it did bring however, is hope for lines of communication to be re-established with the homeland. Happier faces are now a contrast with the drab makeshift, mud-rendered, thatched buildings of this seeming impermanent shantytown of Sydney.

Geoff visits the well-built, but small, government office. Symbolising the future, it is constructed of brick and has a shingled roof like the Governor's house. He receives a payment of seven shillings and sixpence, due to him as part of his release contract.

Fifty yards along the road, a crowd gathers at a store. Intending to buy some goods for Mary and the children, Geoff goes in to join the throng of marines, sailors, officers and members of the clergy who, in spite of the exorbitant price of the goods, are obsessed with making purchases. He can't believe his eyes. 'No!' he says aloud, as he sees shelf after shelf of stores and clothing originating from the *Neptune*. He can't bare it and gets out as fast as he can.

'That bastard Trail is selling off dead men and women's supplies,' he says to himself. 'I just can't believe the man would stoop *so* low.' He is furious. His first impulse is to upend the shelves and throw everything on to the muddy road. He goes to find another store.

Seeking permission to visit Mary and the children, Geoff goes in search of an officer.

'They're not 'ere anymore, they've bin taken up river to that new place at Parramatta,' informs one of the convict women, giving Geoff the glad eye.

'She went off with 'im!' calls another. 'She gettin' married to 'im … Smiffers. That's what she tells me she gonna do.'

This is also the official answer to Geoff's inquiry at the convict women's camp when he asks to see Mary and the children. He walks back to the grassy playing area. No sign of the children there.

'Smithers, that dark horse.' he says to himself. Jonathan *won't know any difference, but Christie will think I've deserted her. That poor kid*, he thinks.

As he wanders back through the settlement he makes up his mind to go to Parramatta and see the children. He stops, turns and takes a long look at North Head.

CHAPTER FIFTY EIGHT

There comes a time in a man and a woman's life where a series of circumstances, be they accidental or destined, leave core personality traits exposed and with nowhere to hide.

Geoff understands how the bigotry of some men, the rigidity and dogma of the church and the structure of society back in England, disenchanted Claire. He is also seeing more clearly that his lack of support for his wife, together with the conditional nature of his generosity towards her, added to her anguish. Before all this, it is now obvious to him that his life has been subject to influences beyond his control. While he rejected his father's ways, he realises that the patriarchal attitudes and selfish, power hungry empire building of his own country England, are even now still part of him. He knows there is a better England inside him. He also knows very clearly that England's past will catch up with her as his has caught up with him. England has been his teacher and his nemesis.

Geoff is alone, but far from defeated. He has a fleeting fantasy that, given a chance, he would rather live out his life in the outback than settle into the routine of colonial life.

For its part, the new colony is already adopting, in addition to English ways it brought with it, new prejudices and norms uniquely its own. The marines hate Port Jackson and the convicts, and scorn the Aborigines. The convicts, in turn, resent authority. And those Aborigines, who have been given food and clothing, lounge about the settlement coming and going as they please.

Geoff approaches the perimeter of the convict work area. He has permission to speak to Horace. He finds him looking grubby and tired but with a sparkle in his eyes. From his enthusiastic handshake, Geoff knows he has acquired new strength. Horace inquires after the children. Geoff tells him Christie and Jonathan have been moved to Rosehill and that tomorrow he will be going to see them.

'Then what 'appens, then what 'appens, Geoff?' Horace knows Geoff, he reads him well.

Geoff moves closer to Horace. 'Now listen to me. This is as far as it goes. Promise?'

But Horace does not commit himself.

'In six days I'm going to North Head.'

'Way over *there*! Ya mad, Geoff. There's nobody out there but those good for nothing blacks. Dose ladies are just in your head. They're not there. Do you hear me? You will find nuthin' out there. Don't go Geoff. *Please* don't go. You love her so much don't ya? Miss Claire must have been really somethin' special.' He pauses while Geoff nods slowly.

'Don't worry,' he goes on, puffing his chest a little. 'I be here when you get back. I know you be going. I know'd all the time.' Horace looks at the ground, trying to restrain the tears escaping from his eyes. 'I be with you Geoff, no matter wherever it be.'

'Trust me Horace. Whatever happens, please trust me.'

Looking down, Horace nods. Then he slowly lifts his head and smiles a teary smile. After all they have been through on the ship this latest development worries him the most. But then the new Horace resurfaces.

'I warn ya … Don't say you luv me. I'm not a fancy boy you know that. I love you like a bruvver, Geoff.' Horace manages a wink and a brave smile.

'I love you like a brother too, Horace. Now be off with you.'

'No Geoff, be off with *you*,' jokes Horace. 'I'm staying put, I will have me own farm. I didn't get to steer the ship, but I will have me own land.'

Horace goes and rejoins his work gang. Geoff stops for a moment and watches him, thinking, how he is one of the men now. Horace turns, looks at Geoff, and waves a half wave as he is dragged back into his group by a new Aussie mate. Horace and Geoff's eyes meet one more time.

*   *   *

Jane pauses while writing a letter to her mother and father.

'I feel so empty today. Oh *hell* I can't do this.' She puts down her pen and switches on the television.

"… the bomb killed twelve Israelis, including four children under five years. Mr Arafat is claiming he is doing all that's possible to stop the suicide bombings …"

My God, the Middle East has more problems, but then I suppose it always has. Many have predicted these things, Jane thinks to herself.

'Jane, if the Bible says it's going to happen that could actually cause it to happen. Geoff and I spoke about this often.'

'Is that you, Claire?'

'The Arab people are not happy with us are they, Jane?'

'That's exactly what Mr G said, and I too can see many reasons why they feel let down and used. We have treated them badly for centuries.'

'Why can't people see both sides?'

'Why can't any of us see both sides? It's just so hard. That's human nature I suppose, we just keep coming back until we learn our lessons,' Jane reflects.

'North Head, Claire,' Jane goes on. The *Neptune* and Geoff are never out of Jane's mind although she does her best not to think about this strange fantasy. 'I'll just have to visit North Head again and put this all to rest.'

'That's probably a good idea, Jane.'

*   *   *

Geoff goes back to the Government office and asks advice about travelling to Rosehill.

'It's twenty-two miles,' says the officer and advises it's a journey not without risk. On the other hand official policy is to encourage the opening up of the route.

Geoff is unsure exactly where the children and Mary are situated, but he considers they should not be hard to find once he reaches the general area.

The last eight miles of his journey is relieved with a slow, but very welcomed ride on a horse drawn cart. The driver, Jim, is glad of Geoff's company for he is well aware that two riding together are more formidable than one if natives or escaped convicts set up an ambush.

The cart is carrying mail and meagre supplies for the outlying areas. Jim is a First fleeter and, like Geoff has been granted emancipation along with some special privileges like the exclusive lease of the government horse and wagon.

Jim tells Geoff about the conditions he suffered on the government-operated First Fleet and thought they were bad enough until he heard about the brutality and disregard for human life aboard the *Neptune*.

As the wagon bumps and sways slowly towards Rosehill, travelling at a speed Geoff could probably walk, his mind thinks back to a previous carriage ride. Although seeming like one lifetime away, it is only just on three years since Claire and he took that jubilant ride through the streets of London.

The crunching and grinding of the wagon wheels over the

resistant rocky surface of the bush track are playing their part in the consolidation of the new route into the interior of the vast Australian continent.

Arriving at Rosehill, Jim shows Geoff the little settlement. 'There are only three small farms, if that is what they could be called, 'ere at the hill. Your friend and the children should na be 'ard to find.'

After some consideration, Jim makes Geoff an offer. 'I be coming back through 'ere the day after next when the sun be at there.' He points to the midday position. 'Dat sun,' he says, his eyebrows lifting and lengthening his face like an expert, '*dat sun* would be in the south skies if we be back home. If ye be not 'ere, the wheels of this cart will keep on.'

Geoff shakes Jim's hand, picks up his swag and leaps from the wagon. Jim is completely oblivious to Geoff's tripping and falling onto the dusty road. Geoff brushes himself off and makes his way to the first farmhouse. They cannot help with any information on the whereabouts of Mary and the children. The second farmer cannot throw any light on where they may be either, but the woman offers Geoff a cup of black tea and some freshly baked damper.

'A few wagons go by. There was some children,' she recalls, 'the day before yesterday, I think, but they could 'ave been bound for who knows where. It will all turn out fine for you, I'm sure,' says the woman. 'Would you be as so kind to take a small parcel to Port Jackson for me and my husband on your return journey, Mr Blake?'

'Of course.'

The warm and peaceful afternoon is interrupted by a screeching flock of white sulphur-crested cockatoos as they land in the top branches of a large gum tree near the riverbank. Geoff decides to rest under the tree for a moment. The moment turns into minutes, quarter, and then one hour as he sleeps soundly.

Only yards away a young girl passes quietly along the road.

Geoff awakes and gathers his senses, takes a drink from the river, then sets out for where, he is unsure. The bush thickens and he realises that maybe he's passed all the farms.

'Tis that *you Geoff?*' an excited voice comes from behind.

He spins around.

'The man on the wagon *said* it was you. It is you.' Christie runs to him and throws her arms around his neck as he bends down to greet her. She holds him tightly.

'He said you was just down the road. I went way up the hill, I did.' Tears pour down her little red cheeks. Geoff is thrilled to see her. She throws her arms around his neck again and he hugs her close. On a dusty road, in the middle of nowhere, they hold each other, talking non-stop.

'Jonathon is getting *bigger* and *bigger,* he is. And Mary is good, and Mr Smithers, he's good *too.*' Christie's droops a little.

'So, Mary married Mr Smithers?' He's a *good* man, love.'

'She was going to marry you, I was thinking. And how is Horace?' she says, leading Geoff by the hand. 'We live in an old tent for now. Over there, see.'

Geoff cannot help but smile, *she's a proper little lady now, grotty but proper,* he thinks. 'Horace wanted to see you but they wouldn't let him come.'

'You can build your *little* house over there, near the pond, Geoff,' she says, hopefully.

'Geoffrey *Blake!*' Edward Smithers appears out of the tent with one hand outstretched in a warm welcome, the other holding baby Jonathan.

'Congratulations on your pardon, *Mr* Blake. Old Trail did one thing right, eh? If it wasn't for you we would all be at the bottom of the Atlantic now. That galley fire was a bad one.'

'*Good* to see you again, Mr Smithers.' Geoff shakes his hand enthusiastically. 'You don't waste any time, do you?'

'No, certainly not. Had to make her mine. Mary and I got messages to each other. Couldn't do much else with Trail and Ellington on the prowl, *you* know what I mean.' He gives Geoff a nudge.

Geoff smiles and nods. 'Hello little man,' he says and reaches for Jonathan's small hand.

'He doesn't remember ya, Geoff,' says Christie in a very matter-of-fact manner. Jonathan pulls his hand away and, taking hold of Edward's shirt, buries his face into his new guardian's woolly chest.

Mary appears at the tent flap looking relaxed and at ease. Edward puts his arm around her and draws her close.

'Welcome to our 'umble home, Geoff,' she says cordially with a slight hint of how things could have been in her eyes.

After Geoff has wished Mary well with her marriage to Edward, they reminisce all afternoon about the voyage, each of them getting a chance to vent feelings and feeling better for it. It is now that Geoff learns that Edward Smithers, a marine aboard the *Neptune*, had taken a shine to Mary but due to Captain Trail's strict rules of non-fraternisation, the soldier's interest in a relationship with Mary was kept under wraps.

When the shortage of women at Port Jackson became obvious to the men aboard the *Neptune*, expectations were quickly moderated and all available women were snapped up.

Mary has fine features; she is strong, healthy and reliable. She has two boys, one of her own and Jonathan, Sarah's son. Mary was given one opportunity, one chance alone, to join Corporal Smithers as his wife on an allocation of land at Brickfield Hill, near Rosehill. She accepted. It all happened as quickly as that.

'Something smells good.' Geoff can't remember when he last ate fresh meat.

'I shot a kangaroo. That's roo stew you can smell.' Edward is clearly proud of his marksmanship and his developing self-sufficiency. 'We have to make do, Geoff, there are few supplies.' He mentions Trail's store and, like Geoff, is disgusted.

Geoff stays two nights helping Edward with the erection of a small house frame and spending some special time with Christie and Jonathan.

'Horace has been asking after you, Christie. Mr Smithers can easily find him for you when you visit town. He is going to have his own farm, just like you.'

'I'm going to get my very own horse one day. Mr Smithers promised me. Where will you be, Geoff?' she asks now accepting that he will not be staying with them.

'Probably at Sydney Cove, love. Though this is good country here at Parramatta. We'll see. I'll have to do some careful thinking, won't I?' he says, squeezing both of her hands together in his. Wherever it be, you can come to stay with me. Come on, let's take Jonathan down by the river.'

*　　*　　*

As arranged, Geoff meets Jim, the wagon driver, at the agreed place and time. Christie, holding Jonathan, stands in front of Mary. She waves her hand and one of Jonathan's, simultaneously. Geoff watches the sadness on her little face as the wagon moves away.

'I'll see you both soon,' he calls, throwing them kisses.

CHAPTER FIFTY NINE

t is midday, four days later. A small rowboat approaches the wilderness of the harbour's north shore. As Geoff leaps out onto the beach he looks back at the settlement. He is glad to be on his way but anxious about his journey and whether he'll make it back. He gives a quick wave as the boatman pulls away, leaving him to commence his trek to the north-east. It will take one and a half days to reach Middle Harbour, the main obstacle he will face before he can reach the promontory of North Head.

He makes his way to the highland area of the northern shore and then follows the ridges in a north-easterly direction. As he moves through the bush he checks his position from glimpses of the harbour through valleys and inlets to the south. Surprisingly, he has only seen two kangaroos and a small brown snake. He fights off thoughts about the natives attacking him, his body speared many times and left to rot in the dry bush. *I know they're in the area. I wouldn't stand a chance*, he thinks.

The voyage has left him unfit and it is not long before tiredness catches up. He calls it a day and opens his swag. He sets out a meal of stale bread, dried fruit, a piece of salt beef, two biscuits and tea tree tea. The mid winter sun disappears as he sits beside a log fire he has built to last the night through.

The dead quiet of the bush contrasts with the sporadic sounds of nocturnal activity. Snapping and crunching of twigs and bark, howling and hooting, the rustling of possums in the trees overhead all play on a sleepy mind. Against the pitch black of the night the fire takes centre stage. He is mesmerised by the crackling, popping chunky logs which burn profusely.

The following morning, Geoff wakes to the vibrant sounds of a rejuvenated nature and a burnt-out fire of hot coals. He notices smoke in the next valley. Accepting the Aboriginals are aware of his presence, he fuels a roaring fire to warm himself and boil his billy. His breakfast consists of toasted bread with lard, an egg, a small potato baked in the coals and a serve of precious China tea he has been saving.

In five hours I should be at Middle Harbour, he estimates, scratching a rough map in the dusty ground.

After crossing some magnificent dry country, he approaches the downward slopes of the eastern shoreline. Above the tree-line he can finally see the majestic cliffs of North Head. *I have no option,* he thinks. *I will somehow have to cross the water.*

Following the arm of the harbour north to where it narrows, Geoff decides to stop for the night. He works on a plan to cross the harbour as he makes his camp next to an old tree stump uprooted by floods. From the evidence of piles of burnt shells and remnants of fire making, he is not the first to use this camp-site. It is clear that other humans have been here many times before him.

Making another fire, he boils his two remaining eggs, one for now and the other for later. As he leans back against the stump and begins to eat, he realises the solution to his crossing is right behind him. If he can get this tree stump to the water at high tide he can use it to cross the channel.

The following morning his plan to move the log on wooden slides becomes a reality. He drags the stump across the sand and floats it in the water. Strapping his gear to the upright roots, he wades out and pushes the makeshift raft to the edge of the channel. With a length of cord he anchors it to a rock where it will wait for the low tide.

Testing for ebb tide by throwing sticks into the water, he makes his move. Holding the raft with one hand, paddling with the other and kicking his legs he edges slowly across the narrow channel. The water is painfully cold and the log is cumbersome, but these are minor considerations when he becomes aware there are two Aboriginal men with spears and clubs waiting on the other side. He manoeuvres the log around to paddle back and can't believe his eyes for, standing near his camp fire, is an Aboriginal wearing the old coat that Thomas had given him.

'It's Colbee! Can't be. Yes, *it is.*' He waves, excitedly.

Throwing off the coat, Colbee runs to the water and helps Geoff out. He then stokes the fire, continually looking back at Geoff smiling. Geoff attempts to dry himself.

Unbeknown to Geoff, Colbee is in fact a protégé of Governor Phillip. He is one of a few aborigines selected, restrained and groomed in the ways of the white-man. It is the plan of the Governor to train and use these men to bridge the gap between the two cultures. This courageous plan was doomed from the start. Colbee's loyalty to the Governor and his officers was not strong enough. Just when it was thought progress had been made, these men would throw off their western clothes, return to their tribes and invariably become antagonistic towards the British.

At the settlement, Colbee watched Geoff's departure. He followed him and protected him from a distance.

Colbee points. Two dug-out canoes, and three men smiling the characteristic toothless smiles, are waiting. Colbee strips Geoff off, laughing as he does so. He then industriously attempts to dry Geoff's clothes over the fire, burning a hole in the trousers. At which point he looks at Geoff expectantly and then at his swag. Geoff gets the hint and offers Colbee some of his supplies. Colbee eats and then, much to Geoff's dismay generously offers the remainder of the rations to the other men.

Colbee hands Geoff's half-dried clothes to him and signals

it is time to go. He loads Geoff's gear into one of the canoes. He points, and Geoff climbs into the other canoe seating himself down amongst a smelly, black slurry of half-cooked fish and charcoal from a small smouldering fire on a rough clay base.

The men paddle profusely and the crossing of Middle Harbour channel is made within minutes.

When they reach the other side, Geoff thanks Colbee and waves. But Colbee has other ideas. Sending the canoes on their way he makes signs he will accompany Geoff who, gladly accepting his help, has the strange sense he understands how important Geoff's journey is to him.

For the next couple of hours, Colbee leads Geoff along well-worn tracks beside the harbour and across two pristine beaches until they are almost at North Head. Geoff has trouble keeping up and only catches Colbee when he stops just short of their destination.

Colbee indicates for Geoff to go on. Geoff moves a few paces and then looks back to see that Colbee has not moved. He indicates he will go no further. Geoff walks back to shake him by the hand.

'*You go*,' says Colbee, takes off the coat and hands it to Geoff. Geoff tries to return it but Colbee insists.

When Colbee sits down, Geoff realises his friend intends to wait for him. Looking around he sees that the vegetation has changed and there is something different about the whole area. *I have heard there are sacred areas out here*, he thinks, it would explain Colbee's reluctance to go any further.

The sunny, windless winter's day allows the strange atmosphere of the promontory to settle around Geoff like a feathery blanket. He moves along a labyrinth of sandy tracks surrounded by dense, low growing tea tree and Banksia bushes as he draws nearer to the mysterious cliffs of North Head.

Pure excitement and anticipation overcomes his tiredness

as he approaches the area where he thinks the women would have been standing as he watched them from the deck of the *Neptune*. He wonders if Claire will be there as she was at Tintagel Castle.

The dense scrub opens up along the cliff edge. Before him lies an incredible sight. The deep blue ocean stretches to the edge of the earth. To his right is the entrance to the harbour and hundreds of feet below the white ocean surges over the honeycombed rocks. Way in the distance is smoke from the Port Jackson settlement. A soft, salty sea breeze mingles with the warm land air. He has often dreamt of this very moment. *I never thought I would make it out here*, he thinks. *I feel like an explorer. Maybe I'm the first white man to set foot here.*

He makes his way along the top of the cliffs, continually looking over the edge as he did on the Tintagel Promontory. 'Are there any rocky areas, sandy beaches or pools?' he says to himself, reliving the moment when he discovered Claire bathing in the sea at Cornwall.

Looking down at the soft-caked earth he can see evidence that somebody, wearing shoes, has been here recently. A large, unusual vertical stone confirms his position. He is now near where the women stood.

Sounds of an ancient didgeridoo, like he's heard at the colony, surround him. He also imagines music from the tavern at Port Isaacs, and the flute on the *Neptune*.

There is nobody to be seen. He doubles back and confirms the exact place where he saw Claire standing. If nothing else, he has made it to this point. He looks intently at some Aboriginal stone carvings covering the sandstone rocks realising they have probably been here for many thousands of years.

His mind becomes fixated on Claire swimming in the rock pool at Tintagel — as if that very special day is somehow only minutes away. He moves to the edge and again looks for her.

His hand reaches to one side carefully holding onto the large stone to balance himself. He remembers the stone in the garden — Claire's stone. His hand feels the smoothness, the strength, the permanence and the timelessness of the stone. Energy in the area of his solar plexus builds to an overwhelming level and then shoots all around his body as he turns and stares intensely at the rock.

Clouds above him are flashing from dark to light as they swirl past while the sun moves across the sky like a fiery comet and the moon follows just as quickly. The trees quiver, changing colours from green to bluish-grey and then to gold. Fine rain strikes his cheeks and a sensation similar to pins and needles runs through both his legs and arms. The sounds of many didgeridoos are now real and constant around him, building in their rhythm and intensity. Suddenly a silver object streaks across the sky, he remembers seeing something similar from the deck of the *Neptune*. In the distance small structures dot the countryside and further in the distance buildings like child's play blocks rise high up into the sky. He grimaces as his bones and muscles ache, but the discomfort quickly goes.

Unusual watercrafts looking quite alien to him crisscross the harbour. Close to where he is standing, portions of the cliff are breaking away and dropping to the ocean. He feels part of himself inside breaking away. He thinks of Horace's caution. *'Don't go out there Mr Geoff.'*

Despite having no regrets about his journey to the Heads or the dangers involved, he temporarily looses faith in his vision of the two women standing on the cliff. It could be a selfish fantasy or something special beyond all belief. Maybe he will never know.

Then Claire's desperateness, her world-weariness and solitude come back into his mind even clearer than before. He must find her. He will find her. He must talk to her. Involuntarily, he follows his vision from the ship and moves along the cliff top to continue his search.

'I did the best I possibly could. I did my best, Claire!' he calls out, over and over.

As he was in his dream of the menagerie, Geoff is now, at last, at the crossroads in his life. He can see that the despicable treatment of the convicts, the persecution of the Australian Aboriginals and his journey into the unknown were all symbolically foretold in his dream. Now, more than ever, he identifies and celebrates his relationship with the persecuted ancient man deep within himself. *Like the animals in the menagerie dream the convicts were packed into crowded pens*, he thinks. *Like my caged ancient man the Aboriginal men, women and children of this land are tormented and killed. Why have I had to see all this?*

As a child he never shied away from anything, always investigating the unknown. His journey to the Heads is a confrontation of any remaining fears he has within.

'*I want to be free!*' he cries out. '*I want to be free!*'

Without any warning there's a slight jerk and the ground under him begins to slide. A gigantic portion of the cliff top on which Geoff is standing is breaking away. It slips slowly at first and then begins to fall more rapidly. In one huge slab, like a ship sliding down the face of a monstrous wave it plummets downward but, unlike a wave, there is no bottoming out and rising again. The slab of cliff just continues to fall with him perched precariously on top. He drops to his knees for fear of being sucked off. When he dares to look up, he sees the cliff face moving further and further away. His world is rushing by him. His dream flashes again into his mind. '*The ancient man is me!*' he screams. The cobblestone crossroads that appeared in his dream are now parallel paths. He is no longer looking down compassionately and patronisingly at his caged instinctive self. He has walked alongside the freed ancient man in his life.

I'm so sorry Claire! My fears tried to stifle you. I was so blind. My past, my immaturity held me a prisoner. I added to your sadness and confused you with my self-centred, binding kindness. These thoughts explode through his mind. 'I truly love you. I meant you no wrong!' he calls aloud.

Lying spreadeagle on the falling slab of the cliff he screams out. 'I am free!' Christie, Jonathan I will never leave you. Claire, I love you!'

Knowing that all will be well, he braces himself. There is a deafening roar as the gigantic falling landmass collides with the ocean and rocks.

Geoff's mind goes blank.

*   *   *

When Jane steps out of the bus on her planned revisit to North Head, she hears the sounds of people screaming. A group of terrified Japanese tourists are running back from the lookout area, one calling out.

'Man falling over cliffs! Man falling!'

Running to another observation area she can see the muddied ocean with fingers of silt spreading outwards with the currents and tide. Screeching gulls circle over where an extraordinary act of nature, a massive landslide, has just taken place. One section, acutely tilted, still remains above sea- level. Jane watches while parts of the fallen landmass are still crumbling away into the ocean, hundreds of feet below. She looks where she saw the *Neptune* sail into the harbour, then decides to leave quickly in case of any further subsidence. Several craft are speeding across the ocean towards North Head and a helicopter is already hovering overhead.

Her sentimental visit is over. Jane decides to return another day.

Two rescue vehicles and two ambulances, lights flashing, scream past her and skid to a halt. Emergency teams pour out, moving cautiously towards the edge of the cliffs.

That Japanese man did say somebody fell over the cliff? she thinks.

Looking back over her shoulder she walks into the rear of a parked, blue BMW, striking her thigh.

'I wonder who owns that? What a stupid place to park,' she says rubbing her leg.

She moves away as the commotion at the cliff top is reducing itself to only a distant disturbance.

'That could have been me,' she says. *'Oh,* gives me the creeps!'

* * *

'Geoff, you are doing just fine. I'm Nurse Connelly. You've had an accident. You're in Manly Hospital. You've probably got several fractures. We'll know when your X-rays come back. Meantime you won't be able to move your left leg because it is temporarily splinted and you may also have a broken rib. Apart from your fractures and a possible slight concussion, everything else seems fine.'

Geoff nods his understanding.

'Your children are outside. Would you like to see them?'

He nods again.

The huge ward door opens and two small figures walk apprehensively towards their father.

'Daddy! Daddy!' calls the youngest as he breaks ranks with his sister and runs to his father's side. He places his small hand hesitantly on the big, sterile bed.

'I'm okay, guys,' are the only words Geoff can manage. He is weak, drugged and confused.

Christine a quiet, sensitive red-haired eleven year old is at first lost for words as she looks at her father's bandaged body. Jonathan is six, but he is sure he is all of eight. He is also sure his father is unbreakable and very brave. This time he is probably right.

'You were on TV, Dad,' Christine half whispers in Geoff's ear.

'Yeh, the helicopter lifted you way-y-y up into the sky, Daddy,' explains Jonathan, his hands and eyebrows rising with his excitement. 'Why did you jump, off Daddy?'

Christine gives Jonathan a nudge. 'Don't be silly, Daddy did *not* jump off!' she says firmly.

As uncomfortable as he feels, Geoff cannot resist giving a short laugh, abruptly terminated by pain from his damaged rib cage.

'Paul brought us here to see you,' says Christine, anticipating Geoff's next question. 'He's waiting outside.'

'Just as well you guys didn't come with me today,' says Geoff. 'I just needed to get away.'

'Don't talk too much Daddy, it must be so hard,' says Christine.

Geoff seems to rustle up a little more energy. 'Would you ask Paul to come in, kids?'

Paul, Geoff's good friend, looks grave as he walks towards Geoff's bed. Paul works for a television news team and they have been mates for many years.

"MAN FLAUNTS CERTAIN DEATH!" He reads, unfolding a copy of the previous day's *Daily Telegraph*.

"Geoffrey Edwards, a thirty-three year old businessman escaped almost certain death when a section of the cliff he was standing on broke away and fell into the ocean at North Head on Tuesday," he continues. 'You certainly made a splash Geoff. You've been on every TV channel in the last twenty-four hours and yesterday there were no less than eight reporters here waiting to interview you. Though they're all gone, today.' This seems to worry him.

'I'm glad. I can't stand reporters, *present company excepted*, you know.' Geoff struggles for words.

'You may be relieved about that, but when you hear about why you're not so popular today, you'll probably feel like the rest of us — still shocked out of our minds.' He produces today's paper, and reads. "WORLD TRADE CENTRE DEMOLISHED." 'Yesterday as your cliff at North Head collapsed, the Twin Towers in New York were wiped off the face of the earth.'

Geoff looks at the newspaper headlines in disbelief.

Even Jonathan seems to understand the gravity of the devastating news who, with his sister, is sitting silently staring at the photographs of two of the highest buildings in the world crashing down into the streets of New York.

'The whole world is in shock, Geoff,' Paul tells him. 'There are initial estimates of up to four thousand people killed.'

Geoff's own miseries are minor by comparison to this devastating news. 'The Bounty?' He manages a few more words.

'Your business has been unaffected. Gary is doing a great job. He sends his best wishes and will be in to see you, probably later this afternoon.'

'*This news will affect tourism.*' Geoff murmurs softly as he sinks off to sleep.

'Come on kids. Dad needs to sleep.' Paul ushers the children out of the room. 'How about some McDonald's?' he whispers into their ears. They both agree, but with only half of their usual enthusiasm.

Geoffrey Edward's father was a leading Australian politician and his mother a politician's wife. Geoff shunned privilege and financial security from an early age, but there was no denying it was there.

After the turmoil of his teens, an inner feeling of reality tugged him and his sensitive disposition into a world of over-compensation. His confidence was many times mistaken for arrogance, but that was far from the truth.

An ardent need for self-satisfaction ran parallel with empathy for others, especially those who had not experienced the lifestyle he had himself. At twenty six his emotional pendulum was steadying. From twenty eight to thirty one, he was married. What he had to offer his wife many women dream about. She left him and the children for a man whose psyche teetered on the edge of devilishness, a trait which some women find enticing.

Nearing his thirties, each year began to expand in its time, as it may when sensibility, a reasonable amount of discipline, good diet and the absence of an accumulation of a life of shortcuts are present. He has also developed an ability to go within himself and find answers that have a different truth about them. These answers are not always to his liking, but they contain a balance he has learnt not to ignore.

*   *   *

A spunky waiter escorts Jane to exactly the same table she sat at on her previous visit to the Manly Pacific Resort.

The restaurant is only one third full. The streets are empty tonight. *The terrorist attack in America yesterday has certainly had an effect on everybody*, she thinks.

'Fish and chips', she laughs. 'That's what *Claire* would say.' Jane holds up her glass and toasts Claire. 'And here's to North Head, lovely, scary North Head. God, it seems the whole world is falling apart.'

How can so many thoughts fit into three sparkling glasses, she giggles to herself, watching the individual champagne bubbles float to the surface of yet another glass. *Everything in here tonight is so clear and distinct,* she thinks.

'Claire, where are you? she says out loud. 'Why did you have to go?'

Jane's waiter comes along to try to rescue her from the attention of several patrons.

'Is there something I can get you?' he asks.

'Please *sit* down.' She looks carefully at him.

'Mal is my name.'

'Sit down *Malcolm*.'

After looking at his superior for the nod, for the sake of peace and quiet, he sits down.

Jane quickly finishes her fourth glass.

'The world wasn't ready for you, Claire' she says, to the waiter's bemusement. 'Was it? Maybe that's why you returned … How unlucky was that guy falling over our cliff today?'

'I thought I heard somebody call out, "help", comes the voice in Jane's head.

'Claire, you did not, you fibber.' Jane taps the waiter on the wrist and giggles.

'Maybe if we both go back to North Head, you wear your dress, and if I wish hard enough, we can find that time again.' The waiter pulls his hand back. The voice comes again.

'Maybe he is somewhere out there waiting.'

'Claire, is that you?'

The waiter, speechless and embarrassed, stands up.

'I will get you some water, miss,' he says, and escapes to the bar.

The maitre-d returns with a bottle of mineral water and a fast-tracked seafood platter for Jane. He obviously thinks Jane has consumed too much alcohol, too quickly, on an empty stomach.

'I used to sell mussels,' giggles Claire, starting up again, 'but what on earth is this?'

'*Squid*,' says Jane wiggling her fingers in the air like a swimming octopus.

'Kak! We would never eat such things.'

Jane drains her glass of champagne and is looking for a top-up. The waiters keep their distance.

'Do you believe in past lives, Jane?'

'Is that some kind of joke? Of course I don't. Nobody has ever put forward any evidence for that, have they, Claire? Do you know anybody, apart from yourself Claire, who has come back in a later time?'

'Yes, I believe I do.'

'Who?'

'You Jane, you have.'

'Me! What is *everybody* looking at?' she says out loud. 'Now, when I have finished this delicious meal, can I treat you to some 2001 music, Claire?'

'Gosh … do you … call this music?' Claire nonetheless begins to sway from the hips up.

Jane is intoxicated enough to overcome her inhibitions and makes her way onto the dance floor. With movements that can find no roots in conventional dance, she is off and away.

In complete contrast to her intimate dance, an energetic elderly man sweeps onto the floor with arms outstretched like that of Zorba the Greek. He proceeds to peacock around and around Jane, the dance floor, and everybody on it. His eyes and the cheeky supercilious look on his face are trying to catch Jane's attention but Jane is oblivious. He finally cottons onto a teenage girl instead.

In spite of the alcohol Jane feels good about herself, and it shows. She has left fear and self-doubt behind and her individual self is beginning to blossom.

Jane whispers to Claire. 'We must visit Sydney. I'll take you there soon.'

'The Big City!' says Claire.

Jane moves to the bar, sits and looks back over her shoulder. As she knew, Claire is nowhere to be seen.

'I think, in fact I'm sure I've had enough to drink for one night.'

CHAPTER SIXTY

ane has decided to take the slow boat to Sydney, so boards one of the old Manly ferries. The thumping diesel engine sends a shudder through the whole craft as it starts up. Standing at the rear, she watches the crew cast off. However, the romance of the moment is washed away as silt and debris is churned up by the ferry's propellers. She decides to go to the front. *There's nobody here,* she thinks. *I have it all to myself.*

The ferry cruises past small bays and beaches and then begins to cross the open water between the Heads.

Jane stares up at the towering cliffs of North Head.

'Passengers are not permitted on the front section of the ferry,' bellows the PA system.

She looks around. Out of nowhere two large waves loom.

'My God!' she calls out.

The bow of the ferry drops and ploughs into the large swell. Heavy spray saturates the front of the ship.

'Oh! Here comes another one!' she shrieks. 'How exciting.' A second wave blankets the bow as she quickly moves aft.

The ocean swell is left behind as the ferry turns into the main section of Sydney harbour following the exact route the *Neptune* sailed when it arrived in Australia over two hundred years before.

The houses and old churches are so beautiful, she thinks. *It looks like some of those churches were built not long after this country was settled. The old religious attitudes are just begging to be changed. It's the same back home.*

* * *

As Jane enjoys a pot of tea and scones in a café overlooking the quays, close to where Michael met her when she last came to the city, a sad, lonely feeling overtakes her. Mal the waiter from the Manly Pacific comes to mind. Then her thoughts switch. *Claire, I'll take you to The Rocks. It's one of the oldest, original areas in Sydney.* She pauses, *why do I think these things? I'll have to stop this nonsense,* she berates herself.

Jane leaves the Circular Quay area and walks towards the Harbour Bridge. She visits the Rocks Museum, and just for a sticky beak, walks through the lobby of the Regent Hotel. After wandering rather aimlessly through some market stalls, she makes her way around to the harbour-side. And there's the Bounty, the ship she'd seen from the ferry. She suddenly feels listless. Like an overexposed photograph. Everything around her momentarily whitens. *I must be in for a migraine,* she thinks

'He's hot,' she whispers to herself, looking at a guy on board the Bounty, standing near the main mast.

'*What do you mean, hot, Jane?*'

'Good looking, handsome, look at him.'

Jane can't believe it she's done it again. She quickly looks to see if anybody can hear her talking to herself.

'Jane he has his back to us for goodness sake. How can you tell he's hot?'

At which point he turns and looks directly at Jane.

'My God, he looks like, Geoff, Jane! Jane! It is Geoff.'

Using her peripheral vision Jane swears she can see Claire standing behind her, just back to her left.

Oh my god, here we go again, Claire seems to be here with me. This is impossible, she thinks, as she turns around. And there is Claire smiling and pointing discreetly at the Bounty.

As if hypnotised Jane goes along with what she sees, hears and feels while the guy stands staring at her.

'Don't be silly, Claire. How could he be Geoff?' she says. She does not believe any of this, but she wants to so much. Her mind shoots back to the flight from London, and Margaret. *This guy does resemble the one in her dreams*, she thinks. But, even more than the resemblance, the same feelings she experienced then are now flashing about her and are intensifying.

'Jane, he's waving.'

Jane looks around the immediate area.

'He's waving to *us*, silly.'

The two women wave back, Claire wholeheartedly, Jane a little sheepishly.

He walks confidently to the edge of his ship.

'Are you joining us today?' he calls out across the small expanse of water separating the Bounty from the wharf.

Claire nudges Jane, who is wondering, is he talking to me or both of us? What exactly is this guy seeing?

'Are, yes…' Jane calls back. She turns to Claire. 'Joining him, *where?*' she asks her.

Claire points to a sign above a small box office at the end of the wharf that says: CRUISE THE HARBOUR ON THE HISTORIC BOUNTY.

'Oh, I've never been on a sailing ship before. Look at those dark clouds over there. It's a little scary.'

'I *have*, many times,' says Claire smugly. 'It will be *just* fine.'

'You've sailed with us before?' he calls, and then quickly clutches his chest.

My God, he's so happy to see us he's having a heart attack. 'Are you alright?' Jane calls out.

'Yes, just a cracked rib or two. Are you twins?'

Jane is dumbfounded. *He's talking to both of us,* she thinks.

'We probably know you from another life,' calls Jane, unable to think of anything to say.

'I'm not married!' he shouts back over the sound of thunder in the distance.

'Life! *Life!*' Jane calls back. 'Not *wife!*'

They shrug their shoulders and grin at each other.

The wind has come up and rain is beginning to swirl through the towering city buildings on the other side of the harbour.

'Come aboard!' he calls, clutching his chest again, it's going to rain!'

Jane takes a good look at Claire and then gives her a sharp pinch.

'Ouch!' says Claire. 'What did you do *that* for?'

They look at each other with a 'will we or won't we' expression and then without any hesitation move towards the ship. The rain-squall sweeping around the harbour's edge herds them through the gateway, along the pier and up the gangplank to be met by the guy who ushers them quickly into the main cabin.

'In here quickly, don't slip.' He closes the cabin door securely behind them. The hustle and bustle of modern Sydney is locked firmly outside. It's as if there has been a slippage in time. He turns towards them.

'Geoff it is you!' says Claire unable to hold back the words. He's taken aback. Jane nudges Claire.

'I must have hit my head harder than I thought in the fall,' he says jokingly.

The two women stare at each other.

'It's obvious I should know you, know of you both, but I'm sorry my memory eludes me at the moment.'

Several claps of fierce thunder, now directly overhead, split the clouds wide open. Hail is falling on the city and approaches the ship like a veil of angry, noisy snow, smashing at the water's surface. The isolated thud and clopping of individual pieces of large hail striking the upper deck soon builds to a roaring climax, then exhausts itself as the hailstorm peaks.

For several minutes, three minds and psyches swirl about with the untamed intensity of the storm and then settle together with the commencement of steady, consistent heavy rain. In a cabin capsule, in a time where all is known, the safety net that protects minds from centuries of accumulated selfishness, sadness, violence, of love and selfish bliss, is dropped. Three souls have momentarily come together as one.

'Well, this is cosy isn't it?' Geoff speaks first. He looks puzzled.

'Now where were we? Tell me, are you psychic?' he says looking at Claire. 'How did you know my name is Geoff?'

'Then your name really is Geoff?' says Jane.

'Yes Geoffrey Edwards at your service,' he jokes.

Claire does not say a word. Geoff made the same kind of comment on the breakwater at Port Isaacs, '*Geoffrey Blake at your assistance ma'm*'.

'It's just you look very much like somebody we both know,' says Jane.

'You're not the first you know,' he says.

'What do you mean by *that?* asks Claire, getting her Irish up as she is reminded of Geoff's attitude the first time they met.

'No, no, please don't misunderstand me. Ever since I went over the cliffs at North Head and my photograph appeared on the front page of the *Telegraph*, I've had women contacting me from as far away as England.'

Jane looks at Claire in disbelief. That creepy, magical feeling she experienced on the aircraft is starting to well up inside her again. Claire appears relatively unaffected by the developments.

'We came across you today quite by coincidence.' She hesitates. I was at North Head just after the cliff accident,' says Jane, momentarily forgetting how unbelievable her comment would appear.

'You were there on that day? What were you doing there?'

'If I told you I was there looking for Geoff, you wouldn't believe me would you?' Jane says, provoking him.

'That's got to be a joke,' he says, wondering what these beautiful twins are actually doing in the cabin of the *Bounty* anyway. The way they present themselves, their genuineness and something he just can't put his finger on is balancing against their outrageous story.

I bet he's wondering who on earth we are and whether he shouldn't just toss us off the ship, Jane thinks.

'What were *you* doing at the *Heads* anyway? You weren't going to jump, were you?' Jane asks, pushing her luck.

'He smiles genially. 'That's exactly what my little boy Jonathan asked me. I don't really know why I was out there, I just …'

'It's all a bit of a mystery if you ask me, Jane smiles.

'Are you English?' asks Claire.

'My family tree does apparently originate in England. I could be from good convict stock. I checked once,' he laughs.

Jane can see Claire is convinced that this man is Geoff and the more she looks into his eyes the more he resembles the man in her visualisations aboard the aircraft. Though their whole meeting is probably a farce, he doesn't seem to want the women to leave. Claire and Jane don't want to leave either.

'Well …' Geoff begins.

'Do you always say "well" when you are thinking of what to say?' asks Jane.

'Well, I suppose I must,' he replies and they all laugh. 'Let's go back to where it all started,' he says. The two women wait bewildered wondering what he might say next.

'I was on the ship facing the main mast. I turned around and there you both were. I asked if you were sailing with us today? Will you sail with us on the sunset cruise, this afternoon, as my guests?'

'Yes,' they both answer spontaneously.

There is a knock at the cabin door. It's Gary.

'Weather's up. We sail on the hour, JC.'

Geoff opens the cabin door. His best friend, and second-in-charge, Gary, stands wordless at the sight of the two women in Geoff's cabin.

'Sorry mate,' he says, obviously misjudging the situation.

'Sorry JC,' mimics Jane and they all laugh again.

'Would you show Claire and Jane around the ship and make them comfortable, my good man. They sail with us this evening.'

'Yes Captain, sir,' he gives a comical salute. 'Walk this way me dears.' He does a poor imitation of John Travolta. Jane immediately copies his walk.

'It is great to have you both onboard, Claire,' says Geoff.

She nods. *It's good to see you again Geoff, it really is*, Claire thinks.

Jane looks back over her shoulder. Claire catches up to her.

'Stop it Jane you look silly,' she whispers.

'He said to *walk* this way,' Jane laughs. She stops. 'Claire I'm so bamboozled about all this. I'm not going to get too serious.'

Claire just smiles with a bit of a chuckle and watches Jane and Gary walking in front of her.

After a detailed tour of the *Bounty*, Gary settles Claire and Jane in the VIP section at the stern of the ship. Dinner is served.

'All sailors drink rum, ladies,' he says, placing a glass in front of each of them.

'I don't like rum,' whispers Jane to Claire.

'Drink it, it will do you good,' replies Claire, already halfway through hers. 'It is Geoff, Jane. It's Geoff alright, but he doesn't know me.'

'I have a definite feeling he knows both of us.'

'Is he still hot, Jane?'

'No, no, don't be *silly*.'

'You don't like him then?'

'Well …'

'Now *you're* doing it.'

'What am I doing?'

'The *well* thing.'

The rum is now starting to take effect.

'Do you like him, Jane? Do you?'

'Claire, how can I answer that? Here you are saying he could be *your* husband and me thinking, after what has been going on, that maybe he *is*. What do you *want* me to say? I've been in some unusual situations in my life, but this certainly takes the cake.'

'How are we, sailors? Would we like another double shot?

'Double? *My God*,' laughs Claire. '*Yes*, I'll have another. And another for my husband's *friend* here.' Claire is feeling a little tipsy and mischievous.

We've got a couple of wild ones here, thinks Gary. The main deck is filling with tourists, but Jane and Claire are in a world of their own.

'Your friend Margaret is right, Jane, the mind does adjust to things rapidly. Here we are sitting on a ship which represents the past. And just over there is one of the most modern cities on earth. My goodness. And it's beginning to feel quite normal to me.'

'Husband's friend, ha, ha.' Jane is still stuck back there.

Geoff is approaching. Claire prods Jane trying to warn her.

'Whose husband, whose friend?' asks Geoff as he sits on the edge of their seat. 'Are you enjoying the calm after the storm — hasn't the afternoon turned out great?'

'Yes it has been gorgeous,' says Jane.

'We're ready to leave. I'll get things under way and see you both a little later on.'

'Fine,' says Jane. 'Husband's *friend* — *what* did you say that for Claire?' she whispers, quickly giving Claire another pinch.

'Ouch! Don't Jane.'

The rum is working and so is the ship's engine. The smell of diesel fumes mixes with the salt air all adding to the marine experience.

At four pm the ropes are cast off and the *Bounty* floats unrestrained for a short time before the back-up engine connects with the prop which in turn bites firmly into the water and gets the ship on course.

Claire is in a world of her own, distracted and distant as she looks up through the sails.

Jane knows deep in her mind that all this is an impossible dream, but it feels so good. With the help of the rum she decides to stop fighting what she is seeing and feeling and to run with it.

With the storm receding into the northern sky, the *Bounty's* sails are set and the vibration of the diesel engine gives way to quiet. All the passengers aboard stop talking and join in the silence of sailing as if an order has been given to them.

The setting sun drops below a line of dark grey storm clouds. Their undersides reflecting in the harbour's waters slowly change from gold to golden-orange and then to scarlet pink. This late afternoon certainly has a magical feel about it.

Jane has just now finished her second drink and is looking around wondering when her captain will return.

'Look at that sunset, Jane,' says Claire.

Jane nods. She is taking it all in. But it is the ship, the crew and their Captain Geoff that have completely captivated her. In the distance she can see him and Gary speaking to the paying customers. They have to entertain everyone, she acknowledges to herself.

Just then, Geoff looks up and smiles, looking relaxed. The two women wave back. Claire puts her arm around Jane.

'It's him. I don't know how or why, but it's Geoff,' she says.

In her minds eye Jane, too, is seeing the resemblance between this guy and the one who appeared in her dreams and visualisations on the jet.

Concentrating on Geoff speaking to the visitors, Jane has the strangest feeling of leaving her seat and walking slowly towards him. As in her dream on the aeroplane she moves beside him, slightly back to his right side. She touches his hair. Moving her hand down to the back of his neck and then to his left shoulder a flow of energy moves through her hand and streams into his body. He turns and is now facing her. Her face is only inches from his. His face is strong and true, his eyes so sure, but a little sad and lonely. She moves even closer and melts into him — their energies combine.

Geoff waves to Jane and Claire.

'Here he comes, Jane.'

'What? … What did you say?' Jane is off with the fairies.

'Here comes Geoff.'

He makes his way back to the women.

'I'm so sorry I have been neglecting you both. All the passengers have had their meal and I think I have satisfied all their questions.'

'The Captain is very popular, isn't he JC?' says Jane mockingly.

He laughs. 'Have you both eaten?'

'We've had our vitals, Geoff, thank you,' replies Jane, looking at him with doe eyes.

'I must confess ever since you came aboard, I have been having the most captivating and strangest feelings and I can assure you I am not in the habit of saying this to other women, let alone two women at once. We've had the most unusual discussions, haven't we? Be honest, do you know me from somewhere else or have you made enquiries about me for some reason? Has Gary put you up to this? He can be a joker sometimes. He didn't pay you both did he?'

If Jane and Claire did not have a deeper knowledge about this situation, they would probably feel very insulted.

'No Geoff,' says Jane. 'Everything we've told you is the honest truth.'

He still looks puzzled, but a little relieved at the same time.

'Geoff, could you tell me what type of car you drive?' asks Jane.

'Well …'

'There he goes again,' giggles Claire.

'Well,' he laughs. 'It sounds like you already know. You tell me.'

'A blue BMW,' Jane shoots back.

'How do you know that?' Geoff is fascinated.

'It was the only car parked at North Head,' says Jane. 'Look.' She lifts her skirt revealing where she bruised her thigh. 'I did that on *your* car.'

'So you must have been there then. What a coincidence.'

'Coincidence, you might call it that. Tell us what happened to you. It must have been horrible.' says Claire

'Business has been very good, and as I do from time to time, I went to the Heads for a break. I'm also writing a book and I go out there sometimes for peace and inspiration. North Head is a romantic spot. It features in my novel. Maybe what happened to me out there could make a good ending to my story. I was standing in my usual place and feeling quiet hyped. I'd just made a few decisions about my life when part of the cliff face broke away and took me with it. The whole world knows the rest thanks to the newspapers.'

'I don't think that's the ending to your book, maybe just another start,' says Claire.

'Oh, you don't … No, you're probably right Claire. It was nearly the end of me though. It's amazing what goes though one's mind as …' He stops speaking and pulls himself together.

'Tell us about yourself, Geoff.' Jane gives Claire a quick knowing look. She is trying to catch Geoff off his guard.

'On one condition, you both have dinner with me on Friday evening.'

'That depends on how good your story is, Captain JC,' says Jane. Claire nods her agreement.

'You realise I'm at a distinct disadvantage here. You are both a little sloshed and I haven't touched a drop.'

'We'll soon correct that,' says Claire, waving her hands at Gary, who drags himself from the other end of the ship.

'Yes ma'am. What can I do for thou?'

'One of your special drinks for the Captain, my good man.'

'Can the Captain drink on duty, sir?' he asks looking at Geoff.

'The Captain is off duty, please take over, squire.'

In a flash, Gary returns with refreshments for his mate. 'Bottoms up, JC.'

'That's enough of that, be off with you my man.'

'Don't talk to your Captain in that way, sir,' says Gary as he pivots on one leg, pretends to topple then moves away to take control of the vessel.

'There should be no more interruptions. And please note I didn't say *well*,' he says as the *Bounty*, after doubling back, slips silently past Bennelong Point on the main harbour channel.

'Let me see, you both know about the *Bounty*. I have two children, Christine who's eleven, and Jonathan who's nearly five. I write. My current book is about the complexities of time. I married in '79. My wife left when Jonathan was two.' He pauses. 'My dad was a controversial politician. He's now retired. He and mum live in Sydney. The rest of the tribe live in Melbourne and Adelaide.'

'I have an idea,' says Claire. 'Let's all meet at North Head on Friday afternoon before we go to dinner. What do you think, Geoff?'

'I vowed and declared I would never go out there again, but I am not one for running away and I should face up. Why not?'

'That would be a good place for us to start,' Jane agrees.

'There's a large stone near the second lookout. We can all meet there at four pm.'

Claire looks at Geoff and Jane warmly.

'By the way Geoff did Gary or you choose your nickname JC?' asks Jane.

He smiles. 'No, my little boy Jonathan came up with that. He's convinced his dad is just like the intrepid Captain James Cook.'

CHAPTER SIXTY ONE

s the Manly ferry moves away from Circular Quay, Jane and Claire look across at the *Bounty*.

'It all seems like a dream. Claire what's wrong? You're different. Are you upset?'

'No,' Claire replies in a distant voice. 'Jane, do you think there is any difference between dreams and reality?'

Jane tucks her hands up under her armpits and makes a gesture like a chicken. 'What comes first the chicken or the egg? What are dreams and what is reality? I'm not sure, Claire, and after what we experienced over the last few weeks, I don't think I'll ever be sure again. Do you really believe that was Geoff on the *Bounty*?'

'It was him. There's no doubt about that.'

'Why didn't you *say* something to him?' asks Jane, touching her on the shoulder.

'What? Tell him that I'm his wife from two hundred and thirteen years ago. On top of everything else that happened on the *Bounty* today, he probably would have made us walk the plank. You don't just say to somebody, *I was with you in a dream once, here I am*. Jane, he *knows*. There will be a time and place to talk with him about all this, you wait and see.'

'Will he come to North Head, do you think?' Jane looks perturbed.

'He's already there. The three days between now and Friday will seem just like seconds. Life is nothing but a few important dreams connected by heartbeats of days and a few chicken feathers thrown in.'

'Gosh, Claire, you're sounding so much like Margaret.'

'As Margaret would probably say, we're all connected at a certain level. Surely, if nothing else has happened since we met, you've seen that.'

Jane is feeling like a real novice.

'You're not you know,' says Claire.

'What?' asks Jane.

'You're not a beginner and you're not alone.'

Jane looks at Claire with love and surprise. 'You have all the experience of your sisters and brothers before you, going right back to the start of time. At this very moment you're at the pinnacle of human existence. You are it.'

'What about you Claire?'

'Can't you see? I can. Nothing that's happened to me is in vain. I've been fortunate enough to have another chance to see what my life and efforts have contributed to. It's you Jane … it is you. I'm so fulfilled and so proud. Please take all I can give you and spring from me into the future. Remember …' Claire has a look about her Jane has never seen before. 'Remember that as long as Geoffrey and people around you are trying, that's the most important thing. Mistakes come before growth. They're part of it. Claire turns and faces the *Bounty*. I am you, Jane … can you *see?*'

Jane nods. 'Yes I can.' She quickly glances back at the *Bounty* in the distance. 'Yes, I can see, and I can feel it too.'

Jane wonders, looking at the city, *what would Captain Cook think if he could see all of this?* She imagines all the buildings gone. She imagines the early settlements and thinks of the *Neptune* sailing through the heads. She sees Geoff waving from the deck of the *Neptune*. She thinks about all the past conflicts within the world — all the mistakes in time — all the mistakes she has made in her life.

'Hey, anybody home?' Claire interrupts. 'Take note of the mistakes of this world Jane, but don't take responsibility for them.' It's as if Claire knows Jane's every thought. 'That's what I've had to learn. I tried to change the world. I sacrificed my life and my baby's life for that, and lost a good man in Geoffrey.' Claire puts her arm around Jane. 'I was selfish and didn't love enough. I expected too much of myself and everybody else. That prevented me from seeing that a good man doesn't have to be, and can't be, perfect. And that everybody is growing and no person's inner flower can be forced to open until it's ready.'

*　　*　　*

It's a calm warm Friday afternoon as a cab approaches the parking area at North Head.

'We're late. I can't see Geoff's car. There are no cars. There's *nobody* here.' Jane is uneasy.

'He will come. Don't be a *worry-wort*.'

'Will we let the taxi go?' Jane doesn't want to be stranded.

'Pay the man. Have some trust, my girl.'

The cab pulls away slowly as if the driver is apprehensive about leaving the two women in such an isolated place. Immediately, silence edges forward like elves from a deep forest as the taxi disappears from earshot.

'Look,' says Jane as she stares at a sign warning about landslides.

'The second lookout platform. This way. Next to the stone on the cliff. Remember?' Claire is undeterred.

The Flannel flowers are in full bloom, lizards scatter across the warm pathway. The air is still. A flat lazy ocean stretching to a glazed horizon comes into view. To the right, the metropolis of Sydney — busy and vibrant — is held silent by the distance.

'Where's the stone?' says Jane, looking around.

'Over there,' Claire points.

'What an unusual formation. Can we get closer do you think?

Look, a track, just over that fence. That's where Geoff will be, let's go that way.'

'No Jane! Do you think we *should*? It's not *safe*.'

'Why not?' says Jane, straddling the top rail ignoring the danger sign. 'Help *me* Claire, my legs aren't long enough.'

Claire giggles, trying to assist.

'*Ouch*, I'm stuck.' Jane has a painful look on her face. 'If this didn't hurt so much, it might be fun.'

Claire gives her a bit of a slap on the back. 'Don't be rude.' She lifts Jane off the rail by placing her hands under Jane's armpits.

'That's better, come on.'

Claire, an accomplished horse rider, side-straddles the bar and flips over effortlessly.

The rarely-used path to the unfenced cliff area is overgrown. The two women crouch down as they move through the dense scrub.

'Whoops!' Jane stops.

'Jane! *Be careful*. What is *it?*'

Claire moves forward. They are both staring over the cliff face — a sheer drop of hundreds of feet.

'*My God!* Come back Jane! *Come back!*'

Jane sinks to her knees, both fascinated and petrified as she watches the waves crash across the rocks below.

'Come away, Jane! Over here! *This way*.' Claire pulls at Jane's arm.

'Hello!' calls a voice.

'*Jane*, Geoffrey's here somewhere.'

Moving back from the cliff edge, they take another track. Jane is the first to see him.

'Look he's there, over to the right,' Jane whispers.

'*Hi*, I wasn't sure you were coming,' he says, holding back a laugh at the two women emerging from the scrub. They brush themselves off.

'I'II just get that spider out of your hair, Claire.' He reaches out.

Claire lets out a small scream and shakes her head.

'He's only joking with you, Claire. There's *no* spider.'

Claire manages to smile. She loathed spiders and Geoffrey knew it all those years ago.

'How did you get here?' Jane asks. Her question lingering — a nervous substitute for a hug or a kiss.

'Along that path. It leads back to the car park. One of the original tracks. I've been here to this spot often, although this time I must admit I *was* apprehensive approaching the cliff area.' He glances warily over at the collapsed section.

'*We* know what you mean. We were just at the edge — it's a *long* way down,' says Jane.

'Tell me about it. I surprised myself coming back out here. It's only a few weeks since I went down the side of that damn cliff. Just give me a minute and I'll be right back,' he says as he heads for the car park.

'He's here, Claire, *he's here*.' Jane touches the rock. 'God, I hope he hasn't taken off.'

Jane dances round on the spot, full of excitement much as Claire would have been when she met Geoff for the second time at Tintagel.

'What do we do, what do I say,' Jane whispers, a little anxiously.

'*It's* time for dinner,' Geoff says, returning with two rugs, a picnic basket, a bunch of flowers, and a cooler. Like a magician, he produces two bottles of wine. The magic continues. From the picnic basket a never-ending procession of goodies are placed on the rug he has spread out on a flat rocky area. The flowers, which consist of one pink rose and two yellow, are placed in a plastic vase in the centre.

Jane stares at the sweet perfumed flowers. *They are identical to the ones the flight director gave her on the jet,* Jane thinks as she remembers Margaret's words. *The flowers you have just received Jane, are not the way they seem.*

'Can we help?' asks Jane.

'She'll be Jake, I packed everything and I know exactly where it all is,' he says, as he puts down a Thai seared beef and papaya salad, rice and pork rolls. 'Mineral water … coffee,' he says, producing a thermos. 'Who's for lemon passionfruit cheesecake and King Island cream?'

'This is lovely!' Jane is impressed. 'Did you make this?' she asks, sampling the beef.

'Yes, all except the cheesecake.' he says, feigning pride as he puts down plastic knives and forks.

Again silence, but the thoughts and feelings are as varied and as interesting as the delicious meal they begin to consume.

Claire is given the task of opening the wine, but she can't get the cork out.

'Didn't they teach you how to open a bottle of wine where you come from?' He smiles and professionally removes the cork for her.

'You remind me so much of someone I once knew,' she says cautiously. 'We met on a seawall and had a *great* old yarn.'

He looks at her, bemused.

'You said you come out here often?' asks Jane.

'I do Jane. I have this fantasy that I'll meet a beautiful, mysterious woman in a sexy old world dress,' he says, half seriously. 'She'll appear and slowly move towards me out of the mist. We then embrace,' he explains as he bites into a pork roll.

'Apart from being beautiful, what other qualities would this mysterious woman have to possess?' asks Jane boldly.

'Well,' he says, obviously not expecting his light-hearted comment, to be taken seriously. 'She would need to …' He stops.

Jane and Claire look at him.

'What colour hair would this woman have?' Jane lets him off the hook.

He clears his throat. 'Blonde,' he says looking at Claire differently.

As Jane fiddles a little distractedly with her salad, he then asks. 'Why did you come out here?'

'I was waiting for my ship to come in.' replies Jane.

'Now *what* ship would *that* be?'

Claire and Jane exchange glances agreeing to push things along.

'The *Neptune*,' says Jane. 'the largest ship of the Second Fleet that came to Australia.'

'The *Neptune*? I know most of the early ships. *Oh* yes, that was the flag ship of the Second Fleet, back in the seventeen hundreds' He thinks for a moment then looks at the two women with a questioning stare.

'What part of England do you both come from?'

'London,' Claire replies.

'So you are both on holidays in Australia? You're travelling together?'

'No, we each came out here separately,' says Jane.

'Separately, and met here? But you are related, aren't you? The two of you look identical.'

'We are *sort of* related. But we had never met before coming to Australia.'

Geoff looks more confused by the moment. Jane is wondering where all this will end up. It feels like lots of pieces of a story are coming together a bit like a jigsaw puzzle.

It's a balmy summer's night. The conversation continues, the food is great. A soft warm breeze increases as air is sucked from the land carrying the smell of the bush out over the ocean to where a change is brewing.

Where the rocks meet the sea is where he will be. Jane looks at Geoff as she remembers another of Margaret's poignant comments.

'You said you're writing a book, Geoffrey. Can I ask you what it's about,' says Claire.

'Well …' he pauses. 'Funnily enough, it commences in England. It's a tragic love story set against the rise and fall of the British Empire and the decline of the traditional Christian church. I've been thinking about it for years. I've written the first eight chapters.'

Claire and Jane glance at each other.

'Let's have another drink.' Jane begins to open the second bottle.

Without any warning, Geoff begins to look strange and seems to lose control.

'Are you all right, Geoff?' Jane puts her hand on his shoulder. He has gone very pale.

'I'm sorry. I'm feeling quite weird. I've been through a great deal in the last two weeks.' He straightens up a little. His hands are shaking and he appears limp.

'I'm *really* sorry … I, I don't know what's come over me.' He touches his chest and slumps. Claire catches him and lowers him into her lap.

'*Geoffrey,* I'm *so sorry,*' she says impulsively, holding him close.

Jane takes his and Claire's hand. The two women look at each other not knowing what to do. But something tells them just to hold him and relax.

An electric rush flashes through the three of them. The trio are lifted away from all words and feelings into an area of the mind which needs no explanation, reflection or understanding.

Claire squeezes Jane's hand and they look intently at each other. Jane can see a weight lifting from Claire's shoulders as she holds Geoffrey tenderly. She senses that all the knots in Claire's mind are unravelling. Her face becomes fully relaxed. Jane's own mind is rocketing through her past. All the tangled stitches in the tapestry of her life are unravelling and separating into several bands of bright colours.

Geoff stirs, whilst he lies weakened, and seems to be dreaming.

Claire and Jane close their eyes and all three of them hold each other like children lost in an unusual but haunting dream.

'My God, I don't know what came over me.' It was as though chapters in my book were writing themselves, flashing through my mind like the lighted carriages of a fast moving train — if only I could have jotted it all down.' Geoff says with a laugh, sitting up. As quickly as he lost control, he has now regained it.

But now for some strange reason there are no more questions, no more doubts. The only concern now is the dark southerly change which is looming. From Geoff's sailing experience he knows they have a little over an hour before the wind and rain reaches them. But Jane's only concern is to hold on to the moment.

'Jane, it was there before, it is still there and it will stay,' Claire says mysteriously.

Jane and Geoff look at her wondering what on earth she is talking about.

'We can have desert and coffee at my place,' says Jane. 'You wouldn't leave us out here would you, Geoff?'

'Well, let me see …' he says, teasing for a moment. 'Let's go,' he says taking each of the women by the hand.

'Look, over there,' he laughs as he points out to sea. 'That must be the *Neptune*.'

Claire and Jane stare with astonishment as the ship sails closer.

Then Jane twigs. 'That's *your Bounty*. You think we're gullible, don't you?' She gives him an affectionate slap on the arm.

'I didn't know anything about this, honest. Damn Gary. He knew we were coming out here this afternoon.

The three of them watch as the *Bounty* sails close to the cliffs, comes about, and hurriedly sets sail for Sydney to avoid the southerly bluster.

CHAPTER SIXTY TWO

Jane is sitting next to Geoff as they drive through Manly. Claire contentedly takes the back seat.

The evening rush is over. Manly begins to draw another veil of dusk from its easterly ocean horizon. The restaurants project their usual nightly romantic image as the city's mood progressively relaxes.

'We're in a one-way street Geoff!'

'My God, we are too! I must have been off with the fairies.' He does a quick u-turn.

'Speaking of fairies, that was lovely of Gary to sail the *Bounty* over to see us.'

'I'm going to tell him you said that, Jane,' laughs Geoff.

'It's that walk he does — like this.' Jane wobbles around in her seat, imitating Gary. They all laugh.

The car pulls into Jane's driveway.

'I can't stay very long,' says Geoff

'*Why?*' asks Jane.

'You may not want me to. And I want to so much. To be quite frank with you, I'm not sure of my motives for coming to see you both today,' he says.

'*Well*, we'll have to look into that, *won't* we,' says Claire.

'We certainly will,' agrees Jane. 'We mightn't even let you go. You may have to stay *forever*.'

Geoff is outnumbered, enthralled and curious.

'Let it all hang out, Geoff.' Jane realises what she has said. They both laugh. Claire looks puzzled.

'What's so funny, you two?'

'I'll tell you later Claire. It's a 2001 joke,' she whispers.'

Geoff grabs the picnic gear and they all make their way into the house.

'You'll feel more at home when you get some of my Russian brew into you,' Jane says as they move inside. 'Don't expect too much of my digs, they're very basic.'

'This is *cosy*. Have you a brandy?' asks Geoff as they sit down.

'Sure have.' Jane pours drinks. 'Back in a minute,' she puts on some music and walks to the bedroom giving a split-second imitation of Gary as she closes the door. Geoffrey looks at Claire and they both grin.

'Claire, I have never been so mystified in my entire life. Being with you and Jane has been an experience I'll never forget. I feel I never want to leave you. Both of you.'

'You never have left, Geoffrey, and you never will,' says Claire softly.

He is now accustomed to the women's unusual comments. He boldly moves across, sits and takes her hand. 'I feel I have known you and Jane for ages, yet it's only been one week.' He looks down at her hand in his.

'Maybe you have. Do you believe in life after death?'

'Now, that's an interesting question,' he says, taking another mouthful of drink. 'No, not really. I need proof about these things. Funnily enough though, the novel I'm writing is about love across time. I'm discovering more and more about myself as I write.' He pauses. 'Do you know I don't think I've ever spoken to anyone about these things before. I *do* feel I'm a product of all those who've gone before me. The positives and the negatives are passed on from one generation to the next and it is up to each of us to choose which path we follow. We all have free will. I see it as a re-birthing of energies.'

Claire sits back.

'Well, that was good for me, Claire. How was it for you?'

Her smile says everything. 'Brings back lots of memories for me', she says, contentedly.

'Coming, ready or not!' Jane calls out. At that precise moment the phone rings. She picks it up. 'Hello,' she says hurriedly.

'Guess who this is?'

'Margaret!'

'How are you, love?' replies that familiar voice, warmly.

'I feel good, really good Margaret; I've *so* much to tell you.'

'Don't let him go now, will you?'

'What do you mean, Margaret?'

'I'll call again before I go home. Gordon tried to ring you. He asked me to say goodbye. He flew out today. I have his address for you. I love your dress … '

'How do you know I'm wearing my dress Margaret? *Margaret* — she's gone, damn.'

Claire and Geoff watch spellbound as Jane makes a dramatic entry. She is bewitching and beautiful.

'Don't take any notice of this,' she says rubbing at the hem. 'That's the grey sand from North Head.'

Geoff stands and walks toward her and then stops.

'That's the most beautiful dress I have ever seen … I can't believe it, it's so much like the dress I was talking about this afternoon. That's *impossible.*'

'She will come out of the mist in an old world dress and we will embrace …' teases Claire, repeating his afternoon comment.

Jane turns where she is standing. The dress swirls out, wraps around her legs and then drops into soft folds. Then, for reasons she does not understand she puts her hands on her thighs and pushes her bottom out provocatively. She straightens.

'*Sorry* about that, it must be the Vodka,' she says, feeling a little embarrassed as she stands upright.

'The blue suits you so much.' Geoff is captivated.

He takes both her hands and leads her back to the sofa. He sits down between the two women and the three of them sit there staring at the blank TV screen.

'Don't go Geoff, don't *ever* go,' says Jane. She cannot believe she's said this.

As if he did not hear her, he asks, 'were you both serious about waiting for the *Neptune?*'

The two women look at each other wondering whether to tell him more.

'This is all amazing,' he goes on. 'We all three frequent North Head. You said,' he looks at Jane, 'you went out there to find Geoff and to wait for the *Neptune* to arrive …'

'Geoff, stop … I went to North Head, not knowingly mind you, to re-meet the person I have known since the beginning of time.' Jane leans across and gives him a soft, short kiss on the lips. 'If we were to tell you, you were married to Claire in another life, and that we are sisters through time, would you believe *us?*'

'I'm not sure,' he replies.

'All right then, let's pretend,' she suggests.

'I must say, I've never had an offer like this. This is quite a fantasy.'

'Close your eyes, Geoff, listen to my voice and count down from twenty, imagine you are on the *Neptune* in the year 1790. You have just completed a voyage from England and you are sailing towards Sydney Heads.' Jane takes his hand and immediately his eyelids begin to flicker. Margaret has taught her well. 'You look up at the North Head cliffs and see Jane and Claire waving to you. Nobody else on board can see us. You wave back and they all think you're nutty as a fruitcake.'

'Horace doesn't believe me either.' Geoff opens his eyes. 'Who the *hell* is *Horace?* Why did I say that? I've had too much to drink.' He stands up and heads for to the bathroom. 'Excuse me a moment won't you?'

He returns with a smile on his face. 'I was just checking to see if Horace was in there. He wasn't,' he says, and sits down.

Claire puts her hand on his shoulder and Jane moves closer to him.

Claire carries the story further. 'See yourself on a seawall, say, on the Cornish coastline, in the south of England. I'm standing before you; there is a mess of fish around my feet spilt from a fisherman's basket. As Jane would put it, you are an arrogant prick.' She looks at Jane to confirm the phrase.

'Arrogant would *do*, Claire,' Jane winces.

Claire continues unaware of the coarseness of her expression. 'Have you heard of Tintagel Castle?' she says, 'the birth place of King Arthur of Camelot.'

'No,' replies Geoff.

'I am swimming in a rock-pool at the base of the cliffs below the castle ruins. You wave to me.'

He opens his eyes. 'This is great material. Can I use it?'

She continues the story.

'We both hold each other on the rocky platform as waves crash around us.'

Geoff puts his arm around Claire.

'Oh my,' says Claire with conviction. *It is him*, she thinks. 'We marry and live in London,' she adds. He again closes his eyes to focus.

Claire touches his arm and continues the yarn. 'In the garden there is a stone, my stone, a permanent symbol of my love for you,' she says.

'I'm not comfortable with the stone, am I? Why?' says Geoff, opening his eyes.

'You tell me, you're the writer.' Claire waits for his reply which is a bit slow in coming.

'The stone comes between us,' he says.

'Why does it?' asks Claire.

'An excuse he could give is that it's against his religion, that it's dark and sacrilegious. But he's not religious in the conventional sense. What he is not saying is he is probably scared and threatened by your developing individuality. He's not the only one to be affected by your persistent need to be your own person. Your beliefs clash with the Church and Geoffrey fails to stand by you. Torn between his incredible love for you and his insecurities he … he's passive, in fact he's *gutless*. He doesn't trust you enough '

Claire has waited two centuries to hear this.

Geoffrey continues. 'Claire, at this point in the story you have several choices, live a life of anger and placation being contained by men. Or be assertive and practice some empathy for us mere males, us little boys. You could leave the relationship and try another, live alone or just do away with yourself.'

Claire looks at him speechless.

'I *tried Claire*! I *tried* so hard!' he calls out.

The two women stare at each other.

Then seemingly oblivious to what he has just said, he goes on. 'I think we are all products of the past. All is set out before us and we make the choices. Apart from small travesties of the law there are no rights or wrongs, just decisions that will impact upon us and lead to inner freedom, or set negative energies in motion that will impede our growth. It's all, and only, a matter of time. You know, there is only one answer in the end.'

The women look at him.

'I can't say any more. You probably already think I'm nuts.' He takes another drink.

Jane pokes him in the ribs. 'Come on spill the beans, Geoff.'

He pauses. 'Guilt. We're all bogged down by guilt and fear.'

'The answer, maestro?' Jane tops up his glass.

'Love,' he replies.

Jane laughs. 'The old love cliché. All you need is love … da da, da da da, dah.' She has heard talk of love many times before.

Unfazed, he looks firstly at Claire, then at Jane.

'I believe we all do the best we can using what we have learnt from our life and those that have gone before us. I try not to make judgements, *try* being the magic word. I stuff up all the time. But that's it, we learn from trying and failing. On one hand I cut myself some slack, but I also reach for the stars. *God* only knows how long it has taken, but I actually like myself.

Geoff's last few words have clinched it for Jane. She has had three drinks and is very relaxed. Free from any concerns now of upsetting Claire she puts her hand on his.

What the ... she thinks. Images of her schoolyard flash into her mind. *Where did that come from? — at a time like this?*

Her special friend John is sitting next to her. The other children are nowhere to be seen. She can feel his leg touching hers ... She has a funny and warm feeling in her chest. Her legs are swinging back and forth. She can't stop them. His hand moves along the railing seat reaching for her hand, she moves it away slightly. He tries again. Their fingers touch. He smells different to girls, she thinks.

'So what are you looking for in a woman Geoffrey E?' asks Jane staring at her hand holding his.

'I've met women who gave me what they thought I needed. And that was my fault as much as theirs. Many times I accepted their mirrored responses without thinking.'

Jane nods. It echoes her experience.

'I need somebody who can ...' he stops.

'You need somebody who could see the real you,' says Claire, rather sadly placing her hand on his shoulder.

'That's what we *all* want,' says Jane, softly. 'What I'm looking for is somebody who is true blue. Somebody I can share *every-thing* with.' She looks up and straight into Geoff's eyes.

'I don't think I'll be driving home just yet,' he says.

'Come with us,' says Jane, tugging at his shirt.

Like the blind drunk, leading the blind, she takes him to her bed with Claire following. The three of them lie down. Geoff holds Jane close and Claire, lying beside Jane, wraps her arms around both of them. Geoff begins kissing Jane. As Jane begins to move in a warm, intense rhythm of love, Claire hugs and moves with her. Claire's hand is now over Jane's, supporting the back of Geoff's head. Similar to the hands on the statue in Claire's garden, their fingertips interlock. Joined at the hips like Siamese twins they are moving as one. Lips kiss.

'I love you both,' whispers Claire.

Jane feels a warm tingling sensation all over as Claire and Geoff cuddle even closer to her. Jane's body quivers, and then … Claire is gone.

'Claire!' calls Geoff.

Jane answers him. 'I am here forever.'

* * *

Two and a half hours later, rain is falling gently outside.

'*Geoffrey*, let's go have some fish and chips.'

ACKNOWLEDGEMENTS

Watkin Tench's 1788, Tim Flannery, Text Publishing Co.
The Fatal Shore, Robert Hughes, Harvill
Orphans of History, Robert Holden, Text Publishing Co.
The Floating Brothel, Sian Rees, Hodder

ABOUT THE AUTHOR

I am a family man. I met my life mentor when I was twenty-three. That's when the trouble started. He was a man who believed all religions have a common goal of good and that the development of the individual within a communal structure is where it is at.

Carl Jung has also been a life-long inspiration to me.

I am a businessperson, qualified in Social Welfare and have undertaken formal studies in Professional Writing.

My writing career commenced at seven years of age. I was presented a first prize, on television, for a short story I wrote.

I believe that everyone can achieve anything they set their mind to, but in saying that, I never underestimate how tough life can be.

I feel nobody, including myself, can be completely original for we are a product of the positives, the negatives and the discoveries that have gone before us.

Through the higher aspects of myself, I trust the past and the future and firmly believe that there is a reason for everything that happens.

Noel Harding, 2010

Noel Harding

Living with the Other Side

Answers to Life are Within You

9 781922 954152

W e all have untapped potentials and psychic abilities. With a deep exploration of our minds, it is possible to unlock these potentials.

In understanding our egos, our 'I, Me and My' levels of consciousness, time can expand and the world of opposites becomes less daunting.

Noel Harding may have started life as a regular working-class boy, but has spent years studying, exploring his own unconscious mind and his part in the universe. He has also applied what he has experienced in owning and operating many retail businesses with his wife, in addition to his studies in Social Welfare work and Professional Writing.

In *Living with the Other Side,* Noel shares some of his own personal experiences, as well as guiding the reader to think constructively about their own life, in order to demonstrate how to access one's most inner self in relation to the world around us and possibly beyond.

Also included are some exercises that can be done to provide questioning and exploration of one's self.

When we begin to calm the turbulence of the mind, our real self shines through.

> Through our lives we care, we aspire, we love, we pain, we accept and we grow. The true and real we seek; the best is always within and known.

> *Living with the Other Side* is for anyone interested in understanding and unlocking the power of their own mind.